THE MOOSE JAW BOOK III

GRIZZLY HARVEST

A NOVEL BY MIKE DELANY

Authors note:

This is a work of fiction. Moose Jaw Creek, the town of Chekov, The Varmitage and the Rainbow Lodge are fictitious places. All the human characters in this novel are fictitious as well. Sadly, the practice of poaching bears for their bile and gallbladders is all too real. Over the centuries, this fluid and the organ in which it is stored, has come to be highly valued in the Far East as a remedy for everything from headache to epilepsy. The ursodeoxycholic acid (UDCA) found in bear bile is also reputed to restore the vigor of youth to the aging male libido.

Bear poaching, despicable though it may be, is perhaps more humane than "bear farming" which is quite common throughout Asia. In China, Viet Nam and South Korea, over ten thousand "bile bears" are kept confined in individual cages and milked of their bile via a catheter surgically implanted into their gallbladders. Many of these "farms" are owned and operated by the state.

Although synthetic drugs are now readily available to address male sexual disorders, many men still prefer the natural remedies provided by practitioners of Traditional Chinese Medicine. Thus, bears will continue to be illegally killed in the wild – or worse, legally exploited on the "bear farms" of the orient.

Of the eight species of bear still found in the wild, all but the Giant Panda have experienced population reduction due to the market for their gallbladders. In South Korea, the black bear is on the verge of extinction. It is now illegal to sell bear organs in that country, with one exception – it is still legal to sell bear organs harvested in the United States. Consequently, bear poaching in Alaska has been on the rise over the past few decades.

Occasionally, one of these poachers gets careless and becomes an organ donor himself. I take some comfort in that.

Mike Delany
Brookbend
November 2014

Acknowledgements:

Once again, I must thank my old friend, Jim Hagee, for his help in creating this novel. I consulted him whenever I needed an Alaskan's viewpoint or phraseology to make the story ring true. He never disappointed, whether my question was about animal taxonomy, snowmobiles, aircraft or bushcraft. I must also thank him for inspiring my Haywood Jennings character in the Moose Jaw saga.

I should also like to thank Lisa O'Hearn for her work on the cover of this book. She and her husband Sean are both good friends as well as enthusiastic fans of the Fergus O'Neill series. Lisa does professional graphic design from her studio in Evergreen, CO. She is very good at what she does and I'm delighted she agreed to create the front cover for this novel.

I would be remiss if I failed to mention Corey Colombin (a fellow local author), Kappy Kling (HearthFire Books in Bergen Village), and an ever-growing readership for their help, support, encouragement and insistence that I complete this novel and get it into print. Thank you one and all.

Finally, heartfelt thanks to my wife, Cynthia, and my daughter, Shannon for their tireless efforts in reading, rereading, editing and grooming the manuscript for this novel. Thanks also to my grandson, Nino, for his help in finding the image of a bear worthy of representing the "ghost bear" in this story, and also for his photograph of me which appears on the back cover.

Mike Delany
Brookbend
November 2014

Prologue

"Maybe we've been out here too long," the old shaman said to himself as he made his way down Moose Jaw Creek. He had often heard it said that white men too long in the bush went crazy. Perhaps this was true of his own people as well. It seemed that way, if his dream had been true.

He had but one good eye. It was glacial blue. He focused it now upon the tracks of the bear his dream had told him to follow. He knew this bear – had known him forever it seemed. When he had been a young man he had called him 'the bear with the broken foot' because the ancient grizzly had lost two claws of his right forepaw to a steel-jawed trap. He felt an affinity with this bear since he too had a crippled right hand with only three remaining fingers. Many years had passed since he had first seen this bear, and over those years he had come to think of him simply as 'Broken Foot'. His truncated track was unmistakable, not just because of the mangled foot, but because of the size – this bear was truly a monster.

The old man followed the bear's tracks downstream through a fresh dusting of snow. Wherever the Moose Jaw rounded a bend, the bear crossed the ice to the other side, keeping to the gravel bars as opposed to the steep cut banks that defined the outside of the bends. Passage across these open stretches of shoreline was unimpeded by the mazes of downed trees and tanglefoot one encountered along the high banks. The old man appreciated the bear's wisdom. He too preferred to maintain a stately pace across country that allowed him to see more than just a shadowy trail through dense forest.

On the open bars the new snow was already crosshatched with the trails of many creatures. The old man stepped over each one as he came to it – an ancient superstition that had settled in his spirit too long ago for him to remember. But he knew there was a practical side to this ritual too; if he did not tread directly upon an existing track, it would be difficult for anyone studying his trail to determine if he had passed this way before or after the other creature. He even took care to keep his paces evenly spaced to leave no indication that he had stepped wide over an older trail. It occurred to him that perhaps this was a childish game he played, and he smiled and shrugged his shoulders. 'I suppose it is,' he thought. 'I've been doing it since I was a child.'

1

The bear, of course, played no such games. He maintained his ponderous gait untroubled by such nonsense. The old man crossed the tracks of wolf, arctic hare, fox and porcupine, some had been made prior to the bear's passing, some after. He noted that a cow moose and her calf had come out of the willows and made their way to the other bank not long before the bear had cut their trail. The bear's steady progress indicated he had no interest in moose today. Perhaps he was not hunting. That was a good thing; it suggested he was not hungry. It was not wise to follow a hungry bear too closely. He did not fear this bear, it was just the duty of a man to act with prudence in the presence of such a beast. So too was it the duty of the bear to act with aggression when humans failed to show respect for Alaska's most fearsome carnivore. The old man understood these things and acted in accordance with them.

Not far upstream of the place where Dead Man Creek joined the Moose Jaw, the bear had left the gravel bar and struck inland. Under the trees there was just a light dusting of new snow atop the pack that had accumulated over the winter. The old man could see the grizzly had turned to follow the trail a snow machine had carved sometime before the last snow. He slowed his pace and stopped to listen. It would not do to surprise the bear in this heavy cover. When he was satisfied that the only sounds were the stirring of the wind and the call of birds, he pushed on.

He had traipsed these woods many times over the years so he knew of the cave in the side of the hill just where the ground began to rise. Generations of bears had used it for their den in winters past. The snow machine had stopped inside the trees not far from the mouth of this cave. The old snow and the dark earth beneath it was disturbed in a manner that showed two men had gone to the cave and returned to the machine. Two yellow holes in a snow bank told him they had stood side-by-side and urinated before departing. Broken Foot had stopped near the yellow snow before visiting the cave. The old shaman was certain the bear had paused long enough to log the essence of these humans in his memory – his sense of smell was extraordinary and he would know them by their scent the next time he encountered them.

The old one-eyed man stood quietly among the mixed birch and spruce trees and allowed his spirit to probe the interior of the cave. He could hear no movement from within, nor could he feel the

2

presence of a living being anywhere in his immediate surroundings. He went closer to the cave's mouth, knelt and studied the ground to verify that the big bear had indeed come and gone, then he went inside. He had no torch, but he did not need one – his good eye could see as well in darkness as ordinary people could see in daylight.

He saw the dead bear, stiff and cold on the floor of the cave near the back wall. It was an adult black bear, not a grizzly. He did not have to examine the carcass to know what had happened here. Men had found the hibernating bear, killed it, and taken a single organ. This was troubling, because he knew the men who had done this awful thing. They were of his family. They shared his blood. And he knew the bear with the broken foot would someday punish them for the sacrilege they had committed. He closed his eye and allowed himself to float in darkness while he contemplated what he must do.

Chapter 1

March, 2001
Fairbanks, Alaska

Fergus O'Neill could not remember when the dreams had begun. At first there had been only the ancient shaman, Old Blue Eye, beckoning him home. The following night the old man had been accompanied by a raven. And the night after that, the three-toed bear was with them. Sometimes the old man would speak the words, sometimes the bear or the raven. They always said the same thing.

"She is waiting."

He would try to speak to them, but he had no voice. Then, in the last dream, Morgan herself appeared to him. She stood naked in the snow on the banks of a frozen creek. Her long red tresses stirred in the wind, sometimes obscuring her lovely face. Then the air currents would shift and he could see the sadness in her green eyes.

"I am waiting," she said softly.

And his voice came to him. "Soon," he promised her.

***

Fergus had spent the winter at Haywood Jennings' home in Fairbanks. Gus, as almost everyone called him, had a place up on the Moose Jaw, but it was just a one room log cabin, with no central heat or indoor plumbing. He had opted for the comparative comfort of civilization.

His host, Haywood Jennings, was one of Gus' two best friends. Haywood was a well-regarded veterinarian with a small animal practice in Fairbanks. He was also a seasoned bush pilot. "Seasoned" in Alaska's flying community often meant the pilot had survived at least one plane crash. He was a tall, lanky Missouri farm boy with a mane of silver-white hair, a big toothy smile and a predilection for outrageous hayseed eloquence. One never knew what he might say next. In any event, he had graciously insisted that Gus avail himself of the guest bedroom until the spring thaw.

Gus' other best friend, Kees Calis, had dropped by Haywood's place that evening after work with a bottle of excellent single malt whisky. "Kees," it should be noted, is pronounced Case. Although officially retired, he had retained his position with the Alaska State Troopers as a hired consultant. He was Alaska's most celebrated crime scene investigator and had risen to become top dog in the Fairbanks detachment of the CIB, their Criminal Investigation Bureau. The contractual arrangement he now enjoyed allowed him to do what he loved best – investigate crime scenes while some poor nine-to-fiver dealt with budgets, personnel matters and a myriad of other mundane chores that had plagued his days while still in uniform.

Early in his career, he had been given the nickname "Hard Case" by his boss and mentor, Pokey Brewster. Pokey had insisted that he had bestowed that moniker upon him due to his ability to solve the hardest cases. Some of Hard Case's peers and subordinates suspected it may have been more in recognition of his gruff personality and his take-no-prisoners approach to life, job, criminals, acquaintances, and inanimate objects. No one called him Hard Case to his face; anyone foolish enough to cross that line would receive an immediate invitation to his office where they would endure what had commonly come to be termed "Case hardening".

Unlike Haywood, Hard Case was of medium height and was heavily muscled beneath an insulating layer of subcutaneous fat which served him well in the brutal Alaska winters. There was perhaps a bit more salt than pepper in his bristling flat-top, but on official documents he still wrote "black" in the box designated "hair color".

Gus was slightly taller than Hard Case, but carried considerably less bulk. He was solidly constructed, broad of shoulder and narrow at the hip. His Alaska driver's license stated his eyes were blue and his hair was black. His eyes actually were quite blue. As to hair color, he was relatively certain there had been just a dignified sprinkle of gray above his ears last year when he'd filled out his application. The new ones hadn't appeared until after his fight with the bear.

Despite their physical differences, the three men were very much alike at heart. It was inevitable that they would become best of friends. The bond that had formed between them was strong. Gus' father had often said, "You don't know who your friends are until the chips are down". When the chips had been down for Haywood last autumn, he never doubted his two pals would move heaven and earth to save him. They had not let him down. And, when Gus had been mauled by a huge grizzly Haywood had found him and mended his wounds with fishing line before flying him back to a Fairbanks hospital. They knew who their true friends were.

**

As the spring equinox approached, Gus became eager to return to The Varmitage. He had come to realize he could not endure life without Morgan. He loved her. Never mind that she had brutally killed a man. She had done so to protect Haywood and himself. And, in retrospect, who was he to frown upon a little justifiable homicide? He was not without the stain of blood on his own hands. He had killed for her – she for him. He knew now that all he wanted in life was to spend his remaining time on earth with her out there in the bush. He realized he would have to accept her for what she was, and just be happy to have her. He told Haywood and Hard Case he'd be heading back out to his cabin for St. Patrick's Day. They didn't object; they had seen it coming and thought it was probably for the best. Haywood had met Morgan in the flesh. Hard Case knew strange things happened in the bush, but he had yet to make her acquaintance. He wasn't certain he wanted to. He was an old cop, with his feet firmly grounded in reality. Still, he never doubted her existence – not for a minute.

"I'm sure you've thought it all through, Gus," Hard Case said. "But keep in mind the ice doesn't break up on the Moose Jaw until mid-May. You're looking at two months of sub-freezing temperatures. For the most part you'll be cabin-bound and spend half your time next to the stove melting snow for your drinking water. And, if memory serves, you still haven't chinked the gaps in the outhouse wall."

Gus nodded. "You're right of course. But, when you weigh those minor hardships against putting up with Haywood's poisonous cigars and cornpone wit, it doesn't seem too high a price to pay."

Hard Case grinned. "There is that."

Haywood returned from the kitchen with three whisky glasses and the bottle of Oban 14 Hard Case had brought.

"I believe that was a miscast aspersion that just buzzed me in the hall." He handed the bottle to Hard Case and placed the glasses on

6

the dining table. "Pull the cork, Case. We'll give Gus a proper send off."

Hard Case poured two fingers of good malt in each glass. Haywood raised his to the table in general.

"To Gus," he said, "Varmitage bound."

Hard Case added, "Keep your wits about you and your rifle handy. Remember, weird things happen out there on the Moose Jaw."

Gus grinned. "You don't need to tell me that," he assured them. Then he raised his glass and said, "Here's to The Varmitage."

Toast toasted, Hard Case went back over to his easy chair in front of the television. Haywood refilled their drinks and slid one across the table to Gus.

"I believe we were in the midst of some philosophical ruminations before the call of demon rum interrupted us. What pearl had you just cast before us swine?"

Gus loved the way Haywood could go on when he assumed his professorial persona. He was full of shit, of course, but Gus loved to listen to him anyway.

He sipped his drink and took up where he had left off. "I had just postulated that time, at least along the Moose Jaw, was anachronistic."

"Isn't 'anachronistic time' an oxymoron?" Haywood countered, sipping his own whisky.

"You're both oxes and morons," Hard Case grumbled from across the room.

"That would be *oxen* and morons," Haywood protested indignantly.

"I stand corrected," Hard Case said. "Now shut up and let me hear what the reporter is saying. The siren just went off in Nome, so Jeff King must have passed the two mile mark; he'll be coming up Front Street shortly."

They were gathered in Haywood's living room, watching television coverage of the 2001 Iditarod and enjoying a roaring fire while warming their insides with Hard Case's excellent scotch. Doug Swingley, a musher from Montana, had won the race, crossing the finish line during the wee hours of the morning. Linwood Fiedler, from Willow, Alaska, had come in second at about two o'clock that afternoon, and Jeff King, another Alaskan,

7

was making the final dash down Front Street toward the burl arch as they watched. The burl arch had served as the official finish line since 1973, when it was erected for the first "Last Great Race".

"I had my money on King this year," Hard Case said dispiritedly. "Who's that musher won the Yukon Quest last month? Weren't you guys pulling for him to take the Iditarod too?"

"Tim Osmar," Gus said. "We got to spend some time with him while he was stopped for his mandatory thirty-six hour rest at the Dawson checkpoint this year. He's a good man, but no one's ever won both the Quest and the Iditarod the same year."

"Yeah," Haywood said. "But if anyone could do it, I figured it would be him. He's a musher's musher."

"Well, you gotta hand it to Swingley," Hard Case said. "I didn't think he could pull it off again." Doug Swingley had won it in 1999 and 2000 also. Susan Butcher was the only musher to have ever won three in a row before.

Haywood said, "Yeah, back-to-back-to-back is pretty rare. Even Shakespeare's beast only had two backs."

Gus smiled and raised his glass toward Haywood in appreciation of his smutty literary reference. Hard Case caught the gesture and glowered. "What the hell are you two yammering about? You sound like a couple of sophomoric nincompoops."

Gus couldn't help himself. "Isn't sophomoric nincompoop redundant?" he asked giving Haywood a surreptitious wink.

"I give up," Hard Case knocked back his whisky and held out his empty glass for Haywood to refill.

***

Haywood volunteered his services as checkpoint veterinarian every year for either the Yukon Quest or the Iditarod. This year, since Gus was wintering with him, they both volunteered at the Quest's halfway point in Dawson City, Yukon Territory, Canada. Gus was delighted to discover they were being put up at the El Dorado hotel, downtown. Granted they had to hot-bed it with three other volunteers on a rotating schedule set up to assure there would be a vet on duty round the clock, but it certainly beat twenty-below in a sleeping bag on the ice of the Skwentna River. He was even more delighted that Dawson boasted a genuine beer hall where mushers and volunteers could all get together for a chat and a brew.

8

As they were packing their gear to return to Fairbanks, Hard Case had called Haywood on his mobile to ask a favor. Haywood owned half-stake in a played out gold mine just over the border in Alaska on the Fortymile River. Six dead bears had been found within a few miles of his digs and the State Trooper dispatched to investigate reported that the gallbladders and claws of each carcass had been surgically removed. Poachers had been harvesting organs and body parts for several years. But recently it had become more and more widespread in Alaska. Hard Case asked Haywood to fly into the Fortymile and check his cabin on their way home. It was well known that Haywood never locked it up and it was just possible that a poacher or poachers had been using his place for their base of operations. If so, there might be an opportunity to lift a few prints. Hard Case had told them to just look around, and if it appeared someone had been there over the winter, to leave everything as they found it and report back to him.

They did as he asked and found evidence that someone had indeed spent several days there. They called Hard Case and Haywood gave him permission to send in a Trooper to see what could be learned.

***

The doorbell rang and Haywood went to the front door and invited the pizza delivery guy from Big Al's to enter. The young man lifted a snow covered boot, obviously reluctant to leave a mess on the customer's floor.

Haywood laughed, "Don't worry about it, just put the boxes on the table."

Gus extracted some bills from his wallet and paid the man. "My treat tonight, gentlemen. Haywood's fire, Case's whisky, the pizza's on me."

"You're a good man O'Neill," Hard Case said approvingly. He handed the delivery man a five dollar bill as he passed on the way to the door. "For your trouble," he said.

The guy from Big Al's smiled and accepted the tip.

"Careful on those steps," Haywood warned. "They're worse going down than up." He closed the door behind the young fellow and crossed to the table where Hard Case was busy opening boxes and laying out napkins.

Gus went to the kitchen and returned with three cold bottles of Alaska Amber Ale.

"Gotta have beer with pizza," he observed. "Can't be drinking Scotland's finest with pub grub."

"Indeed," Hard Case said, helping himself to a large wedge from the 'Carnivore Special'. "You sophomoric Shakespearian oxen would probably consider that to be très gauche."

Haywood cocked an eyebrow at Gus. "French yet!"

Gus nodded, "Me thinks he's more than just a pretty face."

Hard Case beamed with pleasure and tucked into his beer and pizza. He enjoyed the verbal swordplay with his two pals – more so when he was able to give the proverbial blade a little twist.

When the pizza was gone Haywood poured a round of after-dinner drinks. The next musher due into Nome was projected to be Rick Swenson, and he wasn't expected for another eight or nine hours. Gus turned off the television and they settled in near the fire.

"What time you leave for Hawaii tomorrow?" Hard Case asked his host. Haywood was scheduled to attend one of the mandatory continuing education courses required of all veterinarians in Alaska. Of course, he could have enrolled in the same course which was available in Anchorage or Fairbanks, but he preferred Hawaii in the winter. Then too, since the state mandated the training, the trip was deductible as a business expense.

"Connecting flight down to Anchorage departs at ten o'clock in the morning," he replied. "I'm on Alaska Air's direct flight to Honolulu that leaves Anchorage at two in the afternoon. Booked the last seat in first-class."

Hard Case snorted, "Alaska State Troopers have to fly Economy Class, even retired top-shelf back-in-the-fold-under-contract super dicks like myself. I didn't bother begging this time; I just paid for an upgrade out of my own pocket. I'm on the eleven o'clock to Seattle. Can't get to San Diego non-stop from here."

"Want a ride to the airport with us?" Gus asked him. "We can swing by and pick you up on the way."

"That'll work," Hard case accepted. "Mournful George is my designated driver tonight. When he comes to fetch me, I'll tell him he can scratch tomorrow morning's airport run."

"You planning to visit your old boss while you're down there?" Haywood asked.

Hard Case nodded. "Yeah. Last I heard poor old Pokey's going downhill fast. Probably won't be around next winter."

They were quiet for a while, just enjoying the fire and the peat-smoke flavor of the single malt and the camaraderie. Bosworth, Haywood's big Maine Coon cat, waddled into the living room and hopped up in Hard Case's lap; he never asked permission, and he never apologized. Before Hard Case could move his glass out of harm's way Bosworth dipped the tip of his tail in it.

"Christ almighty, Haywood," Hard Case said, "I wish you'd teach Bosworth some manners. Cat hairs do not improve single malt whisky."

Haywood chuckled and watched his big cat ease himself off Hard Case's lap onto the ottoman, then drop gracefully to the floor and plod off into the kitchen – both nose and tail erect as he made his slow and dignified exit from the living room.

"Now you've offended, him," Gus chided Hard Case. "His highness does not appear amused."

Hard Case brushed at the hairs Bosworth had deposited on his lap. "His highness would do well to shed some bulk instead of hanks of his royal mane. His damned shadow must weigh five pounds."

Haywood went to the sideboard, poured a dollop of whisky in a clean glass, and took it over to Hard Case. "Here," he said, "no hairs in this one."

Hard Case accepted it, but did not hand Haywood his original glass until he'd drained it, cat hairs or no. "You're a gentleman and a scholar, Jennings," he expounded. "And, a gracious host."

"Here, here," Gus toasted. "I've been imposing on his hospitality all winter."

Hard Case said, "So when do you leave for The Varmitage?"

"Friday," Gus told them. "I booked a morning flight with Bush League."

Haywood said, "Why don't you hold off until Case and I get back. We were figuring on going out for a grouse hunt anyway. It's only another week. I could fly you out then and save you the bush taxi fare. Besides, if you hang around, I won't have to put Bosworth under lock-and-key at the clinic."

"Bosworth will manage," Gus told them. "And I appreciate the offer, but I need a little time alone with Morgan. I haven't seen her since that thing with Lindsay. I didn't handle that very well; I want to put it right with her. Besides, she's never had my corned-beef and cabbage, and I can't think of anyone I'd rather cook it for."

Haywood looked at Hard Case and shrugged. "It's your call, Gus. And, I guess I can't blame you for wanting to get back to Morgan. You sure she'll be there?"

Hard Case was wondering the same thing himself. He'd never actually seen the mysterious redhead, but both Haywood and Gus insisted she truly existed. And, as he liked to remind Gus, strange things happened in the bush; he'd seen enough weird stuff out there to make him a believer.

Gus didn't have to think long about Haywood's question. "She'll be there," he said with absolute certainty.

Hard Case watched the sparks pop off the blazing logs onto the blackened bricks of the fireplace. "How about taking along my satellite phone this trip?" he suggested. "You can call us when you're ready to receive guests and give us a shopping list of supplies you want us to bring in."

Gus had refused to take any communication device into the Moose Jaw with him last summer, but in retrospect it definitely would have come in handy. He decided to quit being an "asshole about the radio" as Haywood had so succinctly pointed out.

He nodded his agreement. "Good idea, Case. Thanks."

"Don't mention it. I'll feel better knowing you can contact us in an emergency. I'll have it ready for you in the morning, and I'll charge up two extra batteries."

Haywood looked puzzled. "Why don't you just rig up an outlet to LaGrange's magic box. You've got electricity now; you don't need extra batteries. Hell, you could take out a little space heater too. You'd save a lot of firewood that way."

Gus laughed and shook his head. "And a toaster and a television, and an electric blanket? I don't think so Haywood. You can't get away from it all if you take it all with you. Besides, I'm still a little gun-shy of that generator. I think I'll just muddle through without it for the time being."

Hard Case said, "If it's still in the cabin, you might want to find a better place to stow it. I don't think we're out of the woods on the LaGrange situation yet."

They both looked at him for a moment. Haywood said, "You know something we don't, Case?"

Gus went to the fireplace and took his pipe off the mantle. He studied Hard Case as he filled the bowl with tobacco. "It didn't occur to me when you suggested I take along the radio, but now you've piqued my interest. What's up?"

Hard Case placed his glass on the side table and slowly patted his knees with the flats of his big hands. "Just something that came up today at the office. A guy I know over at the Bureau dropped by for a cup of coffee and a chat. He wanted to flag me, off the record, that someone at the Russian Consulate General down in Anchorage has been asking questions about the three of us. My visitor didn't offer any details about the inquiry, but what else can it be?"

Haywood sipped his drink. "I see what you mean. The old Eastern Bloc team knew LaGrange and Inga were with me when the plane went down. Your rescuing me was all over the local news for a few days, so it wouldn't take their top analyst to put two and two together."

Gus lit his pipe and nodded. "Haywood, LaGrange and Inga together in the plane with the generator – LaGrange and Inga are dead. Who does that leave with the magic box?"

Hard Case rubbed his face with both hands. "That's the gist of it. I'm sure they've come to the same conclusion as Lindsay did last fall. Haywood and I didn't return to Fairbanks with it, so it must still be out there on the Moose Jaw somewhere. Your cabin is the first place they'd check."

Haywood looked troubled. "You think they've already been there?"

"Almost certainly," Hard Case told them. "But I don't think they found it. If so, why ask about us?"

They both looked at Gus. "Was it still in the cabin?"

Gus grinned. "No. I put it where no sane person would ever look."

They waited for the rest, but Gus just continued puffing on his pipe. At length, Haywood said, "Come on, come on – where'd you put it?"

Hard Case held up a meaty palm. "Keep it to yourself, Gus. I don't want to know."

Haywood looked at him in open mouthed astonishment. "What the hell…?"

Gus cut him off. "Case is right, Haywood. If they haven't found it yet, and they're determined to do so, they'll want to talk to us. You're better off not knowing."

Haywood let out a sigh. "That's comforting. They won't shoot me after I tell them where it is – they'll shoot me because I can't tell them where it is."

Hard Case summed it up. "Bottom line is, take the damned radio with you this time, Gus. And don't go anywhere near wherever you hid Pandora's Box."

Gus knocked the ashes out of his pipe against a log in the fireplace. "I'll take the radio. And I'll check in on a regular basis, just to let you know all's well."

***

Sergeant George Gleason, a.k.a. Mournful George, arrived as scheduled at nine o'clock to collect his boss. He had been Hard Case's right-hand man, friend and faithful retainer for the past twenty-five years. No one could remember when he'd acquired the nickname, but his bloodhound eyes and funereal expression left no doubt as to why he was dubbed 'mournful'. Haywood greeted him at the door and ushered him into the living room.

Hard Case tossed back the last of his drink. "Right on time as always, George. I believe you're acquainted with these celebrated rogues."

George had exchanged greetings with Haywood at the door. Now he nodded to Gus. "Evening, Fergus," he always used a person's given name. "Good to see you again, sir."

Gus thought it only proper to return the formality; he saluted him with his nearly empty glass. "Sergeant Gleason. Always a pleasure."

Hard Case rested one of his big meaty paws on Mournful George's shoulder. "George," he said, "these kindly gentlemen have offered me a ride to the airport in the morning, so you're off the hook. See me home tonight, and you can sleep in tomorrow."

Haywood saw Hard Case and Mournful George to the door, waited until they were safely down the steps and seated in their full-sized State Trooper SUV, then switched off the porch light and came back into the living room. "It's snowing again, but there's

14

only an inch or two in the forecast. The roads should be clear in the morning," he said.

Gus was tearing apart the pizza boxes and adding them to the fire a little at a time. "You all packed?" he asked.

"Pretty much," Haywood said, rounding up glasses and bottles and heading off to the kitchen. "You know me; I travel light – toothbrush and a credit card," he continued as he came back into the living room.

Gus nodded. "Like I said, I'll take as much as I can into the Moose Jaw this run. Bush League Air Taxi Service has a Helio Courier they can set down on the ice right in front of The Varmitage. I'll haul in as much heavy stuff as I can while I have the chance. Saves me packing it all up the overland trail from the landing strip after the thaw," he said.

Haywood rubbed his chin and considered what Gus had said. "I flew the State Troopers' Helio Courier last autumn," he said. "Damned fine aircraft; they're an old Porter design, specially fitted out for STOL (short take off and landing); great bush planes, and they can handle an impressive payload. Until I get my little Clipper put back together, I'll have to rent something when I want to fly. If you compose a big enough shopping list, I just might rent one of them when Case and I come in for the grouse. There'll be three of us to shift the cargo up to the cabin, so it would be the perfect time for a big load."

Gus agreed. "I'll put together a laundry list."

***

When Gus came up from the guest room in the morning, Haywood was already showered, shaved, dressed and was busy preparing breakfast.

"I smell bacon," he said approvingly.

"Never travel on an empty stomach," Haywood pronounced. "I cleaned out the fridge and cooked up everything but two eggs and three strips of bacon. You can break your fast on them tomorrow before you head out to the Moose Jaw."

"I'll do that. I booked the air taxi for ten o'clock. That'll give me plenty of daylight to pack everything from the river up to the cabin and get a rick of firewood stacked on the porch."

"Gives you plenty of time to, ah… get reacquainted with Morgan too, eh Fergus?"

15

Gus grinned. "That too," he admitted happily.

Haywood used the spatula to load eggs and bacon onto Gus' plate. "You think you're over the Snow Viper thing?"

Gus poured a cup of coffee to go with his breakfast. "Can't say for sure. I won't know until I see her. All women change according to what a given circumstance may require. Morgan just has the ability to change a little more than most."

"You can say that again." Haywood brought his plate of bacon and eggs over to the breakfast table and joined Gus. "I think, once you lay eyes on her tomorrow, you'll forget all about that other business."

Gus smiled. "I hope so, Haywood; we'll see how it goes."

Chapter 2

March, 2001
San Diego, CA

From the terrace of his Mission Bay hotel room, he looked down at the surfers that dotted the clear blue waters off the white sand beach. Southern California was beautiful, but he wished he was home in Fairbanks. Spring was his favorite season in Alaska because the ice was still solid on the rivers, but the promise of long days and warm weather spiced the air with an optimism you could actually taste. Mid-March meant St. Patrick's Day debauchery to most of the residents of the Lower Forty-Eight. In Alaska, it meant the equinox – equal days and nights. That was a big deal in the frozen north. The thaw was coming, the ice would soon be breaking up on the rivers; the days would grow longer and longer until the night was chased over the horizon. Alaskans were already rejoicing.

Not so in San Diego. People here took their balmy climate for granted. They insisted their coastal city enjoyed four seasons, but Hard Case had always felt their seasons were nothing more than summer's mood swings. Nevertheless, a lot of retirees moved to southern California for that very reason; old bones like heat. Maybe that's why Tobias "Pokey" Brewster had moved down here after he retired from the Alaska State Troopers. Pokey had been Hard Case's boss back when Hard Case was just a rookie. He had been the one who gave young Kees Calis his nickname. He'd given him more than that moniker though. He'd taught him how to be a good cop in Alaska – how to understand the people who lived there, both native and newcomer, and what it meant to be a peace officer in America's last frontier. That had been thirty years ago, but Hard Case still lived by the old code of ethics Pokey had instilled in him. Those principles had served him well in a career that began in the newly formed Alaska Criminal Investigation Bureau in 1971 right up to his retirement as Bureau Chief last year. Although he too was officially retired now, he still worked for the State Troopers under contract. He was considered the best Crime Scene Investigator in Alaska – perhaps in the entire western United States – when he'd finally turned in his badge. He had declined several lucrative contract offers from states all over the country, opting instead to remain in Alaska.

The Crime Scene Professionals Conference he was attending in San Diego was an annual affair hosted by a different city's police department each year. He had missed the last few, but decided to sign up for this year's gathering so he could catch up on the latest CSI technology and visit his old boss. Pokey, who turned ninety-two years old last month, resided in an assisted living facility in La Jolla, just a half-hour drive up the coast from the hotel where the conference was being held. After a leisurely breakfast at the terrace restaurant, he took a taxi over to the downtown SDPD headquarters and borrowed an unmarked pool car. By ten o'clock he was on the coastal highway headed north with all the windows open. He could have cranked up the air-conditioning, but he hated recycled air and a visitor from Fairbanks had to take advantage of warm seaside weather whenever he got the chance.

***

Pokey was not looking good. It had been over four years since Hard Case had seen him, and his old mentor had clearly gone downhill. A nurse had met Hard Case at the door of Pokey's apartment and warned him what to expect – still he had not been prepared for the sight of the cadaverous old man sleeping upright in his recliner, plastic tubes running from his nostrils to the portable oxygen bottle beside the chair. Pokey's eye lids were closed and his lower jaw hung slack. There was spittle glistening at the corners of his open mouth. His once full head of dark hair was now reduced to a few wispy strands of gray. They resembled the brittle stalks of corn in a frozen field long after the harvest. Hard Case walked to the window and looked out over the rooftops to the west. The ocean was not part of the view, but he could see palm trees and tropical greenery and red and purple flowers dotting the landscape below.

From the room behind him came a rattling cough, then the old man's voice croaked, "Kees Calis – I will be damned. Is that really you?"

Hard Case turned from the window and smiled. "It's really me, Pokey. How you doin' old-timer?"

"Big shot detective like you oughta be able to see that for himself," Pokey chided. "How you think I'm doin', boy? I'm waitin' for the damned bus."

The bus was, of course, a euphemism for death. As young men, they had both scoffed at the idea of ever waiting for that bus themselves. They fully expected the bus to take them by surprise. Alaska State Troopers didn't anticipate surviving to become decrepit old men. They lived in a violent place. Alaska was an unforgiving land inhabited by brutal men and savage beasts. They would die in a plane crash, or get mauled by a bear, or stabbed by a drunk, or shot by a poacher. They might drown in an icy river, or freeze to death in a snow storm. They wouldn't sit quietly, waiting for death to come take them. Yet, here they were – Pokey waiting at the bus stop, and Hard Case wondering how he could avoid a seat on the same bench.

"Are you in any pain?" Hard Case asked, more curious than concerned.

"Nah," Pokey shook his head. "They keep me doped up all the time now. They give me pills for pain, pills for anxiety, water pills, and pills I don't even know what the hell they're for. I used to manage all my own medication, but I got confused a couple of times so the nurse runs the pills now. They're afraid I might accidently O.D. and kill myself. Think about that. Wouldn't that be better than just rotting away?"

Hard Case nodded, but said nothing in reply. There wasn't really any way to answer that question.

Pokey went on, "It's all about the money, I reckon. They keep me alive and the Medicare money keeps rolling in. I go toes up and they gotta find another cash cow to milk."

"How much longer they give you?" Hard Case asked him. There was no point in pretending death was a long way off.

"They never come right out and say it," Pokey snorted. "But I'd bet you could measure my future in weeks rather than months."

"Anything I can do for you? You know, help make sure you've put your house in order, and all that?" Hard Case offered.

Pokey removed the oxygen from his nose and motioned for Hard Case to come closer. Hard Case pulled a straight-backed chair over next to Pokey's recliner and leaned his head close to the old man's so they could speak in private.

"I had a lawyer help me with the will. That's all taken care of. As to the disposition of my mortal remains, I'm going to be cremated. I don't want a fancy funeral; the American Legion will be handling the ceremony at the cemetery. They'll shoot off their rifles, then a bugler will play taps and the captain of the honor guard will present the flag to my nephew. He's the closest thing I've got to kin. Hell, you're the closest thing I ever had to a son. Maybe I can arrange to have them send the flag up to you."

Hard Case felt a tear forming in the corner of one eye. "If you want," was all he could manage to say. Then, after taking a deep breath, "You know I'd like that."

Pokey extended a claw-like hand and patted Hard Case's knee. "I'll see what I can do."

The effort of conversing had worn Pokey out and he nodded off to sleep. Hard Case sat quietly beside him and thought about those early years when Fairbanks was still a frontier town and he was just a young buck, and Pokey Brewster was the bull of the woods. He recalled how Pokey had done all the crime scene investigations out in the bush until personnel issues, budgets and politics had forced him to delegate that role to an up-and-comer. He remembered the pride that threatened to burst his chest when Pokey had trusted him to be that guy.

After a short nap, Pokey opened his eyes and seemed a little surprised to see Hard Case there with him. Then he gave a slow nod and crooked a bony finger, indicating that his protégé should lean in a little closer.

"There *is* one thing you can do for me, Kees, if you will."

"Name it," Hard Case said.

"You remember those cold cases I used to have you guys go through every now and again?"

"I remember," Hard Case assured the old man.

"Well, one of them always troubled me. It still does. I'd like you to have one more go at it. Would you do that for me?"

Hard Case shrugged his beefy shoulders. "I don't see why not," he conceded. "I still have access to all the old files. Which case was it?"

Pokey's breaths had become short and labored, so he replaced the oxygen tubes in his nostrils and leaned his head back against the headrest for a moment. When his breathing had returned to normal he went on. "You remember that double homicide up in the Moose Jaw country back in the late fifties? The two brothers – can't recall their names – got themselves killed and burned up in that fishing lodge?"

To cover his discomfort, Hard Case rose and walked over to the window and gazed out into the southern California sunshine. He remembered the case, alright – the Rainbow Lodge murders. Just last autumn he had occasion to unearth the old file on those homicides. He had done so because his two best friends, Gus O'Neill and Haywood Jennings had flown in from the Moose Jaw in early September and told him a tale of kidnapping, rape and murder that had reminded him of the old case Pokey had just mentioned. The two victims of those 1959 murders were a nasty pair of brothers named Roy and Larry McCaslin. Some "person or persons unknown", as stated in the case file, had stripped them naked, wired their nuts together through an eye bolt in the log wall, given each brother a dull hunting knife, and left a "timed incendiary device" right there in the room with them. The curious thing was neither of them had died in the fire. One had been shot and the other stabbed to death before the fire even started. They had been found by two moose hunters who noticed smoke from the still smoldering ruins of the lodge as they were floating past the confluence of Moose Jaw and Rainbow creeks. They reported what they had found when they returned to Fairbanks, more than a week after the crime had been committed. Pokey had been the trooper dispatched out of Fairbanks to investigate. He had written up the original report on the murders, including some very odd physical evidence he discovered at the scene. He'd found what appeared to be two plastic shot-shell wads, and later the coroner's report stated the shot pellets removed from the gunshot victim's body were made of bismuth, not lead or steel. In 1959 no munitions manufacturer used such components in their shot shells. They represented a mystery within a mystery – one that had never been solved.

But, just last September, Hard Case discovered the story behind the plastic wads and the bismuth shot. He learned who had blasted them into Roy McCaslin. His reason rejected what he knew in his heart to be true – Fergus O'Neill, his good friend Gus, had been the killer. But that was impossible his reason reasoned. Oh, indeed it was – but nevertheless, it had happened.

***

When Hard Case turned from the window, he saw that Pokey was enjoying another of his frequent naps, so he sat back down on his chair. He was glad to have a little time to decide how to handle the request. Pokey had asked him to have another look at the Rainbow Lodge murders. The fact that Hard Case had officially closed the case last year presented no problem. He could always reopen it. And, in truth, there were still a few loose ends that should be tied up. For instance, who had been there before Gus? Whoever it was had wired the brothers scrotums together through the eye-bolt and rigged the incendiary device. He, or they – after all, it was still one of those "person or persons" sort of cases – had intended to kill both brothers in the most gruesome fashion imaginable; Gus had just blundered onto the scene and shot Roy as he was fleeing the lodge after mutilating his own brother. Wasn't it worth another look? What if he could actually solve that last part of the mystery? Wouldn't it absolve Gus? Might it not remove the burden of failure from Pokey's old shoulders? For a lot of reasons, he guessed it was the right thing to do.

"Kees?" Pokey's weak voice interrupted Hard Case's thoughts. "Would you fill my straw cup with ice water?"

Hard Case did as he had been asked and placed the water on the tray next to Pokey's chair. "There you go."

"Thanks," Pokey took it in a bony hand and sipped at it delicately. When he had had enough, he set it back on the tray and took up the conversation where they had left off.

"You remember the case I'm talkin' about?"

"I do," Hard Case told him truthfully. "The Rainbow Lodge murders. Roy and Larry McCarver, a.k.a. the McCaslin brothers; wire, fire; one stabbed, one shot. I also recall there were some weird shot-shell wads and loads. We never solved it."

"That's the one," Pokey said emphatically. "Still drives me nuts thinkin' about it. I questioned the father of those Athabascan boys. If the rumors about Larry molesting them were true, he had the best motive. But, he had a good alibi. You know how it goes, Kees, after a while the trail just goes cold. I had a lot of other irons in the fire back then. Yet, I never got over the feeling I missed something there. Will you have one more go at it? I gave you that nickname because you could always figure out the hard cases. This should be right up your alley, son."

Hard Case rubbed his beefy jaw and tried to think of a way to side-step the request without hurting the old man's feelings. He said, "Forty-two years is about as cold as a case can get. I wouldn't even know where to begin. Besides, whoever punched the McCaslins' tickets did the world a big favor. Can't you just let this one go, Pokey?"

"Could you?" Pokey asked. "If you were in my shoes, wouldn't you want to go out knowing? I don't expect an arrest. The killer's probably dead by now, anyway. I just want a name – who did it?"

"I can't guarantee any…"

Pokey interrupted him. "For Christ's sake. I know you can't. I'm just asking you to have one more look. Do it for me, Kees – so I can rest easy."

Hard Case nodded. "Alright, Pokey. One more look. I'll let you know what I find out, one way or the other."

Pokey gave him a weak smile. "Thanks, Kees. I just have a feeling you'll get to the bottom of it." Then, he laid his head back on the headrest and closed his eyes. Hard Case let himself out.

He passed the nurse in the hall. "How much longer has he got?" he asked her.

She shrugged her shoulders. "We can never say for certain, but if you intend to visit him again you shouldn't put it off too long."

Hard Case thanked her and took the stairs down to the lower level. He exited the building through the rear lobby and crossed the parking area to his borrowed car. Perhaps it was the blinding sun in the deep blue sky that made him think of the old shaman. He could see the wizened face clearly in his mind. One blind eye – one ice blue.

Questioning Old Blue Eye gave him another reason to visit the Moose Jaw when he returned home. Since the old boy had mentioned seeing Gus at the murder scene, he might be able to shed some light on what had happened before Gus arrived there that night.

He had planned on going out to The Varmitage for a bird hunt anyway. He already had an official reason for the trip since he had been investigating a new rash of bear poaching reports. Now that Gus had spent a week out there, he may have seen some snow machine activity on the river. Pokey's request gave him another official – or semiofficial – reason to fly out to the bush. A promise

23

to an old friend on his death bed was not to be taken lightly. He thought of the lines from Robert Service's *The Cremation of Sam McGee*:

"…Now a promise made is a debt unpaid, and the trail has its own stern code.

In the days to come, though my lips were dumb, in my heart how I cursed that load…"

He sincerely hoped he would not come to curse the burden he'd shouldered for Pokey.

Chapter 3

Friday, 16 March 2001

The Varmitage

Moose Jaw Creek, Alaska

The pilot helped Gus offload the buckets and river bags that contained all his supplies. When he had confirmed that Gus required nothing further of Bush League Air Taxi Service, he climbed back into the cockpit, fired up the engine, set the nose into the wind and roared off down the snow covered ice of the Moose Jaw. As soon as the aircraft's skis had lifted off the frozen river and cleared the treetops, Gus looked up toward the small log cabin he had built last summer and was filled with the joy of homecoming. A thin tendril of smoke materialized above the chimney, became a dense white column and rose into the clear blue sky. Gus strapped on his snowshoes, tramped straight up the bank, entered the cabin, took Morgan in his arms and kissed her long and hard. Before she could say a word, Gus put a finger to her lips, looked her straight in the eye and said, "Don't ever do that again. I've always had a thing about snakes."

She didn't feign ignorance, or deny her part in Lindsay's death. She just smiled at him and gently stroked his cheek with a soft, fragrant palm. "You'll never see another snake in Alaska," she assured him.

That had been all he'd needed to hear. Gus was hopelessly in love with this unearthly beauty, and the months he had spent without her had been unbearable. Although he had been filled with fear and revulsion for the white, fur clad serpent that had killed Lindsay, he could not imagine life without Morgan. Her promise was enough. He thought he could probably deal with any other side of her persona that may appear – as long as the Snow Viper remained deep in the mists of legend.

It was good to hold her in his arms again. He leaned back a little so he could see her beautiful face. She smiled up at him, and he brushed aside her long red hair and looked deep into her soft green eyes. God, how he'd missed her.

She kissed him gently on the lips, "I missed you too," she replied to his unspoken thought. "I didn't expect you to come back so soon."

"You came to me in a dream," he said. "I couldn't stay away any longer."

She squeezed him tighter. "I know."

They held one another in contented silence for some time. At length he said, "Did we have any visitors while I was gone?" He tried to put it as a casual question, but there was an edge to his voice.

She leaned back in his arms and studied him for a moment. "Yes. Two locals came up the river ice on a snowmobile early in the winter. They announced themselves before entering the cabin, and they did not disturb anything while they were here. They just built a fire in the stove and warmed themselves while they ate a lunch they had brought with them. They spoke of hunting bear. They came again a few weeks ago, but another man came with them – an oriental. He went through all your things and took two bottles of whiskey and your long bladed boning knife when they left. He will be back, and you must be very careful around him."

Gus put great stock in Morgan's read on people. Nevertheless, bear hunters were not his main concern. It was the Russians that worried him.

"Anyone else?" he asked.

She nodded slowly. "Yes. Not long after you left for Fairbanks a helicopter landed down by your boat launch. Two men came into the cabin and searched the place quite thoroughly. They were looking for the generator, but of course they didn't find it. One of them told the other they were on a fool's errand. He said there was compelling evidence it had been destroyed when Cahill's plane crashed and burned near Tok."

She could see Gus was relieved by her report. Still, she reassured him. "I think you can rest easy regarding LaGrange's engine."

He managed a weak smile. "I suppose you're privy to where I hid it," he said, although she had not been present when he'd taken it into the woods.

She kissed him on the lips. "It's hard to keep a secret from me."

He had had a feeling, that past autumn when the bear was waiting for him back by the beaver ponds, that Morgan was not far away. He had followed the old three-toed monster deeper into the trees until they came to the place where they had fought one another in the waning days of summer. A large pile of brush, branches and leaves stood heaped in the middle of the clearing – an unmistakable grizzly's cache. The bear stopped beside it, lifted a corner of the mound with the hooked claws of its rake-like forepaw and waited dispassionately while Gus settled the polished aluminum case as far back under the thatch as he could reach. Gus knew as he did so that he was exposing himself to certain death if the bear chose to kill him. But, he also knew the time for killing between them had passed. They were travelling new ground.

When he was satisfied that the generator was situated where he wanted it, he stood up and stepped back. The bear allowed the corner of his cache to drop back to the ground, then turned and disappeared into the woods. Gus had returned to the cabin and prepared to depart, all the while, sensing that Morgan was close to him.

He brought his mind back to the present and returned Morgan's kiss. "Yes," he told her. "I don't think I'll ever be able to keep anything from you."

"Good," she said with finality. "Now – enough talk. The cabin's still rather chilly; maybe we should get under the covers and wait until the fire warms it some."

Gus smiled. "Maybe we should, at that," he said.

She turned her lips to his ear and whispered, "You should probably take off those snowshoes first. They might prove awkward in bed."

***

Later, when he went back outside to bring the supplies up from the river a gentle snow was falling. It took him nearly an hour to transport everything up to the cabin, and in that time perhaps an inch more had accumulated in the tracks he had made. It had never occurred to him that Morgan would not need the stove in his absence, so he was somewhat surprised to see at least two week's supply of firewood still stacked on the porch. His work done, he took out his pipe, filled it with tobacco and lit it. He stood there for a while, just soaking in the landscape around him – the gravel bar in front of the cabin, the bare birch trees and willows along the frozen stream, and tall dark spruce standing sentinel above it on the far bank – all covered with a delicate shroud of virgin snow. He felt himself embraced by the silence and the savage beauty of the Moose Jaw.

Morgan came out to join him. She sensed the peace that had settled upon him and remained quiet, respecting the sanctity of his oneness with the winterscape that surrounded them.

He puffed gently on his pipe and the delicious aroma of Captain Black mingled with the falling snow. He turned, and their eyes met; she came down the steps to stand beside him, and slipped her arm through his. They remained there, arm in arm, not speaking, spiritually bonded in a chaste coupling for what seemed an eternity. The breeze shifted imperceptibly, a raven squawked somewhere upstream, and the snow swung slowly on the breeze until it came full-face into them and powdered their eyebrows and lashes.

"I feel it too," Gus said quietly. Then he realized Morgan had not spoken. He looked at her, mildly puzzled – yet knowing something magic had transpired.

She smiled at him. "Of course you do," she said. "Welcome home."

***

That evening after dinner Morgan poured them each a splash of Tullamore Dew and rejoined Gus at the raw plank table he had constructed last summer out of lumber he had milled with his chainsaw. She loved the solid simplicity of that table, and she loved these quiet moments when they just sat together, enjoying one another's company. There had been a time, last autumn, when she thought perhaps she'd lost him – driven him away with her dark side. She'd had no choice, of course. It was show him her worst possible face – her viciousness, her unbridled wrath, her murderous fury – or allow him and Haywood to die at the hands of a ruthless killer. She had become what she had to be – done what had to be done. And Gus and Haywood had survived. Somehow Gus had come to terms with who she was, and returned to her. A small tear of joy moistened the corner of one eye.

"Don't be wasting precious water," Gus admonished her. He reached across the table, took her teardrop on the tip of his finger and touched it to his tongue.

She smiled, stood and came around to sit on his lap. He slid the chair back from the table to make room for her. She settled in and rested her head upon his shoulder. "It was a tear of gladness," she told him. "I'm so full of joy at your being back, I just want to burst."

"I could tell," he nuzzled her neck. "It was the sweetest tear I ever tasted."

They sat that way for a long time before Morgan gave him a quick peck on the cheek and stood. "I'll clear the table," she said. "You do something with all that paraphernalia you brought in with you. The old copper bathing tub is charming, but an ice auger…? Really, the cabin is taking on the look of an old general store."

He admired her from behind as she took the dirty dishes over to the counter. 'Lovely,' he thought. 'Absolutely lovely.'

She came back to the table with a damp cloth and wiped down the surface. "Thank you," she said. "I'm glad you approve of my derrière."

He laughed, stood up and gave that lovely bottom a pat on his way over to address the "paraphernalia". She returned to the counter and began filling the sink with hot water from the small green woodstove's water tank. As she went about washing up the dishes, she glanced over her shoulder and caught him watching her. Her cheeks flushed with pleasure and she flashed him a bright smile. She knew full well what was on his mind and couldn't resist teasing him.

"I think you'll find there's still a half can of goose grease back there somewhere," she said. "Maybe you should move it closer to the stove so it can soften. My skin tends to get a bit dry in the winter."

He felt an immediate stirring in his loins and his mouth went a little dry.

"Shameless hussy," was all he could muster. She batted her eyes at him and moved her hips seductively.

He was on the verge of abandoning his unpacking duties and dragging her to the bed when his hand discovered a gift-wrapped box in the open throat of one of the river bags.

He extracted it slowly and held it up for her to see. He could do a little teasing himself.

"For me?" She was drying her hands on the dish towel while trying to contain her excitement.

"Maybe," he allowed. "If you promise to be good."

"Oh, I'll be good," she assured him. "I'll be very, very good."

'I don't doubt it a bit,' he thought. He went to her, took her gently by the elbow and guided her over to the rocker near the stove. When she was seated, he placed the box in her hands and said, "Take your time. I've got something else for you, but it's in another bag; it will take me a few minutes to find it."

Before he could begin his search, she reached an arm up around his neck and pulled him down for a hug. She placed her forehead against his and held him there for a long, poignant moment before releasing him. Both her eyes were tearing now.

"You're leaking again," he said as he went over and began opening the other river bags. He found what he had been looking for in the top of the yellow one, but left it there until she had seen what was in the box she held. She was watching him intently, still cradling her unopened gift in her lap.

He nodded that she should begin. "Go ahead," he told her. "Open it."

She looked down at the box, then slowly pulled at one end of the red silk ribbon. When the knot loosened, she slipped the ribbon off the shiny silver wrapping paper and placed it delicately across the arm of the rocker. She turned her moist green eyes to Gus, and flashed him another smile. Then she removed the wrapping paper, folded it carefully and tucked it under the box in her lap. She took one long breath before opening the lid of the box, then let out a small squeal of delight when she saw what was inside; a Waterford crystal vase. It was an exact replica of the one Haywood had given her – the one Lindsay had broken just before he died. She took it out of its box and held it to catch the candlelight. Pinpoints of green and violet light exploded from the prism of its faceted surface and danced upon the log walls and in the rafters of the cabin – a miniature Aurora Borealis. Her thoughts harkened back to the past autumn and she understood what Gus was telling her with the gift of the vase. He accepted her for what she was, in whatever form her spirit might take. He loved her unconditionally.

She brushed aside a tear and looked at him. "Thank you," she said – and meant it.

He brought her another box, opened it himself and handed her a dozen roses. The unopened buds were tight but Morgan could see the faint outline of red at the edges.

"The other ones made you so happy…" he told her. There was no need to finish the thought.

"Where on earth did you find roses in Alaska in March?" Morgan asked as she took them and the vase over to the counter.

"FTD," he told her. "I ordered them last week," he confided. "I didn't tell Haywood or Hard Case, but I already knew I was coming back out to the Moose Jaw."

While she snipped the stems, put water in the vase, and arranged the roses to her liking, Gus found the can of goose grease and put it on the shelf behind the stove. Morgan pretended not to notice, but Gus saw her cheeks color slightly and knew she had.

When she had placed the vase of roses in the center of the table, she blew out the candle, went to the bed, sat, and began undressing in the flickering light from the stove.

"I think you can leave that unpacking until morning, don't you?" she said in a throaty whisper.

Gus popped a button while removing his shirt. The music of her soft laughter filled the cabin and Gus' soul as well.

As he slipped under the blankets beside her she playfully fended him off. "You forgot the goose grease," she protested.

"It'll keep," he said.

***

Their evening activities lasted well into the wee hours, so they slept late in the morning. When they awoke, the sun was already over the treetops and streaming in the east window. Gus felt Morgan stir beside him and he shifted so he could get his arm around her. Her naked flesh was warm and silky. He nuzzled the back of her neck.

"Look at the roses, Gus," she said, wonder evident in her voice. "They're beginning to open."

Gus raised his head so he could see the table over her bare shoulder. The morning sun refracted into shards of colored light as it passed through the prism of the crystal vase. And the inside of the cabin was still warm enough that the roses were, indeed, opening.

Just a hint of their fragrance blended with the perfume of Morgan's hot skin and the mustiness of recent sex that clung to the bedding.

He cupped one perfect breast with a calloused palm. She sighed and pressed her bare bottom against him. He put his lips close to her ear and whispered, "Top of the mornin' to you my love. It's St. Patrick's Day. You're in for a whole day of Irish tradition: full Irish breakfast; a little Irish whiskey; and Fergus O'Neill's special recipe corned-beef and cabbage for dinner tonight."

"I do share your Celtic heritage, Gus, but I'm mostly Welsh," she said. "I don't think I have any Irish in me."

"Easily remedied," Gus assured her. "I'll inject you."

Chapter 4

Spring Equinox, 2001
Moose Jaw Creek, Alaska

When, at length, the old shaman opened his blue eye he was not surprised to find himself standing outside his hut, many miles upstream from the cave of the dead bear. Sometimes he wondered if he had actually traversed the distance on foot while in a trance or if he had entered an altered state of being and travelled through some wormhole in time and space. A raven croaked on the other side of the clearing and the old man smiled and sent forth an unspoken greeting across the open ground toward the trees. The raven responded with a gabble of clicks and clunks. The old man acknowledged the bird's reply with a nod, then ducked into his hut.

His hut was not the typical semi-subterranean barabara favored by the Athabascans for their winter dwellings. Those structures were almost completely below ground level, with their bark and moss covered roofs appearing as small mounds beneath the snow. There were still a few that were habitable up on the high plateau near the caribou fence. His family had lived in one when he was a boy. They had wintered there each year with several other families from their regional band. There had always been enough caribou in the area to support a large group. But that had been many years ago; the caribou were not so plentiful now. This is why the settlement had fallen into disrepair and ruin.

After the families had stopped coming to the area in the winter, the old man had taken up residence in an old trapper's cabin on a braid of the Moose Jaw where he was close to the water. It was colder down in the bottoms than it was up at the settlement, and the cabin was not nearly as snug as a barabara. But the cold no longer troubled him; he was past that now.

What did trouble him was the killing of the bear in the cave. He knew the sons of his nephew had been responsible. They no longer lived in harmony with the land and the beasts that peopled it. They had abandoned the old ways and lived now in pursuit of money. Someone was paying them to kill the bears. He wondered who that might be. In his travels he had heard they were living over in

Chekov with an Asian stranger. Maybe he was the one who paid them. It didn't matter though; if it wasn't him, it was someone else.

The boys were young fools, but they were family, and they still lived off the land – in their own way. They came often to the Moose Jaw now, for the gold in the summer and the bears in the winter. Sometimes they used one of the still serviceable barabaras in the settlement for their base camp. Old Broken Foot patrolled this river from its headwaters thirty miles upstream in the high country to the mighty Yukon a hundred miles downstream in the flats. He always haunted the high ground near the old caribou fence when he returned to the area. If the boys continued to plunder this valley, he would cross their path eventually. There was nothing he could do for them now. Or was there?

He thought of the big State Trooper who had come to his cabin last autumn with the man called Gus. This policeman had an unusual name – Gus had called him Case. They had come looking for their tall friend who had crashed his airplane in the old dry channel. These three were all good men – it was important to have good men in the valley. They had restored balance in a time of great chaos. Old Blue Eye, as he knew Case called him, was aware that the big Trooper would soon come to visit. Perhaps if he were to tell him about his nephew's two sons, he would arrest them and put them in jail where Broken Foot could not kill them. It was something to consider, but not today. He had been travelling for what seemed a very long time. He was weary.

He settled his old bones on a weathered spruce round near the cold stone hearth, closed his good eye and allowed his mind to relax its grip upon his spirit. He often spent long spells like this, in a state of suspended animation. It seemed to him that when in this state his blind eye provided him with unique vision. With it, he could see the Moose Jaw in its entirety and observe all that came to pass in its valley – all that had ever happened, or ever would. This blind eye saw everything that transpired on the here-and-now side of the curtain. But it could also see beyond the curtain. This was its special gift. It was a beautiful omniscience revealing all that comprised the valley of the Moose Jaw – the river itself, the hills and wetlands, the woods and the wind and the creatures – all things that lent their individual essence to the overarching spirit of the place itself throughout the course of time.

On this day, his blind eye told him all was well along the Moose Jaw. The grayling and burbot and eels were untroubled beneath the ice; the moose bulls were shedding their antlers to make room for new ones; the caribou had halted their south migration and were turning their noses to the north; the bears would soon be leaving their winter dens; and the fox vixens were preparing nests for their coming litters. Broken Foot was far downstream near the new cabin where the red haired woman had recently been reawakened by the return of her man – the man called Gus. Perhaps the ancient grizzly had been awaiting Gus too. It was said that Gus and Broken Foot had once fought and killed one another. The old shaman knew this was possible, but wasn't certain it had happened that way. It was odd, he mused: how could a man be omniscient and still be uncertain of anything? It was something to think about, but not today.

Chapter 5

Historically most of the illegal animal parts exported from the Pacific Northwest found their way into Asia via Hong Kong. There they were processed into various ingredients before being distributed to the Traditional Chinese Medicine market throughout China and neighboring countries. By the time they reached the most remote points in the distribution chain, these products had passed through a considerable number of middlemen, each adding to the cost. The cost of a given ingredient in Korea was nearly double that of the same item in Hong Kong. As the new millenium dawned the Koreans decided it was time they established a more direct way to import these precious goods. This came about, primarily through the efforts of one Jong Min-jun.

As a youth, he had been homeless, and although small he was extremely quick and street smart. He had served his criminal apprenticeship in the back streets and alleys of Seoul, where he had matriculated in a curriculum which featured simple burglary, armed robbery, felonious assault, auto theft, drug running, rape and attempted murder (twice). The two failed murder attempts were the only blemishes on his unofficial record. As his skill and cunning developed, his attempted murders began to meet with unparalleled success. Consequently, he had acquired a modicum of notoriety among the most dangerous elements of Seoul's underworld. Because of the cobra embossed on the gold ring which he always wore, some had begun referring to him as "The Cobra". He liked the sobriquet – he liked snakes. He had an affinity for the cobra in particular.

Early in life, he had come to detest cats and rats and the carrion birds with whom he had to compete for discarded food scraps in the putrid trash bins behind restaurants. He took great pleasure in dispatching them with a lightning quick slash of his razor sharp knife whenever they dared challenge him for a morsel.

It was said that he was devious and treacherous, and always ready to use that knife – qualities considered pluses on his undocumented Curriculum Vitae. However, it was also widely known that he was impetuous and often took foolish risks. Perhaps it was this recklessness, more than his positive attributes that launched him into a new career,

His life had taken an unexpectedly fortuitous turn one evening when an old herbalist found him burgling his apothecary. Jong Min-jun produced a knife – the old man, a pistol and a blackjack. The young thief dropped his knife, whereupon the old man dropped him with the cudgel.

When Jong recovered consciousness, the old man had offered him a choice: prison or indentured servitude. The young man had opted for the latter. A wise choice. Over the ensuing fifteen years, he had become indispensible to the old pharmacist, and was now in charge of a growing network of black market wholesalers who shipped their wares directly into Korea.

It had been at the behest of his mentor that Jong Min-jun had set out to create this new supply line. The old man had been more than a mere herbalist; he had also trafficked in the esoteric ingredients favored by those who concocted traditional oriental remedies. The boy had demonstrated a remarkable aptitude for intrigue and violence as he scoured Asia's underbelly for horns, teeth, claws, bones and organs to feed the ever growing demand for such items among those wealthy enough to afford them.

As the market for aphrodisiacs doubled each year, and the supply of bear organs in Asia slowly dwindled, it was only natural that the old man search further afield for these staples. In the spring of 1999 he summoned his young protégé to his small office in the rear of the apothecary.

"How is your English?" he asked in that language.

The young man did not hesitate. "Very good," he answered in a respectable American accent. As his old mentor had insisted, Jong watched two hours of Hollywood soap operas every evening. Early on, he discovered that American porn was the perfect genre for the beginning student of English. The dialogue was absurdly simple and repeated viewings never became tiresome; he could recite most of their vapid scripts verbatim. Consequently, he became quite masterful in the use of American slang and idiom.

"Excellent," the old man smiled. "I'm sure it has not escaped your attention that it is becoming more and more expensive to purchase the bile and gallbladders of bears." The old Korean had switched back to his native tongue.

Jong nodded, but remained silent.

"Some of my colleagues who share this burden with us have approached me. They know of your language skills, and are willing to help finance a foreign venture in which you will play the lead role. Would you be willing to go to America and establish a new source for the ingredients that have become so precious here? It would serve us well if we did not have to bid directly against the Chinese for these essential components."

The young man smiled broadly. This was a dream come true. "Of course!" he said, not trying to conceal his excitement. Then a cloud passed over his features. "But I have no papers. It will take some time to get them in order so I can travel."

The old man opened the top drawer of his battered wooden desk and withdrew an envelope. He closed the drawer and slid the envelope across the desktop to Jong.

"Passport, driver's license, Social Security card – everything you'll need."

Jong opened the envelope and slid out the documents. He was astounded to see the passport and Social Security Card had been issued by the United States in the name of John Young. There was also a driver's license issued by the State of Washington in the same name.

He looked up at the old man. "So from now on, I am John Young, an American from Seattle." He did not state this as a question.

"It's a good name, I think," the old herbalist told him. "It is very much like your own."

"Yes," Jong Min-jun said. "And I have heard that the most desirable products imported from North America come from Canada and Alaska. Seattle is well situated to conduct business with both. Is my base of operation to be there then?"

"Yes," his employer told him. "I do not want you to be too close to the harvesting activities. You will travel to Canada and Alaska to recruit local natives to work in the field and deliver the organs to middlemen in Anchorage and Vancouver. You will meet with these go-betweens periodically to inspect the product and negotiate price and shipping terms. Then you will return to Seattle and await confirmation from me that I have received the shipment."

Jong nodded appreciatively. "Am I to use the same recruiting methods that I use here?"

The old man leaned back in his chair and studied his protégé. "Yes. It is best to stay with a successful approach. A young man's desire for money, drugs and lovely girls is the same everywhere. But you must avoid disciplinary violence when dealing with your American poachers and prostitutes. They are more inclined to go to the authorities than our outlaws."

"And extreme violence?" John Young already knew the answer but he wanted the old man to speak the words – just to be sure.

"When necessary. If, for example, you suspect betrayal you may wish to call upon the services of The Cobra. I understand he has a way of dealing with such matters."

***

Jong Min-jun had exceeded the old man's expectations. Within a year of his arrival in Seattle, he had recruited twelve "field agents", as he preferred to call them, to harvest bear bile, gallbladders and claws. All were young natives, either Alaskan or Canadian, and all had been drawn to the Korean's metaphorical flame for the same reasons – sex, drugs, alcohol, and money.

When these local poachers had harvested sufficient product to make up a shipment, Jong would make the necessary arrangements with a smuggler who operated out of Sitka. The smuggler's name was Alexi Malachenko, whose family had engaged in the movement of contraband across borders for many generations. He was expensive but, as the old apothecary had pointed out, "one gets what one pays for". Still, Jong Min-jun quietly seethed with resentment each time he paid Malachenko's exorbitant rate. While consigning the final shipment of the year 2000, Malachenko informed him there would be a ten percent increase in the price of his services in 2001. Jong decided to cut ties with the Russian and seek a lower cost carrier.

Only by keeping his "harvesting costs" down, could he manage to maintain his own profits at the desired level. In order to minimize overhead, it was necessary for him to stay in close personal contact with his troops on the ground. This meant, of course, that he could not remain as far removed from the harvesting activities as his old mentor had advised.

Then too, one team of his field agents operated out of the small town of Chekov in the remote north of Alaska. The density of the bear population in their immediate vicinity afforded them a particularly target-rich environment. And, it had not escaped Jong's notice that the bile of bears from their territory was of surprisingly good quality. A typical black bear's gallbladder, full of bile, was roughly the size of a small melon. The gallbladders harvested in the Chekov region were significantly larger and contained a much higher concentration of ursodeoxycholic acid (UDCA), the main active ingredient. Top quality goods always translated to high profit margins. He did not know if diet or genetics produced this unexpected bonanza, but he realized he would do well to visit his Chekov agents. He made a command decision to spend a good part of the winter with them, and acquire some hands-on experience in the poaching of bears.

***

The Chekov team consisted of Damon and Jackie Sam, two native Alaskan brothers who knew several tributaries of the Yukon River as well as Jong Min-jun had known the back streets of Seoul.

The Sam brothers were both in their late twenties, and had spent their entire lives in the Alaskan bush. It was common among the Athabascan peoples who inhabited the Yukon-Koyukuk region for a wife's brother to bond with his new brother-in-law and welcome him into the wife's family. After his sister had married Henry Sam, Daniel Frank had done his best to form such a bond with her new husband. Brother and brother-in-law typically became best friends, confidants, hunting and fishing companions and, in most cases, they became closer than blood brothers. Not so with Henry and Daniel. When male Athabascan children came of age, their mother's brother was expected to take them under his wing and guide them toward manhood. So, when Damon and Jackie Sam were old enough, their uncle Daniel taught them to hunt, fish, trap, track and survive in the unforgiving Alaskan bush.

Daniel knew that Henry disapproved of his cavalier attitude toward life, and suspected that had been the reason they had never connected. Henry was a stickler for clan tradition and he was deeply spiritual. Daniel, on the other hand, while understanding the old ways, considered them to be mere guidelines as opposed to hard and fast rules. Nevertheless, the two were always civil to one

40

another, and Henry was happy to have Daniel guide his sons down the path to adulthood.

Henry's wife died when the boys were still quite young, and he began devoting most of his time to religious pursuits. As time went on, he withdrew more and more from any involvement with his sons.

That was okay with Daniel as it gave him a free hand to show his nephews how to become men without interference from their father. And show them, he did. By the time Jackie, the eldest, was sixteen, Uncle Daniel had introduced both boys to the wonders of the bush, not to mention the delights of alcohol, marijuana, and pay-as-you go sex. It gave him a warm glow to see them enthusiastically embrace every new experience he shared with them. They were good boys. He would help them become good men.

Chapter 6

Hard Case spent his first day back in Fairbanks clearing his desk of all the paperwork that had accumulated while he had been in San Diego. Over lunch, Mournful George brought him up to date on all the latest happenings in and around headquarters during his absence. George had always been as competent as he was loyal. Whenever Hard Case was called away from headquarters for any length of time, he left George in charge. By seven o'clock that evening, Hard Case was satisfied he'd addressed all the issues of urgency, and decided everything else could wait until tomorrow. He stopped by the file room on the way out, and withdrew two folders containing closed cases from the archives – the Rainbow Lodge double homicide and the missing persons case he now knew was related.

He reviewed the old Rainbow Lodge murder file at his kitchen table that night while he ate a bowl of soup with crackers for dinner. The suspect Pokey had interviewed was an Athabascan gentleman named Charlie Henry. He had worked at the Rainbow lodge when it had been a going concern in the nineteen-fifties. His whole family worked there with him, stocking firewood, filling the water tank, waiting tables, tending to the boats, and any odd jobs that needed doing. Two brothers from Missouri, Roy and Larry McCaslin, were also employed there at the time, guiding fisherman mostly, but also moose and caribou hunters in season. Rumor had it that Larry, big as a bull moose and dumb as a post, had a taste for young boys. He was always after one, or both of Henry's sons. A staff member Pokey had interviewed said Larry got the youngest boy alone one night and raped him. Shortly thereafter, Larry received midnight callers while he was sleeping off a drunk. They beat him within an inch of his life with axe handles and fish clubs. No one saw or heard anything, including Larry's brother Roy, who was sleeping off his own drunk in the next room.

In the morning, after one of the doctors that owned the place found Larry bloodied and senseless, the Henry family were paid back wages and sent packing. That had been in 1957 so it was inconceivable that any native Alaskans could go unpunished for assaulting a white man. Pokey figured Charlie waited a couple years and let enough time pass to distance himself from the situation

– then he went back out to the lodge and exacted his revenge on the McCaslins. Trouble was, Charlie Henry had a rock-solid alibi for the approximate time of the murders. He and his family had been attending a potlatch in conjunction with a naming ceremony for one of his sister's children.

Hard Case cleared his dinner dishes, put them in the dishwasher, and poured himself three fingers of Dalmore, another of his preferred single malts. He took his drink into the den, settled his ample rump in his leather recliner, and called Chekov.

When the duty sergeant manning the Chekov office identified himself as Mike O'Kelly, Hard Case smiled and said into the phone. "I didn't know they allowed the Irish north of Fairbanks."

"Only those of us in perpetual rut, my friend. They need to breed some charm into the local population," O'Kelly boomed in a very good imitation of the lilting Irish brogue. "And, to what do I owe the honor of a call from the infamous Kees Calis on this fine evening?"

Hard Case grinned. He'd known O'Kelly since the old days when Pokey had been top dog in the CIB. "Hello, Michael. How're things with you?"

"Can't complain," O'Kelly answered in his own soft voice. "Just putting in my time, waiting for that glorious day when I can become a man of leisure like yourself."

"Retirement?" Hard Case asked, genuinely surprised. "I thought they'd have to skin you out of that uniform."

"All good things must end, Kees. Time I stepped aside and let the next generation take their lumps."

"What will you do with yourself?" Hard Case inquired, remembering that Mike's wife had died two years back, and his only child was a nurse down in Cleveland or Detroit, or one of those rust belt cities. He couldn't recall if she was married or not.

"Travel a little at first, I suppose. Then I'll just have to see where the wind blows me. I've got a place down in Eagle River, you know. I might just hunker down there and write my memoirs. But, enough with the pleasantries. What can I do for you?"

Hard Case told O'Kelly about his visit with Pokey. He also told him he was trying to track down Charlie Henry. "You remember that old double homicide we had to review every year or so – the Rainbow Lodge killings? Pokey questioned Mr. Henry back then.

He was his prime suspect but he was whooping it up at a potlatch over in Circle. Big clan affair, whole village was there. Everyone remembered Charlie because he sprained an ankle dancing and after they got him a crutch, he rejoined the dancers. It was a good enough alibi to get him scratched off the list. I don't know where else to start. There are no other names in the file to follow up on. Anyway, see if you can locate Charlie for me. He hails from around your parts; maybe he still has family up there that can tell you where I might find him."

"Yeah, Henry is a local name. I know a few of them. I'll ask around and call you if I turn up something. Anything else?" O'Kelly asked.

"Nope," Hard Case replied. "That'll do it. Thanks, Mike, I'll wait to hear from you. Good talking to you."

O'Kelly said, "Night Kees, take care of yourself," and they both hung up.

***

Katiana Henry answered the door and was surprised to see Sgt. Michael O'Kelly standing there, hat in hand. Mike's wife, Brigid, and Katiana had gone to the same church and volunteered at the same food bank until Brigid had passed away a couple of years ago.

"Michael!" she said, pleased to see him looking so handsome in his uniform. "Come in. I just made some tea; will you join me?"

Mike wiped his feet on the doormat and stepped inside. Katiana gave him a quick hug and bussed his cheek. "I'd love a cup," he said truthfully.

Katiana was about the same age as himself; perhaps a few years younger. She was a round-faced, full-bodied woman with a happy disposition. He had never realized how pretty she was. He looked around for somewhere to put his hat. Katiana noticed and said, "Here, let me take that for you."

He handed it over and followed her down the hall to a well-ordered kitchen. She hung his hat on a rack near the back door. "I heard from Auntie Em you've been asking around about Uncle Charlie. Is that why you finally decided to come see me?"

"No!" Mike protested. "I mean – well, yeah, I guess." His cheeks were always ruddy, but now they were leaning toward red.

Katiana laughed. "Sit down, Mike. I'm just pulling your leg." She came to the table, placed a mug of tea in front of him and went to the stove to pour one for herself. "So, you're looking for my uncle?"

"Yeah, nothing important. Friend of mine down in the Fairbanks office is trying to tie up some loose ends so he can close an old cold case. Do you know where I might be able to locate Charlie?"

She came to the table and sat down across from him. "No. I couldn't say. I was never very close to that side of the family. I know he had some trouble up in the Moose Jaw country back when I was in grade school. I remember he and his family lived over on D Street when his two boys, Joshua and Isaac, were in high school here. If I recall, they moved to Circle after they left Chekov. I think Uncle Charlie worked at the Circle Hot Springs for a few years."

"How about the boys? Any idea what became of them?" Mike asked her.

"Joshua, the older son, was killed in Vietnam. I heard Isaac went to seminary after his brother died. Auntie Em said those boys were real close before Joshua joined the Army. She thinks poor Isaac felt all alone after his brother died. Maybe that's why he decided to become a priest. I couldn't say for sure."

Mike sipped his tea. "You think Charlie might still be living around Circle somewhere?"

Katiana shook her head. "I don't even know if he's 'living' at all. He'd have to be almost ninety by now. If I were you, I'd check with the Yukon-Koyukuk records people. They just took a census survey last year. Maybe they know where he is."

Mike nodded. "That's a thought. If he's still alive and living around there, the Public Health and Safety folks probably have a line on him. There can't be more than a couple hundred residents over there now."

"Only a hundred, I think," Katiana told him. "They just put some of the census results in the paper a few weeks ago."

"Kind of sad isn't it," Mike said. "Back before the Klondike gold rush, Circle was a thriving port on the Yukon. It was the heart of Alaska gold country back then. Now there're only a hundred residents. All good things must end, I guess. Anyway, with such a small population, I imagine all the Public Health records will be kept right here in Chekov. I'll swing by there today and see if they have anything on Charlie."

"They might. And you're right, it's sad in a way – about Circle," Katiana said. "But, it's also sad that Fairbanks and Anchorage have become so big. Don't you think?"

"Yeah," he agreed. "Sadder, maybe."

He finished his tea, carefully placed the mug on the table, stood up and said, "I guess that's it for now, then. Thanks for the tea and the information. If I think of anything else, I'll drop by again – if that's okay, I mean." He went to the hat rack and retrieved his hat.

Katiana stood up and came around the table. "Of course," she assured him, then led him up the hall to the front door. "You don't need to have an official reason to visit. Just stop by again, whenever you want."

He placed his hat squarely on his head, then stood awkwardly for a moment before thrusting out his hand in her direction. "Well, ah – thanks, again. Be seeing you, Katiana," he stammered, then blushed.

Katiana took the offered hand in one of her own, and placed her other on top. "You're welcome, Michael. I'm always happy to see you; I hope you know that."

He didn't know what else to say, so he just said good bye and went out the door. She stood in the open doorway and watched him until he drove off in his patrol car, then she closed the door and went back down the hall, humming a little tune.

Chapter 7

Both Gus and Morgan had gone out on the porch when they heard the plane arriving and recognized Haywood in the cockpit of the green-and-white Cessna 170 as it buzzed the cabin. He had told Gus he might rent something larger until he could get his wrecked Piper Clipper back to Fairbanks for repairs. He had put it into a stand of spruce trees last autumn up at Hermit's Camp and was lucky to have survived.

Like the air-taxi, Haywood's rental was fitted with skis, and he landed it out on the frozen river, then swung around ninety degrees and parked it where the river bank began its assent from the channel. Gus and Morgan walked down to greet him. It was no longer necessary to put on snowshoes, as Gus had packed down a decent trail in his daily trips down to the river. By the time they reached the riverbank, Haywood had completed his post-landing routine. Satisfied all was well, he deplaned and swept Morgan up into his arms and kissed her lips, eyes, cheeks, forehead, and appeared ready to have another go at them all. Morgan squealed with delight.

Gus crossed his arms and commented, "When you're done ravishing the womenfolk, you might at least have the courtesy to say hello, you big oaf."

Haywood squeezed Morgan even harder, lifted her off her feet and kissed her on the neck. He leered over her shoulder with one eye focused on Gus. "Hello, you big oaf," he boomed.

Gus laughed, stepped closer and threw his arms about both Haywood and Morgan. She favored them with her musical, throaty laugh and hugged them as tight as she could.

Gus said, "I thought Hard Case was coming in with you. What happened to him?"

"He's up to his flat-top in an investigation. Caldwell will be bringing him out tomorrow."

A distinctly unhappy noise issued forth from the back seat of the aircraft. It sounded very much like an angry cat.

Gus grinned. "Is that who I think it is?"

"None other," Haywood confirmed. "I've got to run up to Fort Yukon tomorrow after we're done murdering birds. I'll be visiting a couple of kennels up there, so I need to leave Bosworth with you while I'm gone."

Morgan's face lit up. "Oh, yes!" she almost clapped her hands. "Gus told me all about Bosworth. I love cats. Of course he can stay with us! Is that him making all that noise?"

"That's him – seething mad in a pet transport. He hates being cooped up. He also hates little ankle-biter dogs. That's why I can't leave him at the clinic again. A client's Pomeranian got a little too close to his cage last week. Twenty-three stitches; the client was not amused."

Morgan looked thoughtful for a moment. "Perhaps I should go back to the cabin before you bring him out of the plane. Cats are very sensitive to anything – or anyone – out of the ordinary. I don't want to, ah – spook him, for lack of a better word."

Haywood looked at her speculatively. "I see what you mean. We'll bring him up to the cabin in the carrying case. It might be best to introduce the two of you while he's confined."

Morgan trotted back up the bank and went inside. Gus lit his pipe and waited while Haywood unloaded Bosworth from the rear of the plane. Then Gus squatted beside the cage and talked soothingly to the big cat while Haywood unloaded a few buckets and river bags full of supplies.

"Let's each take on a handle on Bosworth's case and walk him up to the cabin first. He's a load for one man alone. We can come back down and fetch the rest of this later."

Gus nodded. "Sounds like a plan," he said, and gripped the handle on his side of the box. They lifted together and set off up the well packed snow of the path. Bosworth stretched out on his side and assumed the attitude of Cleopatra being transported upon her royal litter.

Halfway up the bank, Gus said, "You know we're happy to look after Bosworth for you, but why didn't you just leave him with Donna?"

Haywood chuckled. "He doesn't get on well with little ankle-humper dogs either. That perverted Chihuahua she rescued last year

48

tried to force his carnal lust on The Boz a couple nights ago. As you might imagine, that did not end well."

They slid Bosworth's carrying case up on the porch, then sat down on the steps for a breather. Morgan's voice came through the closed cabin door. "Is he still in a huff, or has he settled down enough for me to present myself?" she asked.

They looked at Bosworth, still fully reclined and apparently relaxed.

"He looks okay," Haywood answered her. "Come on out."

The door opened and Morgan stepped out onto the porch.

Bosworth didn't appear to move, but his transformation was instantaneous. One moment he was a sleek, well groomed feline – the next he was a fur-bearing blowfish. He looked positively electrified and a low, blood chilling growl emanated from the stiffened hairball that now filled the cage.

"Will you look at that?" Gus observed. "I think he likes you."

"Resembles a cross between a porcupine and a medicine ball," Haywood said. "Something seems to have upset him."

"Oh, stop it, you two," Morgan said, clearly displeased with their sarcasm. "Go back down to the plane and fetch the supplies. And please take your time about it. We'll get acquainted while you're gone."

Gus went into the cabin and came back out with two cold bottles of beer. Then he and Haywood walked back down to the Cessna. Gus relit his pipe, Haywood fired up one of his disreputable cigars, and they chatted while they enjoyed the sunshine, the music burbling from beneath the ice of the creek, and the cold beer.

When they returned to the cabin a while later, Bosworth's cage stood empty on the porch. They went up the steps, pushed open the door and peered inside. Morgan was seated in the rocker by the green enamel stove; Bosworth was curled up in her lap. She looked content. Bosworth looked smug.

Beyond them, Haywood could see all the bags and buckets stacked along the back wall. He also spotted the roses on the table in the new vase.

"You dog," he said. "You beat me to it. I've got another Waterford hiding in my travel bag. I'll take it back and get her something else. Looks like you brought in quite a load with you too. Where you figure on storing all the stuff I just brought in?"

Gus pulled the door closed, sat down on the top step, removed his hat and ran a hand through his hair. "Good question. I guess we'll have to take all the food back up to the cache. Tools and what-not will be okay under the porch if we cover them with a tarp. I notice you didn't bring in the upper bunk for the camp bed this trip; I guess we'll get by without it if you're flying up to Ft. Yukon tomorrow. You've got a bed for tonight, and I imagine Hard Case will want to go back to Fairbanks with Caldwell tomorrow after the hunt."

"Hard Case said he'd bring the bunk in with him, but he's not planning to stay overnight."

Gus nodded. "Good. Let's have another beer, and then we'll move the foodstuffs back to the cache. After that, we'll see how much of the rest we can stow under the porch. Do you have that plastic sled in the rental?"

Haywood nodded. "Yep I've got all the survival gear I kept in the Clipper."

"Excellent," Gus said. "We can probably get all the food back to the cache in two or three loads. We can take a light load on the first run while we break trail with the snowshoes. When the snow's packed down, we'll have a lot easier time pulling bigger loads."

Haywood stood up from the porch steps and brushed a little snow off the seat of his pants. "Sounds good to me. I'll go fetch the sled from the plane, and I believe you mentioned something about another beer."

"Right," Gus agreed. "You go get the sled, and I'll get the beer."

Chapter 8

When Gus and Haywood had finished their beers, they left Bosworth in Morgan's capable hands and shifted the foodstuffs from the cabin up to the cache. The cache was located back in the woods a few hundred yards downstream of the cabin. It was nothing but a ruined jumble of poles atop five tall upright logs when Gus bought the property just over a year ago. Most bush cabins had a cache somewhere nearby to keep food stores out of reach of the local bear population. Haywood had helped Gus rebuild the cache, repair the roof and construct a new ladder when they came in the first time last summer. It already held a frozen moose ham, some caribou steaks, a few smoked salmon, and an extra corned beef Gus had brought in with him just before St. Patrick's Day.

It took them three trips to transport all the buckets of beans, rice, coffee, flour, and boxes of dehydrated potatoes, milk, and instant oatmeal from cabin to cache. Haywood had even thought to bring in a few multi-packs of toilet-paper, which were so large, there was nowhere else to store them.

When they finally had everything stacked at the bottom of the ladder, Gus said, "Okay, let's start with the buckets. Once I have them arranged, I'll put the boxes and the toilet paper on top of them."

Haywood uncoiled a length of rope with an S-hook attached to one end. He handed Gus the other end. "Up you go. Let me know if you get tired of hauling up buckets; I'll spell you."

Gus went up the ladder, removed the hatch cover, and crawled inside the cache. "Okay," he called down to Haywood. "You can move the ladder."

Haywood took the ladder around one corner of the cache and leaned it against the wall so the buckets could be hoisted aloft without bumping against it. He went back around to the front, positioned the bucket labeled 'RICE' on the ground where the feet of the ladder had rested, and secured the hook onto its wire handle.

"Haul away," he said. He waited until Gus had taken the slack out of the rope, then helped lift the bucket until it was over his head. "She's all yours."

"Got it," Gus said, then hand-over-handed the bucket up into the door opening, dropped the hook back down to Haywood and arranged the bucket against the back wall, label facing out so he could read it. By the time he'd returned to the door opening, Haywood had another bucket ready for the ascent.

When they were finished with their work at the cache they towed the empty sled back down to the cabin. They went in to warm up before dealing with the items to be stored beneath the porch. Morgan had set out the bottle of Tullamore Dew and three whiskey glasses on the table.

"Told you she was a mind reader," Gus said.

Morgan turned from the counter where she was already busy preparing dinner. She flashed them both a bright smile.

"You were certainly tuned into my frequency this time," Haywood told her as he hung his coat on a wall peg and proceeded directly to the table. He poured a generous measure of amber fluid into each glass, then took his over to enjoy by the warmth of the glowing stove.

Gus visited the table and took up the two remaining glasses; he went over to stand behind Morgan as she worked. He placed his cold nose directly on the back of her warm neck. She laughed, set aside the paring knife, turned and placed her arms around his neck. He was holding a whiskey glass in each hand, and could not return the embrace. She kissed him on the lips and relieved him of one of the whiskies.

"Water?" she asked him as she drizzled a small dollop into her drink.

Gus held out his glass and she did the honors. After she replaced the water jug back on the counter, they touched glasses and sipped the Dew.

"We'll clear all the rest of this kit out of here before dinner. Then we'll have some room to move about," he promised.

She took her drink over to the plank table and sat. Gus joined her. "That will definitely be an improvement," she observed. "The cabin was getting a little cramped."

"You need to build a storage shed," Haywood suggested. "You could keep all your tools and reloading equipment and fly-tying gear out there and bring it in as you need it. You could also build in a little hiding place for that damned whirly-gig of LaGrange's."

Morgan brightened. "That's a wonderful idea, Haywood." She turned to Gus. "If you build a big enough shed, you could keep your canoe and the game gurney out of the weather too."

Gus smiled and opened one of the river bags and withdrew a yellow legal pad. "Great minds think alike," he quoted, and tossed the pad on the table for Morgan to see. "Have a look."

Haywood left the stove and came to the table. He stood behind Morgan and looked over her shoulder.

"Is this what I think it is?" she asked hopefully.

"I believe it is," Haywood said.

"If you're thinking it's a bunkhouse with an extra room for storage, you're spot on," Gus told them. "I began mulling it over last autumn when we had Hard Case, Caldwell, Uncle Jack, Haywood and myself all needing a place to sleep. Anyway, I decided on a bunkhouse big enough to accommodate three bunk beds, a stove, a sink and a table. If I partition off another room, it can be used for storage or the double-decker camp bed when needed."

"It's perfect, Gus," Morgan told him. "Now if we have guests sleep over, we'll have our own private quarters here in the cabin."

"What do you need privacy for?" Haywood asked innocently.

Morgan's cheeks flushed red; Gus laughed. He raised his whiskey glass. "To privacy," he said. "And all those who take full advantage of it."

They sipped their whiskies. Haywood said, "When will you begin construction?"

"As soon as the river thaws and I can float logs down from the burn. I hiked up there last week. The snow's still a little too deep to get back into the logging area but it's rotting fast. I could be harvesting timber sometime in April and floating it down after the ice breaks up and the river calms down."

"The ice will go off the river the second week in May," Morgan told them.

They both looked at her. Gus said, "You know this for sure?"

She nodded. "Of course."

Haywood asked, "Could you pick the exact day?"

She nodded.

Haywood and Gus were thinking the same thing – The Nenana Ice Classic! Before they could pursue it, Morgan said firmly, "No, I don't know when the ice will break up down in Nenana. I know what will happen here in my own valley, not everywhere in Alaska. And, I wouldn't tell you if I did know. That would be cheating."

Gus pulled a face. "Cheating is a harsh word. I prefer to think of it as informed speculation."

Haywood joined in. "Yeah, or insider gambling. The jackpot was $335,000 last year."

Morgan scowled at them both. "Cheating," she said uncompromisingly.

She could see Haywood's mind churning. He was incorrigible. "That won't work either," she informed him. "I'm sure there is a library full of information regarding the winning dates and times down in Nenana. But, you'll be hard pressed to find corresponding records for the Moose Jaw. Furthermore, I know enough about this river to tell you it is not subject to the patterns or cycles of any other watercourse in Alaska. The Moose Jaw has its own timetable."

"Damn it, Morgan," Haywood said. "I wish you'd stop doing that."

She didn't have to ask what he meant. "Then stop trying to figure a way to cheat," she told him in no uncertain terms.

"Yeah," Gus couldn't resist adding to Haywood's discomfort. "Where's your sense of fair play?"

Morgan gave him a withering glance. She was well aware he had been contemplating the same scheme as Haywood.

Gus finished his drink and decided it would be a good time to move the remaining cargo out of the cabin. "Come on, Haywood," he said. "Help me get all this stuff out on the porch. Then we'll store it underneath and cover it with a tarp."

Haywood didn't need to be prodded. He was as keen as Gus to escape Morgan's mental scrutiny. He downed the last of his whiskey, quickly put on his coat and hat, hefted two river bags and headed out the door. Gus was right behind him. Morgan remained at the table sipping her whiskey. Bosworth sauntered over from behind the stove and curled his tail around one of her ankles. She smiled and reached down to help him onto her lap.

***

As they brought out the items for storage, Gus arranged them in two piles. Gear he wouldn't need until summer, they staged to be deployed first, and things he'd require soon were to go under last so they would be ready to hand when he needed them. Gus noticed Haywood was uncharacteristically quiet as they worked. He shoved one of the canoe totes as far back under the cabin as he could manage and straightened up.

"Okay, Haywood, spit it out. I see your mind churning."

Haywood settled his rump on the top step and cast his gaze upstream beyond the treetops. "Second week in May..." he let the thought dangle in the gloaming.

Gus looked up at him, smiled and shook his head in resignation. "You can't let it go, can you?"

"What?" Haywood asked, all wounded innocence.

"If you won three hundred thousand, you'd just buy more expensive airplanes to wreck. Probably kill yourself in the bargain."

Haywood gave him one of his wolfish smiles. "You wrong me, Fergus O'Neill. I was just thinking what a shame it is you have to wait a month and a half before you can start on the bunkhouse. If you had a snow machine you could start moving timber down from the burn today. By breakup you could have all the logs you need right here on site."

Gus dragged a big canvass Cabela's bag over to the edge of the porch. He straightened and looked at his friend. "That's not a bad idea, Haywood. You may have something there."

Haywood grinned. "I bet you could move a dozen logs a day if you had a big old Polaris."

"Yeah," Gus said pensively. "When you get back to Fairbanks, why don't you see if one of the dealers in town will deliver out here?"

"Done," Haywood promised.

"Good," Gus nodded. "Now stop loafing and give me a hand with this tent."

Chapter 9

The Chinese New Year in 2001 began on the twenty-fourth day of January. They celebrated it as the year of the golden snake. Had Jong Min-jun been in Korea, where this special day was called Gou-Jung, he would have enjoyed the festivities in Seoul even more than in years past. He was, after all, known as "The Cobra" by fellow travelers in that city's underworld. Did he not wear a gold ring bearing that serpent's image as his calling card? He was certain that the year of the golden snake would be a prosperous one for him.

Since he was in Anchorage to meet with a gathering of his field agents from the Kenai Peninsula and the Wrangle Saint Elias territory, he had hosted a raucous celebration with them to usher in the Chinese New Year. It had been quite a party by Alaska standards. Jong had rented the upper hall in a backstreet Chinese restaurant and provided an impressive variety of food and drink for his guests – not to mention illegal substances and "local talent". The establishment had even surprised them with a midnight pyrotechnic display launched from the street below.

The following day he had returned to Chekov with two young ladies of dubious virtue whom he had found particularly enthusiastic in the orgy that followed the fireworks. Both were buxom, blonde, uninhibited, and always ready to "party down" as they so eloquently put it. The Sam brothers, Damon and Jackie, were delighted when Jong made it clear he had imported these "hotties" from Anchorage exclusively for their nighttime enjoyment. January north of Fairbanks could be bitter cold, and the nights were very long. With these two nubile lovelies in residence, midwinter promised to be a little hotter than usual.

Danielle, newly arrived in Alaska, committed an innocent breach of etiquette upon meeting the Sam brothers. She dropped her bags at the door, marched straight up to Damon and rubbed noses with him. Damon was not offended, but somewhat taken aback by the forwardness of her gesture.

"Whaaat?" she whined in a nasal twang, seeing the consternation in Damon's dark eyes. "I thought that's the way Eskimos kiss. Nicky told me Alaskan natives love to rub noses."

Nicky chewed her gum with renewed vigor and rolled her eyes. Damon was speechless. 'Eskimos?' he thought. 'Eskimos!'

But Jackie, an old hand at dealing with stupid Cheechako chicks, came to his rescue. "We like to rub bellies more." He leered at Danielle's impressive cleavage as he delivered this witticism.

She squealed with delight. "Oh my god!" she shrieked, looking at Jackie for the first time. "You're a hoot! We'll have some fun tonight, for sure."

Jong's black eyes masked his contempt for his hand-selected associates as he crossed to the table and deposited a one kilo brick of marijuana on its scarred and battered surface.

"You ladies will want to freshen up," he said. "Take your things up to the guest room at the end of the hall. It's small, but it has its own bathroom, and the bed's big enough for two."

Danielle giggled, "I bet we can get three in it if we really try." She shimmied her shoulders a little to underscore the naughtiness of her suggestion. Her voluptuous breasts swung with the rhythm of her movement. Jackie's eyes followed them with unabashed lust. Nicky gave another eye-roll, then focused her attention on Damon, still mute and immobile in the center of the room. 'Cute,' she decided.

After the girls had gone upstairs, Damon regained his composure and followed Jackie and Jong into the kitchen. "How was Anchorage, John?" he asked the Korean.

"Okay," he said. "Our shipment went out on schedule, and I hooked up with those young ladies at a party last night. You like them?"

"Oh, yeah!" Jackie said, and meant it. Jong had never seen him so enthusiastic about anything. 'Pig,' he thought to himself. 'But, I won't need either of them much longer. Until then, I must do whatever it takes to keep them around.'

He had never shared with them any details regarding his arrangements for exporting product. His old mentor had struck the deal with the Malachenko clan of Siberia, and had set up Jong's first meeting with their kinsman in Alaska. The old man had admonished his young protégé to keep the identity of their exporter secret, and to never trust any of his field agents with information they did not need to know. He had followed those instructions faithfully. It was second nature to him; he had never trusted anyone anyway.

He expected to hear back from the old apothecary within the next few days. He'd sent him a coded email after his last meeting with Alexi reporting the pending price increase, and asking him to arrange for a more affordable shipper. He was certain there was more than one family engaged in the smuggling trade along Siberia's coastline. He just hoped they were not all part of a cartel that fixed prices across the board. If the old man could provide him a new contact in Anchorage, he would be able to curtail relations with Malachenko. He thought what pleasure he might derive from cutting the Russian's heart out. In the meantime, he had enough to keep him occupied for the next month or so. He had to restock his inventory in preparation for the next export consignment. And it was time to get some hands-on experience in the harvesting side of the business. Jackie and Damon had invited him along on their last few excursions. Perhaps he would accept their next offer. It might be useful to know how to find and kill bears, and how to remove that precious organ where they stored their bile. It just might come in handy in the near future.

Chapter 10

As was his custom when staying at The Varmitage, Haywood awoke just after dawn. He eased himself out from under the covers, trying not to jostle Bosworth who was curled up at the foot of the camp bed. He needn't have worried; Bosworth never stirred. Haywood donned his clothing, rebuilt the fire and slipped into his boots and heavy coat. Then he retrieved his shotgun from the corner and pocketed half-a-box of bird loads. He could see Gus now had his eyes open and was watching him.

"Off to bleed the weasel," he announced sotto voce. "Then I'll take a walk up to the beaver ponds to see if there are any spruce hens or ptarmigan about. I'll be back in an hour or so."

Gus smiled. Haywood was a gracious guest. He always devised some reason for absenting himself from the cabin in the morning. It was his way of giving Gus and Morgan a little privacy to – well, to do whatever it was they did when alone.

On his way out, he said, "I'll knock when I get back." Then he closed the door behind him.

Morgan rolled on her side and threw a bare arm over Gus' chest. "Bleed the weasel?"

Gus chuckled softly. "Another of Haywood's colorful terms from his Missouri childhood. It means he's going to pee."

"Good lord," she laughed. "And the weasel would therefore be his…" She didn't have to finish.

"Exactly," Gus confirmed. "His schwanzstücker."

Morgan laughed out loud. "His what?" she cried.

"Schwanzstücker," Gus told her. "You know," he wiggled his eyebrows lasciviously, "the old pork sword."

"Oh, my god," she said, scandalized, and buried her face in the pillow.

***

As he had promised, Haywood knocked on the door when he got back to the cabin. Gus and Morgan were already up and dressed and sitting at the table enjoying a cup of coffee. Only Bosworth remained abed.

"I didn't hear any shooting," Gus observed.

59

Haywood propped his shotgun in the corner and hung his coat on a peg. "I could have bagged a few," he said, "but there was something in the quiet back there this morning I didn't want to disturb."

Gus readied a derisive reply, but kept it to himself when he saw Haywood was serious. He had often experienced the same feeling there was some quality in the serenity of the woods that was sacred – and perhaps dangerous. "I've felt that before, too," he told his friend truthfully.

Morgan looked over her shoulder and smiled at them. They were both good men. Anyone that could feel what they felt in the woods had more good in them than bad. She brought a mug of steaming coffee over and gave it to Haywood.

"Take the chill out of your bones," she said.

Haywood accepted the coffee and sat on the edge of his camp bed. He sipped the hot liquid. "Ah," he said appreciatively. "Someone made a fine pot of coffee. I would have set one to perk before I left, but didn't want to make a lot of racket."

Gus smiled. "You're going pretty easy on the quiet this morning," he said. "How was the path up near the ponds?"

Haywood nodded. "Pretty good footing. I broke through a couple of times, but if I kept to the trail you packed down with your snowshoes, it was firm enough."

"Any tracks worthy of notice?" Gus asked.

"Just the usual suspects: moose, caribou and wolf…a lot of wolf tracks."

"How do you want your eggs, Haywood?" Morgan was busy at the stove cooking breakfast. "Gus and I have already eaten."

"Easy over, please."

The sound of eggs popping and sizzling in a hot skillet filled the cabin momentarily. The cooking sounds were accompanied by the delicious aromas of coffee and bacon.

"Did Hard Case give you any idea what time he was coming in?" Gus asked.

"About noon, I think. He was going to stop up at Hermit's Camp on the way. He wants to see if he can catch up with Old Blue Eye. While he's there, he'll check to see how deep the snow is around my wrecked plane. Come spring, I'll have to hire a big chopper to sling it back to Fairbanks for repairs."

"What's he want with Old Blue Eye?"

"I'm not sure. He was a little vague about it. Said he'd fill us in after he's talked to him," Haywood said.

Morgan placed a steaming platter of bacon, eggs and fried potatoes on the table. "Come and get it, Haywood," she said. "Specialty of the house."

Haywood sat down and tucked in. "Perfect eggs," he complimented her. "Perfect everything."

***

Caldwell feathered the State Trooper's four-seater down on the ice just before eleven o'clock. Gus and Haywood walked down to greet them and help offload the camp bed's upper bunk Hard Case had promised to bring in with him.

"Mornin' boys," Hard Case called as they made their way down the bank. "Looks like a good day for a bird hunt."

"It's a keeper," Haywood agreed. "Am I going to be able to pull my wreck out of there anytime soon?"

Hard Case shook his head, "I'd say another month, at least. The snow's still pretty deep back in the trees."

"Ah, well," Haywood told him, "I've got plenty to keep me busy 'til then." He noticed Caldwell had already begun to unload. "Hold on there," he called to him. "Let me help you with that bunk." He ducked under the wing and went to the open rear door of the plane where Caldwell was struggling with the metal bed frame.

Hard Case presented Gus with a full case of Tullamore Dew. "A little something for your liver," he said with a wink. Then he effortlessly slung a heavy-looking backpack over one shoulder and picked up his gun bag. "See you boys up at the cabin," he called out to Haywood and Caldwell as he headed up the bank. "I've got to make a pit stop."

Gus followed him up the grade. Hard Case deposited his gun bag and backpack on the porch, then quick-stepped it up the path to the outhouse. Gus carried the whiskey inside and slid it under the bed. Morgan had removed herself to wherever it was she went when visitors dropped in, but Bosworth was still curled up atop the blankets on the camp bed. He looked up just long enough to see who had the audacity to disturb him, then dismissively closed his eyes and resettled his chin on his oversized forepaws.

61

Gus studied the big cat's face for a moment. Had he imagined it, or were Bosworth's eyes green? He shook his head, and went to the stove and added a couple chunks of wood to the firebox.

Gus heard Hard Case come up the steps, then stomp snow off his boots on the porch before entering.

"Haywood said you were going to stop up at Hermit's Camp this morning," Gus ventured.

Hard Case walked to the stove and rubbed his hands over the warm cook-top. "We did. I wanted to have a chit-chat with the old one-eyed bugger, but he wasn't around so we came down here."

"Chit-chat?"

Hard Case nodded. "Yeah. If we pair up on the hunt today I'll give you the whole story. But, something he said to us last year has been bothering me. I need to talk to him about it."

Gus knew what had been bothering Hard Case. "His seeing me at the fishing lodge?"

"You got it," Hard Case confirmed.

"Well," Gus continued, "since you're out here on official business anyway, I stumbled on something up beyond the burn you might be interested in."

Hard Case left the stove and eased himself into one of the chairs at the table. "I'm listening," he said.

Gus joined him at the table. "You remember those bear carcasses you told us about – the ones poached for their gallbladders and claws?"

Hard Case had told Gus and Haywood about the underground market for wild animal parts that was picking up steam all over Alaska. Bear gallbladders were in great demand in the Traditional Chinese Medicine business.

Hard Case nodded, "I remember. You find a dead bear?"

"Yeah," Gus told him, "just upstream of Deadman Creek. I went up to the burn a few days ago for a scout and came across a Ski-Doo track. Morgan had mentioned two local bear hunters had stopped at the cabin in early winter, then came again a few weeks ago with some oriental prick that made off with two bottles of Dew and that fancy Eagle River knife you gave me last year. I got to thinking they might be the poachers you've been looking for. Anyway, I followed their track up the Moose Jaw and back off the river to a cave. I found a bear carcass inside – long time dead, I'd say.

Appeared to have been shot in the head point-blank. It was frozen stiffer than Haywood's proverbial 'wedding dick', so I couldn't tell if it had suffered any posthumous surgery. But, I can't imagine anyone just killing a hibernating bear for any other reason."

"You think Caldwell can set the plane down on the river up there?" Hard Case asked.

"Maybe," Gus speculated. "The ice is certainly strong enough. I guess it depends on how long a straight stretch of river he needs."

Hard Case nodded. "Fair enough. Maybe we'll have a look on the way out."

"She said we also received a visit from a couple guys in a helicopter not long after the Lindsay ordeal," Gus told him.

Hard Case studied his friend for a moment. "And…"

"And you figured it right. They tossed the cabin looking for LaGrange's generator. When they didn't find it, one of the guys said it must have burned up in Cahill's plane wreck. She says we don't have to worry about anyone coming around looking for it again."

Hard Case thought about that for a bit. "How could she…" he began, then shook his head in exasperation. "Never mind, I guess she'd know. I take a certain amount of comfort in that."

Chapter 11

Over the course of the following weeks after Jong Min-jun returned from Anchorage with Nicky and Danielle he had come to enjoy the killing of bears. He had killed his first one in a mountain cave just off a small stream that fed Wolf Creek, the river that ran through town. Jackie and Damon did not like to venture too far afield in the sub-zero days of February. A man could die out there if anything should go wrong. Accident, injury, or simple equipment failure would prove fatal if one could not get back to civilization.

Jong had accompanied them a few times before, but had remained with the snow machines while the brothers had done the killing and harvesting. He had not been overly eager to take his involvement to the next level that day, but he did not wish to appear afraid when Jackie had suggested he make the kill himself. Damon had stayed with the machines while Jackie led him through the snow to the bear's den. They stopped several paces back from a small opening at the base of a rock escarpment. Jong could barely make out a few weathered tracks in the snow pack near the entrance to the lair. It suggested the bear, if it was in there at all, had not been active for quite some time.

Jackie had handed Jong a flashlight, a pair of earmuffs and a heavy pistol. He whispered, "These places are never deep. You can see if there's a bear in there from out here. Just get up close and shine the light inside. If you see a bear, go in quick and shoot it in the head. If it moves, shoot it again." He gestured to the earmuffs. "Put those on under your hood. The gun makes a lot of noise."

Jong had done as Jackie had directed. He cinched the hood down tight over the earmuffs, approached the entrance slowly, his heart sounding louder in his ears than his footsteps, and stopped just outside. He took off his left glove to afford him a better grip on the pistol, then snapped on the flashlight and shone its beam inside the cave. At first he did not recognize the inert mound of fur as a bear, but when he did, his mouth went dry and his knees nearly buckled. Nevertheless, he knew Jackie was watching him closely so he did not hesitate. Quick as a snake, he ducked into the opening, stepped close to the bear, placed the pistol inches from its head and fired.

Jackie had been right. The roar of the handgun was deafening inside the cave despite the hood and the ear protection. He watched the bear for any hint of movement as the muzzle blast echoed and died around him. When he detected no sign of life in his victim, he took a deep, shuttering breath and exhaled.

He was dizzied by the rush of adrenaline that coursed through his veins so he took another moment before stepping outside. Jackie greeted him with a grudgingly appreciative nod as he emerged into the dimness of arctic midday. Jong was still unsteady on his feet so he leaned against the rock face of the entrance and waited for Jackie to approach.

"You want to do the cutting too?" Jackie asked.

"No," Jong said. "You do it. But, I want to watch so I'll know where the cut should be made."

Jackie nodded again. "Okay, you hold the light and watch. Maybe you can do it next time."

***

And Jong had done it next time. There had been three days of bad weather after his first kill, but as soon as it had passed, they'd gone out again. Just over the mountains, on the Moose Jaw side, the brothers had taken him to a different place they knew of where he had killed another sleeping bear. Removing its gallbladder had been unpleasant, but not difficult. Knowing where to cut was important, but knowing how deep to cut was crucial. It was absolutely critical to slice through the skin without nicking the membrane of the precious bile sac. Such carelessness would result in a significant loss of profit. The organ itself was valuable, but the bile it contained was priceless. And when it came to quality bile, the bears of the Moose Jaw represented the mother lode.

As the spring equinox approached, bears began leaving their dens to forage for food. The rivers were still frozen so there were no fish to be had, but their noses led them to the carcasses of animals that had perished during the winter. Those bears whose instincts had urged them to cache the remains of a moose or caribou in the autumn, now returned to the places where they had buried this bounty and feasted upon it.

Jackie and Damon had begun shooting any game they saw along the river systems and leaving the dead animals for bait. They would return to the spot sometime within the next few days in hopes of

65

finding a bear on the carcass. This tactic produced limited results, but as the days grew longer, Jong realized it would be much easier to locate his prey during the coming months. He would no longer need the Sam brothers to lead him to dens their people had known of for generations. He also anticipated that he would need to buy a rifle and become proficient with it soon. Pistols were adequate for killing comatose bears in caves, but he would need a rifle for shooting them at a distance.

"Where can I buy a rifle?" he asked Damon one morning in early March.

"What you looking for?" Damon responded.

"I am not sure," he confessed. "I don't know anything about rifles. I've never even shot one. What would be best for bears?"

"We like bolt actions," Damon told him. "Jackie shoots a 30.06. It's a good caliber for most big game around here. Mine's a 7mm Mag. If you never shot before, you better not get anything smaller than that. I know some guys who sell guns. I can ask around. But if you buy one, you need to go out to the range west of town and practice. You gotta be good before you start shooting at bears. You wound one and he might come at you. Then you gotta be real good."

Two days later, Jong took his new rifle out to the range. A friend of Damon's had sold him a .300 Winchester Magnum. It was a secondhand Savage fitted with a scope, and came with a sling and a hundred rounds of ammunition. Jong had no idea how much one would cost and experienced a moment of sticker-shock when the seller told him the price. It seemed quite high for a rifle that was in less-than-mint condition. Damon, however, had assured him that the price was fair, and the sale would go unrecorded.

Jackie stayed back at the house with the girls, while Damon went along to provide some coaching. He set up a paper target at a range of fifty yards, then returned to the bench. The Korean watched him approach through the lens of the scope. Damon had taken the precaution of keeping the ammunition with him while he was downrange. It was good that he had. John appeared juiced on something this morning – probably cocaine. Damon was aware he had a personal stash somewhere and that he never shared it. Getting accidentally shot by a coke-head was not in Damon's plans for the day.

"You're not supposed to do that, man," he said, clearly out of sorts.

"Do what?" Jong looked puzzled.

"Point guns at people you don't want to shoot."

Jong protested. "It's not loaded! Besides, I was just checking out the optics – they're a little fuzzy."

"Okay," Damon said. "Just, don't do it again." He was beginning to wonder if this was a good idea.

He extracted a box of cartridges from one of the deep pockets of his parka, opened it and took out a single round before returning the box to his pocket.

"First thing you gotta do is take a shot at the target just to get used to the noise and the kick. If you happen to punch a hole in the paper, we'll know it's shooting straight."

He handed over the cartridge and said, "Just open the bolt, put this in the receiver and close the bolt like I showed you this morning. Then rest your arms on the bench here, get the bull's-eye in the cross hairs and pull the trigger. It's easy – just keep the muzzle pointed downrange."

"Where?" Jong Min-jun asked, confusion apparent in his round face.

"That way," Damon told him, pointing in the direction of the target.

"Ah, yes." Jong laughed. "I told you I've never done this before. Should I shoot now?"

Damon took a deep breath and nodded. "Whenever you're ready."

Jong pointed the rifle at the ground very near Damon's foot and opened the bolt.

Damon moved a step to the left and said, "Sit down at the bench before you load it, John. And keep it pointed downrange when you do."

"Down-range, yes," Jong said, becoming a bit flustered.

He sat on the stool, rested his elbows on the bench and pointed the rifle downrange. The fact that he was left-handed made an awkward situation even more so.

"Remember, if you want to shoot left-handed, you'll have to reach over the top of the receiver to work the bolt. It's like we practiced back at the house. Now – open the bolt. Good. Drop in the cartridge and press it down a little with your thumb. That's it. Now close the bolt and lock it. Okay, you're ready to shoot."

Jong placed his eye against the scope. "Wait!" Damon shouted. "Jesus, man, back your face away from the scope! If your eye is against it when you fire, the metal ring will cut you bad. Remember, it kicks backward. Besides, you can't see anything clear when you're up against it like that."

Jong slid his cheek back along the stock for a few inches and the target materialized in the scope. "Yes," he said excitedly. "I have the target in focus but it seems to be moving around a lot."

Damon was sweating now, despite the frosty air. "Spread your elbows apart more, it will steady you." Jong did as he had been instructed and barked out an appreciative laugh. "Much better. It's still moving a little, but not a lot."

"Okay," Damon told him. "Now center the crosshairs on the bull's-eye and…" He never finished the sentence. The unexpected boom of the rifle caught him completely off guard and staggered him.

The rifle jumped out of Jong's hands and clattered across the bench and dropped over the edge. Jong toppled backward off the stool. He sat in the snow and looked up at Damon in open mouthed disbelief. "Holy fuck!" he laughed out loud, very near hysterics.

'Definitely high on something,' Damon thought. 'And getting crazier every day.' In spite of himself, he had to smile. "I told you it kicked," he said, reaching out a hand to help Jong to his feet. "Let's go see if you hit the target – and, by the way, you forgot about the safety."

Jong nodded his head vigorously as they walked downrange. "Yes, of course – the safety."

Chapter 12

When Haywood and Caldwell had finished offloading the cargo from the Helio Courier, they left it on the snow covered gravel of the bar and trudged up to the cabin. Gus was at the stove repositioning a fresh pot of coffee that had just finished perking. "You guys hungry?" he asked the room in general. "Morgan made up a big pot of ptarmigan soup for us."

"Who's Morgan?" Caldwell asked.

There was a long moment of uncomfortable silence before Haywood jumped into the breach. "Gus' little joke, Caldwell. He's embarrassed to admit he can cook and do all the kitchen chores, so he has this imaginary maid-servant that does it all for him."

Hard Case rolled his eyes and looked for imperfections in the rafters, Gus lifted the lid off the soup pan and studied its contents longer than seemed necessary, but Caldwell appeared satisfied with Haywood's subterfuge.

"Just coffee for me," he said. "We ate a big breakfast before we left Fairbanks and we brought in a bag of submarine sandwiches for lunch."

"I'm good, too," Hard Case said. "We probably ought to get after the birds pretty soon, then meet back here for lunch. How you want to run the hunt, Gus?"

Gus set four coffee mugs on the table, brought the pot over and poured, "Well, Haywood saw some activity up at the beaver ponds this morning. Whenever I hunt that section, the spruce hens usually bust cover and fly across that open meadow toward the willow thickets upstream. One of you should walk up there with me. The other two can go up to the beaver ponds and work the woods toward us."

Hard Case said, "I'll go with you. The snow's not so deep and the walking is easier."

"Okay," Gus said. "Haywood, you and Caldwell should give us about fifteen minutes head start. Then take your time going up to the ponds. Grouse season ends in three days so let's focus on them. Limit's fifteen each; I doubt we'll exceed that. There's still another month of ptarmigan season, so I'd prefer to give them a pass today. You'll probably put out some arctic hares while you're traipsing around in the tanglefoot. They're fair game, and I wouldn't mind a couple for the larder." He turned to Hard Case. "Any new rules or regulations we need to know about?"

"No," Hard Case shook his head. "The same day airborne hunting regs only apply to big game and fur animals; we won't be taking anything like that today." Hard Case surveyed the room, "Caldwell, you're the newbie; any questions?"

Caldwell looked at Haywood. "Do you know where they'll be set up in the willows? I'd rather not shoot the boss before lunch if I can avoid it."

Gus liked young Trooper Caldwell. He liked him even more now.

Haywood nodded. "I know where they'll be. We won't push that far through the woods anyway. It's best if we send the birds their way, then retreat to the ponds and wait. Maybe they'll chase a few back toward us. At any rate, we'll be well out of shotgun range."

"Right, then," Gus declared. "Drink your coffee Case, fetch your fowling piece, and we'll head upstream."

***

They didn't talk much as they made their way up the Moose Jaw. Gus stayed in the lead, as he always did, studying the snow-covered gravel bar for tracks. There were plenty to see – mostly moose and caribou, but there were also tracks of the weasels ranging in size from mink to marten, and there were a few made by porcupine, hare and wolf.

Hard Case stopped to examine some saucer sized tracks through the willows. "Lynx," he said. "Have you seen this guy?"

Gus walked over and looked down. "Not this year. I saw him a couple times last autumn. He's not as big as his tracks suggest. I'm sure Haywood would be delighted to expound upon the evolution of the Canadian Lynx's oversized paws to facilitate living in snow country. All we'd have to do is ask."

Hard Case chuckled. "I'll have to shoot you if you ask."

When they rounded the bend where the long meadow came down to meet the willows just upstream of the "landing strip" Gus brushed the snow off a driftwood log and sat down. Hard Case sat beside him.

70

"Haywood says you're planning to build a bunkhouse this year," he opened.

Gus nodded. "Yeah, the cabin's a little small when the whole crew is aboard."

Hard Case put a meaty hand in one of his side coat pockets and it came out empty. "He said you might be looking for a snow machine." He checked another pocket and came up empty handed again.

Gus smiled quietly to himself. This was one of Hard Case's endearing eccentricities – he always had to give himself a full pat down to find his smokes or matches.

"Yep," Gus confirmed. "Haywood came up with a good one there. With a big enough snowmobile, I can be setting logs as soon as the snow melts."

Hard Case discovered his crumpled pack of Camels hiding two layers beneath his hunting coat, in a shirt pocket. He extracted a bent cigarette from it, straightened it out with strokes of thumb and forefinger, lit it and sighed his contentment.

"You may be a seasoned bush rat already, but you need to pick up the lingo. We call them snow machines up here."

"Yeah," Gus lit his pipe. "I picked up on that when Haywood first brought up the subject. They call them snowmobiles down in the Lower Forty-eight; snow machines are what ski resorts use to make artificial snow."

"In that case, I'll deign to overlook your ignorance this one time," Hard Case said.

Gus smiled. "Big of you."

They sat quietly for a while, just smoking and listening to the wind stir the trees. When Hard Case finished his Camel, he ground out the butt in the snow covered gravel.

"Your three-toed bear been around lately?" he asked.

"Trilogy?" Gus said. "No, but he found that carcass I mentioned too. His tracks went into the cave, then came out and headed downstream."

Hard Case lit another cigarette and watched the smoke waft into the chill air. If they were hunting bear or moose, he would not have risked smoking. But, with upland birds, it didn't seem to matter. Then too, there was a gentle breeze coming straight down the riverbed, so the smoke was carried away quickly.

Gus puffed on his pipe and said, "I don't know how you can smoke two of those things back-to-back. Don't you worry about your lungs?"

Hard Case looked at him out of the corner of his eye. "You're worse than Mournful George. I don't know if it's occurred to you but that bowl full of perfume soaked ragweed you're sucking down lasts longer than three of my coffin nails. Not that it's any of my business, of course."

Gus chuckled to himself and studied his pipe. He couldn't argue with Hard Case's logic, so he didn't try. "You were going to fill me in about Old Blue Eye," he said instead.

Hard Case nodded. "Oh yeah," he said. "You hit the nail on the head when you asked if it was about the fishing lodge. Him saying he saw you there raises a few questions."

Gus nodded. "Yeah, I've thought about that quite a bit this winter. He must have been talking about the McCaslins' place. That's the only fishing lodge I can think of around here."

"That's the way I read it too. So, I had Caldwell take me up there this morning to see if he might be willing to expand on that a bit. He wasn't around. At least, it didn't appear he was, but you know how it is with him – now you see him, now you don't."

Gus puffed gently at his pipe. "I thought you closed that case last year. Why the renewed interest?"

Hard Case finished his Camel, then dropped the butt in the snow at his feet. "I'm sure you recall me mentioning my old boss, Pokey Brewster. Well, I went to visit him while I was in San Diego. He doesn't have long to live, Gus. By way of putting his house in order, he asked me to reopen my investigation into that little murder you committed last September. Of all the cold cases we never solved, that's the one that he wants closure on before he dies."

Gus protested. "It wasn't really murder, Case. It was more like self-defense."

Hard Case shook his head. "Your first shot may have been self-defense, Gus. I'll give you the benefit of the doubt on that one. The second shot was sort of like backing over a guy you just ran down in the street. That's murder in my book."

"Mercy killing?" Gus suggested. "I mean, he was clearly going to die from the blast that blew his – well, his manhood – off."

Gus knew very well that his second shot was not motivated by altruism. Hard Case knew it too. He decided to change the subject. "Haywood and Caldwell should be halfway to the ponds by now. They'll probably start kicking up birds anytime now."

Hard Case, however was not to be detoured. "While we wait for the shooting to start, why don't you refresh my memory about that night at the lodge? You know cops; we love to hear a story over and over again – just in case we missed something the first time."

Gus shrugged his shoulders. "Like I told you last autumn, the McCaslins had come across Morgan and her friend Jason upstream of their lodge. They'd been stranded without their raft after Trilogy attacked them in midstream, clawed Morgan in the back, and tore a hole in one of their floatation bladders. Jason doctored her wounds, but she was in a bad way. The McCaslin brothers took them back down to their place. Larry, the big one, got drunk and raped Jason in a back room. Roy went after Morgan, but she fought him off. She remembered Jason escaped into the night and the brothers went after him. She heard a shot, but never knew for certain what had happened to him.

After I found her on the riverbank and took her back to The Varmitage, she came around and told me the whole story – as much of it as she could remember. She thought the brothers must have knocked her on the head and dropped her in the river. I went up to their lodge looking for Jason, and that's when Roy came at me with a knife and I shot him."

"You did indeed," Hard Case sighed. "The physical evidence – those plastic wads and the bismuth shot pellets – confirmed it. How you came in here and built a cabin in the year 2000, and managed to kill a guy in 1959 will always remain a mystery to me, but I know that's what happened. I know you killed that damned bear too, but he's still walking around like he doesn't know he's dead. And, then there's Morgan. She disappeared back in '59 but you seem to have found her last year – alive and well. Now Haywood tells me he's met her too. Remember I warned you about strange shit happening out here, Gus? Well, I'm beginning to suspect I didn't know the half of it. The Moose Jaw takes the cake when it comes to strange."

"That it does, Case. That it does," Gus agreed.

"All that aside," Hard case went on, "I promised Pokey I'd try to figure out who it was that wired the McCaslin's to that eye-bolt and left the fire-bomb for them to ponder before they died. You sure you never saw anybody else around the lodge when you were there?"

Gus nodded. "I'm sure. I heard some rustling in the trees, and I called out Jason's name a few times, but no one answered, or appeared. After I read the old case file last year, I realized someone else must have been there, but I didn't really want to think about it. I was afraid Morgan might have had something to do with it."

Hard Case pursed his lips and looked off through the willows toward the meadow. "Another Snow Viper sort of thing?"

"Yeah," Gus conceded. "Something like that. But, after Old Blue Eye said he'd seen me there, it made me wonder. You think he could have been the one that did the wire work and arranged for the fire?"

"It crossed my mind; if it wasn't him he might know who did. If he was there before you arrived, maybe he saw someone. That's why I need to talk to him. The only other lead I had was a guy named Charlie Henry, Pokey's primary suspect. Our Chekov detachment informs me he died four years ago. He had a son who might be a priest now, but we don't know where. My contact up in Chekov is asking around the Henry clan to see if anyone knows where he is. But, even if we find him, I doubt he'll be able to tell us anything about that night out at the lodge. Which brings me to the point of this visit; I need you to do me a favor, Fergus."

"Name it," Gus said.

"I can't believe I'm going to ask you this, but will you see if Morgan would be willing to help me out? I need her to make contact with Old Blue Eye and arrange for him to meet me and talk. You think she'd do that?"

"Why don't you just go back up to his cabin and leave him a note or something?"

"Look, Gus," Hard Case reasoned, "you and I – Haywood too, I reckon – know Morgan, the bear, and Old Blue Eye are somehow connected. Without putting too fine a point on it, I think they all dwell on the other side of that gossamer wall I mentioned in my notes regarding the spirit world. Think about it – he was an old, old man the first time I met him back in '72. He's still old – but he hasn't aged. Somehow he's expecting me every time I show up, and he clearly has something going on with Morgan and the bear.

74

You see him when he wants you to see him, but if he doesn't want to be seen, you don't. All I'm saying is I suspect he might be closer in nature to Morgan than he is to us. She'd have a better chance of making contact with him than I would."

Gus noticed his pipe had gone cold. He knocked the dottle out against the log. "I know what you mean. I've more-or-less come to the same conclusion about him myself. It can't hurt to ask her."

"Thanks."

Gus was quiet for a moment then said, "Maybe she'd talk to you face-to-face. You want me to ask her?"

Hard Case looked across the creek, but his focus seemed to be on something too far away to be seen. "No. I don't think so, Gus. I'm tempted, but I'm afraid meeting her would be more than this old cop could handle. I know there's a world on the other side of the wall, but I've lived my life on this side. I don't want to see the other side for myself. I might not find my way back."

Gus nodded his understanding but kept silent.

Hard Case went on, "Besides, it's a pretty exclusive club you and Haywood have joined. I don't think I can afford the price of admission."

Gus gave him a wry smile. "It's not so high," he responded. "All you have to do is go find Trilogy and kick him square in the balls. Haywood and I will sponsor your mortal remains for membership."

Hard Case made a show of considering Gus' suggestion for a moment. Then he gave his friend a sidelong glance. "I've never been a joiner anyway," he demurred. "How about you just ask her if she knows who visited the McCaslins before you shot up the place. You can pass along any info she shares."

Gus nodded. "Discretion being the better part of valor, I'd say that's a more prudent approach."

Two shotgun blasts echoed across the snow-covered meadow. A third followed a few seconds later. Hard Case and Gus stood up, cradled their guns in the crooks of their arms and watched the meadow intently. No birds came into view.

"Sounds like they must have knocked down a couple," Gus observed.

"Yeah, I haven't hunted with Caldwell before, but I've seen him on the trap range. He can handle that over-and-under," Hard Case said.

"I'll bet he can," Gus agreed. "He handles himself pretty well all around for a young fellow."

"That he does."

They waited another ten minutes; when there were no further shots, Gus said. "Our turn to walk, I guess. Let's see if we can flush a few spruce hens out of those willows."

***

They gathered back at the cabin at three o'clock that afternoon for a very late lunch. Hard Case and Gus had beer with their sandwiches; Caldwell and Haywood, who would be piloting aircraft later, stuck to ginger ale. They discussed the hunt while they ate.

"Not a bad day, all-in-all," Hard Case commented.

Haywood nodded. "Twenty- one grouse and four hares; a respectable haul for a few hours sport."

"Just leave me three of the spruce hens," Gus told them. "We saw more hares out there today than you can shake a stick at. I can pot one whenever the mood takes me."

Haywood asked, "Why don't you just set a few snares back there in the meadow?"

Gus laughed. "I tried all last summer. Never got the hang of it, I guess; and I made it a point of honor not to shoot one until I'd mastered the trapping technique."

"I used to snare all sorts of animals when I was a kid," Caldwell told them. "I'll be happy to rig a couple out behind the cabin before we leave. If you like, that is."

"I'd like that. And I'd be obliged if you let me watch," Gus told him honestly. "Maybe you can show me what I've been doing wrong."

Hard Case finished his beer and stood up. "Caldwell," he said, "Haywood and I will dress the birds and those damned rodents while you school Fergus in the fine art of setting snares."

Haywood cleared his throat, "Actually, Case, rabbits and hares are not of the order Rodentia. They belong to the order Lagomorpha."

Hard Case shot him a exasperated glance. "Thank you Dr. Jennings." Then, to Gus he asked, "Any place special you'd like us

76

to scatter the remains of these recently departed fowl and Lagomorphs?" He smiled smugly at Haywood.

Gus concentrated on finishing his sandwich without choking. When he'd swallowed the last bite, he said, "Downstream of the planes a hundred yards or so, if you don't mind. The magpies and ravens will be happy to clean up, and the fox patrols the banks every morning and evening. She's probably got a litter of kits in her den to feed."

"The fox, of course, is of the genus Vulpes, family Canidae. Just thought you'd want to know, Case," Haywood offered, giving Gus a surreptitious wink.

Hard Case shook his head in disbelief. "I give up," he said. "The man's an encyclopedia of dubious zoological trivia."

Haywood grinned. "I'm somewhat an expert on scatology too," he informed them.

"That's good to know," Hard Case parried. "I'll be able to defend you next time I hear one of your detractors say you don't know shit."

***

Gus thanked Caldwell for the pointers he'd given him about setting snares. "Maybe I'll be able to harvest some hares this year without working too hard at it," he told the young Trooper.

"You bet. Just keep the loop small and well concealed in the set. You'll catch 'em."

With that, Caldwell closed the door of the plane, and Gus ambled over to join Haywood. They watched as Caldwell revved the engines and swung the nose out onto the river ice. Hard Case waved to them from the front passenger seat. Then, they heard the engine wind up to full power as Caldwell opened the throttle and the aircraft shot down the riverbed and lifted off into the blue sky. They watched it disappear into the clouds on its way back to Fairbanks.

"Well," Haywood said, "there's no point putting it off. Time I got on up to Fort Yukon. I'll swing back by to pick up Bosworth day after tomorrow."

"Will you stay the night?"

"Not this run. I've been away from the clinic too much lately, what with the Yukon Quest and that week in Hawaii. Not to

77

mention this little four day jaunt. The staff will be after my hide if I don't start pulling my weight."

"Alright, then," Gus rested his hand on Haywood's shoulder as they walked down the bank to the rented Cessna. "I'll see you in a couple days."

Haywood climbed aboard, said, "Don't let the bears eat you," then closed the door and began his preflight routine.

Just as he was lifting off the Moose Jaw, Morgan came out onto the porch of the cabin and waved. Haywood saw her, banked into a turn and waggled his wings as he passed over The Varmitage on his way north-east to Fort Yukon.

Chapter 13

Caldwell had taken off upstream, into the wind, and the Helio Courier was at no more than two hundred feet elevation as they passed over the confluence of Deadman Creek and the Moose Jaw. Hard Case considered mentioning the dead bear in the cave, but it was getting late in the day and he wanted to stop in Chekov before returning to Fairbanks. There was really no need to inspect the bear; he was certain Gus had it right. He'd just report it to the wildlife guys when he got back to the office.

While they were still climbing to reach altitude, he asked Caldwell if he thought they had time to make a stop in Chekov.

"Don't see why not," the young Trooper responded. "It's just over this ridge to our north. We can be there in a half-hour. The strip is well lit there so taking off in the dark is no problem."

"Good," Hard Case told him. "I'd like to pay my respects to Sgt. O'Kelly. Have you met him?"

Caldwell took the Helio Courier up to four thousand feet so they could cross the range between the Moose Jaw and Wolf Creek drainages.

"He conducted a seminar when I was in the Academy. And I've bumped into him a few times in Fairbanks. He's old school, like you. Me too, I guess."

Hard Case gazed at the landscape passing beneath them as they crossed through a saddle in the ridgeback and smiled to himself. He said aloud. "Caldwell, I wouldn't wish it on a lesser person, but I do believe you're right. You are as old school as they come. For what it's worth, I approve."

"Thanks boss. That means something."

Hard Case studied the terrain below them and was surprised when he saw the little gravel strip on the outskirts of Chekov growing in the windscreen.

"That didn't take long at all," he observed.

"Haywood said Gus is going to get a snow machine," Caldwell said.

"Yeah." Hard Case confirmed. "He wants to haul logs down the frozen riverbed to build a bunkhouse this summer."

"He'll be able to bring in supplies overland too," Caldwell added.

"I suppose so," Hard Case agreed. "Pretty long run though; there's a lot of river miles between The Varmitage and the nearest town."

"He wouldn't have to stick to the river," Caldwell told him. "He could cut through the mountains on that snow machine trail a few miles downstream of his cabin."

Hard Case searched his memory. "I don't recall there being a snow machine trail."

They were still above two thousand feet so Caldwell banked the plane into a full one-eighty turn. "I'll show you," he said to his boss.

He took the plane back up to four thousand feet and set his course a few degrees to the east of where they had come through the saddle.

After a few minutes, Caldwell directed Hard Case's attention to a thin ribbon of dirty snow cutting through the trees below them. "Look down there," he said.

Hard Case looked but did not see anything of significance. "What am I looking at?"

"A well travelled trail," Caldwell said. "It follows a little stream down both sides of the mountain. It goes straight from Chekov to the Moose Jaw. If Gus bought a machine in Chekov, he could drive it home to The Varmitage in about four hours."

Hard Case clapped a meaty paw on his pilot's shoulder. "As Haywood would say, Caldwell – you're more than just a pretty face."

Caldwell blushed. "Chekov, boss?"

Hard Case realized he may have embarrassed his young protégé. "Chekov, Caldwell."

***

Hard Case phoned the Chekov office from the airstrip and Mike O'Kelly picked them up and drove them back to the station. They sat in wooden chairs around a battered metal desk and drank coffee from thick mugs that sported the seal of the Alaska State Troopers.

The two old troopers agreed it was too bad about Charlie Henry dying. It didn't leave Hard Case many more trails to follow. When they had exhausted the subject of Pokey Brewster and their old boss' final request, Hard Case told his friend about the snow machine trail Caldwell had shown him.

"Pretty well travelled, you say?" Sgt. O'Kelly wondered aloud.

Hard Case nodded his head. "I'd say there's been quite a bit of traffic on that trail this winter. It makes me wonder if our Moose Jaw poachers are operating out of Chekov."

"It would make sense," O'Kelly reasoned. "It's a long haul into the Moose Jaw from Central or Circle. I'll keep an eye out for anybody spending more money than I figure they should have."

Caldwell finished his coffee and walked to the sink and rinsed his cup. "Any new faces in town?"

Mike O'Kelly smiled his appreciation at Hard Case. He liked the way young Caldwell's mind worked. He said, "Now that you mention it, there's talk of a couple new young lovelies making the rounds of our local dens of iniquity lately. Unusual, I'd say. The normal migratory pattern for beautiful young ladies is from the bush to the cities. They rarely wind up here. I'll ask around about them."

Hard Case began patting himself down. Sgt. O'Kelly shook his head sadly. "Are you still smoking, Kees Calis?" he said with obvious disapproval.

"Occasionally," Hard Case said sheepishly.

"Like a chimney," Caldwell chimed in. Hard Case glared at him.

"They'll kill you, you know," O'Kelly predicted. Then he dropped the subject, knowing it was a lost cause. "How many bears have been poached along the Moose Jaw, you think?"

"The one I just reported is the only one I've heard about so far, but it's a long river. I'm sure there have been others," Hard Case responded, glad to discuss any subject other than his tobacco habit.

"Gus O'Neill was on foot when he discovered it. He's looking for a snow machine now, so he'll be covering more ground. I'll ask him to let me know if he comes across any more bears."

"He the guy that got tore up by the big grizzly last year?" O'Kelly asked.

Hard Case said, "Yep, the same. He's a good man and a close friend. You wouldn't happen to have a line on a snow tracker for sale here in Chekov would you?"

"I would," O'Kelly laughed. "My next door neighbor is moving to the Lower Forty-Eight. He's selling everything he owns, and he has a big Polaris 500, maybe two years old, that can pull more than

Paul Bunyan's Blue Ox. He'll sell cheap if he can unload it this week."

"Sled?" Hard Case asked.

"I think so," O'Kelly told him. "Want me to call him?"

"Sure." Hard Case turned to Caldwell, "You got anything going you need to get back early for tonight?"

Caldwell shook his head, "Nothing that can't wait."

Hard Case stood up. "Make your call, Michael. I'll just step outside and foul the air while I wait."

He went out the door patting his pockets.

Chapter 14

April, 2001
Deadman Creek, Alaska

The day that followed the full moon in April, Old Blue Eye appeared in the clearing where once had stood a fishing lodge. He still thought of the creek upon which it was situated as Rainbow Creek. It had been called that because of the big, colorful trout that teemed in its waters. But the trout were gone now, and the lodge had burned to the ground the night the McCaslin brothers were executed. That had become a famous event in Alaska. The newspapers had described it as 'The Rainbow Lodge Murders'. After the "murders" the creek had come to be called Deadman Creek.

As he often did, the old shaman closed his good eye and was transported back to the night of the killings. He refused to think of them as murders. He knew that was not the proper word to describe what had happened that night. He knew because he had been there.

****

Jason looked down in horror at his mangled, bleeding hand. It still held the knife that had severed two of its fingers. Larry McCaslin's grip had been powerful enough to break several bones as well. The knife slid from his palm and dropped into the puddle of blood now spreading atop the spruce needles that littered the forest floor. Larry kicked the knife aside and slammed a ham-sized fist into Jason's face. Jason felt the socket of his right eye collapse as a supernova of light exploded in his brain. A tooth cracked as his face made contact with the ground. An enormous weight pressed down in the middle of his back and the air was forced out of his lungs. He was nearly unconscious but he could feel Larry fumbling with his belt, and knew what was coming next. He groaned and struggled for breath. He had to fight back – had to make Larry just kill him outright. He couldn't bear thinking about the alternative. Being Larry's plaything for any length of time would be far worse than death. He'd already experienced enough of the giant's savagery. He couldn't endure any more.

Roy, who had stood by with a rifle while his gargantuan brother brutalized the young man, said, "Christ almighty, Larry, you're one sick homo. I ain't gonna stan' here and watch you corn-hole him. I'm goin' back inside. And make sure you dump him a ways down the Moose Jaw where we took the redhead."

Jason felt his pants being pulled down over his legs and began to weep. 'No,' his mind screamed. 'Please, God – No!'

The door of the lodge slammed shut, then there was a resounding thud that sounded like a piece of solid limb wood thumping the trunk of a hollow tree. Like a meteor striking earth, a huge body crashed to the ground next to him and, with his one good eye, he stared into the slack features of Larry McCaslin's monstrous face.

"Wire his thumbs together behind his back," a man's voice said calmly. If he moves, don't kill him, just whack him again. We'll do this the way Charlie said."

Another man said, "Roy's alone inside now; we'll go take care of him. You boys stay here and make sure Larry doesn't get loose. And see how bad this guy's hurt while we're gone."

Jason heard footsteps, then felt strong, but gentle hands roll him over onto his back. Lights flashed inside his skull. A young voice gasped, "Oh, shit, Josh. His eye is hanging right out on his cheek."

Then Jason heard the sounds of retching, and knew the sight of him had sickened the boy. But, who were these people? Would they help him? He lost consciousness for a time, but when he came to, the first man voice he had heard said, "Okay. We got Roy tied up inside. It looks like Goliath the sodomite is coming around. Leave him to me. You three take this guy (he must have indicated Jason) into the lodge and bandage him up. You know where the medicine box is."

Jason felt himself being helped to his feet, then guided across the clearing, up the steps, across the porch and into the lodge. His vision was clear out of his left eye, but not so the right. Hands helped him into a chair near the table. The man with the boys wore a red wool jacket; he said, "Turn up all those lamps. We need more light." Then he took Jason by the wrist above his bleeding right hand and held it while one of the boys wrapped a roll of gauze bandage around and around the palm and finger stumps, then secured it with tape. The other boy wrapped his head and damaged eye in a similar dressing.

"What in hell you assholes think you're doing?" roared a voice from one of the back bedrooms. Jason recognized it as Roy's. He sounded drunk, as well as angry. "I know who you are! I'll report this you fuckin' heathen bastards! You can't treat a white man this way!"

Larry came stumbling through the door, hands wired behind his back, the barrel of a shotgun pressed against his head. "Roy!" he cried out. "They hurt me, Roy! Help me!"

The man holding the gun shoved him toward the back room where Roy was being kept.

"Shut up, Larry!" Roy screamed as loud as he possibly could. "You fuckin' queer! This is all your doin'!"

"Stop making noise," Red Jacket said quietly. "We will give you a fair chance. First, you go to sleep. When you wake up you will know the test you must pass to live."

"What do you mean by 'go to sleep'?" Roy asked in a voice choked by fear.

"Ether," the voice said.

"You're going to kill us!" Roy cried.

"We will if you don't take the ether," the voice agreed calmly. "Now, tell your brother to keep his head still or we'll just cut his throat and let him bleed to death."

Jason's head felt as if it was being split with a white-hot poker, and the pain in his hand was excruciating. He caught the faint chemical odor of ether on the air, then an enormous crash shook the floor of the lodge and rattled the windows. Larry had succumbed. Then Roy's voice pleaded, "Wait!" he whined, "let me sit down on the floor first."

A few moments passed, followed by a gentle thud from the back room. Roy was down too.

"Okay, boys," shotgun man said. "Come in here and strip them. You were right about the eye-bolt; it'll hold them for sure."

The boys left Jason's side and went into the back room. The man in the red jacket came out and knelt by his chair.

"I don't know you, mister, but you owe us for saving you from Larry. He raped that young boy in there two years ago. Tonight he will pay for that. His brother too. If you help us, we won't have to kill you. You understand?"

Jason nodded. "What can I do?" he slurred through bruised and bleeding lips. He lifted his bandaged hand to illustrate his point.

The man smiled. "It only takes one hand to squeeze the crimping pliers."

Jason said, "I'll help you any way I can. I'd kill them myself if I could."

The man nodded his understanding. "What is your name?"

"Jason," he told him.

"Come, Jason," the man helped him to his feet and across the rough boards of the floor to the back room.

When they entered, Jason was amazed to see both Roy and Larry were stark naked and each boy was twisting wire around one of their scrotums. The wire had been passed through a heavy eyebolt which protruded from one of the thick logs of the rear wall.

Red jacket was supporting Jason; he said, "Snare wire. Very strong. You cannot cut it with a knife." He placed a pair of crimping pliers in Jason's left hand and pointed to the notch in the jaws. "Put this over the crimp sleeve and squeeze hard," he told him. "Do it on both of them before they wake up."

Jason did as he said. The youngest boy had wrapped and twisted the wire around Larry's genitals, and he unabashedly held it in position so Jason could make the crimp with no difficulty. The boy nodded his head with satisfaction when the job was done. "This big guy, he hurt me bad. You know what I mean I think," he said, tears in his eyes.

"Yes," Jason told him. "He hurt me the same way." His voice shook as he said this.

The boy looked concerned. "You gonna be okay, mister?"

"Probably not," Jason told him truthfully.

"This one's coming around," the older boy said. The shotgun man walked over and pressed the muzzle against Roy's forehead. "Stay put," he said. "We're almost done with you."

Roy was still groggy from the ether, but he understood. He did not move a muscle as Jason applied the crimp to his wire.

"Good," the man said. "You boys go bring in the cans now. We'll rig the candle."

Jason returned to the table where he sat while the boys brought in five jerry cans and took them into the back room. A few minutes later, the man with the red jacket came out and said to him, "You should be a part of this. Can you walk?"

Jason said he could, stood slowly and followed the man into the back room. The smell of kerosene was very strong in the tight quarters.

The boys stood against the side wall where Jason could see the jerry cans had been arranged in a row on the floor. The cap of one of the cans had been removed and the wick of a fuse had been inserted into its spout. The other end of the fuse was stuck into a candle perhaps an inch below the flame. The candle was on the floor in the corner, and a chair had been tipped over and placed as a protective shield in front of it so a thrown object couldn't snuff its flame.

Jason watched as the man in the red coat nodded to the boys and they unscrewed the other caps from their cans and began pouring puddles of kerosene here and there about the room. They took care to avoid the area around the candle.

"That's enough," the second man said. With that, he took two hunting knives out of his belt and walked to the door. He waited until Jason and the others had passed out into the main room, then he turned to the McCaslins, both now awake and fully cognizant of their predicament, and said, "The knives are not sharp, but they are your only chance." He nodded toward the candle. "You got maybe ten minutes."

With that, he skidded a knife to each of the brothers, turned, crossed the main room and went out into the night. The others followed. Jason exited last, leaving the door standing open behind him and the light from the many lamps in the great room pouring out the doorway.

As they left the porch, they could hear Larry's voice behind them. He was blubbering, "What's goin' on Roy? Why they doin' this to us? You gotta get us out'a here, Roy!"

They crossed the clearing and stopped just inside the tree line. As they waited there a dense frozen fog came crawling up the forest floor from the waters of Rainbow Creek.

"What will you do if they manage to get loose?" Jason asked the man with the red jacket.

The man shrugged his shoulders, "Shoot them I guess. We can't leave them to come after us."

Jason saw the wisdom of this. He also understood why the young boy had been allowed to exact his own retribution from Larry. He had felt the cathartic release himself when he applied the crimp. He saw the beauty of this form of punishment. As a lawyer, he had been bound by the letter of the law. But, out here in the bush, there were no loopholes to be exploited. Punishment usually fit the crime. He wondered how long it would take the McCaslin brothers to attack the eye-bolt, the wire, or one another. 'Justice,' he thought, 'is a beautiful thing when properly administered.'

Moments later, the fog-shrouded forest around the fishing lodge was pierced by a brain-numbing scream. It continued and grew in its awful intensity. The boys covered their ears; the men stood transfixed, staring at the light flooding out the doorway of the lodge and filling the foggy landscape with an eerie luminescence.

Just as the scream began to fade into a whimper, Red Jacket started at a sound that came from down by the river. "Quick," he commanded. "Deeper into the trees – and keep quiet!"

They had just hidden themselves in the shadows of the forest, when a man burst out of the fog in front of the lodge. He carried a shotgun at port arms, like a soldier attacking a fortification. He came in low and fast – very fast. His quickness startled Jason and he caught his sleeve on a tree branch while trying to duck behind the trunk. The branch didn't snap, but it swooshed through the air when it pulled free from the fabric of his coat. The man instantly tucked and rolled and came up with his shotgun trained directly upon Jason's position. Jason froze and held his breath. He was sure the man could see him.

Just then, Roy McCaslin, bloody and naked, came howling out the open door of the lodge with a knife clutched in one hand. The man in the clearing seemed not to move, but his shotgun roared and its muzzle flash lanced through the mist of fog, and Roy buckled and sagged back against one of the porch's railing posts. He clutched at his midsection, trying to keep his intestines from spilling from his lower abdomen. It was a wonder he was still alive. The man with the shotgun had racked a fresh shell into the chamber while the echo of his first shot still hung in the frigid air. He approached Roy slowly and, without so much as a word, lifted the muzzle of his gun within inches of Roy's open mouth, and squeezed

88

the trigger. Roy's head exploded and his dead body dropped to the porch boards.

None of the party in the trees moved until the man went into the lodge, shotgun leveled and at the ready. As soon as he disappeared through the doorway, all five made their way deeper into the forest. They were at least a hundred yards upstream when they heard the man shouting something. They stopped and listened.

The man shouted again. It almost sounded like he said "Jason!"

"I've got to go back there," he told Red Jacket. "I think he called out my name."

"I thought he said Nathan," Josh said. "It didn't sound like Jason."

Shotgun man laid his hand on Jason's shoulder. "We cannot let you go back there, Jason. You helped us kill the McCaslin brothers. If that man is the law, he will arrest you and you will tell him about us. We cannot let that happen. Come with us and we will take you to our settlement where there are people who can deal with your injuries."

Jason tried to think what he should do, but the pain in his head made it difficult to concentrate. He shook his head to clear it, became dizzy and his knees buckled. Red Jacket caught him and eased him to the ground. Suddenly it seemed he was looking straight at the sun. Light exploded in his brain and then there was only darkness.

Chapter 15

The old man opened his good eye and took a moment to make sure he was still in the clearing where the fishing lodge had burned. He never knew where he might emerge from one of his trances. 'I must be getting better at this,' he thought. It pleased him that his feet had not moved from the place he had stood before his journey to the past. But, it was now time to address the reason he had come to this place again.

He had travelled here today because his blind eye had seen the sons of his nephew kill two bears where this stream joined the Moose Jaw. He had come to see the desecration with his good eye, just to make certain he had not dreamed or imagined it. He had not. The carcasses were still warm when he found them. This told him two things: his blind eye could still see with great clarity, and he could not have come by foot. He had often wondered about this; now he had the answer. He was beginning to get a better sense of his own nature and this, he thought, was a good thing. He took the time to inspect each carcass carefully. Both had been male black bears; both had been shot with a heavy caliber rifle; both had been incised on the lower abdomen, and their gallbladders had been removed.

There was still enough snow on the ground that he could see sufficient evidence to confirm his two grand nephews had committed this crime. But there had been another party with them. Two snow machines had come up the Moose Jaw this time, and there were three sets of man tracks. They were getting careless. Killing these bears on an open gravel bar so close to the creek showed arrogance as well as stupidity. Any aircraft following the course of the river would certainly see the dead bears. The Alaska State Troopers still patrolled this area regularly and they would land and take pictures and study the tracks of the killers and their machines. Perhaps he would not have to tell the big one called Case about the nephews – people in the villages always noticed when someone came into new money. There would be talk, especially now that the boys had brought another into their circle. The old Trooper would hear the talk.

He thought about this possibility for a little, and he concluded that it would be best to wait a bit longer before getting involved. Breakup would happen soon and when the ice was gone the boys would stop killing bears for the summer. They would turn their energies to taking gold out of the valley. This was a legal enterprise, at least most of the time. The authorities would lose interest in them for a while. Of course, that may be a bad thing too – Broken Foot would not forget them. If he came upon them while they were busy panning nuggets from the stream, they would never hear him coming. The old shaman shook his head sadly. Maybe he shouldn't wait. Maybe now was the time to go to the big Trooper. He would have to think about it – but not today. Today he had to visit a place farther down the Moose Jaw where his dream told him of another dead bear. The nephews had gone crazy since this third person came.

He closed his good eye and began to sway gently, side to side. His dream came back to him and the old man felt as if he were floating.

Chapter 16

After Hard Case heard back from Mike O'Kelly, he informed Mournful George that Isaac Henry had joined a seminary in the late sixties, and asked him to track him down. While the boss was out in the bush trying to hook up with Old Blue Eye, George went about the search in his own deliberate, if plodding fashion. Since he was the product of a rather large Irish-Catholic family, "seminary" suggested he begin with the administrative offices of the Catholic Church in Alaska. The archdiocese of Anchorage covered a lot of territory. Archbishop Francis Thomas Hurley was prelate of the Cathedral of the Holy Family in Anchorage, but he also was the spiritual shepherd for the Catholic diocese of Fairbanks, as well as the original Alaskan diocese in Juneau.

After enduring several minutes of recorded choir music while on hold, a young clerk there came back on the line with disappointing news. They had no record of anyone named Isaac Henry.

"No, not even as a parishioner. Yes, Chekov did, indeed have a Catholic church, and there were some Henrys in the parish, but no Isaac Henry."

Just before the young cleric hung up, he suggested that George try the Alaska Orthodox Church. Some of the native Alaskans subscribed to that denomination.

It took him all afternoon, but in the end he learned that young Isaac Henry had enrolled at St. Herman's Theological Seminary when it opened on the Kenai Peninsula in 1972. And when the campus moved to the island of Kodiak the following year, he was still registered as a seminarian. Upon completion of his studies he did graduate, but declined ordination as a priest. This was not uncommon. Many young single seminarians chose to postpone their ordination until they wed. The Orthodox Church allowed married men to become ordained priests, but once a young man was ordained a celibate priest, he could not marry. The registrar at St. Herman's had no further information regarding Isaac's current location, but was able to assure Mournful George that he had never become a priest.

***

The next day George was waiting in Hard Case's office when he returned from the briefing room.

"Looks like we hit a dead end on Charlie's youngest son," he told Hard Case. "He was Orthodox, not Catholic – graduated from St. Herman's Theological Seminary over on Kodiak, but never took the cloth. The registrar had no idea what became of him after he left the school. I also checked the 2000 Census for the Yukon-Koyukuk territory, just in case he went back up there. I found a lot of Henrys in their database, but there was no Isaac on the list. He could be anywhere. You want me to keep looking for him?"

"Doesn't sound like there's anyplace left to look," Hard Case said. "I assume you already ran him through NCIC, such as it is."

"First place I checked, just in case he had a sheet. His brother Joshua popped up for a D&D in Fairbanks right before he joined the Army. Nothing on Isaac, though," George reported.

"Every young man's entitled to get drunk and disorderly before enlisting," Hard Case observed.

"I reckon that's true," George agreed. "Sorry I couldn't find him for you."

"Don't worry about it, George – needle in a haystack. I'll call Mike O'Kelly over in Chekov and see if he's turned up anything new. If not, I guess it's down to Old Blue Eye."

"He doesn't seem to be an easy guy to find," George said.

"Gus is trying to arrange a meet with him. Let's hope he can manage it." Hard Case lit a Camel, leaned back in his chair and exhaled a long stream of smoke.

"You're going to set off the sprinklers one of these days, boss," Mournful George warned him. "Just you wait."

"Then you better skedaddle, George, if you don't want to get wet." He gave his sergeant an exaggerated wink and took another deep drag.

Mournful George shook his head sadly, turned and left the room, closing the door behind him. Hard Case stared up at the sprinkler head which protruded through the drop ceiling of his office. A dense cloud of smoke curled lazily around it. He had been chain-smoking in that office for as long as he could remember and the damned thing had never activated. He wondered if it was broken. He crushed his cigarette in the half-full ashtray on his desk. 'Curse that George,' he thought. 'Now I'll be worried about that damned thing going off every time I light up. I do believe he did that on purpose.'

He smiled, shook his head and reached for his pack. Then he thought better of it.

"A pox on you George Gleason!" he barked at the closed door.

***

When Hard Case got home that evening, he poured himself three fingers of Oban, and phoned the Chekov office.

"O'Kelly." The sergeant's voice always made Hard Case smile.

"Hello, Michael. How're things up there in the frozen north?" Hard Case asked of his old friend.

"Cold enough to freeze the balls off a brass monkey, and ass-deep snow everywhere you look – couldn't be better. What can I do for Alaska's most esteemed detective on this fine evening?" O'Kelly responded.

"Probably nothing, Mike. Just touching base to thank you for hooking Gus O'Neill up with your neighbor. Haywood Jennings flew him up to Chekov yesterday and Gus bought the Polaris and a big sled to pull behind it, as well as an assortment of logging gear. He drove back out to his cabin and called me on a sat-phone. He sounded like a kid on Christmas morning."

"Don't mention it. I was glad to do it, and my neighbor was happy to unload so many big ticket items," Mike told him.

"Well, I appreciate the help. Anyway, I also wanted to see if you had any new gin on the youngest Henry boy, Isaac."

"No," O'Kelly told him. "I haven't had much time to run him down, Kees. We're having our annual end-of-winter surge in domestic disputes. One got out of control over the weekend and resulted in a fatality. If that isn't enough, there appears to be a new supply of crack cocaine finding its way to Chekov lately. Those two young ladies I mentioned may be the source. We're going to keep an eye on them. But, I haven't forgotten Charlie's kid. I'll see what I can find out about him."

"If you would, I'd appreciate it. The info you passed on about him joining a seminary was righteous. He wasn't Catholic, but we found out he graduated from the Orthodox seminary on Kodiak – St. Herman's. However, he left the school before becoming ordained as a priest and dropped out of sight. If you can't pick up his trail there in your neck of the woods, I'm pretty much out of straws."

94

"How old you figure he is?"

"I'd guess he must be in his mid-fifties by now. He was twelve or thirteen back in '59 when the murders took place. I doubt he can tell us anything about what happened out there. He was probably with his family at a big potlatch over in Circle. But, just try to find out if anyone remembers seeing him up there after he left the seminary; that was sometime in the early seventies."

"I'll check it out tomorrow evening. Fact is, I'm having dinner at one of his cousin's house. Katiana Henry – she's the one that told me he went into the seminary."

"Katiana," Hard Case liked the sound of it. "Pretty name."

"Pretty woman," Mike confided.

"Married?" Hard Case inquired.

"Widowed three years. A man could do worse."

Hard Case smiled and sipped his whiskey. He could hear his friend's happiness coming over the phone. "So could she, Michael. So, could she."

Mike said he'd call him back in a day or two if he learned anything, and they rung off.

Chapter 17

As soon as Gus concluded his purchase of a 1998 Polaris 500 Wide Track snow machine from Mike O'Kelly's neighbor, the neighbor drove Haywood back out to the airstrip. Haywood flew back to Fairbanks and left a message with Mournful George that the deal was done, and George promised to pass it on to Hard Case.

While they were gone, Gus had a walk around Chekov and treated himself to lunch at one of the downtown eateries. As arranged, he met the neighbor back at his house to load up all his gear and get briefed on the eccentricities of his new work horse.

"This skid will make log pullin' a whole lot easier," the neighbor assured him. He squatted beside it and went over its features. "The ole' boy I bought it from cut it off the nose of a '50 Dodge pick-up hood with a cuttin' torch. He cut the hole in it too for the tow line. You just put the skid under the butt end of the log and run your tow line through the hole. Sink the barbs of the log tongs good and solid into the log, then connect your tow line to the cinch rings."

He looked up to see if Gus understood. Gus nodded that he did. It was a pretty ingenious set up. "And you've pulled some pretty big logs with this rig?" he asked.

"Bigger than anything you'll find up along the Moose Jaw. If you're just pulling them down river ice, you'll be able to drag thirty footers with no trouble at all. And that sled will handle close to a ton of board lumber if you load it proper."

The seller threw in two coils of polypropylene rope, a heavy nylon tow strap and four five gallon gas cans. Gus offered to pay for them, but the guy refused.

"I'll just have to leave them behind if you don't take them. Besides, you should always have a couple extra cans of fuel with you when you're up there loggin'."

Gus thanked him, loaded his purchases into the sled and drove off toward the edge of town where they had passed a gas station on the way in. He filled all four petrol cans and topped off the snow machine's tank. Inside, he purchased two more gallons of two-stroke oil because he knew the logging runs would eat a lot of fuel. After paying cash at the counter, he went back out to his snow machine, secured the jugs of oil in the sled, and climbed aboard.

Essentially, the trail was nothing more than the frozen surface of Wolf Creek. Gus joined it just south of a parking area outside of town that bore a sign proclaiming "Wolf Creek Trailhead". He took it easy in the early going, getting used to the big Polaris. He'd ridden a snow machine only once before, and he'd been a passenger at the time. But, it didn't take him long to become comfortable with the machine's power and by the time he reached the foot of the hills, he was running at a respectable clip. The sled behind him, although carrying a fair sized load, tracked well and did not slow him down much as he began climbing the grade.

The descent down the Moose Jaw side of the trail was a bit steeper and had a few more switch-backs than the Chekov side, but it didn't take him long to get the hang of the downhill run. The sun hung just above the western horizon as his skis slid down the bank and ran out on the ice of the Moose Jaw. There was a gentle breeze coming down channel, and the air was a little chillier for it. He drove across the creek and parked on the lee side of a downed spruce's dirt-clotted root wad and killed the engine. The silence was a profound pleasure. And the root wad made for a very effective windbreak. He swung off the big machine's saddle, removed his goggles, and stretched his back muscles, taking in the landscape as he did so.

He had floated this river several times over the past five or six years, so he knew he had passed this spot before, but did not recognize any of the terrain. He took out his pipe, filled and lit it, then walked around the sled, checking the load. He tightened the cinch straps and restrung a couple of bungees just for good measure, then concentrated on his pipe. God he loved being out here. He loved this river. 'This is home,' he thought.

He had entered a "milepost" marker on his hand-held Garmin GPS before departing Chekov. Now, before resuming his trip up to The Varmitage, he took the time to add another so he would be able to find the trail again. He would check to see how many miles he'd covered once he got home tonight.

He knocked the dead ashes out of his pipe and stowed it in his inside zipper pocket. He tucked the Garmin back in its padded sack and slid it into his backpack, then fired up the Polaris again and let it run a little before setting off.

The trip up the Moose Jaw took him less than an hour. He had no idea where he was until he rounded a bend and recognized a high cut bank on the north side of the river where he had collected mud, rich in clay content, for chinking his cabin walls. Just around the next bend, he passed the slough that came in from the south and he knew he was only two bends below The Varmitage. He cut back on the throttle and slowed to a gentle crawl over the final leg. It reminded him of the feeling of relaxation one experiences in a speed boat as one roars toward the shore until the last moment, then cuts the engine and silently rides the following swell up onto the sand. It's the crossing of an unseen threshold – perhaps between water and land, or between cacophonous tumult and blessed silence, maybe between the "then" and the "now". Whatever it was, Gus' soul always registered it as a long held breath released.

Up ahead, his cabin stood dark against the forest, golden light spilled out the windows and lit the snow covered terrain. Wood smoke perfumed the frigid air. He took a deep breath, exhaled, then recited aloud the last two stanzas of a Robert Louis Stevenson poem he loved:

"...Home is the sailor, home from the sea
And the hunter home from the hill..."

Chapter 18

Jong Min-jun lowered his light-gathering binoculars. "Who the hell was that?" he asked Jackie Sam after Gus had sped off up the Moose Jaw on his snow machine. They were fortunate they had decided to scout several miles downstream of the Chekov trail after killing the two bears up at Deadman Creek. Otherwise they would have met Gus face-to-face while ascending the grade. They had killed another bear three miles down that afternoon and were coming back upstream when they decided to stop for a drink and a bite to eat before crossing the hills back to town. That fortuitous stop saved them a very awkward meeting. As they stood there in the dim light of evening, the sound of Gus' big snow machine faded in the distance.

Jackie shrugged his shoulders, "Who gives a fuck?"

The man they called John Young studied the eldest Sam brother with barely concealed contempt. He was beginning to wish he had not let Damon persuade him to bring Jackie aboard. Granted, they knew where to find the bears, and they were a dependable team as long as Jackie let Damon do the thinking. Still, there was an undercurrent of hostility in his attitude. Jong Min-jun suspected Jackie resented working for a Korean city-slicker. He'd never actually heard Jackie voice a racial slur specifically aimed at him, but he'd heard him employ other terms of endearment such as nigger, cheechako, and gook. And he made no attempt to hide his disdain for anyone not raised in the "bush".

For the past two months, Jong had accompanied the Sam brothers on their excursions up Wolf Creek and along the Moose Jaw. He enjoyed this cold wilderness and wondered why everyone considered the "bush" such a dangerous and treacherous place. It seemed to him a good deal safer that the festering alleys of Seoul. Although his old mentor had admonished him to keep his distance from the harvesting end of the business, he was drawn to it. He loved it, in fact. He had already killed six bears himself, and could now remove the gallbladder with little difficulty. He had always been good with a knife, but now he could shoot too.

It occurred to him that killing bears was not nearly as thrilling as killing an armed man. Still, it was better than shacking up with those two stoner bimbos he'd imported from Anchorage. Oh, the Sam boys worshiped at their lily-white feet. They couldn't believe such gorgeous white chicks would willingly agree to the kinkiest sexual acts they could imagine. Hell, the girls had suggested many of the perversions themselves! He shook his head in disgust.

'No,' he thought. 'It was far preferable to roar up and down the frozen rivers hunting bear than shagging a couple of dope-desensitized sluts.'

He turned to Damon. "You ever see that guy before?"

Jong was well aware of Damon's exceptional eye-sight; he was certain the Alaskan saw the stranger's face as clearly as he had through his binoculars.

Damon considered the question for a moment. "No. But I think he must be the guy that built that cabin just below where you killed those two bears today. He must have been over in Chekov when we passed his place on the way upstream. There was no smoke from the chimney so I knew no one was inside, but you remember I showed you the tracks of the ski plane on the ice there. Maybe he flew over to Chekov and came back on that machine."

"You know his name?" Jong did not like the idea of someone living on the river in the middle of his best poaching grounds. He had not confided in the Sam brothers, but he had big plans for the summer along this stretch of the Moose Jaw. He anticipated a windfall harvest of bears during the salmon runs. They would all be right there on the water intent upon the fish – easy pickings from a boat. A potential witness would mean trouble.

"Gus," Damon told him. "Old Uncle told us about him. He is some kind of witch he thinks, and very dangerous. He told us to avoid him and his cabin. He said this man once fought with the giant grizzly some call Broken Foot and they killed each other, but they both still live in this valley. I think we should go back to town now."

Jong Min-jun was intrigued, but he said nothing to reveal his interest. 'A giant bear,' he thought to himself. 'Big bear – big organs – big claws. I think I need to hear more of this fable.'

To Damon he said, "Yes, I agree. I don't think he saw us so there is no need to follow him today. Let's go back to town and see what kind of games the girls want to play tonight, eh?"

He noted with revulsion that Jackie actually licked his lips and tugged at his crotch before mounting their snow machine. Jackie would have to go. Pretty soon, he'd have to go.

***

They stopped at The Cherry Orchard, a dilapidated watering hole presumably named for a classic Russian novel, written by the author Chekhov. The Cherry Orchard catered to most of the local bottom-feeders. Nicky and Danielle were seated at a table in the darkest corner of the room. They were smoking filtered cigarettes and drinking a vodka-Kahlua concoction they called "Black Ruckin' Fussians".

'Typical,' Jong thought to himself when Nicky told them the name they'd come up with all by themselves. Jackie thought it was the funniest thing he'd ever heard. "I'll have one of them things myself," he said enthusiastically as he squeezed in next to Danielle.

Damon offered a gentle smile by way of acknowledging the girls' cleverness. "What'll you have?" he asked his Korean benefactor.

Jong did not enjoy alcohol, but he always had one drink just to keep up appearances. He had not stolen the two bottles of whiskey from the cabin for his own enjoyment. He had given one each to the brothers. The knife, of course, he had kept for himself. Still, he knew his "field agents" were the type to feel uncomfortable around total abstainers so he said, "I'll have one of those Ruckin' Fussians too," just to humor the bimbos. 'The things one had to endure…'

He handed Damon a twenty and Damon made his way to the bar. The man they knew as John Young always paid for the drinks; it was expected. He bought the meals too, and kept his associates supplied with their drugs of choice. 'Why not?' He had to be mindful of expenses, but he could certainly afford to scatter a few table scraps to the hogs now and then. It kept them happy, and happy hogs didn't eat the children. 'Now where did that come from?' he asked himself. Then he remembered and an icy chill slithered across his scalp like a frost-rimed snake.

He'd heard the expression in a roadhouse south of Fairbanks – Skinny Dick's Halfway Inn, just north of Nenana. A tall, lanky fellow with bushy white hair was shooting pool at one of the tables near the back wall. A waiter had stumbled on his way to one of the dining booths and pitched forward with a tray of steaming plates and full beer glasses. The diners took the brunt of it full in their laps. There were angry shouts from the table and hoots of laughter from other patrons in the establishment. The bartender hurried over with towels and the wait staff poured out of the kitchen to help clear the wreckage and calm the sodden customers. When things quieted somewhat, the tall guy at the pool table laughed out loud and said, "I haven't seen so much excitement since the hogs ate my kid sister!"

The man he'd been playing pool with laughed too. He had laughed hard enough that Jong had looked at him. The man was the same man he'd just seen over on the Moose Jaw.

When Damon returned from the bar with the drinks, Jong Min-jun accepted his and downed it in one throw. Damon had never seen him do this before.

"Is something wrong, John?" he asked, genuinely concerned.

Jong shook his head. "No," he said curtly. "Nothing wrong." He thrust a wad of bills into Damon's hand and turned to leave. "You keep the party going. I'll see you back at the house."

With that he went out the door into the night. Damon followed him with his eyes. 'He's getting crazier,' he said to himself. 'Ever since he started killing bears, he's been getting crazier.'

Chapter 19

The sound of the snow machine's engine growing in the distance did not surprise Morgan. She had expected Gus at dinner time. She replaced the lid on a steaming pot of rice and slid it to the edge of the stovetop to keep warm. She had built up the fire earlier so the cabin was now quite cozy. The temperature outside was below zero and she knew Gus would want to thaw out a little before they ate.

The noise of the engine died and was replaced by the void of silence akin to that which often follows a storm or the rifle-crack sound of shifting ice. Morgan poured a measure of Dew into Gus' favorite glass and set it on the table; it would warm his core while the fire worked its wonders on his extremities. The crunch of frozen snow and stomping of heavy boots on the porch boards beyond the plank door, confirmed his arrival. He came in, closed the door behind him and looked across the room at her as he removed his hat, gloves and coat.

'God,' he thought, as always, overcome by her striking beauty. 'There's no lovelier site on earth'.

Morgan's cheeks reddened ever so slightly and he was reminded she could read every thought that crossed his mind. He was glad she could – she knew exactly how he felt about her.

"True," she said, mischief flashing in her green eyes. "I do know how you feel about me, and I approve. Your hands always find just the right places."

He snorted a laugh. She never missed a double entendre – even one he had not intended. He hung his outerwear on the wall pegs and crossed the room to where she stood by the fire. He took her in his arms and she kissed him full on the lips as she swung him around so his backside was a little closer to the glowing stove.

"Ahhhh, that feels good," he said. "It got pretty cold after the sun went down. The thermometer on the porch says it's four below."

Morgan went to the table and came back with his whiskey. "Drink this; you'll thaw in no time at all. How do you feel about dinner at eight?"

He couldn't help himself. "I was hoping to feel about you a bit first."

She laughed her throaty laugh. "You're so easy to manipulate. I cued you for that, hoping you might rise to the suggestion."

He opened his mouth to respond with a lascivious witticism.

She pressed a finger to his lips and shook her head. "Too obvious," she told him. "That one is pretty well worn out by now, don't you think?"

"True," he said, tossing back his drink. "Let's just pop in bed and explore our feelings – please forgive my aborted 'rising' cliché."

She unbuttoned the top button of her flannel shirt. "Aborted has too final a ring to it, don't you think," she teased. "Maybe we could just put your 'rising' on hold for a bit."

Gus sat on the edge of the bed and removed his pants. "How nice of you to offer!" he told her.

Morgan let her clothes drop to the floor and slipped under the blankets. "Enough prattle," she said. "Come to bed."

He did as she said. "Your wish is…"

She placed a hand over his mouth. "Stop talking."

He stopped talking.

***

In the morning after breakfast, Gus went outside, topped off the snow machine's gas tank and staged all his logging gear. That done, he placed a small brazier of hot coals from the stove beneath the Polaris' engine and went back inside to enjoy a last cup of coffee with Morgan.

"It's pretty cold still," she observed. "Wouldn't it be better to wait until the sun cooks the frost out of the air?"

Gus sipped his coffee. "It's already seven above," he told her. "It will be positively balmy by the time I get up to the burn. In any event, I won't work too long today. This is just a shake-down cruise. I need to experiment a little with this new logging method."

"Do you think you can drive all the way back into the good trees?"

He shook his head. "I probably could get up the hill okay, but I'm not sure I want a half-ton log sliding downhill behind me on the way out. I'll just cut one tree on the low slope today and try to drop it straight downhill. If I get lucky its momentum will toboggan it down close to the beaver ponds. Then I'll hook it up to the tow line and skid, and see how it goes from there. The guy that sold me the

104

rig had been logging on pretty level terrain so he didn't have a tow-bar. But, just to be safe, I'll fashion some kind of a stand-off between the rear end of the Polaris and the skid just in case the log tries to overtake me coming down the slope. Once I get out on the river ice it should be a piece of cake."

"Would you like me to pack you a lunch?"

"No. I'll be back for lunch. A jug of coffee wouldn't go to waste though."

She went to the counter and came back with a full thermos. "I thought you might need something hot," she said as she placed it on the table.

He smiled and patted her lovely rump. "Always one step ahead of me."

He finished the coffee in his mug and gave it a quick rinse at the sink. Then he patted down his coat pockets to make sure he had all his customary kit: matches, toilet paper, lip balm, pocket knife, band-aids, mini chocolate bars and sunglasses. Satisfied he was fully fitted out, he took down his rifle from the pegs over the door and operated the lever action half-way until he could see there was a round in the chamber. Then he closed the lever, clicked on the safety and propped it against the wall.

"You should take the pistol, too," Morgan advised. "If you're on that machine and some bear comes after you, you'll need one hand to steer and the other to shoot."

"Already aboard," he told her. "I'll wear it on the outside of my coat while I'm riding."

He pulled her close and kissed her, then took up rifle and thermos and went out the door.

"Be careful," she said.

***

The little brazier O'Kelly's neighbor had thrown into the bargain was nothing more than a small portable barbeque the fellow had insisted was indispensible in the frigid winters of the Interior. When you weren't using it as a block-heater, you could heat up a pot of soup. Since Gus had covered the Polaris' engine with a double layered insulating blanket overnight the cocoon it provided trapped the heat radiating from the brazier and the temperature beneath the blanket soon approximated that of a summer's day. Gus was pleased when he pulled the cord and the engine only coughed once before it roared to life. He let it idle while he took the chainsaw out of its case and ran it for a few minutes too.

When he was satisfied that all his gas powered equipment was ready to go, he loaded the chainsaw in the sled with the peavey pole, skid, tongs and gas cans, then secured the load so nothing would bounce around once he left the river and was traversing the rough terrain below the burn. He stowed the thermos in a corner of the sled where it would remain upright, slid his rifle into a scabbard strapped to the side of the engine shroud, strapped on his .44 Magnum revolver and swung into the saddle.

He took it slow, crossing the flat gravel bar to his boat landing where there was a gentle ramp down to the river ice. He headed upstream at a leisurely pace, stopping briefly to inspect the fresh snow machine tracks he had not registered the night before. As he had been intent upon getting home for dinner, he had paid them little mind at the time. He could see that two heavy tracked vehicles had gone upstream and that the same two had come back down sometime later. He didn't recall them being there when Haywood had come to fetch him yesterday, so he reasoned they must have made the round trip in his absence.

Since it was clear they had come and gone, he knew he wouldn't have to be looking out for them today. Reassured, he opened up the engine to half-throttle and maintained a comfortable speed going up the channel. He was somewhat surprised at how quickly he passed his landing strip. Ten minutes later, he realized he was rounding the final bend before the beaver slides that served the ponds directly downhill of the burn where he logged his trees.

The fire that had left all the dead, standing spruce spars on the hillside above the ponds had raged several years ago. He had no idea how long it had been, but the conflagration had consumed several hundred acres of the Moose Jaw high country, and petered out a few miles upstream of his cabin. As it burned its way down the hill toward the Moose Jaw it had apparently run out of fuel in the muskeg bogs that covered the flatlands bordering the river. Its heat had dwindled in intensity near the terminus and the trees standing along that final fire line had been scorched and denuded of their limbs and subsequently died. Yet, still they stood, a legion of skeletal spires, dark and foreboding against the winter sky. It was an eerie place.

Haywood had discovered the burn while flying into The Varmitage last summer and suggested it might be a good place for Gus to harvest his cabin logs. He had been right. The old spars were perfect for building the cabin. They required no brushing out as they were no longer green – and therefore much lighter than live trees. All Gus had to do was fell them on the slope of the burn, roll them down to the pond, then drag them out the water-filled beaver slides to the Moose Jaw and float them down to his building site.

He had planned on doing the same this year, but Haywood's idea of using a snow machine to fetch them allowed Gus to get a six-week jump on the construction of his bunkhouse.

***

Gus drove the Polaris past the highest beaver pond and up into the burn until he came to the first suitable spar. He offloaded his chainsaw, peavey pole and ax, then drove the snow machine back downslope and parked on the northeast side of the beaver pond. He pocketed his tape measure then walked back uphill to the spar he had earmarked for today. He had chosen it because it wasn't long or thick enough for a foundation log, but it was sound and straight and would serve well for his maiden voyage hauling logs downstream.

He was glad he'd serviced the chainsaw and sharpened its chain before stowing it for the winter. The temperature had warmed up some, but it was still in the teens. One had to remove one's gloves to sharpen a chainsaw's chain, and anything below freezing could make that a painful process.

He fired up the Husqvarna, let it run a little to warm up, then felled the spar. There was no reason to drop it in any particular direction, but Gus enjoyed testing his skill whenever the opportunity presented itself. He had made his initial notch cut so the trunk would fall directly downhill. If he got it right, gravity and momentum would send it straight down the slope toward the beaver pond. He wouldn't have to reposition it before hooking it up to the Polaris. The breeze was blowing precisely in the direction he wished the tree to fall so he made his back cut a little shallower than normal, leaving a solid inch of hinge to keep the trunk lined up as it began its fall. Just a few seconds ticked by after he hit the kill switch on the chainsaw before the breeze strengthened, and he heard the first telltale crack of wood fibers splitting. Then the top of the

107

spar slowly tipped earthward and down she came with a resounding crash.

The noise startled a raven that had been sitting atop another spar just uphill of him. It squawked, lifted off its perch and soared downhill where it took up a new station on a rotting stump.

Gus always appreciated an audience so he acknowledged the raven with, "Not bad, eh? Right where I wanted it."

The raven said nothing to this, but cocked its head and studied Gus and his felled tree. The sun played upon its feathers and purple undertones shimmered in its glossy black cape.

Gus smiled and went back to work. He set the chainsaw on the ground alongside his peavey, picked up a hand ax, then took out his tape measure. The raven looked on with renewed interest as Gus secured the metal barb of his tape where a split in the wood of the butt offered purchase, then he walked its length paying out the measure as he went.

He stopped and said aloud, "Eighteen feet should do it." Whereupon he blazed a mark on the trunk with his ax and rewound the tape into its case.

After cutting the log to length he brought his big snow machine up the slope, unhitched the sled then positioned the tail of the Polaris close to the downhill end of the log. It was a relatively straightforward process, rigging the skid and pulling apparatus, and when he had finished he drank a cup of coffee from the thermos while enjoying a pipe. As he did so, the raven left the stump and glided to the far end of the log. Gus watched in amused silence as the bird strutted its length, stopping now and again to inspect a crack or worm hole in the old dry wood. Apparently satisfied that all was in order, the raven returned to its stump and Gus fetched his chainsaw from the slope and deposited it and his peavey pole in the sled. Knowing he would be leaving the sled behind he had brought along a tarp against the weather. After returning his rifle to its scabbard on the side of the Polaris, he covered the load and secured the tarp with bungee cords, then pitched on a few lengths of limbwood to hold it down in the wind.

"Right then," he said aloud. "Mr. Raven, I doubt there is anything in that sled light enough for you to steal, but you're welcome to try. Knock yourself out."

With that he mounted the snow machine, cranked up the engine, and set off for the river, the log, sliding along nicely behind. The small sapling he had affixed to the tow line served to fend off the log and keep it a safe distance behind him.

The raven watched him until he had rounded the pond and disappeared into one of the beaver slides. It cocked its head as if amused by the sound of the engine fading in the distance, then swooped over to the sled for a more detailed inspection of the marvels contained therein.

***

Gus kept to the center of the creek on his way back downstream to The Varmitage. The ice was thick and smooth over the deep water of the main channel and the log offered very little resistance on the gentle downhill pull. That was the nice thing about water, Gus mused – it never went uphill.

When he arrived at his boat launch, he swung to the other side of the creek and brought the log around in a long, sweeping arc and opened the throttle a little to gather sufficient speed for the slight grade up to the cabin. He had already marked out a place for his stockpile just uphill of where he intended to construct the bunkhouse. You pick up a lot of little tricks when you build your first cabin. Gus had had to move all the cabin logs from the low ground near the creek up to the cabin site last summer. But, with the snow machine and a good base of hard packed snow, he was able to stage his building material uphill this year. Thank you once again, Haywood. He'd have to do something nice for Haywood when he visited again. Maybe an aromatic cigar – of course a burning outhouse was more fragrant than his usual brand. Anything less odorous would be an improvement.

Morgan came out on the porch as he was unhitching the skid-and-drag gear from the log.

"That was quick," she said.

He smiled up at her and nodded, "Sure was," he laughed. "It helps to have the proper equipment. I think I'll bring down another one before lunch."

"If that machine can handle the extra weight, maybe I'll tag along with you. Want some company?"

"Sure. Get your coat and climb aboard. I can think of nothing better than a hot-blooded redhead to keep my back warm."

Morgan ducked into the cabin and came back out wearing her beaver parka with the wolverine trimmed hood. He'd surprised her with it his first night back at The Varmitage after...well, after. The dark fur made the perfect frame for the lustrous ivory skin of her face. He took a moment to admire her as she descended the steps from the porch.

'Magnificent,' he thought. 'The very picture of a Celtic goddess.'

"Not quite a goddess," she murmured into his ear as she mounted the saddle behind him. "Just a handsome woman in a fur coat. But, thank you for the thought."

***

They had just rounded the bend above the landing strip when Morgan tugged on his coat sleeve. He looked over his shoulder and she gestured for him to stop.

He throttled down to reduce the engine noise and said, "What is it?"

"Those tracks," she pointed to the compacted snow Gus had studied earlier in the day. "When you mentioned them, I wasn't sure. But I'm sure now. They were made by the same machines that I found in front of the cabin after they took the whiskey and your knife. We should follow them to see where they went."

Gus was in no hurry to harvest another log. "I agree," he told her, and headed upstream.

At the confluence of the Deadman and the Moose Jaw, the tracks turned up the tributary. Gus reduced his speed and swung onto them. No more than a hundred yards in, the machines had stopped. There had been no new snow since yesterday, so it was easy to follow the man tracks up the bank toward the site of the old Rainbow Lodge. Gus knew the terrain well. Just inside the tree line, they discovered the carcasses of two dead bears.

"Damn them," Gus spat the words. "Let's not walk too close until I've had time to study the ground."

Morgan said. "That won't be necessary. I can tell you what took place here – I see it clearly."

Gus studied her for a moment. "Very well. But, before you do, let me tell you what I see, then you can confirm or correct."

Morgan smiled. "Yes. That would be a better approach."

Gus scanned the disturbed snow near the carcasses. "Three men afoot came up from the river and went directly to the dead bears. They must have shot them from their snow machines, then came for the gallbladders."

"Go on," she prompted.

"Trilogy arrived sometime later, inspected each carcass, then headed downstream through the woods."

"You are quite good," she said with a small smile. "But you missed something. Old Blue Eye was here also."

Gus scrutinized the area again. He could see a light depression in the snow near one of the bears. It reminded him of the old man's tracks he had found up in the headwaters last autumn while searching for Haywood. But he could detect no indication of where he had come in or gone out. "The only tracks into the bears were made by the three poachers. If he was here, he didn't walk in."

He looked at her. She fixed her green eyes upon his, but said nothing. They remained silent for what seemed a long time. Gus heard her loud and clear, although she never spoke aloud. At length, he said, "You're serious, aren't you?"

She nodded. "Why does this surprise you? I don't always leave tracks either."

'True,' he thought. He recalled searching the cabin and surrounding area last summer when she first introduced him to her vanishing act.

"I concede the point," he said. "But where does this leave us?"

"We now know who is killing the bears – not their names, perhaps. But Trident and the old man know them too. The bear requires no names. He'll recognize them when he finds them. This barbarity will soon come to an end."

Before returning to their snow machine, Gus had a close look at each carcass to confirm both had been killed for their gallbladders. On the way back down the bank, he asked, "How long had the poachers been gone before our bear arrived?"

"Less than an hour," she told him with absolute certainty. "They would do well to keep an eye on their back-trail."

"Indeed. They cut it pretty close this time."

***

Gus put the logging experiment off for another day. Instead, they decided to go back to the cabin for a quick lunch, then follow the poachers' tracks downstream at least as far as the Wolf Creek trail. When they arrived there, it was apparent that their three 'suspects' had gone further down the Moose Jaw before doubling back. It suggested they were hoping for another bear.

"Want to keep going?" Gus asked Morgan.

"Of course," she enthused. She was clearly enjoying the hunt. "Is there enough day left to find our way back to the cabin?"

"Probably," Gus said. "If not, I'll turn on the headlight."

"Off we go, then." She made a 'giddy-up' sound.

Gus laughed, and opened the throttle. It didn't take them long to find the third dead bear. It was just a few miles below Wolf Creek, on the left bank of the Moose Jaw. It too, had been shot from the ice midstream, and had suffered the same posthumous desecration as the first two. Gus registered the spot as another milepost on his Garmin. After making certain the poachers had ventured no further downstream they climbed back aboard the big Polaris and headed home. There was still an hour of daylight left when they arrived back at The Varmitage.

Morgan laid a fire in the stove and poured them each two fingers of Dew while Gus rung up Hard Case on the satellite phone.

"We've three more dead bears out here," Gus told him. "Two up near the old Rainbow Lodge, another maybe three miles below the Wolf Creek trail turn-off." Gus gave him the GPS coordinates.

"Give me a minute." Gus could hear Hard Case shuffling papers on the other end of the line; he steadfastly refused to peck at a 'goddamned keyboard'.

He came back on the line. "Details?"

"The two up at the lodge were both young adult male black bears, each shot once with a heavy caliber round; incisions in the lower abdomens made by a very sharp knife. Whoever did the surgery knew precisely where to cut. The carcasses are atop the high bank a hundred yards up the Deadman on the downstream side of its confluence with the Moose Jaw. It looks like they shot them from the river ice, left their snow machines there and climbed the bank to harvest the gallbladders."

"Any approximation of time?" Hard Case asked.

"Yesterday, between the time Haywood collected me for the run over to Chekov and my arrival back at The Varmitage...hang on a second," Gus told him.

Morgan had interrupted to tell Gus, "Midday – just before one o'clock."

Gus returned the phone to his ear. "Midday," he told Hard Case. "A little before one."

Hard Case grunted. "Been fine tuning your forensics, I see."

"Ah, yeah." Gus looked over at Morgan and gave her a smile. "Collaborative effort."

"You mean Morgan told you," Hard Case guessed.

" Oh,Ye of little faith," Gus objected.

"Goes with the job." Hard Case sounded weary. "How about the one down by Wolf Creek?"

Gus briefed him on the details regarding bear number three.

"Okay, Gus," Hard Case said, "I'll add these to the file. Any idea who might be doing this?"

"Thought you'd never ask," Gus replied, obviously pleased with himself. "You're looking for three males – late twenties to early thirties. Two of them are native Alaskans, one oriental of undetermined nationality. They hunt off snow machines, one single, two riding double. Almost certainly operating out of Chekov."

"Would this oriental of undetermined nationality be the 'prick' who stole your knife?"

Gus grinned into the mouthpiece. "The very same. If I catch him first, I'll shove it up his ass."

Hard Case chuckled. "Mistreatment of suspects is not to be tolerated," he said in a mechanical drone. "Just bring me his gallbladder and justice will be served."

"They seem to be working my stretch of river on a regular basis. I'll keep an eye out for them. Let me know if you come up with names."

"Will do, Gus. I'll flag O'Kelly over in Chekov. He might have some idea as to who might fit their profile. In the meantime, I'll have Caldwell do a few random flyovers in the next couple days."

"Perfect," Gus told his old friend. "I'll wait to hear from you."

Chapter 20

As Jong Min-jun was dressing for the bush, he discovered his belt-knife was not in its sheath. He checked the floor under the bed and the shelf in the closet where he kept his hunting gear. When he could not find it, he thought back to the last bear he had killed and wondered if he had left it there. He had used the knife to remove the bear's gallbladder. He shrugged his shoulders. It was just one more reason to go over to the Moose Jaw today. He had intended to go anyway, as he was eager to begin hunting the three-toed bear, and he wanted a better look at the man who, according to legend, had killed that bear in a face-to-face fight. But his primary reason for going deep into the bush was to rid himself of Jackie Sam. If he could arrange for Damon to stay in Chekov today, he would have Jackie alone out there. He had lain awake a good part of the night working through the details of his plan. When all the pieces had coalesced in his head, he rolled over and slept.

Jong knew Damon would be reluctant to accompany them out to the Moose Jaw to confront the man he had seen at Skinny Dick's. He was also aware of Damon's abject fear of the three-toed bear. Damon put more stock in the "old ways" of his native people than did his older brother. His superstitions made him a perfect target for manipulation. Ironically, his older brother's callous disregard of his peoples' traditions and superstitions made him just as easy to manipulate. The only reason Jackie still hunted was to line his wallet with cash. He cared nothing for the Athabascan traditions of respect for all living things. He relished his current situation where alcohol, mind altering drugs and Anglo pussy were there for the taking anytime he wanted. And that was often – too often. Jackie had become expensive and therefore expendable. Although Jong had abundant resources, Jackie's insatiable appetite for sexual and chemical stimulation had become burdensome. The time had come to cut his losses with regard to Jackie Sam. He smiled to himself as he set his plan in motion.

The devious Korean dispatched Jackie to the gas station to get some take-out coffee and donuts for breakfast. The girls were still upstairs sleeping off the exhaustion of last night's debauch so John took this opportunity to approach Damon.

"Have you seen my knife anywhere?" – an innocent opening that would bring him to the main topic indirectly. He really had lost his knife, hadn't he?

"Which one?" Damon asked.

"My belt knife," he said, turning slightly so Damon could see the empty sheath. "The one I use on the bears. I may have left it out on the Moose Jaw where we killed that third bear a few days ago. Maybe we should take a run over there today and look for it. I was thinking of going anyway. I'd like to see if we can find the tracks of that big grizzly you told me about. What do say?"

Damon had said too much last night and he knew it. He regretted telling everyone the legend of the ghost bear. Now John would never be satisfied with any lesser beast. He wanted to find the mysterious bruin and kill him. And, he was bent on killing Gus also. 'Getting crazier every day,' Damon thought.

He shook his head slowly. "That's not a good idea, I think."

"No?" Jong inquired. "Why not? If he is as big as you said last night, his claws alone will bring a very high price."

"They say those who hunt this bear always find themselves hunted instead. We should leave him alone."

"You're not afraid of him are you?" John asked in feigned astonishment.

"Yes," Damon told him honestly. "You should be afraid of him too. It is said he cannot be truly killed. He has been killed before, but after a little while, his tracks are found in the valley again."

John Young smiled. This was exactly where he had been leading Damon with this conversation. "Perhaps Jackie will not be afraid. You stay here with the girls today. Jackie and I will hunt the bear."

Damon mistakenly thought John was trying to shame him into going with them. He did not care. He had heard about that bear all his life. It was not a normal bear; it was a ghost. He did not want to disappoint John, but nothing trumped his fear of this bear. He would not go. Maybe it was time for him to get away from these people. Yes, that is what he would do. While John and Jackie were hunting today he would pack up his things and leave. His mother had died young and he hadn't seen his father in over a year, but he still had many cousins around Circle and Central. He knew his Uncle Daniel would put him up if he asked, but that would be the first place Jackie looked. He needed to get out of Chekov.

Jackie came through the door carrying two takeout bags. He set them on the counter in the kitchen. "Food," he said simply. He opened the bags and helped himself to a cup of coffee and a donut, and took them over to the cluttered table.

Jong followed suit and joined Jackie at the table. "I want to go look for that big bear with the missing toes today," he said, adding milk and sugar to his coffee. "Your brother won't go. Says he's afraid of this bear. You're not afraid, are you?"

Jackie looked like he was about to spit in John's face. "Afraid? No. I am not afraid of any bear. And he should not be too hard to find; I have seen his tracks around the new cabin all winter. I think he still wants to fight that man they say killed him once."

"You believe that story?" Jong asked him earnestly.

Jackie shrugged his shoulders. "My people have many such stories. They tell them to scare the children and make them behave. But, I don't like messing around that guy's cabin. Old Uncle says he kills men better than he kills bears."

Jong smiled. "Then he and I should get along well; we have something in common."

Chapter 21

Gus checked the snare sets every morning after he paid his visit to the little house behind the cabin. On this particular morning Bosworth accompanied him. The big cat made a habit of checking the sets twice a day himself and had hit the jackpot occasionally. He had developed a taste for snowshoe hare and was delighted that Gus had become so proficient at snaring them. But, today they found both sets undisturbed so they returned to the cabin.

"Any luck?" Morgan asked as they came through the door.

"Not today," Gus told her. Bosworth hopped up on the bed and settled in for a nap.

She said, "There's still a half pot of coffee left. Would you like a cup?"

He hung his coat on the wall peg and left his boots near the door. "I would," he told her. "It's a bit chilly out there today. The ice will certainly stay solid if the nights continue to be this cold." He had checked the thermometer before he came inside. It registered four below zero.

Morgan poured two cups of steaming coffee and took them over to the table. "This will warm you up," she said. "I can make another pot to fill the thermos. You'll certainly need it up at the burn today."

"That can wait," he told her. "Have a seat. Let me run an idea by you."

Morgan sat down and sipped her coffee. "I'm listening," she said.

"I want to give Haywood a little surprise. I'd like to make a run up to Hermit's Camp while the ice on the river is still thick and solid. I think that big Polaris is powerful enough to pull his plane out of the trees into the old river channel. If so, he won't have to wait 'til spring to get it out of there."

"Can you do it without help?" she wondered aloud.

"I believe so," he said. "Some of the logs I've pulled down the river probably weigh as much as his airplane and they don't have wheels. I've been giving it a lot of thought. If I can jack up the tail section far enough to get my log-skid under the rear wheel I should be able to drag it backward out to mid-channel."

"How long would it take you?" she asked.

"Well, if all goes well, I could probably rig the skid and the tow line in an hour or so. I'd have to cut a few limbs off the tree it's stuck in – let's say another hour. Then it shouldn't take any time at all to pull it out. I don't have to move it more than fifty feet, give-or-take. Want to go with me?"

"It's a long way up there," she said. "Would we camp overnight?"

"That's the plan," he told her. "It's about an eighty mile run up to the old hermit's place. Twenty miles per hour would be a safe speed. Barring any obstructions across the river, we could be there in four hours. If we left here by eight in the morning we could be there by noon. You could pitch camp while I dealt with the plane. What do you say?"

She sipped her coffee and thought about it for a few moments. "I think it's a wonderful idea," she said. "We owe Haywood more than we could ever repay, but this would be a fine way to thank him. I think we should do it."

He gave her a big smile. "Tomorrow?" he suggested.

She nodded. "I don't see any reason to put it off," she said. "While you're making your logging runs today, I'll scout the river for trouble. If all's clear we can go up in the morning."

Gus no longer questioned her about her ability to move from place to place along the Moose Jaw. Having prior knowledge of conditions on the river would be very useful if they were to have a safe journey up the ice.

"That's an excellent idea," he told her. "We'll discuss logistics over dinner tonight."

***

The light had faded to the point where Gus needed his headlamp to bring down the last log that day. The temperature was a just bearable six below. While working the logs up at the burn he had not noticed the cold; the vigorous activity had kept him quite warm. However, riding a snow machine moving at a slow clip did not qualify as "active". As soon as he pulled up in front of the cabin, he cut the engine and went directly inside to warm up. Morgan had a pot of tea waiting for him.

"Wow!" he said coming through the door and going immediately to the green enamel stove. "With the wind chill it feels like twenty below out there."

118

"Here, drink this," she said, placing a steaming mug off to the side of the stove top. "Let me take your hat and gloves. The hot cup will warm your fingers in no time."

He did as she had directed and wrapped both hands around the mug. Needles of painful pleasure prickled the skin of his palms as the welcome warmth insinuated itself into his flesh. He sipped the tea and winced as the hot liquid made contact with his purple lips.

"Ahhh," he said. "Just what the doctor ordered."

He returned the mug to the stovetop while he slipped out of his heavy coat and hung it on its wall peg. "I left the log hitched to the tow gear," he told her as he went back to the stove and retrieved his tea.

"Why don't you leave it for after dinner," she suggested. "You look like a little nourishment might do you good."

He turned to look at the pot bubbling on the stovetop. "What are we having?" he asked.

"Nothing special," she smiled. "Just chunks of moose simmered all day in a stew of potatoes, onions and carrots." She knew it was one of his favorites.

"Say no more," he said. "My mouth is watering just thinking of it."

Over dinner he inquired about her scouting mission. "How's the river look between here and Hermit's Camp?"

"There are a couple of tight spots going through the narrows," she told him. "And the ice has heaved and buckled in a few places. But, I think we'll be alright if you take it slow along those stretches."

"Excellent," he said. "If we don't have to stop, four hours should be plenty."

Morgan frowned. "We will have to make at least one stop," she told him. "There's another dead bear on the bank halfway between here and the narrows. We'll have to check and see if it died like the others."

"We'll do that," he said. "If it's the work of the poachers I'll have to report it. Anything else?"

She shook her head. "No, that's all," she said. "Some rough spots, a couple of tight squeezes and a dead bear. The ice is solid and the path is clear otherwise."

"Good to hear," he commented. "Too bad you couldn't pay your respects to Old Blue Eye while you were up there. You could have seen if he was willing to meet with Hard Case."

"I made contact with him," she said.

"Did you indeed?" he looked hopeful. "What did he say?"

Morgan shrugged her shoulders, "I didn't actually meet with him. I just reached out to him. I believe he's thinking about it. He'll let me know when he has decided. You'll just have to be patient."

Gus nodded and ladled another helping of stew into his bowl. "Well, anyway, thanks for trying. And thanks for being so thorough in checking out the river. I can't believe you had time to make your recon run, connect with Old Blue Eye, and cook a pot of stew as well."

She smiled and patted the back of his hand. "I should think a brilliant engineer like yourself would have a better understanding of time."

He put down his spoon and patted the corners of his mouth with his napkin. He'd always been intrigued by Morgan's relationship with time. She seemed to have the ability to move about in it like dust motes through the air.

"Enlighten me," he said, genuinely interested in hearing what she might say.

"Very well," she said. "Since you use that term, let me ask you something. How fast does light travel? I truly do not know."

He shrugged, "One hundred and eighty-six thousand miles per second," he told her. "At least that's our best estimate."

"So how long would it take a beam of light to travel eighty miles?" she asked.

He did not bother to do the math; he got the point. "I see," he said, not sure if he really did. "So a spirit, your spirit for instance, is closer in nature to light than it is to something of substance? It's unencumbered by the constraints of movement imposed upon mass?"

She laughed, "I think I might be getting in over my head here. But yes, I suppose you could say that."

"So," Gus went on, "it's your essence that covers the distance between here and there. You're not physically transported."

"No," Morgan told him. "Not physically, but still, I can observe. The essence to which you refer is conscious, it has cognitive ability. Otherwise, there would be no point in my going."

"I'll need to think about that," Gus said. "It's pretty complicated."

"Eat your stew before it gets cold," she said with a smile. "You've a log to tend to before we go to bed. Having spent the day as an 'essence', I'm looking forward to something a bit more physical."

***

The dead bear was a large grizzly. It was clear that it had been shot twice in the head but they could not determine if its abdomen had been cut; the carcass was quite large and frozen solid. There was no way Gus could inspect the belly. Still, they concluded that it had almost certainly been killed by the poachers so Gus entered the coordinates on his Garmin. He'd include them in his report.

The other information Morgan had gathered on her reconnaissance run had been accurate as well. Except for the narrows and some glaciated ice ridges here and there, they had clear sailing all the way up to Hermit's Camp. Gus unloaded the camping equipment at the foot of the slope upon which the old Welshman, Owen Price, had lived. The crumbling remnant of a stone chimney was all that remained of his cabin, but it was a landmark Gus and Haywood knew well. They had camped there a few times while floating the river over the past few years.

"Let's get all this stuff up the hill," Gus told her. "I'll help you put the blue tarp up for the camp kitchen then I'll go have a look at Haywood's wreck. Think you can manage the tent alone?"

She smiled. "I think so. The airplane isn't too far up the channel. I'll come get you if I need another pair of hands."

"Okay," he said. "Let's get the tarp up, then I'll leave you to your own devices while I rig the tow gear. I'll come back here to get you before I try to pull it out, though. I'll need you to watch and make sure I don't damage anything worse than it already is. Haywood would kill me."

They strung a high line from tree to tree near the old chimney and stretched a tarp overhead. When they had the prop poles in place and the corners tied down with bungee cords, Gus kissed her good-bye and made his way back down the slope to the Polaris.

He drove the big tracker up the snow-covered dry channel through the bare willow shrubs. They were tall and would have impeded progress were they fully leafed out. As it was, he just plowed through, flattening those in his path. When he spotted the tail section of Haywood's little Clipper poking out of the spruce trees that lined the channel he made a wide turn and parked behind it. He killed the engine and walked over to see what he had gotten himself into. While he was making his inspection a raven swooped down from the top of a tall tree and settled on his sled. He smiled and shook his head.

"I hope you're as expert in this sort of thing as your cousin that helps me with my logging," he said to the bird. The raven did not reply, but cocked his head and studied this curious human with what appeared to be amusement.

"Right, then," Gus said and proceeded with his inspection.

As he had remembered, the trunk of one spruce was very close to the right side of the aircraft. Its limbs would need to be removed before he did any towing. There was also the broken spar of a sizable limb protruding through the gap that once housed the windscreen. The left side of the fuselage was free of obstructions but the metal cowling over the engine and the propeller were tangled in a maze of bent and twisted boughs of another big spruce. He decided to cut them away and free up the plane before attempting to jack up the tail section. It might be dangerous to lift any part of the plane while the rest of it was under tension. No telling which way it might shift.

The raven issued a squawk and lifted off the sled as he approached. It perched on the tail of the airplane and continued its vigil.

"So," Gus said as he unloaded his chainsaw and small pruning saw. "You can talk. Good. Let me know if the tail starts moving while I'm cutting. I don't want to get pinned up against a tree."

He went back up the right side of the Clipper and began removing the branches that looked to be troublesome. He decided to leave the big spar in place through the window frame to provide some stability while he worked at cutting away all the smaller branches from the nose.

As he sawed through the last twisted bough, the nose of the plane did shift a little sideways and the propeller gave off a metallic twang as it came free of the limb. The raven cawed sharply and flew back to the sled.

"Thanks for that," Gus told him. "A little late on the uptake, but I appreciate the effort, nonetheless."

He had one more look at the last spar just to make sure it wasn't supporting any significant weight or applying tension to either side. Satisfied it was safe, he cleared a few more limbs to give himself room to work close to the trunk. Then he positioned himself to the side of the tree a little uphill from the bulk of the plane, and cut the spar free of the trunk. Haywood's little Clipper did not appear to move but as he pulled the broken limb out of the cockpit through the window frame he could have sworn he heard a sigh of relief. Maybe it was his own – but he didn't think so.

He returned to the sled and got out the old truck hood that served as his log skid. After positioning it at his feet behind the rear wheel of the plane's landing gear, he placed one hand on the underside of each rear wing and bent his knees in preparation to lift.

"Caw! Caw! Caw!" called out the raven as it swooped close over his head. He abandoned his lifting exercise and looked at the bird, now perched on the roof of the plane's cabin.

"Well," Gus said, taking a step back to reassess what he had been about to do, "that was emphatic enough. What are you trying to tell me Mr. Raven? Am I doing something stupid?"

A vision flashed through his brain. An image of himself lifting the tail of the plane appeared in his mind's eye. The aircraft's front wheels began to roll down the slope.

"Ah!" he said. "Yes, I see. I didn't take into consideration the force of gravity. Very careless of me. I thank you Raven."

He carried his chainsaw up the channel along the line of spruce trees that grew along its old bank. When he found a suitably thick stump, he cut two large wedges from it and returned to the wrecked plane where he secured one behind each of the front wheels.

"That should do it," he said to the bird. "Is that better?"

The raven answered with an impressive medley of clicks, clunks and rattles.

"I'll take that as a yes," he said and returned to his labors.

The airplane still shifted downhill a bit as the rear wheel broke free of the frozen ground, but not much. The movement actually facilitated Gus' efforts to slide the log skid into place. That done, he ran his tow line through the hole in the skid and tied it off to the rear wheel's struts. As he did so he realized he'd still need the come-along when it came time to drag the plane out into the channel. He'd have to rig it to the forward landing gear and take the pressure off the wheel chocks so he could remove them. 'There's always something,' he thought.

He drove the Polaris back out the channel and parked downhill of camp where he unhitched the sled. Smoke drifted lazily out of the old chimney at the top of the slope. It smelled good in the cold air – it smelled warm.

Morgan had set up the tent in the same spot he and Haywood had always used. There was a pot of coffee steaming on the Coleman stove under the camp kitchen's blue tarp, and she was adding limb wood to the fire.

"All the comforts of home!" he said, truly impressed.

She came out from under the tarp and put her arms around him. "How'd you fare?" she asked.

"Piece of cake," he told her. Then he thought of his oversight with regard to gravity. "Well, maybe not as easy as all that, but it went well. Let's enjoy a cup of coffee, then go pull her out of the trees."

"Her?" she inquired.

"Sure," he told her. "All planes are 'her' – ships too. All things we men hold dear to our hearts rate the feminine gender."

"I can accept that," she told him, more-or-less mollified.

***

It took only a few minutes to rig the come-along to the trunk of the tree and attach its cable to the struts of the forward landing gear.

"Okay," he called out to Morgan who was watching the wheel chock under the left tire. "Let me know when it's clear." He ratcheted the lever arm a few cranks, waited, then gave it two more."

"Good!" she called out. "It's free."

He went down the slope, removed both chocks and tossed them off to the side. "Perfect," he told her. "I'll use the come-along to ease her down the slope a few feet until she comes to a stop on the level surface of the channel. You keep an eye on the skid and give a shout if the wheel appears to be sliding off."

124

She nodded that she understood and he went back up the slope and positioned himself near the big spruce. He took a firm grip on the handle and clicked the lever's spring-tensioned pall to the "let out" setting.

"Stay clear," he called out. "I'm ready when you are."

Morgan told him she was ready, so he let out some cable. "How we doing?" he asked.

"The skid moved with the wheel," she told him. "Let out some more slack."

As the forward wheels had only ascended the slope of the old channel's bank a few feet, it took less than five minutes to ease it back down to level ground. Gus chocked the tires just to be safe, then detached the come-along and affixed the tow line to the rear end of the Polaris.

"Climb aboard," he said. "The extra weight will give us a little more traction."

She smiled. "A pity Hard Case didn't come along with us," she said.

Gus laughed. "I doubt we'll need that much ballast."

Morgan mounted the saddle behind him and wrapped her arms around him as he fired up the big Polaris. "This is fun," she shouted over the engine noise.

He nodded and drove off slowly toward mid-channel, taking up the slack in the tow line before opening the throttle a bit more until the airplane began following across the packed snow.

"It's working!" Morgan cried happily.

Gus looked over his shoulder and could see that the Clipper was tracking along behind them like a big bird skating backward on a frozen pond. He laughed out loud.

"Perfect!" he crowed. "I love it!"

When he had it positioned near the middle of the old river bed, he cut the engine and removed all the towing gear. Then they took a three-sixty walk around the ripped and ragged little craft to get a better look at the damage.

"The prop's bent pretty badly," Gus observed, "And I doubt he'll be able to repair the right wingtip. It'll probably have to be replaced; the engine cowling too. Other than that, all she needs is a new skin of fabric and lot of general maintenance."

Gus opened a door and peeked inside. "He's lucky he came out of this with his own skin," he told Morgan as he inspected the interior.

"How will he get it back to Fairbanks?" she asked.

"He said they come in with a big helicopter and 'sling' it back," Gus told her. "They land next to it, rig up a bunch of steel cables and pick it off the ground like a crane. When they get it up to altitude, they just fly back to Fairbanks and set it down at a maintenance hangar. That's why we had to drag it out here in the open."

"Sounds difficult," she said. Then, seeing that Gus had found something under the seat she asked. "What do you have there?"

He slid a one-quart zip-lock baggie out from under the pilot's seat. He held it up in the dim Arctic light. "Hah!" he laughed. "Haywood's idea of a survival kit! A pencil flashlight, matches, toilet paper and two cigars."

***

Gus volunteered to cook dinner that evening while Morgan foraged for firewood. He was at the two-burner Coleman thawing a can of Dinty Moore beef stew over a low flame when she returned to camp with an armload of dead spruce limbs.

"Any chance of your making contact with Old Blue Eye while we're in the neighborhood?" he asked, turning the can over to warm the other end.

Morgan deposited her load near the old chimney and brushed bits of bark off the sleeves of her coat. "I'm sure he's around," she ventured. "Where else would he go? This is where he belongs."

"True," Gus said, giving the can another turn. "I'd sure like to find out what he's decided."

"How long before dinner is ready?" she asked.

He tapped the side of the can he was warming. "A while yet," he said. "It's still frozen pretty solid. Half-hour maybe."

"If you'll give me those two cigars you found in the plane, I'll put them to good use. Our old friend has a taste for tobacco. While you labor over your semi-hot stove, I'll pay him a visit. If he's at his cabin, I'll ask him about the meeting personally; if not, I'll just leave the cigars. He'll get my message."

Gus looked over his shoulder, considered her suggestion for a moment, then nodded. "Worth a try I guess," he said. "I put

126

Haywood's 'survival kit' in my backpack. Go ahead and take the cigars. I'll keep dinner warm until you get back."

Morgan pocketed the cigars, gave Gus a kiss and started down the path to the old dry channel. "I won't be long," she told him.

"Take the Polaris if you like," he called after her.

Her voice came back through the trees. "Too slow!"

He smiled and returned his attention to the frozen can of stew.

***

A light snow was falling when they emerged from the tent the next morning. They made two cups of instant coffee on Gus' little single burner backpacker's stove and had it with jerky and granola bars for breakfast. Then they broke camp, loaded everything into the sled and headed downstream. The wind was behind them and the snow was not falling heavy enough to obscure visibility so they made good time. They arrived back at The Varmitage around midday.

Morgan went inside the cabin and got a fire going in the stove while Gus covered the snow machine and sled with tarps. When he went inside Bosworth looked up from his nest on the bed and yawned.

The fire began crackling as the kindling caught so Morgan added a couple more chunks of wood to it and closed the stove door. "He didn't even hop down to greet me when I came in," she said. "I gather our absence did not meet with his approval."

Gus looked over at the big cat, who now had his eyes closed and appeared disinterested in their presence. "He'll get over it," he said. "Soon as lunch is on the table, he'll come around."

"I'll heat up the leftover moose stew we had the other night," Morgan said. "That should appease him."

"Sounds good," Gus told her. "We didn't have our usual hot breakfast this morning. I'm going to bring a few logs down from the burn this afternoon. A couple bowls of stew will see me through 'til dinner."

"You'd better call Hard Case to tell him about the dead bear," she reminded him. "Maybe he's learned the names of the poachers."

"I'll do that right now," he said and took the satellite phone out of its case. "Too bad you weren't able to hook up with Old Blue Eye. Hard Case will be disappointed."

127

Morgan shrugged her shoulders. "He'll find the cigars and get my message," she told him.

"You think he can read?" Gus asked.

She laughed softly. "I didn't leave him a note, Gus. The cigars are my message. He'll know who left them and realize I came to his cabin in the flesh. He will understand this meeting is important to me."

"So, maybe we'll get his answer sometime soon," he said. "At least I can tell Hard Case that much."

He switched on the phone and made his call.

Chapter 22

Hard Case had thanked him for the information regarding the dead bear, but was unable to tell him the names of the poachers. Nevertheless, Gus discovered their identities later in the day from an unexpected caller. When he returned from the burn that afternoon, a sleek Arctic Cat was parked in front of his cabin. He killed the engine as soon as he rounded the bend below his landing strip, abandoned the Polaris in midstream, and trotted up the slope in a line that would not expose him to fire from any window. He stopped only long enough to make sure each cylinder of his revolver held a live round, then covered the remaining distance at a more cautious pace. As he skirted the Cat, he noted just one set of tracks leading to the porch.

He mounted the steps, crossed the porch and paused before the door for a few heartbeats just to listen. When he sensed no movement from within, he cocked his pistol. Well oiled though it was, the three-stage mechanical sound of it was always louder than he expected it to be.

"No need for that," a rich baritone voice resonated from the other side of the door. "I'm friendly. I'll come outside if you prefer."

Gus walked over to the front window and looked inside. A stout man with a tight cap of curling black hair sat comfortably at the table, hands folded contentedly across his thick middle while he contemplated the chess set Morgan favored as a centerpiece. Morgan herself, of course, was nowhere in evidence. After a quick appraisal, Gus' instincts detected no menace in his visitor. Nevertheless, he still gripped the pistol as he entered, although pointed at the floor rather than his uninvited guest.

"Ah, there you are," the man said, standing. "Viktor Malachenko, at your service." He briefly inclined his head in lieu of a formal bow.

'Russian,' Gus thought. Still, he relaxed a bit, and returned the nod.

"Fergus O'Neill", he introduced himself. "My friends call me Gus." He went to the bed and placed the revolver on the pillow. "Welcome to The Varmitage. I hope you didn't have to wait long."

Viktor Malachenko waved a hand in a dismissive gesture. "Thirty minutes perhaps – no more."

Gus said, "Please, sit down. I'll pour us a drink if you like, and you can tell me what errand brings you out to the Moose Jaw."

Mr. Malachenko reclaimed his seat. "You are too kind," he said. "A drink would be much appreciated. Vodka if you stock it, if not, I'm sure I'll enjoy whatever you serve."

Gus smiled at his guest's turn of phrase. "I'm afraid you'll have to make do with Irish whiskey. That's all I have."

"Excellent!" Viktor gave the impression Irish whiskey topped the list of his preferred spirits – just beneath vodka, of course.

Gus placed the bottle and two glasses on the rough planks of the table. Viktor steadied his with a well manicured hand as Gus did the honors. "Water?" he offered.

"A drop only," Viktor said.

Gus filled a small glass pitcher with water and returned to the table. "I take a little water with it myself," he said. "Please add your own. I sometimes overdo it."

Viktor took up the cruet, added a dollop of water to his whiskey, then saluted Gus with his raised glass. "Nastrovia," he toasted. Whereupon, he took a delicate sip.

Gus tasted his also, and placed his glass pointedly on the table and took a seat directly across from his curious visitor.

"Mr. Malach..." the Russian held up a hand in protest.

"Please, my gracious host! You are to call me Viktor. Already I know we will be friends. May I call you Gus?"

How could he refuse? "Of course, Viktor. I apologize for my formality. Nevertheless, Vik-tor..." (he stressed each syllable of the name), "...I'm sure you hope to return to town before dark. Perhaps we should discuss what brings you here."

Malachenko again raised his glass in appreciation of his host's firm, but well put insistence on his coming to the point. He took another sip of whiskey and smiled. "You are a perceptive man, Gus, so no doubt you think I am here regarding a certain electrical generation device invented by one Dr. LaGrange. Is this not the case?"

Gus nodded. "It had crossed my mind."

Malachenko smiled. "Yes, my friend, but you are, as we say in America, off the mark."

"Indeed," Gus was not convinced.

"Yes," Malachenko gave a short laugh. "Indeed. Of course, you are aware that my country became interested in you during the unfortunate circumstances surrounding Dr. LaGrange's recent death. I can tell you that there are those among our intelligence community who still harbor suspicions that you may have possession of his remarkable little engine. But their voices have become tedious to those who make command decisions. I don't think you will be troubled by them in the future."

Gus wanted to believe him. "Yet, here you are…" Gus let the sentence trail off.

"Yes," Viktor conceded. "Here I am. And you still wonder why. And well you should." He finished his whiskey and suggested, "Perhaps one more?"

Gus refreshed both glasses, but remained silent. Viktor added water to his, sipped, then continued. "First, I should confide to you that I am attached to the Russian Consulate General's office in Anchorage. Therefore, I am privy to most issues of importance with which our delegation takes interest. But let me assure you, I am not here in any official capacity. I am here concerning a more personal matter – a family matter."

Gus nodded and sipped his drink. "Go on."

"Although the Malachenkos all derive from a single ancestral stock, there are now two distinct sides of the family. Over the generations, one chose to dedicate itself to political endeavors, while the other devoted their energies to more entrepreneurial activities. Both branches of the family have been blessed with great success and have accumulated, in Russian terms, vast wealth and power. Currently I find myself in a rather delicate position due to a rift between the two. And, of course, it would not go unnoticed at the Consulate should I allow a personal issue to distract me from my diplomatic mission."

Gus was certain Viktor would arrive at a recognizable point in due course. He said, "Please continue."

"Sorry," Malachenko apologized. "I do go on at times. I beg your indulgence; this is most difficult for me."

"I'm listening," Gus prompted gently.

Viktor realized it was time to place his cards on the table. "My cousin, Alexi, with whom I was very close, was recently murdered.

He was found in an Anchorage trash bin, naked and disemboweled. Since there was no money, jewelry or identification on his body, the police classified it as a simple homicide with robbery as motive."

"I'm sorry for your loss, Viktor. But how could Alexi's death lead you to me?"

Malachenko took down half his whiskey in one swallow. "I'm getting there. Please hear me out."

Gus nodded his acquiescence, and Viktor explained. "As I'm sure you've surmised, I belong to the political arm of the family. Alexi, the other. He was engaged in several ventures, some legal, some not. He had been arrested many times over the years, so the police had compiled an impressive dossier regarding his activities. When such a man is found murdered, it is not simple robbery."

"And the rift between the two branches of your family?" Gus inquired.

"Alexi's father, who lives in Sitka, insists he knows who killed him. He is applying tremendous pressure on my side of the family to demand action from the Anchorage District Attorney. Russian politics is tricky business. The Malachenkos within the government are reluctant to become involved in a dispute with the American justice system. Since I was his friend, as well as his cousin, Alexi's father has approached me to do something. My father forbids my involvement. So you see, I find myself between the proverbial rock and a hard place."

"Awkward," Gus conceded. "Still..."

Malachenko was becoming agitated. "Yes, yes! I know – come to the point. Very well. I come to you because the LaGrange incident alerted us to your close relationship with a well-regarded Fairbanks detective. We are also aware that he is investigating a case with which Alexi's murder is connected."

Gus was intrigued. "How so?"

"Alexi was involved in, shall we say, the sub rosa import-export business. He moved goods between Alaska and certain cities in Asia. Some of the goods would be considered contraband."

"He was a smuggler," Gus put it bluntly.

Malachenko nodded.

"And what did he smuggle that got him killed?" Gus pressed.

"Bear organs, primarily." Malachenko's distaste was evident.

Gus thought he'd heard enough to cut to the chase. "I see. So, Alexi's father knows the name of the man who packaged shipments of these organs, and paid Alexi to smuggle them out of Alaska to the orient."

Malachenko looked relieved. "Precisely."

Gus filled a pipe with tobacco, and held it up for Viktor to see. "Mind if I smoke?"

"Not at all," Malachenko said. "I have no objection to smoking."

Gus struck a match and held its flame over his bowl until the contents were burning to his satisfaction. "Some difficulty arose between Alexi and his client, and the client killed him?" Gus suggested.

"We are certain of it," Viktor stated passionately.

"And you are here to give me the name of Alexi's killer?"

"Indirectly, yes," the Russian admitted. "I noticed a scrap of paper under an axe on your wood splitting stump outside. There appeared to be three names on it. If I were to venture a guess, I would say those are the names of the poachers who base their operations in Chekov. You should have a look outside after I leave."

Gus assumed the diplomat in Viktor would not allow him to speak the names aloud or pass him the note personally. "Plausible deniability" was not unique to American politicos. "How will I know which name is the killer's?" he asked.

Malachenko smiled. "Two of the surnames are identical. The other is the killer. If that is not enough, I might speculate that the third name has a Korean flavor to it."

Gus felt his heart increase in rhythm. "That should be helpful," he said, trying to keep the excitement out of his voice. "You realize, of course, that the vengeance Alexi's father seeks will not be satisfied with a mere arrest for poaching."

Malachenko finished his drink and stood up. "The Korean and his minions occasionally harvest bears here on your river," he said. "If he should meet with an accident out here in the wilderness, both sides of the family would pay handsomely for proof of his demise. I believe he wears a gold ring on his right hand. It is embossed with the image of a cobra. He has a fascination with snakes. The cobra is his personal talisman. He produces this ring as proof of his

133

identity when meeting others engaged in his business for the first time."

Chapter 23

Viktor Malachenko thanked Gus for his hospitality, donned his fur parka and riding gloves and went out the door. Gus followed him down the steps, and waited while the diplomat got situated in the saddle of his Arctic Cat.

Before switching on the engine, the Russian said, "I doubt we'll meet again – a pity, but it could prove awkward for me. If you should happen upon the remains of the Korean after some fatal misadventure, do not contact me. Get in touch with Alexi's father. You'll find his business card on the stump beside the note a mysterious previous caller left there. He will give you instructions regarding the ring."

"If events unfold as you describe, I'll do just that," Gus assured him.

Viktor settled his helmet on his head and fastened the chin strap. He flipped up the face shield. "A final caution," he said. "The Korean is left-handed, and the knife he prefers is often concealed in his right sleeve. He's never been known to carry a gun, but he always has a second knife. Should he approach you, do not allow him to get close. He strikes without warning. They do not call him 'The Cobra' without reason."

With that, he lowered the face shield and roared off down the slope to the river ice. Before he rounded the first bend he shot Gus a gallant salute. Gus waited until the sound of his engine faded into the distance, then walked over to the stump and retrieved the business card, as well as the note left there by "some mysterious previous caller".

Morgan came down the steps from the porch as he scanned the names neatly written on an index card. "Who are they?" she asked breathlessly.

Gus read her the names. "Damon Sam, Jackie Sam and Jong Min-jun a.k.a John Young."

"Jong Min-jun," she repeated the name. "There can be little doubt as to which one is the Korean."

"No," Gus told her. "I better get on the horn with Hard Case. I imagine he'll still be at the office."

"I wouldn't mention the business card your mysterious caller left," Morgan cautioned him. "You never know – maybe you will have a reason to contact Alexi's father some day."

Gus hadn't even looked at the card, he had been too focused on the names of the poachers. He glanced down at it. It was a simple business card, black ink printed on white cardstock. The name printed across the top was Yuri Malachenko. Below it, in smaller script it said simply "Import – Export". There was an address in Sitka and a telephone number below that.

***

They had just finished dinner and settled in for a game of chess when the satellite phone rang.

"Okay," Hard Case said without preamble. "My pal over at the Bureau faxed me a copy of John Young's passport. He arrived from Seoul early last year. I'll have Caldwell bring you a copy tomorrow when he does his flyover. I want you to know what he looks like if you run across him out there. As to the Sam brothers, they're both from Chekov so we can round them up anytime we like, but I'd rather hold off until we have the Korean in custody."

"What did you learn about Malachenko?" Gus had asked Hard Case to give him some background on the Russian.

"I didn't look at him tonight, but I think he really is attached to the Consulate General down in Anchorage. I've heard him mentioned a few times. I'll see what I can find out about him tomorrow. In the meantime, I've passed your information along to O'Kelly. He'll get an address for the Sams and quietly keep tabs on them until we nab Mr. John Young. My gut tells me he's the kingpin of the operation."

Gus said, "Your gut's probably right. Anyway, tell Caldwell I'll be back and forth between here and the burn tomorrow. I'll see him if he flies in while I'm upstream. I'll come straight down to the cabin. If he doesn't want to wait, just tell him to leave the papers on the table. Oh, and ask him to bring in twenty gallons of gas for the Polaris, will you? I'm going through it pretty fast with all this back and forth to the burn. I'll leave four empties on the porch he can take back with him for next time."

"I'll tell him. Anything else?" Hard Case asked.

"Nope. Just keep me posted. I'll stay on my toes out here."

"Fair enough," his friend said. "And thanks for the help, Gus. You've done all the heavy lifting on this one. I may have to dip into petty cash and buy you a bottle."

Gus laughed. "It won't go to waste. Good hunting."

They said their good-byes and Gus returned the handset to its plastic case. Morgan poured them each a night cap.

"Let's skip the chess tonight," she said, handing him his whiskey. "I don't think either of us will be able to concentrate on the game."

"We could turn in early and play some other games," he suggested.

She smiled. "Great minds think alike."

***

When Gus awoke the sun was not yet above the ridgeline, but he could make out the muted silhouettes of the spruce trees through the east window in the soft first light of morning. Morgan stirred next to him so he rolled over and nuzzled her ear.

"Mmmm," she responded snaking a warm bare arm around his neck and holding him tight.

"I demand a rematch," he whispered.

Her eyes opened wide. "What?" she said, not yet fully awake.

"A rematch," he told her. "Our game last night – you came out on top."

It didn't take her long. "Your insatiable lust is one of the things I like about you," she said, throwing a naked leg over his stomach.

"Randy as a ten-peckered billy goat," he boasted.

She pushed off and held him at bay. "Haywood?" she asked.

"How'd you guess?" he asked innocently.

"Good lord," she moaned, "will it never end?"

***

Later, after a breakfast of reindeer sausage, eggs and toast, Gus brought in a couple loads of firewood and restocked the hopper next to the stove. Over the last of the coffee they discussed plans for the day.

"I'm hoping to bring down a dozen logs today," he told her. "I'll keep an eye out for Caldwell and come straight back when I hear his plane. I'm anxious to see what our knife thief looks like."

"I had a good look at him in person," she reminded Gus. "But, I'd like to know more about him. I hope Hard Case came up with some history on him."

"Yeah," Gus said. "But I doubt he can add much to what Malachenko told me. And I already knew he was a prick."

Morgan laughed. "You're not going to forget about that knife, are you?"

"No," he said. "I hate being robbed, and I hate having my cabin violated. I may just shoot him on sight if he turns up here."

"Considering his reputation, that might be the sensible thing to do. I won't tell."

Gus smiled, finished his coffee and kissed her. "I'm off," he said. "Better keep the door barred while I'm away – just in case."

"I will," she promised. "And you be careful up there."

Chapter 24

Jong Min-jun never drove a snow machine when he hunted with the Sam brothers. He would always ride double with either Damon or Jackie, so Jackie thought nothing of it when he climbed aboard behind him as they prepared to set out for the Moose Jaw.

Before Jackie switched on the key, he turned his head and sniffed the wind. "You wear those same clothes last night?"

Jong bristled. He had always been fastidious and prided himself on his cleanliness. "Of course not. Why do you ask?"

Jackie was never one to mince words. "You stink like the bar. You were wearing that coat last night. It stinks like tobacco and old booze. The bear will smell you a mile away."

Jong Min-jun was livid. The tone of contempt in Jackie's voice was intolerable. He closed his eyes and took a deep breath. 'Just a little longer,' he thought. 'I must be patient.' But, he also knew Jackie was right. Bears had a remarkable sense of smell. He patted Jackie on the shoulder as he swung off the saddle.

"Be right back," he said.

Damon looked up when Jong came through the door and shrugged out of his coat.

"Change your mind?" he asked.

"No," the Korean answered. "Jackie thinks my coat stinks and that the bear will smell me coming."

"He's right," Damon agreed. "You'll never get close. Or maybe you'll get closer than you want. You can take my old hunting coat. It's hanging by the door."

John thanked him, went to the coat tree and exchanged his coat for Damon's.

"I'll try not to get any blood on it," he said over his shoulder on his way out the door. He smiled to himself as he walked down the path to the snow machine. 'Don't want any evidence on Damon's coat, do we?' he thought.

***

Jong did not want to kill Jackie too close to Gus' cabin. In fact, he reasoned, he did not want to risk leaving his body upstream of the Wolf Creek trail. They had worked that stretch of river quite hard during the winter and had left several bear carcasses along the banks. The authorities may be monitoring activity along that section now. As they began their descent down the Moose Jaw side of the trail, he suggested they start downstream of the place where he suspected he had left his knife. He told Jackie they may as well scout some new territory while they were in the area.

When they reached the Moose Jaw, Jackie swung the nose of his old Yamaha downstream and drove ten miles past where they had killed the last bear. They spent an hour slowly scouting the banks in that country, but found nothing of interest.

"We're wasting our time down here," Jackie said. "If you want to find the Ghost Bear, we need to go back upstream. All this winter I see his tracks on that part of the river near the cabin. I think he must have a den somewhere around there. You can look for your knife on the way."

"Good idea," Jong said, his mind making adjustments to his plan. He had hoped they would find some tracks while they were far below the Wolf Creek trail and follow them deep into the woods. If he killed Jackie in a place like that, his body would never be found.

"Yes. We should go up there now before it gets too late in the day. I want to talk to the man in the cabin anyway. We'll look for the knife on the way out."

Jackie said nothing to this, but Jong knew he was thinking of some way he could avoid this meeting without losing face. He climbed on the snow machine behind Jackie and they headed upstream. Jackie opened the throttle to forty miles per hour, a good distance eating speed. They had just passed the trail coming over from Wolf Creek when Jong tapped Jackie on his shoulder and gestured that they should stop on the next gravel bar.

When he had driven up off the river and killed the engine, Jackie turned and asked, "Why we stopping here?"

Jong gestured toward the trees. "Isn't this where we killed that bear last month?"

Jackie studied the terrain. "Up around the next bend," he said with contempt. "You need to remember landmarks better."

The Cobra ignored the disdain in Jackie's words. 'Not long now,' he thought. 'Just keep talking, my friend. You're going to be quiet for a long, long time.'

Aloud, he said, "I remember we saw other fresh tracks near that one's cave. Let's go back in and see if maybe there's another bear in there now. Easy money."

Jackie shrugged his shoulders and restarted the engine. They rounded one more bend of the river, then swung inland. The valley was wide here due to the alluvial plain that had accumulated over the centuries as a result of the eroded material that had washed down Wolf Creek. They had to thread their way through the trees and skirt beaver ponds to get back into the place Jong had chosen. It was a long way off the river.

As soon as they parked the snow machine, Jackie walked off a few paces and began urinating in a patch of snow. He had left his rifle in its scabbard on the snow machine, but Jong knew he kept his pistol in his parka's right side pocket. He knew also that Jackie always had to remove his glove to get to it.

"You don't like me very much do you?" he asked Jackie's back.

Jackie was not finished with his business yet, so he did not turn to look at Jong.

"Not very much," he answered truthfully. He had been mildly surprised by the tone of John's question. Maybe he was trying to pick a fight. Jackie hoped so. Many times over the past few months he had wanted to punch the little bastard in the face, but did not want to jeopardize all the dope and pussy John supplied.

Jong waited until Jackie had zipped up the front of his pants, then walked up to him as he was putting on his gloves.

Jackie turned and misread the look on the Cobra's face. 'Yep, he's looking for a fight,' he thought. 'He can't blame me if he gets his ass kicked.'

"I don't like you either," Jong told him as he came in low with the knife. Jackie was quick, but he was already up on his toes, ready to lunge at the Korean and land a blow before he had time to throw one himself. His momentum worked to Jong's advantage and the long blade penetrated the material of Jackie's parka and the soft spot just below his sternum, then plunged upward through his heart.

The Cobra retreated as quickly as he had struck. He had released his grip on the knife the moment its hilt slammed home against Jackie's chest. He left it as a plug to prevent the gush of blood he knew would pump out of the wound. He took two hasty steps to his right before Jackie sagged to his knees and slowly toppled facedown in the snow.

The Cobra smiled as the first stains of red began to seep from beneath the body. As it spread into an every growing circle, he inspected his left sleeve and the front of the waterproof, stain-resistant liner he had worn especially for today's work. He had taken off Damon's coat and left it on the saddle of the snow machine before he approached Jackie. 'He had done this before,' he thought. 'But, never so well.'

Jong knew some of his breed liked to stand over a victim and talk rubbish to the dead man. He was not of that ilk. He considered urinating on Jackie's corpse instead, but decided against it. 'DNA,' he thought. He had done this before.

Chapter 25

The ghost bear, as Damon thought of him, followed his nose into the gentle wind that came down the Moose Jaw. There was something on this breeze that triggered recognition in the old grizzly's brain. Something... He tasted the air currents and added this new sensory input to the olfactory data already being processed through his memory banks. Yes. He knew this human being. His essence was an exact match for a human he had been waiting for. He continued upstream, keeping to the cover of the willows just outside the tree line. His instinct told him the human he now stalked was dangerous. He associated his scent with that of a dead bear. The man was a killer of bears. It was second nature to Trilogy, as Gus O'Neill called him, to proceed quietly, and with no sense of urgency. There was no need for hurry. He would find this human today, or tomorrow, and kill him.

The breeze freshened momentarily and Broken Foot, as Old Blue Eye thought of him, caught just the hint of a change in the essence of this human he sought. He came to a halt and slowly swung his enormous head side to side a few times until he registered the significance of the change. He stood fully erect, face hard into the wind, just to make sure he had it right. It was extremely subtle, but it was there, and he knew it well – death. He dropped softly back down on all fours and pushed on. The sun was still well above the western horizon when the bear came upon the corpse of Jackie Sam. Old Blue Eye stood motionless near his grand nephew's body and watched Broken Foot approach. He showed no fear of the huge grizzly, and the bear showed no aggression toward him.

***

"I knew you would come," the old shaman told the bear. "At least you will not have to kill him now. Someone else has done that for you."

The bear continued his slow progress until he came to the body. He placed his crippled paw on it and rolled it over so Jackie's unseeing eyes stared into the blue expanse of the universe. The bear again swung his head side-to-side as if to satisfy himself that this human could be stricken from the list.

Old Blue Eye waited quietly until the grizzly had completed his inspection of Jackie's mortal remains. When the bear looked up at him, he said, "Maybe you won't have to kill the brother either. Maybe this will change things."

The bear stared at him with dead eyes. It was as if the old man did not exist. They stood that way for a very long time, an old man and an old bear, one each side of a corporeal entity whose spirit had already departed.

At length, the bear turned away from Jackie's body and ambled out toward the river. Before he had gone far, he stopped and examined another set of man tracks in the snow. A low, rumbling growl issued forth from his chest. The old man knew the bear had recognized the scent associated with these tracks too. He watched as the bear set off upstream, clearly following the snow machine that had carried the other man away.

Chapter 26

Fergus O'Neill had become quite adept at the new logging technique. During the three days since Caldwell had delivered the fuel and an envelope containing copies of Jong Min-jun's passport and driver's license, he had averaged eleven runs per day. His stockpile of logs was becoming rather impressive. At the end of the third day, he stopped at the cabin and had a hot cup of tea with Morgan before unhooking the last log from his towing rig.

"Good day?" she asked as he came in the door and went to stand by the stove.

"It was," he told her. "I had to work higher up today because I've dropped all the good ones that were down low. I skidded the first one all the way down to my normal take-out area, but that took a lot longer than I had hoped. So, I just drove up the hill and pulled the next one down real slow. I broke the stand-off when it started pushing me too hard on the steepest drop so I cut a stouter one and pressed on. I pulled out the rest with no problem. It saved a lot of time."

"How many do you have now?" she inquired as she poured tea.

"Over fifty, last count. I guess I'd better start keeping a log – no pun intended."

She took their tea to the table and beckoned him to join her. When he was seated across from her, she asked, "Do you think you could bring down a few extra logs to build us an extension on the porch? We sit out there often in the summer; if it were big enough for a picnic table, we could dine al fresco in the warm evenings."

Gus nodded and sipped his tea. "I don't see why not," he said. "I think that's a great idea. It wouldn't take a lot of lumber. I could probably mill everything we'd need out of three or four trunks."

***

When they'd finished their tea Gus went back outside and added the last log to his pile. Before putting the Polaris to bed for the night, he made a fresh count of his logs. While he was doing so, the raven – he suspected it was the same one that often visited him at the burn – lit on the porch roof and observed.

Gus smiled and went on with his tally. He'd come to enjoy the company of the bird and had fallen into the habit to talking to it while he worked.

"Fifty-six," he said over his shoulder. When no squawk or clunk was forthcoming, he turned and saw that the raven had departed.

"Fifty-six," he repeated to himself so he would remember to write it down when he went back inside. He was better than half-way there. He had made a material take-off list using his plans for the bunkhouse. He needed ten twenty-four footers for each of the two long walls, ten fourteen-footers for each depth wall, three of medium diameter (twenty-eight feet long) for the floor beams, and another for the ridge beam, four twelve-footers for the stepped gables – he would cut them to size after the walls were in place – and a couple dozen small diameter stock for the purlins, rafters, and divider wall. Then he'd need maybe thirty from which he'd rip planks for the floor boards, shutters, shelves, and Morgan's porch extension. Since he'd been stacking the logs by category and arranging the first-to-be used stacks close to the bunkhouse pad, he would be able to pull them off in order without having to sort through the whole pile each time.

He had not yet felled the longest ones, but he had all four selected up at the burn. He didn't want to bring them down until after all the shorter stock was in place; they would just be in the way. He'd also saved the small diameter timber for the early May runs, to keep the weight down as the ice began to thin. If it remained cold enough he could tow two or three at a time. Running the numbers through his head, he calculated that another week of logging would probably do it.

After filling the Polaris with gas and blanketing the engine, he bounded up the steps, kicked the snow off his boots and opened the door. He was greeted by the delicious aroma of whatever was simmering on the stove. "God, that smells good," he said, stepping inside. "What is it?"

Morgan did not answer. She was seated at the table, staring out the front window. The look on her face was sufficient to wipe the smile off his.

"Morgan," he said, concern apparent in his voice. "What's wrong?"

146

She heaved a sigh. "I've just had a visitor," she told him. "Old Blue Eye. He came to tell me one of his nephew's sons has been killed. He wants us to tell Hard Case and ask him to come out."

Gus was bewildered. "Old Blue Eye was just here, while I was outside? I didn't see him come or go."

"Perhaps he did not wish for you to see him," she said.

Gus sat down across the table from her. "Why does he want Hard Case to come out here?"

"Our old friend found the body down near Wolf Creek. He was murdered. He told me how to get to the place it happened."

"I'll have to call Hard Case right away. What was the boy's name?"

"Jackie Sam," she said pointedly. Their eyes locked for a moment.

"One of the bear poachers," Gus wasn't sure if he was sad or glad. "How was he killed?"

"A knife," she said quietly. "Your knife." She went to the sideboard, where she had placed it to dry after she'd washed it. She handed it to him.

Gus looked puzzled. "How..." Morgan preempted the question.

"The old man brought it to me and asked that I give it to you. I guess he knew it was yours."

Gus shook his head in wonder. "That leaves little doubt who killed Jackie. I can't believe the Korean would be so careless as to leave it at the scene."

"The old one says he thinks he left it in Jackie's heart to point the finger at you if the body was found. Remember, this Jong Min-jun had no way to know he could be connected to the knife. Only Jackie and Damon were with him when he stole it. Neither would be likely to tell."

Gus realized she was right. 'The sneaky bastard,' he thought. Aloud, he said, "This is going to complicate things. That knife was the only physical evidence implicating Jong as the killer."

Morgan sat back down at the table. "Old Blue Eye placed another knife in the wound. Its blade is as long as your knife's. He said he found it near one of the dead bears. He also said he knew Jong had handled it without gloves."

Gus smiled in appreciation. "That old bugger never ceases to amaze me."

147

Gus looked at his watch. "We still have an hour of light left. Let's go."

He began to rise but she put a hand on his sleeve. "No," she said quietly. "You must not disturb the scene. It will complicate things for Hard Case if you go down there and leave evidence that you had been near the corpse."

Gus started to object, but thought better of it. "I'm glad you've got a cool head," he told her. "You're right of course. I'll call Fairbanks and report the death."

***

When he got off the line with Hard Case, he cradled the phone in its plastic box and snapped the lid shut. Morgan brought him a stiff whiskey and he thanked her with a nod and a smile. She went to the stove and stirred whatever dish was simmering in the skillet.

Gus said, "Caldwell's plane is in the hangar for maintenance. They'll try to rustle up another one tomorrow morning. Hard Case said to expect him around noon. He wants me to take the Polaris down to the point where the old man said to cut inland and see if there's a suitable place for them to land. I'm to call him with the GPS coordinates if there is. I'll head out early; do you want to ride along?"

"Maybe," she said. "I'll tell you in the morning. Now wash up and we'll have dinner. I made something special I think you'll like."

Gus sniffed the air. "Smells wonderful – what is it?"

"Hasenpfeffer," Morgan said proudly.

He smiled. "German peppered hare," he remembered. "I love that dish. I haven't had it since I came back from Europe."

"I learned how to prepare it when my father was attached to the embassy over there. I made it with that big fellow you snared the other day. Since you've become so proficient at setting traps, I thought we should celebrate your success."

"Maybe we should save some for Caldwell to thank him for teaching me to rig snares."

"There's plenty," she assured him. "Now finish your drink and we'll eat."

"Sounds good," he said, downing the last of his whiskey. "I'm famished."

***

148

Gus got up at first light, took a scoop of hot coals from the stove and placed them in the brazier before going out into the morning. A gentle snow was falling as he slid the warm pan between the skis of the Polaris and adjusted the insulating blanket over the hood to trap the heat. He went back inside and added kindling and a few pieces of wood to the remaining coals in the stove and filled the percolator with water and ground coffee.

"How much snow fell in the night?" Morgan asked him.

He turned to look at her. She was sitting up in bed. The blankets had gathered at her waist and her lustrous red hair cascaded over her bare shoulders and breasts and obscured the ivory skin of her flat stomach. She was a lovely site.

"Good morning," he said. Then, in answer to her question, "Perhaps two inches, but it's still coming down. I'm going up to the burn and bring down the sled. We'll need it to haul out the body. The fire should catch in a few minutes and the coffee is prepped in the pot."

"I'll have breakfast waiting when you get back." She stretched and swung her legs out from under the blankets. He admired them as he put on his gloves.

She looked up and smiled. She always appreciated a compliment, even when unspoken. "Off you go," she told him. "You can have your way with me tonight."

He went to the bed, bent and kissed her. "If I'm in the mood," he said.

She laughed and pushed him toward the door. "Go," she commanded.

***

Gus went directly to the Polaris, removed the blanket and brazier and started the engine. He left it to idle while he paid his morning visit to the privy and checked the two snare sets. He was relieved to see both were undisturbed. He had enough on his plate for today, and dressing out a frozen hare would have been just one more thing.

The engine was warm and running smooth when he returned, so he swung into the saddle, cinched down his hood, and headed upstream.

It took him less than a half hour to make the round trip. When he arrived back at The Varmitage, he killed the engine, tossed the blanket over it to keep it warm, and took the now cold brazier back inside.

It was still snowing, and the shoulders of his coat were white with powder. He gave it a shake before hanging it on the wall peg.

"Right on time," Morgan greeted him with a hug and a kiss. "The coffee just finished perking."

Gus went to the table and sat down. "What's for breakfast? I could eat a horse."

"Sausage and eggs," Morgan said. She went to the stove and lifted the lid on the skillet. "Almost ready." She poured two cups of coffee and took them to the table.

He accepted his and said, "If it's snowing like this down at Wolf Creek, there won't be many tracks left for evidence. I'll take the tarp along and cover any still unburied."

She considered this for a moment. "Yes," she said. "But, you need to stay out on the river bank so you don't make any tracks yourself. I'll go down with you and place the tarp if there's anything left worth protecting."

Gus sipped his coffee. "I thought you said we shouldn't go anywhere near the body."

"I said your tracks would complicate things. I won't leave any tracks." She went to the stove and returned with their breakfasts.

***

The snow had stopped by the time they arrived at the Wolf Creek trail. Still, enough had fallen to cover any tracks the killer would have left so there was no point in deploying the tarp. The river was wide here and Gus decided the straight stretch would be long enough for a plane to put down. He drove the Polaris downwind as far as the first bend to make sure there were no logs or rocks hidden beneath the fresh snow that could catch a ski. Satisfied it was clear, he returned upstream where the cut in the mountains afforded him line-of-site to the satellite and stopped.

He checked his watch. "Nearly ten o'clock," he told Morgan. "Hard Case will be waiting for my call."

She slid off the saddle and dug the phone's red plastic carrying case out of the sled. After giving it to Gus, she walked back upstream and found the trail Old Blue Eye had described. She waited there while Gus called in his report.

150

Hard Case answered on the first ring. "Mornin' Gus. I was beginning to think you slept in."

Gus snorted. "I had to get up to run an errand for a pal," he said. "Did Caldwell find you a ride?"

"No, everything we have is booked for the day. Haywood's volunteered to bring me out. The Cessna he rents is big enough to transport a body, and he's landed it at your place a couple times this winter. We've just been waiting to get the all clear from you."

Gus assured him there was plenty of open ice for the Cessna and gave him the GPS coordinates. "I scouted it up and back with the Polaris. Just stay in my tracks and you won't get into trouble. I'll wait here for you."

"Perfect," Hard Case replied. "Haywood says you're only good for heavy lifting anyway."

Gus laughed. "At least we won't have to carry out the stiff. I pulled the sled down behind me. But, you might tell Haywood to bring along that little plastic one of his, just in case I can't drive all the way in."

"I'll make sure he brings it. Oh, and he wants to know if he can board Bosworth with you for a while. If so, he'll add him to the manifest."

Gus looked off in the direction Morgan had gone. "Sure," he said. "The Boz is always welcome at The Varmitage."

"I'll tell him. See you sometime around noon. Can we bring you anything?"

Gus thought a moment. "A couple of fresh batteries for the satellite phone might come in handy. I seem to be using it a lot more than I anticipated."

"I'll bring you a solar powered charger. You should have enough daylight out there by now. It'll fully charge a dead battery in less than two hours. Anything else?"

"Yeah," Gus told him. "If Caldwell refilled my gas cans you could bring them with you."

"Already aboard. He gave them to us this morning when Haywood picked me up at the maintenance hangar. Want some lunch?"

"I'd never pass up a free lunch. And a cup of hot coffee would be nice."

He was already chilly and he knew he'd be colder after a two hour wait.

"You got it," Hard Case said. Then he signed off.

Chapter 27

The Cobra was never troubled after a kill. In fact, sticking the knife in Jackie Sam had put him in high spirits. He relived the scene as he guided Jackie's old Yamaha back out the trail they had made on the way in from the river. As he emerged from the trees onto the open bar, he hummed a little tune in his head. It was one of his favorites; Another One Bites the Dust, by the group Queen – "thump…thump…thump…another one bites the dust". The drum beats and lyrics provided a felt-rather-than-heard background for his thoughts as he headed downstream to have a look for his lost knife.

He hated losing a knife. He loved the heft and feel of one in his hands. He thrilled at the lethal potential in the blade of each one he handled. He regretted having to leave Gus' knife back there with Jackie, but it had been the smart thing to do. Maybe it would implicate the man that haunted his thoughts lately. It was a long shot, but one never knew.

When he arrived back at the place where he thought he had left his belt-knife, he went directly to the dead bear. It was clear that wolves and birds had been at the carcass. Little remained but hide, bones and skull. Since his knife was not where he thought he might have placed it after removing the bear's gallbladder, he went over the whole area carefully. He even shifted what was left of the carcass so he could check the frozen ground beneath. No knife.

Still, he gave the whole scene a final look. He stood with his hands in his pockets and allowed his eyes to scan every inch of ground near the bear. There were wolf and man tracks everywhere. He was not particularly good at reading sign, but he knew wolf tracks when he saw them. And he could see that some of the man tracks were larger than the others, but he attributed them to Jackie. He did not take notice of the different treads. Had he done so, he would have realized that there were more than three distinct patterns.

Convinced that further search was pointless, he heaved a sigh and returned to the snow machine. He could always buy another one, but still, losing a knife did not bode well. He needed to be more careful.

***

Jong arrived back in Chekov a little before six o'clock. He noted with some disappointment that Damon's old Ski-Doo was not parked at the house. He had prepared a plausible story to explain why Jackie had not returned with him. But it would keep until Damon came back.

Inside, he found Danielle sprawled on the sofa smoking a joint.

"Hi, sweetie," she said in a dreamy voice. "Where are the guys?"

He remembered both girls were still sacked out when he and Jackie had departed for the Moose Jaw shortly before ten o'clock. "I don't know. They're probably over at The Cherry Orchard."

"We're getting ready to go over there now," she told him. "Nicky's in the shower. Maybe you should surprise her; she'd like that."

Jong did not answer. Something was wrong here. He could feel it.

"I didn't see Damon's ride out back. Where'd he go?"

Danielle took another toke on the joint. "We thought he went with you. He wasn't here when we rolled out this morning."

Jong thought back to his chat with Damon before breakfast. He'd seen something in his eyes that didn't register at the time. Damon had decided something. 'Shit,' he thought to himself.

He didn't respond to Danielle. He took the stairs two at a time and went directly to Damon's room. The door was closed but he went straight in.

"Shit," he said aloud. All Damon's things were gone.

He checked the closet, just to make sure, but it too was empty. Damon had cut and run. Did he suspect what Jong was up to that morning? Had he known that the Korean would come back alone? Damon had been the smart brother; was he smarter than Jong had given him credit for?

The Cobra had to regroup on the fly. Jackie was dead and Damon had chosen to disappear. Jong realized that the Chekov phase of his operation had come to an end. There would be no bear harvest during the salmon runs this year. He had to move on. He considered his options as he stood there.

He heard the shower turn off in the adjoining room. It gave him an idea. He hurried to the top of the stairs, then descended slowly. Danielle was just rising from the couch.

154

"Nicky just got out of the shower. When she comes down, you two go on over to The Cherry Orchard. I'll clean up and come over later." He gave her a twenty-dollar bill. "You can put everything on my tab until I get there, but here's some tip money."

Danielle took the twenty and stuffed it in a front pocket of her tight jeans. "Okay," she said. "You know where to find us."

Jong met Nicky coming down the stairs. She was naked, with a towel wrapped around her head. "Hey," she said. "We wondered when you'd get back. We're going over to the bar. You gonna join us?"

Jong smiled. "Later," he promised. "I want to shower and change my clothes first."

***

Jong went up to his own room and began packing his things. He had everything staged at the foot of his bed when he heard Danielle's voice. "We're gone," she called up the stairs. "See you when we see you." Then he heard the front door slam shut.

'Or not,' he thought to himself as he hurried down the hall to Jackie's room. It took him less than five minutes to stuff all Jackie's things into two river bags and take them downstairs. After he brought down his own gear he ran out to the shed at the rear of the property and fetched an old tow-sled some previous renter had left stored there. It took him no time at all to couple it to Jackie's snow machine and load everything aboard. Danielle and Nicky were just ordering their second drinks over at The Cherry Orchard as he drove slowly out of town.

Damon and Jackie had both known that their friend John must have had a warehouse somewhere close to Chekov where he stored the product they brought him from the field and packaged his consignments for shipment. But, Jong had never told them where it was.

Shortly after arriving in Chekov, Jong had taken space in a heated self-storage unit just west of town. He had rented it using Malachenko's import-export company name, AlexiCo. The Russian smuggler had suggested the arrangement himself. Since Alexi was now dead, no one knew about the place. He went directly there from the Chekov house, opened the overhead door, and parked next to a 1989 Jeep Cherokee he kept hidden there for just such an emergency. He had also taken the precaution to outfit the storage

155

unit with a portable AM/FM radio, folding cot, microwave oven and sufficient water and food to see him through several days. It was not exactly the Ritz, but it was safe, warm and comfortable. He had slept in much worse conditions as a homeless youth in Seoul, where he had spent many winter nights cold and hungry in doorways or packing crates. At least the storage unit was free of rats, cats and vermin.

As he set up the cot, plugged in the microwave, and inventoried his food stores, he thought about the days to come. He was certain no one would discover Jackie's body, but Damon worried him. And the girls would begin to wonder what happened to the three guys that had been balling them for the past couple months. They were just stupid enough to file a missing persons report, but he doubted they would. They'd probably just hook up with someone who could take them back to Anchorage and that would be that.

'No worries,' he liked the Aussie expression. All he had to do was hole up for a few days, then drive south and connect with his field agents in the Kenai, or go east to Tok where he could fall in with his Wrangle St. Elias team. He took his mini-mag flashlight out of his pocket, turned off the overhead light in the storage unit and stretched out on the cot. He lay there thinking for a little while before switching off the flashlight and going straight to sleep. Back at The Cherry Orchard, Danielle was just signaling the bartender for another round.

Chapter 28

Even though Gus had told Hard Case it would be safe to land on the frozen stretch of the Moose Jaw at the foot of Wolf Creek trail, Haywood made a low level fly-over just to make sure it looked good to him. Since he'd put his little Piper Clipper into the trees last fall, he'd become a lot more careful than he'd been before the crash. Granted, that accident had not been entirely accidental. Haywood had intentionally put his plane into a classic ground loop where the tail comes up suddenly after landing and the aircraft tips up onto its nose and a wingtip. Had he been successful, he might have been able to turn the tables on Dr. Curtis LaGrange, who held a pistol trained on him at the time. Unfortunately, the plane veered off the bed of the old dry channel he had chosen for a landing strip and plunged into the trees. Haywood was lucky to be alive.

Gus parked his big Polaris just inside the tree line in order to give Haywood the full width of the river ice upon which to land. After his ten o'clock call to Hard Case to give him the coordinates for the best place to put down, he and Morgan decided to make a trial run into the place Old Blue Eye had told them they'd find the body. The fresh snow had obscured most of the poachers' snow machine trail, but there were places under the trees where it was still visible. As Gus didn't want to destroy any evidence, Morgan guided him on a circuitous route that brought them very near the spot they sought. They did not go any closer to the actual murder scene than was necessary to see Jackie's frozen remains near the mouth of a cave in the hillside. They returned to the river keeping to the same trail they had cut on the way in.

Morgan, as was her custom, had taken her leave when they first heard the sound of the plane approaching. Gus knew he'd find her at The Varmitage when he got back after Hard Case and Haywood flew out with the corpse. He filled his pipe and lit it as he watched Haywood bring his airplane down expertly and glide downstream on its skis. He waited while Haywood swung it around, powered back upstream and brought it to a stop out in mid-channel. After Haywood killed the engine and the prop came to a stop, Gus walked out onto the ice to greet his friends.

Hard Case opened the passenger side door and tossed a paper bag down to Gus. "Meatball sub," he said. "Will that do you?"

Gus opened the sack and reached in. The sandwich was double-wrapped in aluminum foil and was still warm to the touch. "Perfect," he said.

Hard Case descended to the ice and clapped Gus on the shoulder. "There's coffee in the thermos. I imagine you could use a hot cup about now. Let's go sit on your rig and I'll have one with you while Haywood gets Bosworth calmed down. You wouldn't believe how loud that damned cat can be when he's unhappy!"

Gus laughed. "Yeah," he said. "He wasn't real happy the last time he came in either."

They watched Haywood come around the tail section of the plane and inspect the ski and struts on the side facing them. When he was satisfied nothing had sprung or popped loose upon landing, he came up to join them.

"Coffee?" Hard Case offered.

Haywood shook his head, "I've had enough for today." He nodded to Gus. "You're looking a tad bit chilled, Fergus. You're not going soft on us are you?"

Gus snorted. "Just been sitting here contemplating the fate of the proverbial brass monkey," he said. "Did you bring a tranquilizer gun along for the Boz? It sounds like I might need one to get him back to the cabin."

Haywood grinned. "Morgan will settle him down. But, I'd keep him in that cage until she's there to help. He is one angry feline at the moment."

Hard Case had finally come around to accepting Morgan's existence. He had no desire to make her acquaintance, yet he had asked Gus to approach her to help him make contact with Old Blue Eye. Considering this latest development, she might have done just that. The fact that the old fellow had requested Hard Case's involvement in this case boded well for the future.

He finished his coffee and screwed the lid back on the thermos. "How far in to the corpse?" he asked Gus.

"Quarter mile, maybe," Gus responded. "We drove back there this morning, just to make sure we could get to the body with the Polaris."

Hard Case ignored the 'we' in Gus' sentence. "You didn't get too close, did you?" Hard Case asked him.

"No, and we avoided the trail the killer used. I didn't think you'd appreciate me obliterating evidence."

Hard Case smiled and nudged his friend with his elbow. "I'm telling you Gus, you missed your calling. You're getting pretty good at this sort of thing. In any event, the killer's trail is probably too old to tell us much, but you never know. I'll follow it back in to the kill site afoot and see if it's worth preserving. You two ride in on the Polaris and wait for me there. Don't go any further than you did this morning. By the way, how deep is the snow in there? You think I'll need snowshoes?"

Gus shook his head. "It's pretty solid under the new powder. You'll probably be okay in those boots."

Hard Case stood up and headed off into the woods.

Gus turned the key to "ON", pulled the cord and his engine roared to life; he let it idle. "Climb aboard Haywood, time to get to work."

Haywood swung a long leg over the saddle and settled in behind Gus. "Ready when you are," he said. And they angled downstream to pick up the path he and Morgan had carved earlier in the day.

When they arrived at the terminus of the new trail Gus brought the big machine to a stop and cut the engine. "Hard Case will probably need another twenty minutes," he said. "If you brought in any of those foul smelling terrier turds you smoke, you may as well go ahead and pollute the air."

Haywood extracted one of his infamous cigars from his breast pocket and stoked it up. He held the match while Gus lit his pipe.

"I hope Bosworth won't be an imposition," he said, toxic gases billowing off the tip of his stogie.

Gus dismounted the snow machine and walked a few paces upwind. "No. Morgan was delighted when I told her you were bringing him out. What's up? You off on another trip?"

Haywood shook his head. "No. I'm not going anywhere, but Donna is. She and a few of 'the girls' are going to Hawaii for two weeks in what has become an annual getaway. She asked – insisted – that I put up her mutt while she's away. No cage in the clinic for her precious little darling. I couldn't say no."

"No more need be said," Gus laughed. "I gather the Boz would not be a gracious host."

"Most certainly not. I figured it wouldn't set well with her to be called back to the mainland early to attend her dearly beloved's internment ceremony at the pet cemetery, so Bosworth was odd man out. I was hoping Morgan might not mind having him back for a visit."

Gus smiled around the stem of his pipe as he puffed aromatic smoke into the cold air. "Sooner or later she's going to say, 'it's me or Bosworth'. What then?"

Haywood shrugged. "I'll cross that bridge when I come to it. In the meantime, I appreciate you two helping out."

"Anything for a pal," Gus told him.

Haywood puffed thoughtfully on his cigar. "You didn't happen to sneak up to Hermit's Camp and help out your old pal in other ways did you?"

Gus smiled. "Whatever gave you that idea?"

"I took a detour on the way in. I flew over Hermit's Camp to see how much snow was still on the ground, and there was my little Clipper, smack in the middle of the old channel."

Gus made no comment so he went on. "I made another low level run and could see the tracks of a big snow machine. Fess up O'Neill."

Gus grinned and nodded. "I owed you one for coming up with the snow machine idea. Morgan went along with me and helped. Now you won't have to wait for warm weather. You can go get it whenever you want."

Haywood laughed. "I knew it! What can I say? Thanks. I'll arrange for a chopper soon as we get back."

They were still chatting when they heard Hard Case coming through the woods. "Don't shoot officer!" Haywood called out. "We surrender."

Hard Case materialized out of the heavy cover across the clearing from them. He leaned against a tree and glowered in their direction. Even from that distance, they could see that he was sweating and steam was rising off his parka hood into the cold air. They gave him a minute to catch his breath.

When he had, he said in a wheezy voice, "I trust you ladies had a pleasant ride through the woods."

Haywood couldn't resist. "Most uncomfortable," he complained. "Gus should have these shocks replaced. I may have dislocated my ass bone!"

Hard Case took a few more much needed breaths before responding. "Gus," he said, "I thought you told me the snow underneath the powder was solid. I broke through every other step!"

Gus chuckled. "I had based my calculations upon the weight of the average man. I had not taken into account your particular...ah...mass." He winked at Haywood and said, out of the corner of his mouth, "If he goes for his gun, you dive right, I'll go left."

After a bit more breath catching, Hard Case pronounced. "You're a cruel man, Fergus O'Neill. By the authority vested in me, I hereby commandeer your motorized vehicle to transport the deceased back to the plane. Since you're of average height and weight, you should have no difficulty going out afoot."

"Sounds like he's recovered his breath," Haywood said quietly.

"Now," Hard Case went on. "You two just stay put while I get some photos of the scene and do my thing." He withdrew a rather large camera from its case and came a few paces out into the clearing.

Gus and Haywood settled back to watch the show. Hard Case stopped perhaps ten yards from the body and brought the camera up to his eye. After a few seconds, he lowered and studied it with a puzzled expression. His thumb seemed to be exploring various buttons on the back of its housing. He repeated this up, down, study, process three or four times before bellowing, "God damn it! Do either of you smart asses know anything about digital cameras?"

Haywood jumped into the breach. "This is our chance to get back into his good graces, if they exist," he told Gus. He hopped off the Polaris and started across the clearing. "Hang on Case," he called. "Help is on the way."

Gus watched as Hard Case walked Haywood in a three-sixty around the snow-shrouded corpse, stopping every few paces to snap a photo. It was apparent he was trying to capture every possible angle. When they had completed that exercise Hard Case reclaimed the camera and deposited it in its case. He pointed in Gus' direction and Haywood retraced his own steps back to the snow machine.

"Was he civil?" Gus inquired.

"His hostility level diminished as we progressed," Haywood told him. "But, he's not in his normal humor."

They again settled in and watched while Hard Case examined the body. He knelt beside it for several minutes before turning it over and spending even more time studying the side now exposed. At length, Hard Case stood up and motioned for them to join him.

"What do you think?" Gus asked as they approached.

"I think Old Blue Eye was very perceptive," he said.

"How so?" Gus wondered.

"Well," Hard Case said, "if the body was face down in the snow with a knife handle sticking out of its chest, how did the old bugger know it was murder? For that matter, how did he know it was Jackie Sam?" He looked at Gus poignantly.

"How does he know anything?" Gus countered.

Hard Case considered this for a moment, then nodded slowly. "There is that."

Haywood asked, "Are you done here, Case? Can we load up and head back?"

Hard Case looked around as if to make sure he had left nothing undone. "Yeah," he said. "There's no more to be learned here."

To Gus he said, "Will that big workhorse of yours manage the three of us and the stiff?"

Gus took this to mean Hard Case had relented regarding his going out on foot. "Sure," he said. "It's handled heavier loads coming down from the burn."

"Good," Hard Case decided. "You guys help me get the body bagged up, then we'll load it in the sled and head back to the plane."

When Jackie's frozen corpse was strapped down in the sled, Hard Case asked, "You squeamish about riding with a dead body, Haywood?"

Haywood said, "Is it that or walk?"

Hard Case nodded. "Your choice."

Haywood didn't hesitate. "No one has ever accused me of being squeamish."

"Okay then," Hard Case ordered. "Hop in the sled and keep our cargo from rolling around. Gus, I'll ride behind you."

***

162

Gus waited on the bank until the Cessna roared down the frozen Moose Jaw and lifted off. He waved as the plane circled back to the southwest and passed over on its way back to Fairbanks. Bosworth had gone mute in his cage which was now securely strapped down in the sled so Gus didn't trouble him with inane chatter. He suspected the cat's nose had detected the smell of the dead human not long removed from the space he now occupied. Maybe Bosworth had decided it was time to shut up and behave. Gus started the engine, let it idle for a few seconds, then dropped down the bank onto the ice and headed home. The raven, which had been perched atop a spruce across the creek most of the day, watched him until he disappeared around the first bend.

Chapter 29

Sergeant Michael O'Kelly had filled out the paperwork requesting a search warrant for the house of the three poachers as soon as they had been identified, but held it in abeyance until he got the go-ahead from Hard Case. He received the green light the previous evening when Hard Case had called to tell him about Jackie Sam's murder, so he filed it as soon as he got off the line. That done, he began preparing an arrest warrant for Jong Min-jun.

Hard Case had checked in with him early the next morning and said he'd be away from the office for the better part of the day. He had to fly out to the Moose Jaw and work the crime scene before returning to Fairbanks with the body.

It was nearly noon when O'Kelly received the signed warrant for the address on Pushkin Street. He had dispatched Trooper Sven Larson to watch the place at seven o'clock that morning, cautioning him to be careful as there might be a murder suspect inside. Larson had reported "nothing to report" every hour on the hour since.

"Either they're sleeping in or there's nobody home," he'd said before ringing off his eleven o'clock call-in.

O'Kelly got him on the radio. "We got the search warrant. Nolan and I will be there in about ten minutes. Any activity?"

"Nothing," Larson replied. "You sure this is the right address?"

"I guess we'll find out when we get there. Usual routine, we'll park a block away. When we're in place, you drive around into the alley behind the house and watch the back door. Let us know when you're in position."

The road system in Chekov was relatively straight forward. Numbered avenues ran east-west, and lettered streets, north-to-south. The only exception was Pushkin Street, which followed the banks of Wolf Creek as it cut a winding path through the west side of town on its way north to join the Yukon. In fact, Pushkin continued north out of town where it appeared on maps as Wolf Creek Highway, a twenty-eight mile stretch of semi-maintained gravel road which connected Chekov to the Steese Highway.

As they had discussed, Larson raised them on the radio as soon as he was in position in the alley. O'Kelly and Nolan got out of their unit, and walked up to 419 Pushkin. Chekov was a rural

Alaska town. The State Troopers there went about their business without turning it into a Hollywood production. They didn't require swat team backup when they approached the abode of a suspect. Nevertheless, Nolan stopped at the bottom of the porch steps and moved off to the side where he would get a split-second glimpse of whoever was behind the door as soon as it opened a few inches. His service piece was still in its holster, but he rested his hand on the butt and nodded to his sergeant. O'Kelly knocked on the door. After thirty seconds Nolan spoke into his vest-mounted transmitter, "Got any sprinters, Larson?"

His receiver crackled, "Nothing yet," Larson responded.

O'Kelly rapped on the door again, this time a bit harder. "I'm coming – I'm coming!" a raspy female voice shouted. Less than a minute passed before a bleary-eyed blonde opened the door a crack and peered out into the sunlight.

"Oh, shit," she said. Then, over her shoulder, she shouted, "Nicky! We got company!"

O'Kelly came immediately to the point. "Is Jong Min-jun home?" he asked.

"Nobody here by that name," the blonde said truculently. "You got the wrong place."

"How about Damon or Jackie Sam?" Sergeant O'Kelly inquired patiently. The young woman's puffy eyes opened a bit wider.

"What you want with them?" she said in a more civil tone.

"Do they live here?" he pressed on.

"Ah, yeah. But I don't think they're here now. If they are, they're still in bed. Maybe you should come back later." She was clearly becoming nervous. She ran a hand through her hair.

Another blonde appeared over her shoulder. "What is it, Danielle? Why are the cops here?"

O'Kelly addressed the new arrival. "Good afternoon. We're looking for the three young gentlemen who we believe live here – Jackie Sam and his brother Damon, and a Korean named Jong Min-jun. He also goes by the name of John Young. May we come inside?"

The two young ladies held a hasty conference behind the half-closed door. O'Kelly, who could hear every frantically whispered word, turned to Nolan and shook his head in amused disbelief.

Nicky took up station at the door. "You guys got a warrant?"

O'Kelly held it up for her to see. "May we come in? We really don't have to ask your permission, but we thought we'd extend you the courtesy."

Nicky softened a little; she shrugged her shoulders and opened the door. She had a thing for men in uniform, even the older ones. "Okay, but like Danielle told you the guys aren't here. I just banged on their doors and nobody answered. You can look around, but you're not going to find anything to bust us for. We're clean."

Sergeant O'Kelly did not doubt her. He'd heard the toilet flush three times while he was speaking with Danielle. "We got company" must have been their code for "the cops are here".

Nicky stood aside to let them in. Nolan went directly up the stairs, while O'Kelly checked the ground floor rooms.

"Clear," Nolan called down after a few minutes. O'Kelly heard him speak into his radio, "We're good here, Larson. Go get some lunch."

Since it was apparent that only the two young ladies were home, O'Kelly turned his attention to them. They were both seated on the sofa in their robes, smoking filtered cigarettes as fast as they could suck them down. He decided to rock their boat a little before questioning them.

"We're not here to bust you for anything. We're looking for the Korean gentleman I mentioned. An arrest warrant is being processed for him as we speak. He's wanted for the murder of Jackie Sam," he told them, point-blank. He watched with satisfaction as both their eyes and mouths popped open.

"Jesus Christ!" Danielle blurted. "Jackie's dead?"

O'Kelly nodded slowly. "The identity of the victim has not yet been confirmed, but we're quite sure it's Jackie. His body was found over on the Moose Jaw."

"Where's that?" Nicky was near tears.

"Just over the mountains to the south of town. We're told he hunted over there on occasion with his brother and Jong Min-jun. The evidence seems to suggest Jong may have been the killer. You wouldn't know anything about that would you?" O'Kelly smoothly segued into interrogation mode.

"We don't know any Jong...whatever his last name is," Danielle insisted.

O'Kelly turned to Nolan who had just come down the stairs.

Nolan said, "All the rooms are empty, except the one at the end of the hall. I'd say these two young ladies share that one. If the guys lived here, they've cleared out."

Once again, the astonishment on the girls' faces appeared to be genuine.

"So," Sergeant O'Kelly resumed. "Let's get it straight about the Korean. Did one of your roommates go by the name of John Young?"

The girls looked at one another for just a second, then both nodded. "Yes," Nicky confirmed. "This is John's house. At least he pays the rent. We met him down in Anchorage at a party he threw for Chinese New Year. We hit it off so we came up here with him."

Danielle, too, appeared ready to cooperate. "John was here for a while last night. He was supposed to meet us over at The Cherry Orchard, but he never showed. We came home after the bar closed and crashed. I didn't look in the guys' rooms, did you Nicky?"

Nicky was chewing her lip now. "What?" she looked at Danielle – "I mean, no, I thought they were all asleep." She lit another cigarette, took a deep drag, and blew out the smoke. "We haven't seen Damon or Jackie since night before last. You don't think John offed them both do you?"

O'Kelly decided to play it straight. "It's certainly possible. Your friends had been poaching bears all winter. The Korean was probably the ring leader. If he thought the Sam brothers had become expendable, he may have killed them both. We have reason to believe he killed another of his business associates down in Anchorage back in March. We were quietly looking for him regarding that killing, but he had no way of knowing it. He must have had some other reason for departing Chekov so hurriedly."

The old Trooper could see Nicky's mind working. She said, "John killed someone in Anchorage too?"

O'Kelly told her. "It looks that way. Do you know where he was in mid-March?"

Danielle appeared to be searching what was left of her memory. Nicky said. "He wasn't here on St. Patrick's Day. I know that for sure. Jackie and Damon treated us to green beer and some stringy red meat and potatoes over at that Irish place on Ninth Ave. We go there a lot. Everyone asked us where he was, but none of us knew. He came back a couple days later."

"Thank you," O'Kelly maintained his courteous posture. Their information did not put Jong in Anchorage for the Malachenko murder, but it was something. They seemed willing to talk, but he decided to give them another little nudge.

"I should warn you that if Jong is still at large in the vicinity, you could be in some danger. He has a history of cutting ties with his old friends with a knife. If you know anything that might pose a threat to him, he could come back."

Danielle went pale, but Nicky just shook her head. "We don't know anything he's been up to. We never asked, and he never told."

O'Kelly considered that for a moment. "How about Damon or Jackie? They never mentioned the bear poaching?"

"Not to me," Nicky said. She turned and looked at Danielle.

"Me neither," Danielle stated emphatically. "All they ever told us was that they liked to hunt and fish. Who doesn't, up here?"

O'Kelly could see further questions would be fruitless. He turned to Nolan, "We'll put out a BOLO for Damon and Jong this afternoon. Maybe get his passport photo on the wire."

"BOLO?" Danielle thought that was some kind of necktie.

Nicky rolled her eyes. "B-O-L-O! It's cop talk for 'Be On the Lookout'. Duh!"

Danielle wrinkled her brow. "Oh, yeah. I guess I knew that."

O'Kelly ignored them. "Trooper Nolan," he said in his best sergeant voice. "Please contact Larson and have him pick me up out front. You remain with these charming young ladies and take down their personal data. I'll get the search for Damon and Jong rolling."

Nolan keyed his handset to raise Larson.

O'Kelly returned his attention to the girls. "Please remain in town until we've completed your background checks. It shouldn't take long, we'll be in touch."

"Will you tell us, if you find Damon?" Nicky appeared very concerned about the younger brother's disappearance.

O'Kelly nodded. "We'll let you know if he turns up." With that he went out the door.

***

Larson pulled up just as O'Kelly reached the street. "Anybody home, or did you guys just kick in the door?" he asked as he drove to the next intersection and turned left, toward the station.

"Remember those two new girls in town?" Sgt. O'Kelly asked. We looked at them for the crack epidemic a while back. They let us in."

Larson had just joined the ranks last autumn, but O'Kelly sized him up as smart and dependable. The kid didn't miss much.

Larson said, "Yeah, I remember. We just got interested in them when your snitch dimed the Simpson kid as the pusher. Who'd a figured, eh?"

O'Kelly smiled and looked out the windshield. Larson had a propensity for using TV cop jargon. "Same young ladies. Anyway, Jong and Damon seem to have packed their things and departed. In fact, Damon might turn out to be another of Jong's victims."

Larson shook his head sadly. "I knew both the Sam brothers. Jackie was a jerk, but Damon seemed okay. I hope you're wrong about him."

The young trooper dropped his sergeant back at the office then returned to patrol. O'Kelly went inside and immediately put in a call to Fairbanks.

Mournful George was manning Hard Case's desk in his absence. "Gleason," he answered the phone.

"Good afternoon, George," O'Kelly said. "We came up empty on Jong and the younger Sam. Two girls they've been shacked up with over on Pushkin Street said the Korean was there last evening, but they haven't seen Damon in a couple days."

"Not good," Mournful George said. "The boss was hoping we'd have them in custody when he gets back from the Moose Jaw."

"I know," O'Kelly told him. "I was too. Guess it's time to put out an arrest warrant for them both."

"Kees told me to hold off until we get a positive ID on Jackie Sam. He should be back in Fairbanks by five. He'll check in from the Medical Examiner's office. You probably won't see anything on the wire until tomorrow morning."

"Fair enough. Take care, George."

"You too, Michael."

***

Hard Case called him early the next day. "Mornin' Michael. George tells me our boys flew the coop. We just got confirmation from the ME that the body was Jackie Sam. Cause of death was never in doubt, but he confirmed that too."

O'Kelly sipped at a cup of coffee. "Good. Now you can send out the alert on Jong and Damon."

"We're going to focus on Jong for the time being," Hard Case said. "If Damon's with him, we'll pop them both together. But, I have a feeling Damon's either dead, or he high-tailed it before Jong could stick a knife in him."

O'Kelly thought about that for a moment. "Yeah, that's probably the best approach. We don't have anything solid on Damon anyway. He's really just a person of interest at this point. But, something came up in Nolan's interview with the girls yesterday that you should pass along to your pal O'Neill."

Hard Case said cautiously, "What do the girls know about Gus?"

"Maybe nothing," O'Kelly conceded. "But, I just finished reading Nolan's report. He asked them what they could tell him about the bear poaching. Both young ladies denied having any knowledge of the poaching operation. However, one of them said Damon got pretty drunk the night before he disappeared and told them a creepy story about a guy and a bear that killed each other out on the Moose Jaw. He insisted that this guy and the bear are still walking around out there – that neither of them stayed dead. Jong got real excited and said he wanted to go find that bear and kill him right. Damon warned him if he hunted the 'ghost bear' the bear would hunt him."

"Okay," Hard Case said. "What makes you think he was talking about Gus and that three-toed monster he tangled with last year?"

"Well," O'Kelly went on. "The girls said Jong couldn't stop asking about it. In their words, he kept 'obsessing' over it. The last thing they remember was Jackie telling Jong to keep away from the guy's cabin. He told him 'Old Uncle' said the guy's name was Gus, and he couldn't be killed either. Jong just laughed and said The Cobra could kill Gus and the ghost bear so they'd both stay dead. They assumed he was talking about himself because of the ring."

Hard Case's voice sounded tight. "They actually used Gus' name?"

170

O'Kelly confirmed it. "Yep. You know any other Gus that has a cabin on the Moose Jaw?"

"No," Hard Case admitted. "They were talking about O'Neill alright. But, drunken death threats rarely live to see the next day."

"The girls said Jong wasn't drunk. They suspected he may have snorted a little coke on occasion, but he never had more than one drink. And whenever he became obsessed with an idea, he never let it go. If he said he was going after Gus, sooner or later, he would do it," O'Kelly said flatly.

"Ah, shit," Hard Case groaned. "I'll warn Gus. Thanks for letting me know."

Chapter 30

As Gus had expected, Morgan was in the cabin when he returned to The Varmitage late that afternoon. He stuck his head in the door and said, "You have a visitor awaiting your adoration in the sled."

She pushed past him on the porch and bounded down the steps. Gus shook his head, smiled, and followed. "He was pretty quiet on the way up," he told her. "But maybe I just couldn't hear him over the engine noise. Why don't you work some of your magic with him before we open the cage door? I'd rather not lose a limb this late in the day."

Morgan knelt in the snow next to the sled and looked in. "There you are!" she said in her low, melodious voice. "I wondered when you'd come back to see me."

It did not surprise Gus to see Bosworth amble slowly to the front of the cage and begin rubbing his jaws on the bars. She opened the door and lifted him out and cradled him in her arms like a mother with a baby. "Look at you," she murmured. "You've been eating well, I see." She rubbed his exposed underbelly as she crooned softly to him. Bosworth closed his dark eyes in apparent ecstasy and burrowed his head into the crook of her arm. She took him into the cabin.

Gus remained outside for a while to give Morgan a little time alone with her oversized kitty. He stowed the travel cage under the porch, loaded all his logging tools back in the sled with the two jerry cans of gasoline, and covered the Polaris' engine with the blanket before going inside to warm up. It had been a long, cold day. He checked his watch and figured Haywood and Hard Case were probably halfway back to Fairbanks with Jackie Sam's body.

As he hung his coat on the wall peg and kicked off his boots, Morgan held a finger up to her lips and looked down at the sleeping cat in her lap. Gus almost laughed out loud. He wondered how the good Dr. Jennings would ever get him back aboard the airplane.

Since he'd been admonished to avoid making noise, he went to the counter and poured himself a whiskey. He looked over at Morgan to see if she wanted one also. She shook her head and continued to stroke the big Maine Coon cat's fur. Old Bosworth never had it so good.

Hard Case had brought him a copy of today's Fairbanks Daily News Miner so he retrieved it from his coat pocket and sat down for a drink and a read. He didn't have it so bad himself, he thought.

***

He had read through the headline news, the business section, and was scanning the sports page when a heavy thump shook the floor planks. He looked over and saw that His Eminence had finished his nap and was checking out the cabin. Gus assumed he'd find everything in order.

"Now I'll join you for that drink," Morgan said.

Gus folded the newspaper and deposited it in the wood box. They usually banked the fire before they went to bed and there were plenty of coals left in the morning with which to get a new one started. But, sometimes he had to get one going from scratch; the newspaper would come in handy.

He went to the counter, poured two fingers of Dew into Morgan's glass and refilled his own. He took hers to her where she sat in the rocking chair near the stove.

She thanked him and took a delicate sip. "I expected you back earlier. Were there complications?"

"No," he told her. "Not really." He gave her a blow-by-blow of that afternoon's activities while they enjoyed their cocktails. He had just finished telling her about Hard Case's struggling through the snow on his walk into the crime scene when Bosworth reappeared from under the bed.

"Well," Gus asked the cat, "does everything appear to be as you left it?"

Bosworth studied him for a few seconds, after which he ambled back over to Morgan and curled up under her rocker.

She smiled, "I guess you don't rate an answer."

"Guess not," Gus said. "If you rock on his tail, he might have something to say."

They sat quietly for a time, listening to the fire popping softly in the little green stove, and Bosworth's contented log-sawing.

"What did Hard Case have to report regarding the other two poachers?" Morgan asked.

"He called his pal O'Kelly over in Chekov last night and told him to round them up," Gus told her. "I'll check in with him in the

173

morning to see if they had any luck. I'd feel a lot more comfortable if that little Korean prick was behind bars."

Since Gus had lost a full day of logging, he was eager to get at it again. He told Morgan he would head up to the burn right after breakfast in the morning. With that in mind, they ate an early dinner, played a game of chess, had a nightcap and turned in. Bosworth joined them and made himself a cozy nest at the foot of the bed.

Chapter 31

The little Korean prick, as Gus called him, awoke at first light after his second night on the cot in his rented storage unit. He had not slept well. Having spent the previous day cooped up in the windowless steel building had made him restless. He had come to enjoy the excitement of the bear hunts and the rides over the mountains in the bitter cold. The prospect of another day of dormancy weighed heavily upon his spirit. He would have to find something to occupy his mind or he'd go stir-crazy.

Yesterday he had installed a fisheye peephole in the roll-up door just for something to do. It afforded him a view of the area directly in front of his unit but he had no way of knowing if anyone had visited one of the other units in the compound. He kept an ear out for the sound of an engine, but the wind rattling the metal panels of the roof would have covered all but the most powerful diesel. He desperately wanted to get outside and have a look around. He had seen a light snow falling through his fisheye in the afternoon, so anyone coming or going since would have left tracks. If he was going to risk it, he'd have to do it soon. The later it got in the day, the more likely someone would see him. He considered this, then decided to play it safe. He could get through another day.

He turned the radio on and adjusted the volume so it could not be heard beyond a few meters. He had listened to the news broadcast by the local AM station at the top of each hour throughout the day, but there had been no mention of Jackie or himself. He would do so today also. He set a pot of tea water on the hot plate. While he waited for it to boil, he used the chemical toilet in the corner then went through his morning stretching exercises.

He was just pouring his second cup of tea when the seven o'clock news came on. Again, there was nothing to interest or trouble him. He turned the radio off, ate a light breakfast and spent the next two hours cleaning his rifle, sharpening his knives, and checking the peep hole from time to time.

The nine o'clock news hit him like a hammer blow.

"Good morning, Chekov. This is Aaron Hatcher with the news. Our lead story today involves the murder of a long-time Chekov resident, and the manhunt for his killer. Details immediately following this commercial message."

Jong Min-jun sat in stunned silence for a moment, his mind racing. Every second might count now. He wrapped his knives and whetstone in a towel and tossed them in a plastic bucket. He knew he might have to leave quickly so he began frantically loading his things into the rear of the Jeep as he waited for the interminable commercials to end.

'How the hell had they found Jackie's body already? Who had found it? Chill out man – stay calm. Maybe it wasn't Jackie. There were a lot of people in Chekov; it could have been someone else. The reporter hadn't said the murder victim was a man; it could have been a woman. And it sounded like they knew who the killer was – even if they found Jackie, the evidence he had left behind pointed to that guy named...'

Aaron Hatcher's voice came back on the air and interrupted The Cobra's speculation. He was brief and to the point, naming no names, but removing any doubt in Jong's mind that the victim had been Jackie. The body had been found in the woods off Moose Jaw Creek by a snowmobiler who lived nearby.

"Bastard!" Jong hissed. 'That fucking Gus guy found Jackie and got his knife back. He probably replaced it with another one that couldn't be traced to him,' he thought. 'Now he's fucked everything up. The Troopers will have already gone to the house and talked to those two crack-head bitches, so they'll know about me. They'll be watching the road out of town. Shit! I'll have to lay low here until things settle down,' he thought. 'When the time is right, I'll go south.'

* * *

The Cobra suffered through two more days in the confines of the storage unit. He tuned into the local radio station obsessively every hour, on the hour. Each time he heard Aaron Hatcher's voice, his anxiety level soared and he literally held his breath until he was certain nothing new had broken in the case. As soon as Hatcher's report ended, he would click off the radio, and lay spread-eagle with his back flat on the concrete floor until his heart rate returned to normal.

When his vital functions stabilized enough to stop the muscle spasms in his legs and arms, he would go back to the cot, do

176

a line of coke, and plot revenge against the assholes that had so disrupted his life – Damon and the two sluts, and that Gus bastard. 'Hell, he'd even kill the fucking ghost bear if he found him. Kill 'em all!' he thought and smiled. In the background of his mental violence, the music played on. It was Queen again.

'Thump...thump...thump...Another one bites the dust.'

At the end of the fourth day, he had lost all sense of reality. He'd snorted the last of his cocaine after the evening news, just to give himself a boost. It seemed to clear his mind and restore his confidence. 'Gotta get moving,' he thought. 'Yes! Time to roll! Drive all night down to the Kenai. Now!'

He threw open the overhead door, climbed behind the wheel of the Jeep and drove out into the semidarkness of the night. He was nearly to the highway before he remembered he had not closed the storage unit behind him.

"Mother fucker!" he screamed aloud as he threw the Jeep into a skidding one hundred-eighty degree turn. The road surface was still nothing but hard packed snow and the vehicle reversed polarity so quickly, he felt a rush of exhilaration when he realized his headlights were aimed directly back up the compound's entrance road. He let out a howl of delight and pounded on the steering wheel.

"Sweet!" he congratulated himself as he drove back to his rental unit to close and lock the door.

Chapter 32

Old Blue Eye liked to watch Gus work. He spent many hours downstream at the old burn where Gus was harvesting logs for his bunkhouse. Gus could not see him, of course. The old shaman thought it would be bad manners to interrupt the rhythm of his labors. He liked the confident way Gus approached each tall trunk, and the sure, but careful way he moved the heavy logs on the slippery hillside. It also pleased him that Gus took time to speak to the raven. He did this often while he worked, sometimes asking the raven for advice, or explaining what he was doing. He showed great respect for his fellow creatures. Gus, he thought, lived very much according to the old ways of his people. He killed only what he would eat – the old man had seen him give many fish back to the river. His two friends did this as well. It appeared that they would catch them just for fun, then let them go. Curious, but it did no harm. They were all good men. It was important to have good men in the valley.

Gus was more than just a good man though. His spirit was very strong. He recalled the swift and merciless way he had killed the man at the old lodge. When it was time for kindness, he showed it, but when it was time to kill – he killed.

The seed of an idea began to sprout in the old man's mind. Maybe it was time for Gus to kill again. He'd have to think about that. He had to think about talking to the big Trooper too – but not today. Today he had to use all his mental powers to journey back up to the headwaters. It was a long way home, and the trip always tired him.

As he was taking his leave, he heard Gus say to the raven, "Where are you off to you old rascal? I thought you might help me drop another spar."

Chapter 33

As Morgan had foretold, the ice began breaking up on the Moose Jaw in mid-May. Gus had stopped bringing logs down from the burn the previous week. During his daily runs up and down the river he had noticed subtle changes in the character of the ice beneath him. As cracks became visible and the surface softened, he decided it was time to quit. Morgan agreed. There was no point in taking unnecessary risks for a few more logs. He had stockpiled more than enough to build the bunkhouse and extend the porch on the cabin.

When he had staked out the footprint for the bunkhouse he had made sure it was well above the high water mark of the river. He hoped this year's runoff would not set a new record and wash away his logs.

"You needn't worry," Morgan told him. "They'll be high and dry."

"If you say so," he said, "who am I to doubt it. Looks like I can put the Polaris out to pasture for the summer and get cracking with the chainsaw. I have a lot of logs on the rip pile to mill into planks."

She gave him a hug. "You can probably stop looking over your shoulder for a couple of weeks too."

"What do you mean?" Gus asked, knowing full well the answer.

"You've been worried about Jong Min-jun ever since Hard Case told you he was still at large. Now that the ice has broken up he won't be able to come in here on a snow machine, and with the river roaring as it is, he won't be able to come in by boat either."

Gus smiled sheepishly. "You don't miss much do you?" He pulled her to him and kissed her forehead.

She hugged him tighter. "You're pretty easy to read. But, now you can relax. Why don't you take the rest of the day off and we'll have a picnic lunch out on the porch and enjoy the sunshine."

"Why not?" he decided. "I think it only appropriate to celebrate breakup. I believe it's an official Alaskan holiday. If it isn't, it should be."

***

Over the next few weeks, Gus spent the cool mornings ripping logs into planks, and in the warm afternoons he worked on the pad for the bunkhouse. With the runoff from snow melt and the almost daily rains the water rose a few inches each day, and by the first of June the Moose Jaw was in full spate. He would often take a break from his work, settle on a stump and smoke his pipe while marveling at the thunderous power of the roiling river as it swept past The Varmitage carrying huge logs and whole trees downstream. He was relieved to see them pass by. If one hung up on a snag or big rock, others would pile against it to form a log jam. He and Haywood had seen many such jams during their autumn floats down from the headwaters, and inevitably the river had cut a new channel around these natural dams. He was perfectly happy with the current topography of his section of the valley. A log jam would present a significant threat to his property.

Just as he had done while laying the foundation for the cabin, Gus positioned large rocks at the corners of the bunkhouse pad and three more to support the mid-span weight of the girder logs. The ground was soft now, so he had no trouble dislodging them with a long steel digging bar and rolling them into place. He positioned them squarely using the time honored three-four-five formula of the Pythagorean Theorem which he had committed to memory in high school geometry class. No high-tech equipment was required. All one needed was a tape measure.

Leveling them was a bit trickier. He employed the same water-level he had devised the previous year. It was nothing more than a length of clear surgical tubing marked with a black Sharpie a few inches from each end. He secured one end at the corner he used as his baseline and the other at each remaining corner in turn. He had a pretty good eye, so when he thought he had a given foundation rock close to level with his reference point, he'd fill the tube with water then raise or lower his working section until the water at both ends found the black mark on the tubing. Since water seeks its own level, he would set the top of each foundation stone to the water line.

He had plenty of gas and bar oil for the chainsaw so as the mornings grew warmer with each new day, and he had finished the foundation work, he began milling planks fulltime. By mid June, he had laid in enough board stock to floor and roof the new structure and build Morgan's porch extension as well. Whenever he finished ripping a plank that had an interesting grain, or a particularly pleasing color, he set it aside in a special stack to be used for the door, shutters, and two more tables.

Morgan understood he loved the physical labor and was happiest while working with his hands. She knew how much satisfaction he had derived from the building of the cabin last summer, and she could hear the excitement in his voice each evening as he told her of the day's progress.

For the most part she left him to his work, but each day, she would take him his lunch and they would sit on stumps, eat and discuss the ever-changing nature of the river. The Moose Jaw had crested early in the month and receded a few inches each day as the summer solstice approached. Every few days they would walk up the overland trail and check the water level over the gravel bar that served as their landing strip. By the third week of June, they could see the rocks on the upper half of the bar, and it appeared that a plane would be able to land there no later than the solstice – the same day Haywood had brought Gus in the previous year.

As the days passed and she watched the piles of lumber grow higher, she could also see the changes in Gus. He had softened a little over the long winter in Fairbanks, but the hours running the chainsaw and wrestling logs had hardened him. His forearms had become corded with muscle and his grip was positively viselike. Sometimes in the evening as he kneaded goose grease into her bare skin, she would have to remind him to go gently. He had no idea how powerful his hands had become.

She loved the pleasant routine that had settled upon their days in the late spring. Bosworth, who hated the sound of the chainsaw, kept to the cabin until Gus had finished work for the day. Nevertheless, he had a routine too, and would condescend to join them of an evening out on the porch for cocktail hour – and snacks. Late each afternoon, as the sun worked its way toward the western mountains, Morgan would talk quietly to him as she set out drinks and arranged delicacies on a platter. Bosworth would become particularly solicitous toward her whenever the intoxicating smell of smoked salmon perfumed the air inside the cabin. He would abandon his post under the rocker and accompany her as she moved gracefully between counter and porch. She had to take care to not step on him as she went about her end-of-day ritual; Bosworth, wending his way around and through her ankles, wanted to make sure she was fully aware of his presence. Sometimes she would favor him with the music of her laughter and the occasional offering of food. Humans could be tolerated when they observed protocol.

Even Gus was coming around nicely. Every now and then, when he wasn't disturbing the peace with his infernal gasoline engines, he'd come in to the cabin and take his shotgun down from the pegs over the door. Bosworth never missed the significance of this, but he invariably feigned indifference. Still, the sound of a far off shotgun blast would instantly stimulate his salivary glands and he could not help but position himself on the porch steps where Gus would have to notice him as he came down from the woods. Sometimes he would return to the cabin with a hare or game bird, and he'd always give Bosworth the heart and liver. The big cat had found these grizzly morsels to be quite to his liking when devoured raw. They stirred an atavistic savagery deep inside him. As soon as Gus would place them before him, he'd snatch them up and disappear underneath the porch where he would tear and chew while growling a low and menacing warning.

Chapter 34

From the top of the ridge, the bear known to Gus as Trilogy, and to Old Blue Eye as Broken Foot, studied the mountains to the west where his river was born. His eyes followed the shadowy depression coming down from the high country until it was clearly recognizable as the valley over which he had held sway since…well, perhaps from the beginning of time.

Off to the southwest the salmon were just starting up the great river from the sea. They would follow whatever ancient imperative that drove them to their spawning grounds. Soon each tributary, each feeder stream, would teem with them as they pressed on through the gauntlet of bears and eagles on their way upstream where they would spawn and fight and die. As it was every year, the spice of anticipation was palpable in the valley as his tribe began to line the banks of the river. Every fiber of his being told him that this was as it should be. Things were in order. The cycles of the seasons followed their proper patterns. It was neither a good thing, nor a bad thing – it was just things as they should be. There was no chord of disharmony. The bear killers were gone now. There was the man, of course - the man and the cabin he had built. He had been an annoyance for a time, but now that they had tested one another, and let one another's blood, he was beginning to fit into the scheme of things. Soon he would be subsumed into the valley's essence like the woman and all the others that had come before them. In the end, the valley – his valley – was an ever evolving distillate of all things that had happened in the churn of its past.

Down in the valley, the man took time out from his labors to enjoy a drink of cool water as he studied the hills across the creek from his cabin. The woman came out and sat on the top step of the cabin's porch.

"Trident?" she asked the man.

He nodded, still studying the high country.

She followed his gaze to the ridge across the creek. "He's been keeping pretty close of late."

"Yes," the man said. "I'm sure he has his reasons. Perhaps he's just watching over you."

"Or you," she said.

Chapter 35

June, 2001
The Varmitage

Although still quite early, it was full light by the time Gus and Morgan rolled out of bed following their morning dalliance. The sun hardly dipped below the horizon during the long days of summer. Even then, there was always a spectral luminosity that hung in the air over the river so one could discern the soft silhouettes of the spruce trees that lined the far bank. Gus paid his devotions to the little building behind the cabin, then walked the riverbank as he did each morning, checking for tracks. Morgan remained inside and, although the day promised to be warm, she built a small fire in the stove to heat water and cook the morning meal. As hard as Gus worked each day, she liked to send him off with a hearty breakfast.

The river was running clear now, just a few inches above its midsummer depth. Another day or two and he would be able to begin his morning ablutions while standing ankle-deep in the swift current. He had developed this morning ritual last year when he was out here alone. He'd take his pistol, a plastic bottle of biodegradable camp soap and a towel down to the creek, strip off his shirt and wade out a few paces into the streambed. After recovering from the shock of the first splash of icy water in his face, he would lather up head, arms and torso, and give them all a good rinse. It was an exhilarating way to begin one's day.

He recalled the morning after he had found Morgan half drowned on the bank, when he had first encountered Trilogy. He'd been foolish enough to go down to the creek without his pistol, and had just finished washing his hair when he saw the enormous grizzly's reflection upon the water. It seemed so long ago now. So much had transpired since then – the bear had stalked and attacked him back in the woods; he had killed the beast, but suffered a good deal of damage in the fight. Three long ribbons of hard white scar tissue served silent reminder of the bear's perpetual presence. He scanned the ridge across the creek. 'He's up there right now,' Gus thought. 'I don't know how I know – but I know.'

"Ah," he said as he came through the door. "Coffee and bacon – nothing better to start off a morning."

Morgan was flipping eggs in the cast iron skillet. She cocked an eye at him.

"Nothing?" she queried.

"Well," he reconsidered, "almost nothing."

She favored him with a smile. "Two minutes," she said. "Pour yourself a cup of coffee and go to table. His lordship has already broken his fast so I'm free to serve you myself."

Gus shot a glance at Bosworth, who was now enjoying a post breakfast nap under the rocker. He went to the stove, gave Morgan a peck on the cheek, and filled his cup.

"Need a refill?" he asked.

"I assume you refer to my coffee cup." She flashed her green eyes at him playfully.

Gus chuckled. "That I did," he said. "Silly me."

She took time to kiss him on the lips. "Sit," she commanded and filled a plate with eggs, bacon and fried potatoes.

He sat. And while he enjoyed his breakfast, she asked him what he had planned for the day.

"Well," he told her. "I've gone as far as I can go without some imported muscle. All the prep for the bunkhouse is done. But, I'll need help setting the first two courses of logs and the big girders. My plan for the day is charging the batteries for the phone and maybe a little bird hunting up at the beaver ponds. How does ptarmigan and rice sound for dinner?"

"Sounds just right," Morgan told him. "And I'm sure our resident feline would not object. He seems to have developed a taste for woodland fowl."

They both looked over at Bosworth, who graced them with a half opened eye.

"I don't believe I've ever seen him so enthusiastic," Gus said.

Bosworth closed his eye and resumed his slumber.

Gus laughed. "One of these days that cat of yours is going to have to start earning his keep."

"He will," Morgan assured him. "He will."

After dinner that evening, Gus called Hard Case on the satellite phone.

Hard Case picked up on the second ring. "The infamous Fergus O'Neill, I presume."

Gus smiled. It was good to hear the gruff baritone voice of his friend.

"Guilty as charged," Gus admitted. "And how are things with Alaska's most celebrated detective?"

"Could be worse, I suppose," Hard Case answered. "But, I don't know how. I'm ready for a few days away from the office. You up for a visitor?"

"As a matter of fact, my clairvoyant friend, that's the reason for this call. The landing strip has reemerged from the depths, and now stands high and dry above the water. The creek is still running high, but it's clear, disturbed only by the feeding rings of hungry fish. And I'm itching to lay the first logs for the bunkhouse but can't shift them alone."

Hard Case chuckled. "Haywood said you'd be about ready to start construction. He wants to fly in on Thursday to hoist a jar with you to celebrate your first anniversary as a bush rat and get the bunkhouse going. I'll come along too. The three of us should be able to get the base logs set."

"Perfect," Gus said. "I was hoping you'd both come out. I'll get the wall tent set up tomorrow. Bring in your sleeping bags and we'll rough it like I did before the cabin was complete. How long can you guys stay?"

"Haywood's going to stay through Tuesday. I'm due back in the office Tuesday morning so Caldwell will pick me up Monday around noon. Mournful George can handle anything that crosses my desk while I get a little R&R."

"Excellent," Gus told him. "We can get a good start on the bunkhouse with three full days. By the way, anything new on our Korean miscreant?"

Hard Case snorted into the phone. "Not much. We know he cleared out the day we pulled the warrant for him. Our guys down in Anchorage found an old Jeep Cherokee abandoned in the parking lot at Portage Glacier. Either he was wearing gloves or wiped the whole vehicle down real good. But the gas cap had a clear thumb print on it that turned out to be his. So we figure he's down on the

Kenai or he doubled back to Anchorage. If he's still in Alaska, he'll turn up sooner or later."

"Too bad," Gus commiserated. "I'd rest a lot easier if he were in the pokey."

"I hear you," Hard Case agreed. "And now that you've reminded me – were you able to set up a meet with Old Blue Eye? Pokey Brewster probably doesn't have much time left on his clock. I'd like to be able to give him something before he checks out."

"Morgan spoke with him the evening Jackie Sam was killed, but I don't know if she asked him to meet with you. I'll find out and let you know when you get here."

"Please do," Hard Case said. "I want to put the Rainbow Lodge murders behind me once and for all. Anyway, I'm sure you have a long grocery list for us. You talk and I'll write."

Gus consulted his yellow legal pad and read it to his friend, pausing after each item until Hard Case had grunted something that sounded like "got it". When he had finished reading his supply list, he said, "Oh, and add a couple of one pound cans of Captain Black pipe tobacco, would you? I'm down to the fine powder."

Hard Case said, "The white can with the black label, right?"

"That's the one," Gus confirmed. "I'll see you Thursday."

"Yep," Hard Case told him. "It wouldn't hurt to have some libations awaiting our arrival. A bush landing with Haywood always requires an immediate restorative."

Gus gave him an appreciative laugh. "Don't I know it?"

With that they rung off and Gus returned the phone to its carrying case.

***

Morgan brought him a bottle of Heineken. "Thursday, then?"

Gus accepted the beer. The cold glass against the calloused skin of his palm surprised him. "Ice?" he inquired. "I don't recall the floor cooler being so cold. How did you manage ice?"

She smiled and kissed him on the forehead. "I have my ways."

"Indeed you do. Speaking of which – were you able to arrange a meeting between Hard Case and Old Blue Eye?"

She went to the stove and poured herself a cup of tea. "We didn't discuss it," she said. "But I think he knows Hard Case wants to talk to him. When he's ready, I'm sure he'll pop up."

"Perfect turn of phrase," Gus observed.

He stood up and opened the door. "Bring your tea outside. We can sit on the steps and enjoy the evening."

When they had settled in Gus filled and lit his pipe. She loved the vanilla aroma of the smoke and leaned her head against his shoulder so it wafted past her lovely face.

"Ummm," she purred in contentment.

"Ummm, what?" Gus put an arm around her.

"Ummm everything," she said. "These past weeks have been wonderful. It's good to have you back where you belong."

Gus did not respond. He just sat quietly enjoying his pipe and loving the woman beside him. He did belong here, this was home. He thought back to the afternoon last autumn when they had lazed on these same steps and she had given him those special flies she tied. Everything she did was special, he thought.

Aware of his thoughts, she placed her tea cup on the step behind them and hugged him with both arms. "I remember," she said. "You were somewhat dumbstruck when you realized what made them special." She had tied him three caddis flies with one of her own red hairs mixed into the deer hair wings. The red hairs had not been of the long variety.

He laughed. Her ability to see everything that passed through his mind no longer surprised him. "I must admit, I was a bit flabbergasted when I recognized your secret ingredient for what it was. In any event, the grayling were certainly delighted with them."

She gave him a squeeze, then released him and bounded up the steps and into the cabin. "Hold that thought," she said as she disappeared through the door.

When she reappeared, she was holding his fly rod. "I affixed one to your tippet when you were talking to Hard Case. As you told him, the grayling have been feeding all afternoon. Why don't you have a go at them? I'll watch from here."

He finished his beer, deposited the empty bottle on the porch, and accepted the rod from her. "Is this 'Special' as special as the others?"

She gave him a big smile. "Absolutely," she said. "I put a little bit of myself in each one."

***

It had been a good afternoon on the water. The grayling could not resist Morgan's special flies and Gus caught and released a half

188

dozen before invoking the mercy rule on their behalf. He'd enjoyed equal success among the birds and returned to the cabin with two fat ptarmigan for dinner.

That night, as they lay in bed, Morgan said. "Only two nights left before your friends arrive."

"I know," he said wistfully. "I suppose we should make the most of them."

And they did.

Chapter 36

As Gus had promised, he had libations ready to hand on Thursday when Haywood and Hard Case touched down on the landing strip. He had to admit, Haywood was getting better. Just one year ago to the day, in his little Piper Clipper, he had plummeted out of the sky, hit the bar hard, bounced twice and barely managed to bring it to a stop with the tundra tires hub deep in the waters of Moose Jaw Creek. This time, although he came in steep as always, he only bounced once before settling into a relatively sedate rollout. Perhaps the rented Cessna had better brakes.

While Haywood swung her around and taxied back down the bar, Gus poured three glasses of the "restorative" Hard Case had requested. He placed one glass each on three impressive spruce rounds he had arranged in a triangle earlier that morning. This was not simply the thoughtfulness of a gracious host; it was practicality. They were the three largest rounds he had cut out of a thirty foot drift log that had run aground precisely in the middle of the landing strip. Moving them any distance would have required equipment he did not have. It was all he could do to roll them off to the side far enough to provide Haywood sufficient room to land. There had been several other less formidable obstacles among all the post-runoff debris that littered the gravel bar, but the big log had required the chainsaw and peavey. It had taken him all morning to clear the assorted driftwood, sand-trapped brush and large rocks that had been deposited as the flood waters of spring receded. The big rocks, once dislodged and rolled into the creek, left holes that had to be filled. By the time he had finished, Gus thought he too could use a little restorative.

"What God hath brought!" Hard Case's deep voice boomed as he marched up from the parked airplane. "I see you Fergus O'Neill!"

Gus laughed and gave his stout friend a bear hug. "Isn't that *wrought*?" he asked.

"Of course it's rot. I'll be speaking gibberish for the rest of the day. Haywood scared the shit out of me coming over the pass. Damned fool spotted a herd of Dall Sheep and got so excited, he all but climbed out on a wing for a better look."

190

After Haywood completed his post landing routine, he hopped out onto the bar. As always, unfolding his lengthy frame after emerging from the cramped quarters of the cockpit took some time. He performed a few semi toe-touches, then, hands on hips gradually rose to his full height. He grinned and opened his mouth to speak, but Hard Case cut him off.

"Don't say it!" he beseeched.

Gus couldn't help himself. "How stiff are you, Haywood?" he shouted.

Haywood chortled. "Stiffer'n a weddin' dick!" He threw his head back and laughed out loud. "Homo fully erectus!"

"Perfect," Hard Case said flatly. "A homo with a hard on."

***

They sat on the spruce rounds and basked in the midday sun while enjoying ice cold beer and each other's company. They had toasted the coming days with one short whiskey before getting into the cooler. The solstice was the longest day of the year, and Gus wanted to get in four or five hours of construction work before their evening meal. They would officially declare cocktail hour after that.

"Looks like you had a busy morning, Fergus," Hard Case observed, indicating the long pile of driftwood, brush and rocks that lined each side of the landing strip.

"Yeah," Gus nodded. "I should have cleared this bar earlier, but it was still underwater a few days ago. I waited until this morning to let it dry out a little. It's still pretty muddy in spots."

"Well, thanks for the effort," Haywood said. "I've had bumpier landings on tarmac." He could see Hard Case was mentally preparing a witty retort so he quickly added, "Of course, the extra ballast in the passenger seat probably flattened out most of the high spots."

Gus smiled. Some things never changed. He hoped they never would.

Hard Case realized Haywood had trumped his ace before he had a chance to play it so he decided to change the subject.

"Old Blue Eye ever RSVP to my invite?" he asked Gus.

Gus sipped his beer and took a moment to fill his pipe. After it was lit to his satisfaction he said, "Not formally. But Morgan says he'll come around when he's ready. I guess you'll have to wait 'til he decides he's ready."

"I hope he hurries up about it," Hard Case said. "The nurse at Pokey's assisted living facility down in San Diego called me yesterday. He's slipping away fast. Won't take food or fluids, so they're feeding him intravenously now. She says it's only a matter of days."

"Sorry to hear that, Case. I'll pass it along to Morgan. Maybe she can speed things up a bit."

Haywood had remained silent while his two friends talked business. He was intrigued that Hard Case now appeared to accept Morgan's existence without reservation. He was discussing her as if she were just your typical hausfrau. He had brought Morgan a dozen roses, but had kept the box out of sight so Hard Case would not see it. He would present them to her when the time was right. The time would be right when Hard Case was otherwise engaged.

Gus finished his beer and put the empty back into the cooler. "Okay, boys," he stood up and brushed off the seat of his pants. "Party's over. Time to get to work. Let's shift some of your load up to the cabin, then I'll brief you on the bunkhouse project."

***

Bosworth was out on the porch when they came down the slope from the overland trail. Morgan, as was her habit, was not present – that is, she was nowhere to be seen.

Haywood rid himself of the cooler he had insisted he carry himself, went over to the cat and stroked the fur of its head.

"Hello there, old-timer. You're looking fat and prosperous. Someone's been taking good care of you I see."

Gus came up behind him and deposited two backpacks next to the cooler. "You'll break Morgan's heart when you take him back to civilization, you know."

"Won't be this trip," Haywood assured him. "I'd like to leave him here with you a bit longer. Providing, of course, he hasn't made a nuisance of himself."

A muffled whoop of delight penetrated the log walls of the cabin. They both smiled and looked back up the trail. Hard Case had just emerged from the woods at the top of the rise and was clearly too far off to have heard.

"I'll take that as a yes," Haywood said quietly.

"Yes," came a softly spoken reply from the other side of the wall.

"Well, old fellow," Haywood scratched Bosworth under his jaw bone affectionately, "it appears you've smitten another fair maiden – you dog you."

Bosworth stared at him blankly for a moment then dismissively closed his eyes and settled his chin on his big paws. Gus chuckled.

Haywood turned to him and shrugged. "A little veterinarian humor," he said. "Cats never appreciate it."

Hard Case came down the trail, plopped a large red river bag next to the backpacks then went over and settled down on the porch steps. He shook a Camel out of a crumpled pack and began the inevitable pat down of his pockets in search of a match. Haywood tossed him a pink disposable lighter.

Hard Case caught it in one of his beefy hands. He raised an eyebrow as if to say "What's this?".

Haywood said, "I have observed over the years that you suffer from the 'Can't Find My Fuckin' Matches Syndrome'. In my professional opinion, a lighter will ease your pain."

Hard Case looked dubiously at the object in his palm. "Why pink?" he inquired.

"Look around, Case," Haywood told him. "Everything out here is mud brown, tree green, or stone gray. You'll find it hard to lose a pink lighter."

Hard Case shook his head sadly as he lit his cigarette. "I don't lose my matches in the woods, Haywood," he said. "I just can never remember which pocket I put them in. Unless pink shows through my pocket liner, I still won't be able to find the damned thing."

Gus left them to their repartee and went into the cabin to fetch his bunkhouse plans. Morgan threw her arms around his neck the moment he closed the door.

"What...?" he began, but she planted a kiss full on his lips and held it for a long time. When she stepped back, she held a finger to her own lips in the universal signal to shush.

He shushed. He knew how much she had been dreading Bosworth's departure. Now that the cat would be staying on with them, he could see the childlike joy dancing in her green eyes. It made him smile.

He took his yellow legal pad off the shelf, kissed her quickly, and went out the door.

"Follow me, gentlemen," he ordered as he hopped off the edge of the porch and, plans in hand, marched off toward his log pile.

"You heard the man," Hard Case said. "No more dawdling."

They joined Gus at the bunkhouse pad where he explained how he wanted to go about placing the first logs on the stone piers.

"I scribed and notched all the ones we'll be setting this trip. And they're stacked in the order they'll be placed. We'll have to take the first one slow, just to fine tune our method."

Hard Case studied the logs. "They look pretty heavy. You sure we'll be able to lift them?"

Gus nodded. "Yeah. The base logs are the biggest, but we'll just roll them down the slope next to the foundation rocks, then all three of us will lift one end at a time and set them atop the piers. We'll do the creek-side long one first. When we get one end seated, you guys steady it while I wedge it in place – then we'll set the other end. I'll be able to pull the wedges once we get the first four locked in place with their notches."

"Sounds straight-forward enough," Haywood observed. "Let's give the first one a go."

"Okay," Gus said, putting on his leather gloves. "I'll man the safety rope, and each of you guys take one end of the log. Pull the wedge block out from under your downhill edge and gravity will do the rest. I'll let out the rope slowly to keep it from picking up too much steam, but keep on the uphill side of the log, just in case."

He waited while his two friends got in position, then threw a loop of his safety line around a stout spruce that would serve as his capstan just uphill of the log pile. "You guys ready?"

They both nodded that they were.

"Okay. I've got tension – pull your wedge blocks and call out when you're clear," he instructed.

Both men bent to their assigned task. "Clear!" they called out in unison.

Gus eased off on the tension and the big log rolled down the slope, its speed controlled by Gus' manipulation of the safety rope. When it had come to a stop against the foundation piers on the uphill side of the level pad, Gus let out some slack in the rope and tied it off to the 'dead-man'.

194

He walked down to the pad where Haywood and Hard Case awaited him.

"That went well," Haywood said.

Hard Case agreed. "Yeah. It was a lot easier than I imagined. What next?"

"Well," Gus told them, "this one has to go on the downslope side of the bunkhouse so we'll have to lift it over these piers and set it on the other side. Let's do one end at a time."

**

It took them only two hours to get the four base logs placed and locked into their notches. Gus made a few small adjustments to make sure all were level and the footprint was square, then suggested they take a break.

"Smoke 'em if you got 'em," he said, heading off toward the cabin. "Anyone up for a beer?"

"I never say no," Hard Case said as he produced the pink lighter from the first pocket he checked and lit a Camel.

"Same here," Haywood called after Gus. Then he turned his attention to Hard Case. "I do believe that lighter was the answer," he told him. "You located it without your customary full cavity search."

"My ass," Hard Case responded sourly.

Haywood looked hurt. "No need to be unpleasant."

Hard Case shook his head in resignation. "I had it in my hip pocket," he explained patiently. "My ass 'located' it when I sat down on this log."

Haywood unwrapped one of his cigars and began patting down his pockets. "Shit," he said.

Hard Case smiled but did not offer him a light. "Better get yourself a lighter," he said smugly. "They're all the rage. I'd recommend something in chartreuse."

Haywood glowered at him. "You got a problem with pink?"

"Not at all," Hard Case assured him. "I love pink. But, if you had a pink one too, we might get them confused."

Gus rejoined them and handed them each a bottle of beer. "You going to light that god-awful thing, or just chew it all day?" he asked Haywood.

"I can't find my matches and Case won't let me use his lighter."

Gus laughed out loud and handed him a lime green Bic disposable. Haywood was clearly astonished, but only momentarily. He looked at his two best friends with dismay.

"You fuckers set me up."

***

They worked straight through to seven o'clock that evening. When they finished setting the second course of short logs that abutted the door frame they decided to call it a day. With the walls now three logs high, and the door opening defined by thick, heavy planks, they could visualize the bunkhouse as if it were complete already.

"A good day's work gentlemen," Gus told them as they headed for the wall tent. "I think a proper thank you is in order. Let me buy you a drink before we dine."

"Capital idea," Hard Case enthused.

"You open the bar, boys," Haywood told them. "I'll fire up the camp stove and get dinner going. Pasta alla Jennings tonight. I also brought in a pound of last year's caribou burger to beef up the tomato sauce, and of course a baguette to sop up the dregs."

***

Gus had pitched their camp the previous day. The big Cabela's wall tent could easily accommodate three occupants. He had broken down the fold-away metal bunks into two free-standing beds. He intended to let his guests have one each while he slept in his sleeping bag on the inflatable camp mattress. But, they had insisted he spend his nights in the comfort of his own bed.

"Three's a crowd," Hard Case had grumbled. "Besides, I don't want to have to step over you every time I answer the call of nature in the night."

"And Case snores plenty loud enough without accompaniment," Haywood chimed in. "I won't get any sleep at all if you're both sawing logs through the wee hours."

Gus knew their objections were pure fabrication. They were good friends and wanted to afford him the opportunity to sleep in the cabin with Morgan.

"Very well," he told them. "If that's the way you want it, I won't argue."

***

The sun was still well above the western horizon when they finished dinner just after nine that evening. A short squall moved down out of the mountains and drove them inside the tent where they enjoyed drinks and smokes while sitting out the rain.

"Jesus, Haywood," Hard Case fanned the air. "You need to switch to cheroots or a pipe. Those sewer cured walrus turds you favor should be outlawed in civilized company."

Gus laughed. "At least they keep the mosquitoes at bay." He indicated a cloud of large flying insects that loomed just outside the tent flap. "The rains always bring out the big boys."

Haywood snorted derisively. "Hell, Gus, back home in Missouri we'd call these little fellas 'no seeums'. The mosquitoes down there get so big they can stand flatfooted and fuck a turkey!"

Hard Case closed his eyes and tried to dispel the outrageous vision Haywood had planted in his brain. It didn't work. He reopened his eyes and observed a moment of silence before he spoke. "Flatfooted," he said, not actually wanting confirmation.

Haywood winked at Gus. "Oh, I suppose a young one might have to tippy-toe a little if he were romancing a big Tom."

Gus shook his head in wonder at his friend's seemingly inexhaustible repertoire of hay-seed wit. Hard Case sipped his whiskey and studied Haywood as though he were beholding a recently arrived visitor from another solar system.

"Haywood," he said, "you never cease to amaze me. You've truly outdone yourself this time. We can only look forward to the next pearl you cast before us undeserving swine."

When the rain stopped and the clouds moved down the valley, the sun reappeared and the grayling began rolling out in the stream. They broke out their fly-rods and spent the next two hours at the water's edge. As always, the feeding frenzy ended suddenly, and the surface of the creek became calm and flat. They went back to the tent and had a night cap before Gus returned to the cabin.

"Well, ladies," he told them as he finished his drink and stood up, "it's been a long day and we've a longer one ahead of us. I bid you goodnight."

***

"Flatfooted?" Morgan asked, delightfully scandalized. They had just gone to bed and Gus was telling her about his day.

He laughed quietly. "That's what the man said," he confirmed.

Chapter 37

Jong Min-jun's top agent on the Kenai Peninsula was a discredited hunting/fishing guide named Clive Nelson. Clive had run afoul of the fish and game laws on numerous occasions and consequently, lost his license to guide legally. This was a setback, of course, but there were other ways a man could make ends meet if he were willing to take some risks.

He operated an under-the-table air-taxi service out of a ramshackle barn behind his equally dilapidated fishing lodge on Crooked Creek just above its confluence with the Kasilof River. Somehow he had managed to retain his private pilot's license and he eked out a living transporting passengers who wished to avoid the legitimate air-taxis for reasons of their own. Since he flew under the radar, as it were, he ran a cash-only business. In the winter, of course, he poached bears for the Korean. He had been nearly destitute when John Young had offered him a chance to get back on his feet. He was glad he had signed on with him. After one good season of "harvesting" bear organs he was out of debt and could afford some long overdue maintenance on his old Super Cub. Things were looking up for Clive. John Young was his meal ticket and he hoped their arrangement would last for a while.

Jong had stopped to fill up with gas in Eagle River and called Clive's mobile. It was nine o'clock in the morning and Jong was strung out from his all night drive down from Chekov. He knew he couldn't keep going until he reached Kasilof. Clive answered on the second ring. When Jong explained what he needed, Clive suggested they meet at Portage Glacier where they could leave Jong's Cherokee and drive down to the Kenai together.

"You won't have a long wait. I can be there in about two hours," Clive assured him.

Jong consulted his roadmap before leaving Eagle River and committed the route through Anchorage to memory. All he had to do was keep to Highway 1 and it would eventually take him southeast down the Turnagain Arm of Cook Inlet all the way to Portage Glacier. He figured he could be there by ten-thirty if he didn't fall asleep at the wheel.

Clive was as good as his word. Jong parked the Jeep in the middle of the parking lot that served the glacier's welcome center and wiped down the interior just to make sure he hadn't left fingerprints. He also took a few minutes to wipe the exterior door handles and was busy cleaning the lift gate latch when Clive's battered old Suburban pulled into the space beside him. There were tourists arriving and leaving regularly, and some of the others were transferring coolers or fishing equipment between vehicles so they attracted no attention as they shifted Jong's things into the back of Clive's big rust bucket.

"You didn't ever register that thing in your own name did you?" Clive asked as they pulled out of the lot and headed south on the Seward Highway.

"No, it's still in the name of the guy I bought it from up in Central. I never even drove it except to the storage facility where I kept it."

"Good thinkin'," Clive told him. "So, what have you got yourself into that you couldn't tell me about over the phone?"

Jong gave him a reasonable facsimile of the truth, admitting to having killed Jackie, but attributing his action to a quarrel that got out of hand. He told him the law was calling it murder, but it had really been self defense. He didn't want one of his field agents thinking he might be a little too dangerous to work for. He needed Clive in his corner – at least until his trail went cold.

When they arrived at Clive's lodge in the early afternoon, Jong could see he had chosen the right place to disappear for a month or so. He hadn't seen any other structures on the way in, so he felt sure there wouldn't be an issue with nosy neighbors. The road into the property was nothing more than a four-wheel drive trail up a semi-dry creek bed so they'd be able to hear anyone coming in long before they got there. Since the lodge was situated right on the bank of Crooked Creek and there was a johnboat moored to the rickety dock, Jong had an escape route if it came to the point where he needed one.

Clive asked if he was hungry, but Jong said he'd snacked on the way down from Eagle River. He just wanted to get some sleep, so Clive showed him to a back room that was crammed with hunting and fishing equipment, boating accessories, outboard motor parts, giant coolers, and plastic gasoline cans. He waited in the doorway until Clive opened a path to the folding camp bed and cleared it of a jumble of life jackets, waders and coils of rope.

"Sorry about the mess," Clive apologized. "You didn't give me much warning. I'll get all this stuff out'a here after you've slept."

Jong said, "That's fine. I'm so tired, I could sleep on the floor if I had to."

He stretched out on the top of the wool blanket, still in his coat and boots, and was asleep before Clive closed the door.

***

Jong Min-jun did not awake until ten o'clock the next morning. He found the bathroom, brushed his teeth and showered until the water trickled to a stop, then went in search of Clive. He found him in the "galley" as he called it, having a cup of coffee while reading the newspaper.

"What happened to the water?" he asked his host.

"Pressure tank ran down," Clive said. "I should'a told you to take military showers. Sorry."

Jong noticed that the date on the top of the newspaper was today's. "You get the paper delivered?" he asked.

Clive shook his head. "No, I drove into town early this morning and picked up some supplies and the Anchorage Daily News. You better have a look – they got a picture of you on page three. Says you're wanted for murder." He refolded the newspaper and slid it across the table to Jong. "You want something to eat?"

Jong nodded his head absently, while he scanned the article near his picture. They had used a copy of his passport photo which had been very grainy to begin with. The physical description they gave was accurate, but he doubted anyone would recognize him from the photograph. The write up was short on details but it referred to him as Jong Min-jun a.k.a John Young and said he was being sought for the murder of Jackie Sam and also was 'a person of interest' in the death of Alexi Malachenko.

"Cereal okay, John? I can make up some instant oatmeal or something," Clive offered.

Jong set the paper aside. "Just coffee and toast will be enough. I don't eat much in the morning."

Clive lit a burner on the propane stove and placed two slices of bread on a Coleman "toaster" rack and set it on the stovetop to brown.

Jong observed this curiously. "You don't have a toaster?"

"Don't have no electricity if I don't run the generator," Clive explained. "The power lines don't run back in this far. But this little Coleman rig does a pretty good job on toast."

Jong had mixed feelings with regard to this bit of information. On one hand he was not overjoyed at the prospect of spending a month or more without electricity; on the other, he was pleased that the lodge was even more remote than he had realized.

The paper says your real name is Jong something or other. Is that right?"

"Yes," Jong admitted. "My American name is John Young but I think it best that you call me Lee when people are around. It's a very common name in Asia. It shouldn't make anyone suspicious."

Clive turned the toast on the wire rack and brought his guest a cup of coffee. "I'll call you that all the time so I don't slip up when it counts."

Jong smiled. "That's a good idea. From now on I'm Lee."

When the toast was golden brown on both sides Clive turned off the burner, transferred the slices to a plate and brought them to the table. "Here you go, Lee. I got butter or jam if you want."

"Jam," Jong sipped his coffee. It was black and very bitter. "And do you have milk and sugar for the coffee? I like it sweet."

Clive went to a shelf and brought back a tin of condensed milk and some packets of sugar. "This is all I got, but the condensed milk is pretty sweet by itself."

While Jong doctored his coffee and stirred, Clive asked him, "What's up with the Malachenko guy? It says they want to talk to you about his death."

Jong spread jam on his toast and took a bite before answering. "I don't know anything about that," he said.

Clive didn't want to press the issue; he didn't want to offend the guy that was the key to his future financial success. Still...

"Lee," he began hesitantly, fidgeting with a salt shaker. "I'm willing to help you any way I can. But you gotta level with me. I need to know what I'm getting into here. I've heard of this Russian guy before. They say he was a smuggler. I may not be the brightest bulb in the pack, but I know you would need a guy like that to move your stuff to wherever you send it. Was he your pipeline?"

Jong considered stonewalling the question, but he was eventually going to ask this man to help him commit murder. He decided to lay his cards – at least most of his cards – on the table at the outset, and see how Clive reacted.

"You are a brighter bulb than you think, Clive," he stroked the man's ego. "Yes, I did business with Malachenko. He was too expensive to begin with, but he wanted to raise his rates. When I refused to pay more, he told me dependable people were not cheap. If he had to use less reliable mules, some of my shipments might get lost in transit. We argued and I became very angry. I slapped his face and he came at me with a butcher knife. I am small, but very fast. I stabbed him and hurried back to Chekov. I did not know he died from the wound."

Clive nodded slowly and looked Jong in the eye. "I thought it was probably something like that. But what bothers me is that you worked with Jackie Sam and had to kill him. Same with Malachenko. Now I'm willing to go along with anything you say, but I don't want to end up dead. If things get crazy between us, we'll have to part ways. I'll drop you anywhere you want to go, and I won't blow the whistle on you. Fair enough?"

Jong was not pleased to receive an ultimatum from this fool, but he didn't let his ire show. "Fair enough," he said. "If things don't work out, I'll make other arrangements somewhere else, and pay you to fly me there."

"Deal," Clive said. "Now you make out a list of stuff you need to buy and I'll go get it this afternoon. I got some beer and a half-bottle of whiskey but I can get anything else you like. It'll cost some, but I can get it for you."

Jong said, "I remember you enjoyed the cocaine I had at the party in Anchorage. Can you get good stuff like that here?"

Clive shook his head. "I'm not sure if I can. I can't afford cocaine so I never tried to buy none locally. I'll ask around – if we can't get it here I know a guy that makes regular runs into Anchorage. He won't mark it up too much and he'll keep his mouth shut."

"Okay then," Jong finished his coffee. "I'll put together a list and we'll see how it goes. And, I really appreciate your help. If things come together like I hope they will, you'll make a lot of money this summer."

That was just what Clive wanted to hear. If there was enough money to be made, he'd do whatever it took to make it.

Chapter 38

They set the final course of logs for the walls late Sunday afternoon. Things had progressed at a much faster pace after they completed the fifth course, upon which the window frames were set. The girth of the logs was not much diminished yet, but their length was considerably shorter, since they spanned only from the corners to the windows. Gus had precut the slots for the splines in the outside edge of the frames, and he slotted the ends of the window-abutting logs just before they were placed. The splines, already seated in the frames, kept the short sections aligned perfectly as they spiked the notches.

The last course, which sat directly atop the window frames was comprised of full length logs, but the team had their method of procedure finely tuned by the time they were ready to heft the last ones into place. Once the logs came level with the top of the window frames, Gus had constructed some five foot tall tripods as temporary prop-stands close to each of the long walls. These allowed them to rest the full length logs at shoulder height while taking a breather. Then they'd position themselves, one at each end with Haywood in the middle, and lift them into place on top of the wall.

"This calls for a beer, gentlemen," Gus announced, after they were done. "It's all light work from this point on."

They drank Heineken out of bottles while inspecting the structure. Hard Case went inside and took up position at the front window and placed his bottle of beer on the sill plank. He lit a Camel with his pink lighter and blew a stream of smoke out the opening into the warm summer air.

"Considerate of you to place these little bar tops at strategic locations around the perimeter, Gus. Architecture is just another of your myriad talents."

"Yeah," Haywood enthused. "When you get the floor in, Case will be able to lean out the window without tippy-toeing."

"You seem to be fascinated with tippy-toeing images," Hard Case grumbled.

Gus laughed. "Take a window sill for yourself Haywood. Demonstrate your flatfooted technique for us."

Haywood lit a cigar. "Nah, it would only inspire jealousy."

Gus stepped through the doorframe and inspected the interior. "More spacious than one would think," he said. "When the gaps are chinked it will look a lot more like a cabin. I'd say you guys are going to have some pretty cushy sleeping quarters."

"Could do with a roof, though," Hard Case observed.

"Oh?" Gus acted as though he hadn't noticed. He looked at the open sky. "Yes, I see what you mean, Case. I'll have to have another look at my plans – see if I included one."

"Maybe we could start on the gable ends this evening," Haywood suggested.

Gus shook his head. "No. Let's just tear down the tripods and set up some spruce-pole scaffolding outside the short walls. I'll work on the gable logs after you guys pull out. They're not hard to lift in place, but I have to leave them long, then cut them to the proper roof pitch after the ridge pole is in place. It takes a while; there's a lot of climbing up and down."

Gus had cut a dozen straight, slender poles ten-foot long which they used for the scaffold uprights at each end of the bunkhouse, then used the shorter poles from the tripods for the horizontal cross members that bore the weight of the platform planks. They lashed all the parts together with parachute cord and secured the uprights to the top logs of the wall. When they had finished Gus climbed up and walked out to mid-span on the platform.

He grinned down at them. "This will make the high work a lot easier than it was last year. I can prop the gable logs against the wall, climb up here and pull them up one at a time."

"The bottom two look pretty heavy. Are you going to be able to manage them alone?" Haywood asked.

Gus looked over at the log pile and stroked his chin as he considered them. "Probably not," he conceded. "Maybe I'll have you help me get them up here tomorrow after Hard Case flies out. No work in the morning, though. I think we deserve a leisurely breakfast, a little fishing, and a few hours of doing nothing at all. What do you say?"

"Sounds just right," Haywood said. "I'll help you with the gables after lunch."

***

Since Hard Case was due to depart around midday, they observed a longer-than-usual cocktail hour. Haywood had thought to bring in a bottle of fourteen-year-old Oban, one of Hard Case's favorite single malts. They shared it out in front of the tent, seated on some weathered spruce rounds they referred to as their "camp barstools". For once, their conversation was devoid of the customary barbs and taunting banter. They had exhausted their supply of zingers during the course of the work day.

"Haywood," Hard Case had said upon accepting the bottle of scotch from his friend, "you're a gentleman and a scholar. I thank you."

Gus came back from the cabin with three glasses and a carafe of water. "Pull the cork, Case, and we'll see if this is the real stuff."

Hard Case did the honors. "Steady your glass, Gus. Say when."

"Just fill it to the Haywood line," Gus told him. "I'm not driving tonight."

The Haywood line, of course was the rim of the glass. Haywood maintained that if God had wanted you to settle for less than a full glass, he would have put the brim down lower.

"Same here," Haywood said. "You didn't name that line after me for nothing."

The raven, which had followed their progress on the bunkhouse, took up roost on a spruce tree across the creek. He had shown great interest in their activities for the past few days, and now appeared to be equally enthralled with their end-of-the-day gab fest.

They were half way down the bottle when Hard Case broached the subject of Old Blue Eye.

He came straight to the point. "Am I going to get an audience with that old bugger or not?"

Gus shrugged. "Beats me," he said. "Nothing's changed since I gave you the last update."

Hard Case sipped his whisky and smacked his lips appreciatively. "I thought Morgan was going to try and speed things up a bit."

"What can I say?" Gus asked him. "When he's ready, he'll turn up."

"Well, it'll probably be too late when he does. According to that nurse, it looks like I'm going to miss the deadline." When he realized what he had said he shook his head sadly. "Sorry gentlemen – I guess that was a bad choice of words."

Haywood thought it was time for a new subject. "Did you guys see what the jackpot was for The Ice Classic this year?"

Gus shook his head. "No. How much?"

"Three hundred and eight thousand!" he said dreamily.

Hard Case, always the realist said, "Yeah, but there were eight winners. After the split and taxes, each share came to about twenty-eight thousand. Still…"

"Yeah," Haywood said. "Nothing to shake a stick at." He puffed on his stogie for a moment then turned to Gus. "I forgot to ask you – what day did the ice break up out here this year?"

Gus tried to remember. "I couldn't say for sure, but it was somewhere in the middle of May like Morgan said. What was the official date in Nenana?"

"May eighth at one in the afternoon." Hard Case had a good memory for details.

Haywood scowled. "Damn it Gus, I should have trusted my gut. I was thinking Nenana's clock would stop about a week ahead of the Moose Jaw breakup but I outsmarted myself. I went with the fifth because it seemed a little warmer this year."

Gus smiled. "Hell, Haywood. With the rates you charge, you could make twenty-eight thousand a year neutering guinea pigs."

The subject of the Ice Classic behind them, they revisited the logistics for completing the bunkhouse, the upcoming salmon runs, and the prospects for another good season of moose hunting. When the bottle neared empty, Hard Case stood up and stretched.

"One last cigarette before I turn in, gentlemen," he said, lighting a Camel. "Caldwell will probably arrive early so he can get in a little fishing with us before we head back to Fairbanks. It looks like I'm not going to get my face-to-face with that old one-eyed bugger."

The raven, apparently having lost interest in their idle chatter, abandoned his perch in the spruce tree and swooped across the creek toward the cabin. It deposited an impressive load of guano on their tent flap as he passed overhead.

Gus looked at his friends. "Must have been something we said," he observed.

***

The temperature dropped in the night and there was a light frost on the tent when Gus went down to call his guests to breakfast. They ate at the table inside the cabin where a fire popping in the green stove provided warmth as well as ambiance. When they had devoured the platter of ham, eggs and fried potatoes, they remained at the table to enjoy a last cup of coffee.

Morgan had taken her leave after helping Gus prepare the morning repast. Before she departed she took the precaution of removing the fresh roses Haywood had brought her. She had set the vase on the counter, well out of harm's way. With three hungry men at the table, conversation sometimes became quite animated.

As was his custom, Bosworth drowsed on the foot of the bed while they ate, maintaining just enough vigilance to spot any morsel that found its way to the floor. When Gus patted his mouth with a napkin, Bosworth knew he was about to begin clearing the table. Never one to display undignified excitement, he stretched, yawned, quietly slid off the bed and positioned himself near the counter. Gus often required his assistance in disposing of detritus left on plates. Gus came over from the table and deposited his dirty dishes in the sink.

"Sorry old timer," he said to the cat. "I ate it all."

Bosworth settled his attention upon the two men still seated at the table. He decided that Haywood needed a little cat hair on his pant cuffs so he sashayed over and gave them a few cursory passes, applying just enough pressure against the ankle to insure a response.

Haywood laughed, bent down and roughed the big cat's fur affectionately.

"You old rascal," he said. "How did you know I saved you some meat?"

Bosworth nearly allowed the plate to touch the floor before he snatched the scrap of ham off it and disappeared under the bed. The men at the table were then treated to the sound of rapturous chewing accompanied by the menacing deep throated growl.

"Bloody cat has gone positively feral," Haywood said, returning the plate to the tabletop.

"He certainly has," Gus told him. "I had to stop snaring hares because he'd get to them before I could check the traps. All he ever left me was blood and fur."

"Looks like the diet agrees with him," Hard Case observed. "He seems to have added some tonnage since the last time I saw him."

Gus cleared the table and left the dirty dishes to soak in the sink. As he replaced Morgan's roses as the centerpiece, he said, "The dishes can wait. What say we wet a line?"

"I'm game," Haywood said. "I'll go fetch our rods from the tent, Case. See you at creekside."

"You guys go ahead," Hard Case told them. "I want to check in with Caldwell to get his ETA."

Gus retrieved the satellite phone from the shelf and placed it on the table next to the roses.

"Battery's fully charged," he said, following Haywood out the door.

On their way to the tent, Haywood pointed out the raven, which had just landed on the wood-splitting stump near the cabin. "Corvas corax," he informed Gus. "It's Latin for airborne black shitter."

Gus looked at the bird speculatively and recalled the evening Old Blue Eye had dropped in on Morgan while he was busy counting logs. A raven had arrived not long before that visit.

"You go ahead without me," he told Haywood. "I better go wash up those dishes so Morgan doesn't have to deal with them while we're fishing. It won't take me long."

"Take your time. I can find my way to the creek." Haywood said, and set off for the tent.

Gus trotted up the steps, crossed the porch and ducked inside. Hard Case was just returning the phone to its portable case.

"He's due in about ten o'clock," Hard Case told Gus.

"Never mind Caldwell," Gus said. "I think you've got a visitor."

Chapter 39

Old Blue Eye entered the cabin and looked around appreciatively. Gus had moved Morgan's roses to the end of the table and placed an ashtray near Hard Case's elbow. With a gesture of his hand, he indicated that the old man should take the other chair. The old one sat down across from Hard Case. He declined the offer of food or drink and appeared content to just sit and admire the beautiful red flowers.

"I'm afraid I don't know your name, Sir," Hard Case apologized.

"You can call me Sir, if you like. Old Blue Eye is too long, eh."

Hard Case and Gus looked at one another. They were sure neither of them had ever spoken that name aloud in his presence. They also referred to him as "the old one" or "the old shaman", and sometimes as "the old bugger". They hoped he hadn't picked up on those names as well.

"I know all the names people call me, but Sir shows respect."

That answered that. "Okay," Hard Case said, "Sir it is. I'm grateful you came. Gus just now told me you were outside. I need to ask you a few questions."

The old man's eye shifted almost imperceptibly; it seemed to be focused upon something on the other side of the log wall. "You want to know about the night at the fishing lodge." It was not a question.

"That's right," Hard Case told him. "Do you know if anyone else was there before Gus arrived?"

The old one nodded. "Seven men were there before this one came." He indicated Gus with a wave of his crippled hand. "I was one of seven."

"Can you tell me the names of the others?" Hard Case asked.

"The only names that were spoken were Roy and Larry and Josh and Jason."

Gus came over and stood behind Hard Case. "Jason was there? You saw him?"

Old Blue Eye looked at Gus. "He was there. The giant beat him bad. Four others came before the giant could hurt him anymore. They tied the giant and his brother up with wire and left them in a

room with a lot of oil cans and a candle. When they left, this one –
he indicated Gus again – came and shot the giant's brother."

"Who killed the giant?" Hard Case asked him.

"His brother, maybe. I did not see that happen."

"This giant and his brother…" Hard Case began. "Just to be
clear – are you speaking of the McCaslin brothers? Roy and Larry
McCaslin?"

The old man nodded his head.

Hard Case pressed on, "And Roy and Larry were two of the
seven who were there before Mr. O'Neill arrived?"

The old man turned to look at Gus. "That is your name – Mr.
O'Neill?" he asked.

Gus smiled and nodded. "You can call me Gus."

Hard Case remained on track. "The McCaslins counted as two
of the seven you spoke of as being there at the lodge that night?"

The old shaman's eye returned to the big man across the table.
"Yes," he said.

"You also mentioned the name Josh. Do you know Josh's last
name?" Hard Case held his breath.

The old man focused his one blue eye on him. "Henry," he said
quietly.

"Josh Henry?" Hard Case asked. "Charlie Henry's oldest son?"

The old man nodded. "But he is dead now. Six of the seven
who were there at the lodge are dead."

"Was Charlie there?" Hard Case inquired.

"No."

"I have to ask you this because you appear to have seen the
McCaslins wired to the wall, and you described the fire bomb that
was left in the room with them. Were all seven of you inside the
room that night?"

"The old man said, "Yes."

"And did five of you take part in the murders?"

The old man smiled. "No," he answered. "Not one of us was in
the room when the giant was killed. And this one killed the
brother." He indicated Gus with a gesture of his head.

Hard Case leaned back in his chair and picked up his pack of
Camels. He shook one out and offered it to the old man. Old Blue
Eye accepted it and studied its smooth roundness while Hard Case
took one for himself and lit it with a kitchen match. Somehow, he

didn't think this was the time to break out a pink lighter. He held out the match toward the old shaman, who was pleased with the big policeman's courtesy.

It had been many years since he had enjoyed a factory produced cigarette. He bent forward, watched as the flame turned its tip to a glowing coal, then inhaled the rich smoke and leaned back in his chair. He closed his good eye and smiled gently in apparent ecstasy.

Hard Case watched him with pleasure. 'I wish I enjoyed these things half as much as he does,' he thought to himself. He let a little time pass before interrupting the old man's reverie.

"I'll rephrase my question, Sir," he began. "Did all five of you participate in the events that led up to the McCaslin's deaths and the fire that burned down the fishing lodge?"

The old man smiled and nodded. He liked the way this big Trooper had posed the question. "Yes," he said. "We all helped."

Hard Case took another puff of his cigarette. "Before we go on, I have to read you this," he said, holding up a small laminated card. "There is no statute of limitations for murder. And, even though none of your party actually killed either of the McCaslins, the law would probably consider you murderers or at least accessories to murder. So I have to read you your rights."

He began, "You have the right to remain silent..."

When he had finished reading the old man his Miranda rights, he stubbed out his cigarette and continued. "You understand that you don't need to tell me anything else, and that anything you say can be used against you in a court of law?"

The old one smiled, "Oh, yes, I understand. But all that was a very long time ago. I see in your heart that you do not wish to arrest me. Ask me what you want to know."

He was right, Hard Case thought. He had no intention of causing this old shaman trouble. If he had taken part in the McCaslin murders, he'd done the world a favor. Nevertheless, he had to learn all he could about that night.

"I need the other three names," he said quietly.

"If they are all dead, why do you need to know who they were?" the old man asked reasonably.

Hard Case decided there was nothing to be gained in withholding the truth from the old man. "I promised an old friend – the Trooper who investigated the killings back in 1959 – that I would find out who was involved. The case is officially closed. He just wants to know so he can die in peace."

Old Blue Eye nodded gravely. "You are a good man," he said. "You do not need to worry about your friend. He died in peace."

"How…?" Hard Case began, but realized it didn't matter how the old shaman knew Pokey had died. Gus had once said, "How does he know anything?" There were questions to which there were no answers. 'Poor old Pokey,' Hard case took a deep breath, realizing that he had been pressing hard to beat the clock. Now he could relax. The clock had won.

He shifted and straightened in his chair to stretch the muscles of his lower back. His knee knocked against one of the table legs and Morgan's vase of flowers tipped over, spilling water and roses onto the tabletop. It rolled toward the edge and both Hard Case and the old man lunged for it simultaneously. Hard Case reached it first and kept it from falling off the table. But the old man was quick too, and the yellowed nails of his three twisted fingers raked deep furrows in the back of Hard Case's hand.

"Shit!" Hard Case hissed, jerking his hand off the vase.

Gus quickly stepped around him and removed the vase from the table. "Hang on, I'll get a towel." He went over to the counter.

"I'm sorry," the old man said. "I did not mean to hurt you."

"I know you didn't, Sir. It was an accident. It's just a scratch." He stood up and went over to the counter. "Got any antiseptic?" he asked Gus.

Morgan came out of the shadows near the bed. "Here," she said. "I'll take care of Case's hand, Gus. You deal with the mess on the table."

Both Gus and Hard Case were dumbstruck.

"I…" Hard Case began. "What…?" he stammered.

Morgan smiled, "Welcome to the club."

Hard Case looked puzzled. "Club…?" Then he got it and thought, 'Ah, yes – the club.'

"Jesus, Morgan," Gus said. "You sure know how to make an entrance."

None of them heard the door open or close, but when Hard Case looked back at the table, there was only the water and the roses. Old Blue Eye was gone.

Chapter 40

Caldwell arrived just after ten o'clock that morning. The three friends left their fly-rods at the tent and walked up to the landing strip to greet him. He was just taking his rod case out of the rear storage area when they came down the overland trail through the budding willows.

"I hope you brought some 5X tippet," Hard Case called out as they approached. "The grayling are feisty today."

Caldwell smiled and shook hands all round. He couldn't help but notice the bandage Hard Case was sporting. "What happened to your hand?" he asked.

"It's nothing," Hard Case assured him. "Just a scratch."

As they walked back to the tent, Gus said, "The fish have been hitting just about any fly we toss out on the water, but number eighteen mosquitoes seem to be working best."

"That's true," Hard Case told his young Trooper. "But stay with the small ones. We don't want our local grayling sexually violated by mosquitoes with a thyroid condition."

Caldwell glanced sideways at Gus and gave him a "What the hell is the boss raving about?" look.

Gus laughed and slapped him on the back. "Ignore him Caldwell. You don't really want to know."

Haywood laughed too. "I'll fill you in on mosquito breeding techniques later. I've prepared a most enlightening lecture on the subject."

Hard Case gave him a withering look. "Don't be foisting your entomological pornography on the pure of heart, Jennings," he said. "I'll have to arrest you for lewd and lascivious conduct. You're becoming a menace to society."

"You brought up the subject," Haywood objected.

Caldwell said to Gus, "Man, I'm never leaving him out here three days with you guys again."

Hard Case caught up to them and steered Caldwell down toward the creek. "Anything new on the Jackie Sam murder?" Gus heard him ask.

Caldwell shook his head. "No the last word was the positive ID on the thumbprint off the gas cap, but you already knew that."

"I did, yes," Hard Case said. "I have a feeling we haven't seen the last of the little bastard. Anything else?"

Caldwell extracted his fly rod from its case and began piecing the sections together. "Sergeant Gleason called me at the maintenance hangar this morning just after I got off the line with you. Your old boss died last night. I'm sorry to have to be the one to give you the news."

Hard Case smiled gently and patted the young man on the shoulder. "Thank you for telling me." He didn't mention that he had already heard it from another source.

Haywood and Gus came down to join them carrying a cooler. They set it on the gravel of the bar, popped open the lid. Gus said, "Beer and sodas gentlemen – help yourselves."

Caldwell said he'd get in some fishing first, but Hard Case reached in and pulled out a Heineken. He sat on a log and lit up a Camel and told Caldwell, "You go terrorize the grayling. I've caught more than is decent for one morning."

Caldwell couldn't help himself. "Nice lighter," he said.

"Never you mind about my lighter," Hard Case grumbled. "Us seasoned bush rats know pink is the hardest color to lose out here. You'd do well to study up on survival techniques before you go casting aspersions at my fire-starting implements."

"Sure, boss," Caldwell was not buying it. "The color does suit you though."

Hard Case glowered. "Go annoy the fish, boy."

***

Caldwell enjoyed a good two hours of fishing before a rain shower came down the valley and spoiled his fun. He had thought to bring in a bag of submarine sandwiches for lunch, so the four men ate them while sitting out the rain inside the tent. He had been quite impressed with the progress made on the bunkhouse and said as much.

"I'm somewhat amazed myself," Gus told him. "I didn't think we'd be able to get so much done in just a few days. I'll have it roofed and weather-tight in a couple more weeks."

"Gus," Hard Case said, "I think this young gentleman would probably appreciate an invitation to join us on the moose hunt in September. We could use another strong back for packing out the meat. What do you say?"

"Absolutely. Caldwell, I hope you know you're welcome to come out anytime to hunt or fish. Come out for the salmon runs this year if you like. I'll leave the tent up until the bunkhouse is finished. Just make yourself at home. No invitation required."

Caldwell was pleased and his face showed it. "Thanks, Gus. I've floated this whole river a couple of times. You've got the best location for moose and caribou I know of. You can count on me being here in September. I wouldn't miss it for anything."

"Well," Hard Case told him, "now that's settled and the rain's let up, we better be heading back to Fairbanks. Maybe Haywood will help you haul my stuff up to the landing strip. I've got to fetch a few things from the cabin, and I'll be right behind you."

Haywood knew Hard Case just wanted to say a proper good-bye to Morgan. "Sure," he said. "I'll be glad to lend a hand. Caldwell, if you take the big river bag, I'll bring the rest of the gear."

As they started up the overland trail, Gus and Hard Case went back to the cabin. Hard Case rested a big hand on his friend's shoulder as they walked side-by-side down the bar.

"Fergus, that was a fine visit. I enjoyed the physical labor as much as the fishing. And, I can finally put the Rainbow Lodge murders to rest. It's too bad I couldn't tell Pokey before he slipped away, but Old Blue Eye says he died in peace. I take comfort in that."

They went up the steps and into the cabin. Morgan was putting teabags into a glass jug of water to set out in the sun. Gus had taught her to make sun tea that way and she had developed a taste for it.

"How is your hand feeling, Case?" she asked.

"Still stings a little, but it will be fine. I wanted to thank you for the doctoring before I left. And I wanted you to know what a genuine pleasure it was to make your acquaintance."

She smiled and said, "The pleasure was all mine. I'm delighted to have had this chance to meet you. I hope you come back soon."

Hard Case took her hand, bent at the waist and kissed it, European style. Somehow, this outdated formality would have seemed unnatural had anyone but Kees Calis attempted it. But with him, it seemed to be the proper way to say good-bye to a lovely woman.

When he straightened, he said. "I'll do that. Thank you for the invitation."

She blushed a little, but was obviously pleased by his gallantry. She stepped close to him and kissed his cheek. "Have a safe trip home."

***

Caldwell was already seated in the cockpit when Gus and Hard Case arrived at the landing strip. Haywood was fiddling with something inside his rented Cessna. He saw them coming out of the willows onto the open bar, and closed up his plane and joined them.

He gave Hard Case a bear hug and said, "Be seeing you Case. I'll be back in town tomorrow night. Let's try to get together later in the week."

"I might have to fly down to San Diego for Pokey's funeral," Hard Case told him. "I'll give you a call when I know for sure what they've arranged for him."

He checked to make sure Caldwell couldn't overhear him, then said quietly, "Morgan's certainly every bit as beautiful as you two said she was. You're a lucky man O'Neill, but I'm sure you know that."

Haywood said, "He knows alright. I remind him of it on a regular basis."

They walked Hard Case over to the side of the plane and waited while he climbed aboard. They heard him say, "Okay, Caldwell, whenever you're ready," before he closed the door and buckled up.

Gus and Haywood went up to the top of the bar and gave them a thumbs-up. Caldwell waved back and started the engine. After a short warm up and his pre-flight checks, he shot them a salute, swung the nose into the wind, roared down the gravel strip and lifted off well before the end of the bar. He followed the river only as far as the next bend, then climbed above the treetops, brought the Super Cub around in a tight turn and was still climbing fast as he passed over The Varmitage and headed southeast.

Chapter 41

Gus and Haywood spent the afternoon laying in the first two courses of gable logs. As Gus had planned, they left them long so he could cut them to the exact pitch of the roof once they were all in place and the ridge beam tied their peaks together. Morgan brought them a cold beer just as they were coming down the scaffold after setting the last log.

"Ah," Haywood intoned. "You couldn't have timed it better."

"I know," she said, handing each a frosty bottle. "I've been checking your progress every now and again. I saw you hauling up the last log so I thought you might be ready for a little refreshment."

Gus took a sip, smacked his lips appreciatively and said, "Haywood here is wondering if Old Blue Eye might have engineered Case's little accident this morning."

Morgan appeared to give that some thought. "I don't know," she said simply. "It's not beyond the realm of possibility. It could have been his way of bringing him into the fold, I suppose."

"Well," Haywood said, "whether by accident or intent, just having Hard Case know we're not lunatics is a relief. I'm glad it happened."

"I am too," Gus agreed. "It makes things a lot easier in many ways."

"Yes," Morgan told them. "The 'now you see her – now you don't' routine was becoming a bit tedious for me also. I think I'm going to enjoy the new arrangement."

Haywood took another swig of beer and studied the bunkhouse. "It's certainly taking shape fast Gustopher. I can help you with a few more gable logs in the morning if you like. I won't be heading out until late afternoon."

Gus said, "No. I'll be able to manage them alone, but if you'll hold one end of the water level for me I'll set the footings for the porch extension. An extra pair of hands would speed that process up a bit."

Haywood finished his beer and set the empty bottle on a stump. "You got it," he said. "I've heard about that method of leveling, but I've never done it. Maybe I'll learn a new trick."

"Good!" Morgan said excitedly. "I can't wait to have a big porch and a long table so we can all eat outside together this summer. Now there are four of us, it will be perfect."

Gus laughed. "After we get the footing rocks placed tomorrow morning, I'll have Haywood help me with the front support beam. I'm ready to take a couple days off from the bunkhouse anyway. Building the extension will be light work compared to all the heavy lifting we had to do this weekend."

Morgan entwined her arms around his neck and kissed him. "That would be wonderful." She gave Haywood a hug and a kiss as well then retrieved his empty from the stump and waited until Gus finished his beer and took his bottle too.

"I'll go back to the cabin and throw together something for dinner," she said. "I'll leave you gentlemen to work out logistics for tomorrow."

She turned and headed back down the bar toward the cabin. The men watched her depart, admiring the graceful sway of her hips as she walked.

She called over her shoulder, "Stop it, you two; you're supposed to be gentlemen."

They looked at each other. "Damn, I wish she would quit doing that," Haywood said.

Gus laughed, "It can be a bit off-putting."

***

Morgan had "thrown together" a sumptuous dinner of poached salmon with wild rice, steamed carrots and green beans. A bottle of chilled white wine complimented the fish perfectly. Haywood had helped Gus move the plank table out onto the porch, as Morgan had suggested, so they could enjoy dining al fresco and discuss the extension project on site.

"Where did you find flat rocks that big?" Haywood asked.

"They were some of the base for the old chimney that I tore down. I used most of them for the bunkhouse footing, but I saved these two for the porch – mainly because I didn't relish trying to move them up there by myself."

"Don't blame you. I'll bet they weigh three hundred pounds each."

"Probably," Gus said. "But the two of us won't have too much trouble shifting them into place. They're pretty close to where I want to set them now."

"Another eight feet of deck will make quite a difference," Haywood said, visualizing the planned addition.

"It certainly will," Gus said. "When I built this section as part of the cabin, I never expected to be hosting parties. I just wanted enough room to have a store of firewood right outside the door. When I have a half-cord stacked out here, there's not much room for anything else."

Morgan sipped her wine and said, "Had we not used up that last rick, I don't think we could have eaten out here tonight. But, it's been wonderful getting a feel for what it will be like."

Gus said, "It has. And the evening's still warm, but the wine's gone. Anyone fancy an after-dinner drink?"

Morgan stood up and began clearing the table. "You two go ahead and enjoy a smoke. I'll be right back with the whiskey and water."

Haywood and Gus began to help with the dirty dishes. "No you don't," she told them. "I can manage without any interference, thank you very much."

The men resettled in their chairs. Gus got out his pipe and filled it with Captain Black. He lit it and stretched out his legs toward the edge of the porch. "By the way," he said, "what do I owe you for the two cans of tobacco and all the other stuff that was on my list?"

"You'll get my bill in due course," Haywood told him, lighting up one of the infamous cigars Hard Case had dubbed the "moose shit blends". "Wait until I finish hauling in the rest of the building material."

Morgan came back out onto the porch with a bottle of Tullamore Dew, a carafe of water and three whiskey glasses arranged on a wooden tray. She set it on the table and said, "You do the honors, Gus – make mine neat, if you please."

While Gus poured two fingers of Dew into each glass, she popped back inside and returned with her vase of roses. "I don't think I ever thanked you properly for these," she told Haywood.

He added a few drops of water to his whiskey. "Another kiss would probably rectify that," he told her.

She bent down and gave him one. Then she went round the table and favored Gus with one as well.

"What's mine for?" he asked her.

She accepted the whiskey Gus handed her. "For nothing – and for everything," she smiled contentedly and sat down with them.

***

Haywood departed a little before two in the afternoon of the next day. He had helped Gus set and level the footing rocks, and place the support beam for the front of the new porch before packing his things and saying his good-byes. Gus had helped him carry his kit up to the landing strip.

Haywood stowed everything in the rear of the plane and closed the door. "Anything else you want to add to the list?" he asked.

"Yes," Gus told him. "I'm glad you reminded me. I'll need another pair of strap hinges and a latch for a door to the store room. And, see if you can find a pack of mixed lettuce seeds, and a couple packets of flower seeds. Morgan loves flowers as you well know, and she often mentions how much she misses fresh green salads."

"Are you going to build her a fenced-in garden?" Haywood asked.

"Not exactly," Gus said. "Instead of a railing around the new deck, I'm going to build several planter boxes. I'll cover them with wire lids to keep the critters out."

"That's a great idea," Haywood said enthusiastically. "How about some herbs too? A package of seeds doesn't cost much; I'll buy up a good selection and she can plant whatever she likes."

"Perfect," Gus told him. "But, you might want to check with a garden specialist to see what will grow this far north."

Haywood rubbed his chin. "Okay," he said. "I hadn't intended to come back for a couple weeks, but I'm awaiting confirmation on a Thursday haul-out date for my Clipper. The helicopter outfit I contracted will let me know this evening. If it's a go, I'll pick up all this stuff tomorrow and drop it off here on my way up to Hermit's Camp on Thursday. It's not much out of the way and Morgan will need to get the seeds planted asap if she's to have salad this summer. Think there might be another smooch in it for me?"

Gus laughed. "If Morgan doesn't come through, I'll kiss you myself."

Haywood threw an arm around his friend's shoulders and chuckled. "How can I say no to that?"

They gave each other a bear hug and Haywood climbed up into the cockpit. Gus went up near the willows and settled down on a driftwood log. Haywood started the engine and let it idle while he checked dials, twisted knobs and flipped switches. When all appeared to be in order, he waved one of his pitchfork hands out the window and taxied out onto the "runway".

Gus remained there until Haywood's rented Cessna lifted off, climbed above the tree-tops, then made a wide turn and did a wing-wag as it flew over The Varmitage. After it had disappeared into the clouds that were gathering in the southeast, he took the overland trail back to the cabin. On the way he decided to build the planters first so Morgan could start planting as soon as Haywood returned with the seeds.

Morgan was waiting on the porch to meet him as he came down the slope from the ridge. He mounted the steps, put his arms around her and kissed her.

"I've got a new twist I'd like to try out on you," he suggested.

She pushed off to arm's length and gave him a mischievous smile. "I can't imagine anything we haven't already tried."

He laughed. "I mean a new twist regarding my extension."

"You come right to the point, don't you big boy," she murmured in a sultry Mae West voice. "I like that in a man."

"Stop it!" he insisted. "You're going to make me lose my train of thought. I'm talking about the porch extension!"

"Oh," she feigned disappointment and pushed him away. "Why didn't you say so?"

He explained his plan for the planters around the edge of the deck and how she could have fresh lettuce and herbs and flowers right outside the door. Morgan laughed with delight and skipped down the steps and literally danced atop the support beam.

"Pansies here!" she bubbled gleefully, pointing out a spot on the log. "And herbs here!" she indicated another place. "And marigolds on that side over there!"

He walked down to ground level and she hopped off the log and into his arms. She hugged him tight and showered his face with kisses.

"So," he said, "I take it you approve of the idea."

She took him by the hand and led him back up the steps and into the cabin.

"Now I have a new twist I want to try out on you."

Chapter 42

True to his word, Haywood stopped by The Varmitage Thursday on his way to Hermit's Camp. Gus had been expecting him around noon so Morgan had lunch waiting when he landed. Gus went up to the strip to greet him.

"Got time for a quick lunch?" he asked. "Morgan has it ready if you do."

Haywood smiled. "You bet. I never say no to lunch. Besides, I want to see her face when she gets a load of this." He opened the rear door and told Gus to have a look inside.

"Good Lord, Haywood!" he exclaimed. "These are full grown plants! Looks like you ferried in a whole nursery."

"I couldn't resist," Haywood said. "The guy in the garden department said it was too late to plant seeds. He gave me a great deal on starts if I bought them by the flat, so I thought, 'why not?' Let's take the flowers down first and we can come back for the herbs and vegetables after lunch."

Morgan was waiting on the porch when they came out of the woods on the ridge and started down the trail. When she saw the big yellow pom-poms of the marigolds she ran barefoot down the steps and up the path to meet them.

"Oh!" she cried out with glee. "Oh, Haywood, you didn't! Pansies too!"

She threw her arms around his neck and kissed him full on the lips. He had to hold a flat of flowers out at arm's length with each hand to protect them from Morgan's enthusiasm while maintaining his balance in the process.

Gus laughed and proceeded down the trail while Morgan continued pouring praise and kisses on her hero. "I guess I won't have to make good on that rash promise," he said over his shoulder. "She's handling things pretty well herself."

When Haywood had been well and thoroughly rewarded, Morgan disentangled herself and said, "Here, I'll take the marigolds, you bring the pansies."

Gus had already deposited a flat of oriental poppies and two small rose bushes on the edge of the porch. When Morgan saw them she nearly wept. "Roses," she could barely choke out the word. "I can't believe it! Will they do well this far north?"

Haywood placed his flat of pansies next to the others. "That's what the man said," he told her. "They certainly do well in Fairbanks. And the pansies have been 'hardened off' –whatever that means. And even though we get about twenty hours of sun up here, they'll be okay because it comes in at a low angle. He sounded like he knew what he was talking about."

Gus said, "Haywood's on a tight schedule, Morgan. Let's eat lunch and then go back up to the plane for the rest of the load."

"There's more?" she asked, obviously delighted.

"Just a few herbs and veggies," he said. "Nothing to write home about."

She laughed and kissed him again. "I can't wait," she said. "Smoked salmon, pickled eggs, fruit, cheese and iced tea are on the table inside. It's serve yourself today, so fill your plate and we'll eat out here where I can enjoy the flowers."

***

After offloading the flats of lettuce, onion, and kale starts, as well as an assortment of herbs, Haywood gave Gus a box of hardware.

"Here's your strap hinges and latch for the storeroom door. No kissing necessary."

With that he hugged them both, graciously accepting another peck on the cheek from Morgan, and climbed into the cockpit.

"I'll be back in two weeks for the salmon run," he said. "Hard Case will be flying in with Caldwell, I think. Check with him on the satellite phone and let him know anything else you need. One of us will bring it in."

"Good luck with your plane," Gus told him. "I'd love to tag along and see how it's done, but I can't give up another day on the bunkhouse. The porch and planter boxes set me behind a bit."

"I'll take a lot of pictures," Haywood said, and closed the door.

After they watched his plane disappear over the mountains to the northeast, Gus and Morgan carried the herbs and vegetables and Gus' hardware back to the cabin.

"Man, this one smells delicious," he told her, sniffing it to catch the full aroma. "What is it?"

"Rosemary," she told him. "It's wonderful on roast potatoes."

Back at the cabin, she asked Gus to put all the boxes he had built on the porch before he filled them with soil. When they were all arranged to her liking, she began placing the plants, still in their individual containers, in the appropriate ones.

"I want to see how they'll look in the planters," she explained. "And they need a little time to get used to their new homes before I actually plant them."

***

Gus spent the rest of the afternoon working on the new section of porch while Morgan fussed with her "garden" on the old one. Haywood had certainly made her day. He couldn't recall seeing her so happy and excited.

By six o'clock that evening, he was ready to install the floor boards, but decided a break was in order.

"I'm getting a bit hungry," he said. "Why don't we knock off for an hour, eat a cold dinner, and have a drink together? Then I'll lay the planks for the floor and help you move the planters wherever you like."

"Really?" she could hardly contain herself. "Tonight?"

"Yep," he told her. "They're already cut to length. It won't take me more than a couple hours to place them and nail them off."

He washed up while she prepared a plate of cold chicken, marinated mushrooms and olives. Gus poured a beer for himself and an iced tea for Morgan, then followed her outside. They sat shoulder-to-shoulder on the edge of the porch with their legs dangling through the open frame for the extension and ate the food with their fingers.

"What a wonderful day," she said contentedly.

"That it was," he agreed. "Sometimes Haywood outdoes himself."

That night, after Morgan had arranged and rearranged the planters more times than he could count, they watched the sun dip close to the horizon from the new deck, shared a nightcap, and turned in.

He watched her undress in the dim light coming through the west window and was, once again, captivated by her grace and beauty. She read his thoughts and turned to look at him. Her long red hair tumbled down her shoulder partially obscuring her nakedness – partially.

226

When he slid under the covers and pulled her against him he asked, "In your world travels, were you ever introduced to the Kama Sutra?"

"I was," she said.

"Did you read it?" he inquired.

"It was more of a picture book, as I recall," she observed, noncommittally.

"And?" he persisted.

"I wondered how they managed it while wearing all those robes," she confessed.

With that she demonstrated her ideas for a few new pages. It was a very old book. It needed updating.

Chapter 43

The first Chinooks, also called King salmon, had come up the Kasilof in late May. Consequently, more boats had appeared on the river with each day in June. And with each day of confinement Jong became more and more restless. As he had done while hiding out in the storage unit at Chekov, he tuned into the local news regularly to see if there was anything to give him cause for concern. But, as the solstice approached it appeared that he was no longer newsworthy.

Nevertheless, he knew it was absolutely necessary for him to remain out of sight. Anyone coming up or down Crooked Creek might see him and remember the manhunt for the fugitive Korean. No matter how he longed to get outside for a while, he knew it would be foolish to risk it when every day that passed moved him closer to achieving his ultimate goal.

He could not remember when, exactly, he had become determined to kill that bastard who fucked up everything for him. He had been snorting more cocaine than usual, but he felt certain it was not a factor in his obsession with Gus. It went deeper than that. Sometimes he would wake in the night frightened or confused, then he would remember his dream, and Gus' image would flash into his mind, holding that long bladed knife, taunting him with it. 'Come back and get it,' he seemed to be saying.

'Don't worry, you asshole,' Jong thought. 'I'll come back. And I'll cut you open and leave you for the fucking crows and ravens.'

With so much time on his hands, he turned his mind to just how he would accomplish that. At first his plan was really no plan at all – it was simply "get back to the Moose Jaw and kill the son of a bitch". But, as July approached he realized he would have to make his move soon. He didn't know how much longer he could stand hiding out on the Kenai, and he suspected Gus would not remain at his cabin over the winter.

As his plan began to evolve and the details began to gel into a true plan of action, he focused on the logistics. Clive provided him with a wealth of information regarding the salmon runs and the moose rut, as well as the levels of human activity and air traffic these natural cycles inspired. After careful consideration, he determined that the last two weeks in August would be the optimum time to return to the Moose Jaw. The salmon runs would be winding down and moose and caribou season did not begin until the first of September. It stood to reason that this hiatus would be his best shot at catching Gus out there alone. Once moose season began, there would be too much air and water traffic in the vicinity. And, when it ended, Gus would probably be pulling out for the winter, just as he had done last year.

Chapter 44

The old shaman was very pleased with himself. Now that he had become more familiar with his own nature, he saw each new journey as an opportunity to hone his skills. It was remarkable how far he could travel if he put his mind to the task. In the early days he had been content to stay within the confines of his valley, but as he became better at what he did, he ventured further afield. He found that his blind eye could see things beyond the mountains that contained the Moose Jaw and guided it on its journey to the Yukon. His vision extended little by little until he could see things that were happening far away.

He remembered his first glimpse of the world outside his valley. It had been just after he had started finding the dead bears and he began thinking of the sons of his nephew. It came as a surprise to him when he realized he had the ability to peek over the hills to the north where his two young kinsmen were living like white men. He could see them rutting with the blonde women, and conducting themselves like fools. He had concentrated very hard on making contact with their spirits and discovered that he could do so through their dreams. Each night he would appear to them and subtly nudge them back toward the true path. He knew then that the oldest one did not hear his voice – or if he did, he did not care. But he also knew that Damon had begun to change.

It was a sad thing when he had found Jackie's body in the snow, but his heart sang with joy when his ever-expanding vision saw Damon was now lodging with cousins along the Yukon. He could see the cousins lived in accordance with the old ways and that Damon's feet were now following the right path. As "Old Uncle" he continued appearing to him in his dreams, helping him on his journey home.

Recently his powers had become much stronger. He found he could travel the full length of the Yukon to where it joined the sea. And, if he wanted, he could cross water to far distant places. Not long ago, he had appeared to an old Trooper in a dream. The old fellow was very near death, but he was hanging on until he learned the answer to a thing that had troubled him for many years. When he visited this old man in his dream he gave him the answer he had been seeking. He told him the names he wanted to know – and he gave him a vision so he could see what had happened on a night long ago.

The old Trooper had smiled in his sleep and said aloud, "I'll be damned." Then he died.

And the next day, when he went to Gus' cabin to talk to the other Trooper, he was able to tell him that his old friend had died in peace. It was a good thing to do a good thing. It gave him much pleasure.

It was different than the visits he had paid Jackie's killer. Where he had appeared to Damon and the old Trooper to guide them and give them comfort, he insinuated himself into the killer's dreams to torture him. He was not "Old Uncle" to the killer. No – to him he was the raven. He knew if the raven spoke the right words, he would lure this killer of bears and men back to the Moose Jaw. He had seen in the man's heart a deep hatred for Gus. So he poisoned his dreams with visions of Gus finding Jackie's body, and Gus holding a beautiful knife while laughing. It pleased him to see the hatred fester in the killer's subconscious. He would come back – someday, he would come back to kill Gus. The old shaman smiled to himself and thought 'maybe sometimes it is a good thing to do a bad thing'. Yes, he was very pleased with himself.

Chapter 45

As Gus had promised, he had the bunkhouse ready for guests when Haywood, Hard Case and Caldwell flew in for the salmon runs in mid July. The floorboards were not installed yet, but it had a hard-packed dirt floor that was level and free of rocks. And, it had a door, screened window openings and a roof, although it was still innocent of shingles. He had "dried it in" by covering the raw planks of the roof decking with two blue tarps. If all went well it would serve to keep the rain off them for a few days. If not, Haywood was to bring in the roofing felt and rolls of tarpaper on this run. If the tarps sprung a leak, they could always take a few hours off from fishing and do the job right.

Once the structure itself was more-or-less weather tight, he spent two days building one set of bunk beds and a table. He brought the folding two-tier camp bed out of the cabin and set it up in the bunkhouse to accommodate two more occupants. His ultimate goal was to have three sets of built-in bunks with the camp bed set up in the store room for shelving. He couldn't imagine a time when he'd have more than six visitors staying over, but it would provide an extra set of bunks if the need arose.

Morgan had helped him move the camp bed down to the bunkhouse. Without it occupying one corner, their small cabin seemed positively spacious. She was delighted with the new floor space and suggested Gus build them another chair so three could sit at the table together without one of them having to pull up a bucket.

Gus added that to his list. He had plenty of limb wood stockpiled for furnishing the bunkhouse anyway, so another chair wouldn't break the bank. As he worked on the bunkhouse over the past two weeks, he'd stop now and then, to watch her puttering in the little kitchen garden she had created on the porch extension. It gave him great pleasure to see the delight in her eyes each time she discovered a new bloom or blossom. Every day, while they lunched at the big picnic table he had constructed on the porch, she would take him on a "point and tell" tour of the boxes.

"Look at the lettuce, Gus!" or "Can you believe the size of the tomatoes?" Her excitement was infectious and he'd often just sit and wonder at how this beautiful creature seemed to grow lovelier with each passing day. Her presence imbued this wild river valley with a grace and gentility that tamed its feral spirit. Savage beasts, brutal weather, gods and demons raged all around them in the boreal wilderness that was the Moose Jaw. Yet, at the center of it all, there was a core of serenity and pure beauty – Morgan.

***

Haywood never came in empty, and since Hard Case was flying in with Caldwell, he had plenty of room for the usual buckets of food, cases of alcohol, little surprises for Morgan and all his survival and fishing gear – not to mention the roofing material and a light-gauge metal, wood-burning stove for the bunkhouse. Gus had specified that he wanted a stove that wouldn't take up too much room, but big enough to heat the cabin in the moderately cold nights of autumn. He had also insisted it be a front-loader with enough flat cooking surface to brew a pot of coffee and warm a saucepan full of soup. Haywood had found one at an estate sale that met all the requirements and cost less than a bottle of rot-gut whiskey. The selling agent had called it a "vintage Tin Lizzy". Haywood was a sucker for anything "vintage".

Since Hard Case and Caldwell were not due in until later, both Gus and Morgan met Haywood when he landed. As always, he hopped to the ground, compared his stiffness to that of a "weddin' dick", and proceeded to ravish Morgan, who did nothing to fend off his attentions.

"Welcome home, Haywood," she said, laughing while straightening her disheveled garments after he had well and truly molested her.

Haywood gave Gus a somewhat less enthusiastic, but equally hardy bear hug then said, "The bunkhouse looks like you designed it in classic Alaska bush tradition – blue tarp roof and all. I spotted it from three miles out."

Gus laughed. "Did you bring in the roofing material?" he asked.

Haywood opened the rear door and gestured that Gus should have a peek inside. "It's buried under there somewhere."

"Judas Priest!" Gus exclaimed upon examining the cargo. "You must have needed a hydraulic jack to get all that stuff in there."

"No square inch of space wasted," Haywood said. "I even packed the inside of the Tin Lizzy with anything that would fit through its door."

233

As they began unloading Gus asked, "When are our Troopers due in?"

"Around two I imagine," Haywood guessed. "Hard Case had to go over to Chekov Sunday morning for a wedding. Mike O'Kelly and Katiana Henry tied the knot. Then her clan threw them a potlatch over in Circle starting Sunday afternoon and Hard Case attended that ceremony as well. She has a lot of family so it was probably one helluva party. Caldwell is picking him up about noon today and then they'll come straight out here."

"I wish I'd known," Gus said. "I would have sent a gift."

"Taken care of," Haywood told him. "I sent one in your name. Hard Case delivered it for you."

"What did I send them?" Gus inquired.

"What else?" Haywood said. "A bottle of Dew and a Waterford vase. You taught me well!"

Gus nodded his approval. "That should do it," he said.

"Speaking of gifts," Haywood dove into the rear compartment of the plane and began rummaging around. "Come over here, Morgan," he called over his shoulder. "Give me a hand with some of this stuff."

Gus stood aside and served as the last guy in the bucket brigade as Morgan received boxes and packages from Haywood and passed them along to him. Gus stacked them on the gravel as she did so. As always, Haywood's Santa routine brought out the little girl in her. She was literally bubbling with excitement.

When they had offloaded everything from Haywood's rented Cessna, Gus produced his hip flask and passed it around.

He said, "We have four hours to kill before the other guys show up. Let's take Morgan's latest container load of gifts and all your gear down to the cabin. You can stow your kit in the bunkhouse, then we'll have a proper drink while she tears into the presents. If there's enough time left after that, we'll go down to the stream and wet a line. Morgan and I have been knocking 'em dead lately, but we left a few for you."

"I didn't see any bears on your stretch of the river when I did my fly-over. As I recall, you were overrun with them last year when the salmon were spawning."

"They're fishing a few bends below us this year. Morgan says this is Trilogy's territory. He swings a big club in the bear community, as you well know. Remember how they avoided the river between here and Deadman Creek when we went up to scout the burn?"

"I do," Haywood confirmed. "We always wondered why there were no bear tracks along that section. But enough about bears – let's go have that drink you mentioned and let the rest of the day unfold as it will."

***

Hard Case looked a little worse for the wear when he and Caldwell showed up at The Varmitage just after two that afternoon.

"Good Lord," Hard Case told them, "those people sure know how to throw a wingding! I ate more, drank more and danced more than I ever did in my life. I'll sleep well tonight."

"Did you dance with the bride?" Gus asked.

"I danced with everyone," Hard Case told him. "They just get in a big circle and let 'er rip. And, by the way, Mike and Katiana send their thanks for the gifts. I imagine Haywood told you he covered you on that."

Gus nodded. "Yep. Whiskey and a vase to drink it out of. Just what I would have sent myself had I known."

Haywood opened a cooler and showed the new arrivals the two salmon he'd caught just before they landed. "Rig your rods," he said. "They're hitting red-and-black streamers if you have any. If not, I'll loan you a few."

Caldwell didn't have to be coaxed. He put his rod together and headed down to the river. Hard Case begged off.

"You guys go ahead," he told them. "I'm just going to kick back on the porch and enjoy the sunshine – might even get in a little nap."

"There's beer in the cooler just inside the cabin door," Gus informed him. "Hair of the dog, and all that. Help yourself."

He and Haywood walked down the bar far enough to give Caldwell plenty of room, then they spread out themselves.

"Bottle for the biggest?" Haywood challenged.

Gus laughed. "You're on. Since it's not for the first one landed, I'll even give you a head start."

He sat on a driftwood log, watched Haywood cast his line upstream, and lit his pipe. He'd missed these guys. Not like he had last summer before Morgan appeared, but missed the camaraderie and good-natured ribbing. He was glad he'd built the bunkhouse and hoped they would come out and use it often. He knew Morgan liked them too. She'd been swept off her feet with the lavish gifts Haywood had brought her this trip – an Irish linen table cloth and napkins to match, a silver salmon poacher; and a set of garden tools, complete with apron. She rewarded him with hugs and kisses that would have been considered statutory rape in most civilized societies. She certainly knew how to keep the presents coming.

"Ha!" Haywood cried out. Gus looked up and could tell by the arc in his rod, he hooked a big one.

"Don't horse him!" he called down. "He'll take some tiring out before you can bring him in."

The salmon rode the current downstream in the fast water and Haywood played him well, feeding out enough line to ease the strain on his rod while never letting it go slack. He turned the fish and guided him over into the calm water close to shore and began slowly bringing him back upstream. He had him swimming against the current now and Gus figured two more strong runs might do the trick. Halfway back up to Haywood, the big fish bolted suddenly out into midstream and got sideways in the fast current. The line snapped and its tippet floated through the air and settled in a coil at Haywood's feet.

"Damn it!" he shouted. "Didn't see that coming."

Gus laughed and knocked the dottle out of his pipe against the log. "Let me show you how it's done," he said, picking up his fly rod and walking down to the water's edge. "You wouldn't have won the jackpot with a little fella' like that anyway."

***

Hard Case enjoyed a beer and a smoke while inspecting Morgan's flourishing garden boxes. She saw him through the window and couldn't contain herself. Caldwell had disappeared up around the bend above the boat launch so she tapped on the window pane to get Case's attention. He was surprised to see her, but when she beckoned him to come inside, he held up a finger to indicate "one minute", and trotted up to the bunkhouse.

He returned with a gift wrapped box and went straight inside.

"I didn't know if I'd see you this trip," he told her. "But, I brought a little something, just in case."

Morgan eyed the box, clearly pleased. "Oh, Case," she said, and gave him a peck on the cheek. "You didn't need to, but I'm delighted you did."

"I wanted to show my thanks for arranging the meeting with Old Blue Eye. I couldn't have done it without your help."

She accepted the box and opened it while he looked on. It contained a set of four crystal wine goblets. She nearly wept with joy.

"I don't know much about vases," he said modestly. "But, I know my drinking vessels."

She laughed and hugged him, giving him another kiss on the cheek. "They're beautiful," she said. "I've always loved Waterford. Thank you, Case."

He was not normally given to awkwardness around women, but he couldn't conceal the blush that colored his cheeks. Morgan had a way of making him feel like a schoolboy.

"You're most welcome," was all he could think of to say.

Morgan nodded toward the window. "They're coming back up to the cabin now," she said. "Why don't you take the cooler out on the porch. I'm sure they'll be ready for a cold beer."

Hard Case was thankful for the opportunity to gracefully withdraw. He opened the door, carried the cooler outside and set it on the big table.

"Bar's open gentlemen!" he called out as they came up the slope.

***

Gus had constructed a small stone smoker near his meat drying racks, downstream of the cabin perhaps a hundred yards. It was large enough to accommodate six split salmon, hanging from green spruce poles which he poked through the high holes he had left in the stone wall below the lid for just that purpose. He had smoked a few salmon last year using birch chips, but Haywood was a purist when it came to smoked salmon so he had brought Gus a large bag of western red alder chips, native to southeast Alaska, but not to be found in the interior. Gus had to admit, the flavor produced by this hardwood was much better than anything he'd used before.

They gathered at the big table on the new porch and drank beer in the late afternoon and recounted their day's adventures. They had eight fish in the cooler and planned to add to that count in the evening.

"Haywood," Gus said, "how about you grill a couple of these lunkers for dinner tonight? I'll get the others brined and in a couple days we can smoke them for a few hours. You guys can take them home with you when you pull out."

"Sounds good to me," Haywood agreed. "Grilled or smoked, you can't beat fresh salmon." He lifted two of the big fish out of the cooler and took them down to the stream to prepare them for grilling.

Caldwell said, "How do you make your brine, Gus?"

"Nothing fancy," Gus told him. "I just mix a little non-iodized salt with some brown sugar and cover the splits with it. I leave them for a day, then turn them and coat the other side. After they set for another day, I smoke 'em."

"No liquid?" Caldwell asked.

"Nope," Gus shook his head. "The fish exude plenty of moisture. The salt and sugar just soak it up and form a soggy crust around the slabs. I don't even rinse it off before I hang them in the smoker."

"Sounds simple enough," Caldwell said.

"It is," Gus told him. "You split the fish and I'll get the salt and sugar, then I'll walk you through the process."

***

It rained in the night and the occupants of the new bunkhouse discovered there were a few diabolically placed holes in the tarps with which Gus had covered the roof. Hard Case, who was usually the last one out of bed, had the coffee perking on the camp stove when Gus and Haywood emerged into the misty morning. Haywood smiled and prepared to deliver a cheerful greeting.

Hard Case glowered at him. "If you ask me how I slept, Jennings, I'll shoot you dead."

Gus couldn't resist. "Top of the mornin' to you, Case. You look particularly radiant this morning. Nothing like a good night's sleep, eh?"

"That's exactly what I had...nothing even close to a good night's sleep," he growled and turned down the Coleman's flame a little. "With Caldwell in the top bunk, at least I stayed dry. He had the foresight to spread his tent's rain fly over him before he turned in. But, the incessant drip...drip...drip drove me nuts."

The coffee appeared dark enough in the little glass dome on the percolator, so Hard Case poured out three cups and they each took one. Gus looked across the creek at the mist hanging just above the tree tops.

"It's like this most mornings lately," he said. "The sun will burn off the fog in another hour or so. Maybe we should tackle the roof today. I don't fancy another night of water torture either."

Hard Case lit a Camel and settled on a log. "Good idea," he agreed. "The four of us can probably have it rolled out and nailed off before lunch."

Caldwell came out of the bunkhouse and headed off into the woods. Hard Case took a deep drag on his cigarette and chuckled. "Gotta give him credit," he said. "He was the only one of us with enough sense to have a rain fly in his backpack. He was directly under the leak, but I don't think he got a drop on him."

"He's certainly no dummy," Gus said, as he finished his coffee. "Now that he's up and about, we can have breakfast. I'll go down to the cabin and mix up some pancake batter. Why don't you guys get the ham and eggs started while I'm gone?"

Hard Case and Haywood shot each other a quick glance, both of them knowing Gus was going back to the cabin for more than pancake batter. They had been surprised that he'd spent the night with them in the bunkhouse, but he'd said the Captain should be aboard for the maiden voyage.

***

The next two days went by far too quickly. As they had discussed, once the haze had burned off, they removed the sodden tarps from the bunkhouse roof and allowed the planks to dry in the sun and breeze while they spent the morning among the salmon. There had been a good surge of fish just after breakfast, and occasionally they had two or three on at one time. For the most part, they were spaced far enough apart that their lines did not become tangled, but once they lost both fish and tackle when a particularly large male made a strong run and stripped off enough line to tie up with another hooked salmon coming the other way. There was a good deal of splashing, laughter, shouts of encouragement and bellows of outrage. When they broke for lunch they took a head count. They had twenty-eight fish.

"It's a good thing you established residency last summer," Hard Case told Gus as he gutted a large female and deposited her roe sacks in a five-gallon bucket they had washed out specifically for that purpose. "If you hadn't qualified for subsistence living this year, we'd be over our limit. We city dwellers have a bag and possession limit of six fish each, over twenty-eight inches."

Haywood said, "That's true, but now that you are a documented bush rat you can run out a set net if you want, or even a salmon wheel."

"I know," Gus told them, "but I get enough with the fly rod to keep me happy. If I caught many more, I'd be tending the smoker five days a week. It's not as though there isn't enough other game about to keep me fed."

Considering the haul they had made that morning, they put their rods away for the day, ate lunch, then walked down to the bunkhouse and made sure the roof planks had dried sufficiently to apply the felt and tarpaper. Haywood clambered up the scaffolding and had a look.

"Still a few damp spots on the north side," he called down. "But, we can start over here on the front pitch. By the time we reach the peak, the other side will be dry as a bone."

"Let's get after it then, boys," Hard Case said. "How do you want to approach it Gus?"

"Two on the roof, one on the scaffold, one on the ground should do it," Gus told his crew. "Caldwell, since you're young and nimble, you'll be on the roof with me. Haywood, because you're the tallest, you can nail the middle section halfway up from the scaffolding while we nail off the ends. Hard Case, since you're…"

"Yeah, yeah," Hard Case said. "I know you were about to say I'm the strongest and also the only one of you slackers industrious enough to do the tote and carry work on the ground."

"Gentlemen," Gus said, "Case read my mind. That's exactly what I was about to say."

***

It took them only three hours to roof the bunkhouse. With Hard Case handing up the rolls of material and the other three laying, cutting and nailing, the work went fast. It likely would have taken them only two hours, but Gus insisted on getting a section of chimney pipe secured through the roof jack, and seating and sealing the flashing. Once the floor boards were in he would build up a thin stone hearth-pad over them and install the stove. Now that the through-the-roof section of chimney pipe was in place, he could do that alone. It would just be a matter of getting the stove's flue positioned under the drop pipe, add the interior sections of chimney and extend the one above the roof, then top it off with the weather cap.

"That'll do it!" he told the crew as he applied the final coating of roofing tar to the high side of the chimney flashing. "The only rain we'll get inside tonight will have to come in horizontally through the gaps between the wall logs."

Hard Case lit a Camel and sat on a stump while the roofing crew gathered tools and came down the scaffolding.

"I hope you're not suggesting we begin chinking," he said. "The sun's over the yardarm. Time to open the bar."

Gus laughed. "No chinking this trip, gentlemen," he told them. "Thanks for helping with the roof. Let's open a few beers and get into that new set of horseshoes Caldwell was kind enough to bestow upon The Varmitage. There's a good stretch of flat, sandy ground right over there where the gravel bar meets the willows."

Hard Case said to Caldwell, "Let's give these civilians a lesson in the fine art of pitching iron, son. The Troopers against the Perps! They don't stand a chance."

"Sounds like these flatfoots have thrown down the gauntlet, Gus," Haywood said.

"Flatfoots again!" Hard Case laughed. "Troopers versus the Flatfooted Turkey Fuckers!"

Caldwell shook his head. "Every time I bring him out here, he goes a little further round the bend."

They walked together down to the cabin, trading barbs and disparaging comments all the way.

'I wish this summer would never end,' Gus thought to himself.

"So do I," Hard Case said aloud, then looked startled. He looked over at Gus as they approached the porch. Gus made eye contact and gave him a gentle smile.

'Welcome to the club,' he thought.

Hard Case nodded. He understood something of import had just occurred. He just wasn't exactly sure of what it was.

Chapter 46

August, 2001
Crooked Creek
Kenai Peninsula, Alaska

"Five thousand?" Clive asked, mentally calculating how much he would make after fuel costs and landing fees.

Jong Min-jun, now going by the name Lee, nodded his head in affirmation. "Yes," he confirmed. "Five thousand U.S., but you must take me in exactly where I showed you on the map and then pick me up later at the cabin."

Clive gave up on the mathematics, he'd never been very good with numbers. "It's over eight hundred miles round trip," he said. "And I've never put down on the Moose Jaw. I'd have to do a scout run out of the closest town. That's a lot of fuel. How 'bout five thousand plus expenses?"

Lee appeared to consider this for a moment. He had no intention of paying Clive anything beyond the twenty-five hundred dollar advance he would give him before they departed Kasilof. But, he needed a bush pilot and he needed Clive's inflatable raft and survival gear if he were to get back into the Moose Jaw. Still, he did not wish to seem overanxious.

"Okay," he agreed. "But, you must keep your receipts for everything. I will settle up with you when we get back here."

Clive didn't like it; he wasn't sure he could trust Lee to pay up. Then again, the little Korean seemed to have pretty deep pockets. He'd paid for the extra diesel it took to run the generator twelve hours a day for the past three months, and he had covered all the food and booze they had gone through too – not to mention the drugs. If he helped Lee this time, he might become his main man. That would mean a lot more money down the road.

"Done," he said. "I'll pay for everything out of the advance and keep the receipts like you said. But, all I gotta do is outfit you for a one day float, then taxi you in and out. Is that right?"

The Cobra smiled. "You got it right," he agreed. "And, if you do well on this run, there will be more in the future."

This was just what Clive needed to hear. "It won't take me long to put your outfit together. When do you want to go?"

"In a few days, I think," Jong told him. "How long will it take us to get up there?"

"Four hours to Fairbanks, give-or-take," Clive told him. "Have to refuel there so you're lookin' at an hour on the ground. Then I'd say it's probably another hour into the Moose Jaw. Six hours total."

Jong wanted to have the raft inflated and be on the water no later than three o'clock in the afternoon. Clive told him the current probably averaged about five miles an hour along that stretch and he had fifteen river miles to cover. If he began floating at three, he would arrive at Gus' landing strip about six o'clock. His plan was to put into shore, deflate the raft and leave it and his survival gear on the bar while he walked down to the cabin to settle accounts with Gus. He would allow himself two hours on the ground, just in case something went wrong. There would still be plenty of daylight for Clive to land and pick him up at eight o'clock in the evening.

"Good. So six hours to where you put me in means we should leave here no later than nine o'clock in the morning. Today is Friday; can we go on Monday?"

"Sure," Clive told him. "I could be ready to go tomorrow if you said the word. But, we can use the three days to get you checked out on the survival gear. You shouldn't need it on a fifteen mile float, but you never know. There's no sense taking it along if you don't know how to use it."

Clive had shown Jong how to inflate and deflate the raft over the past few weeks. And Jong had made several three mile floats down Crooked Creek between salmon runs, when there had been no one else on the water. He had become quite adept at using the oars to navigate downstream and learned to read the water ahead to choose the best channel. He was confident that he would be able to manage fifteen miles on the Moose Jaw with little difficulty.

Clive had insisted that he remain inside the lodge during the salmon runs – he did not want it known that he had a guest. Most salmon fishermen stayed on the Kasilof River which teemed with big fish, but a few came up the creek from time to time. And some even docked at the lodge, thinking it was still a going concern. Clive never invited any of them inside, but he kept a thermos of coffee ready to hand, which he would always offer just to keep up appearances. He knew, having been a guide himself, that most fishermen had more food and drink aboard than they needed, so the gesture was simply that. He could not remember anyone accepting his offer.

Chapter 47

After refueling at a small gravel strip outside of Fairbanks, they flew northwest for just over an hour. The sky was clear and there was no weather in the forecast.

"Okay," Jong said. "That's where I want you to drop me."

Clive took his Super Cub down to one hundred feet elevation and flew over the bar from both directions. "Yeah," he conceded. "I don't see a problem landing on that."

Jong was getting excited. "Good. Now follow the river downstream about fifteen miles and you'll see where I want me to pick me up."

Clive remained at low altitude for the first ten miles so Lee could have a look at the river he was going to float. It didn't appear to be anything he couldn't handle.

"I'm going to take it up to normal cruising altitude now," he said. "I don't want to spook your friend with a low level fly-over."

"Good," Jong said. "Yes. Very good." Clive could hear the tightness in his voice. He was certainly cranked up. He wondered if Lee had done a line while he was filling up the tanks.

"There!" Jong cried out, pointing down to an unmistakable landing strip on the left bank of the river. It would have been hard to miss considering the log cabin situated not more than a half-mile downstream.

"Got it," was all Clive said, maintaining his course until they were well below Wolf Creek. Then he climbed up to seven thousand feet and crossed over the mountains to the Chekov side before heading back to the put-in.

Clive made one more low level pass over the bar with the wind behind him before banking into a one-eighty turn and landing into a gentle breeze. The bar sloped very gradually down to the river, but there were no obstructions to speak of. He helped Lee unload and inflate the raft, then went over the timing again as they assembled the rowing frame.

"So, I'll do a recon run over the cabin at eight o'clock. If you're ready to be pulled out, stand right there in the middle of the landing strip. I'll dip my wings to let you know I see you and then you go back up to the top of the bar so I can land. If you're not there at eight, I'll make one more fly-over at nine. After that, you're on your own."

"I'll be there at eight," Jong told him with absolute certainty. "Just make sure you are."

He stowed his backpack of survival gear in the bow and was about to put his rifle into the raft also, when he had a change of plan. "Here," he told Clive, handing him the Savage. "I won't need this. It will just be extra weight."

"You need a gun," Clive insisted. "The salmon are still coming up this river. You could have bear trouble."

Jong thought about this for a minute, then said, "You're right. Let me have your pistol. I can wear it on my hip like you do and both my hands will be free."

Clive said, "You ever shoot a handgun?"

"Yes," Jong told him proudly. "Jackie let me shoot his a few times. I was pretty good at close range."

"What did he carry?" Clive asked.

"What?" Jong was becoming impatient.

"Was it a revolver or a semi?" Clive pressed.

Jong wanted to get going. "It was a revolver, just like yours. I think it was a .357 Magnum. Now give me the damned gun so I can push off."

***

Less than an hour below the put-in point Jong approached a place where the river divided into two distinct channels. Had he not seen this fork from the air, he would have been deceived into believing the best way was to the left. Fortunately, he had observed that the left fork split again into two shallow channels. As his raft carried no significant weight aside from himself, it drew very little water, and he probably would have been safe no matter which fork he chose. Nevertheless, he kept to the right.

Clive had been a good instructor when it came to rafting. Jong gained confidence as he successfully avoided the sweepers leaning over the fast water on the outside of the bends, and also the big rocks in the shallows off the other bank. He checked his watch and realized he was making good time. But, just to be sure, he put in on the sandy edge of the next gravel bar he came to. The wind had picked up a little and once the bow nosed up onto the bar, the raft swung slowly around and sat parallel to the shoreline. Jong stepped over the port side into ankle deep water and was on dry land after only one step. 'This is easy,' he thought.

As Clive had instructed, he kept a firm grip on the bow line until he had tied it off to a driftwood log a few paces up the bar from the water. Then, after confirming the time, and comparing his GPS coordinates with those of Gus' cabin, he determined he would reach his landing strip a little ahead of schedule. He considered pushing on, but did not want to arrive early. If things went as he expected, he would have a long wait until eight o'clock.

"What the hell," he said aloud. "A little pick-me-up can't hurt." He fetched his backpack from the bow of the raft, brought it back to the log and took out a small plastic baggie of white powder.

A raven landed in the top of a tree across the creek. He wished he had his rifle; he hated those damned birds. Clive's pistol was holstered on his right hip. Getting it out would have been awkward, and he'd never actually shot a handgun at a distant target before. Jong only wanted to wear it to make Gus think he was right handed. A little edge, but an edge nevertheless.

"You're lucky, bird," he said. "If I could shoot this thing, I'd blow you into a mess of bloody black feathers." He laughed at his own frivolity in speaking to a fucking raven. The coke was kicking in fast.

The raven, apparently not appreciative of his humor, left its perch and flew off downstream. He recalled a raven in one of his crazy dreams and hoped it was not a bad omen. 'Had the raven in his dream spoken to him? Yes, he was sure of it. It had said, "They are waiting." What the fuck was that supposed to mean? Who the fuck were 'they' anyway? Whoever 'they' were, fuck 'em – let 'em wait.' He laughed out loud again.

Chapter 48

Gus was chinking the gaps in the last wall of the bunkhouse when Morgan came running up the bar from the cabin.

"Gus," she gasped, trying to catch her breath. "He's here. Come back to the cabin and get your big gun."

Gus did not have to ask who "he" was. He had been expecting him all summer. He dropped off the scaffold and took Morgan by the shoulders. "Is he at the cabin?" he asked her quietly.

"No, he's a few miles upstream of the burn. He'll be here soon. Go get your gun."

Gus smiled. He remembered seeing the raven pass overhead and land on the roof of the porch. "Did Old Blue Eye bring you the news?"

"Yes. He came and told me. He also told me the bear is coming down from the hills, and that you must not let the bear kill this man."

"Why not?" Gus asked, then realization washed over him like a wave. It all became clear. "You don't have to answer that," he said. "I understand."

"You don't have to understand, Gus. You just have to be ready when he comes and you need to kill him before the bear does." She was clearly beside herself. He'd never seen her so agitated.

"Just like that?" he asked. "Soon as he shows up, I just shoot him?"

"Yes," she said emphatically. "Even Hard Case said you must not let him get close to you. If he shows up, just shoot him."

Gus remembered. Hard Case had indeed said that, but he doubted he meant it. Still… "I'll consider it," he told Morgan, just to appease her.

She was not to be mollified. "No. Don't consider it – do it! Remember what the Russian told you. He's very quick with a knife; he always has one hidden in his right sleeve and he is left handed. If he gets close to you, you don't have a chance. Just shoot him!"

"Easy!" Gus told her. "I'll call Hard Case from the cabin. He needs to know his fugitive is at hand. Let's not go off half-cocked until we've heard what he has to say."

Mournful George answered the satellite phone.

248

"George, Gus here. That Korean you've been looking for is on his way to my cabin as we speak. Let me talk to Case."

George, ever the professional, never wilted under pressure. "He's in a meeting with our esteemed Lieutenant Governor. But, I can interrupt; tell me what you need."

"I need to know how long it will take you to get somebody out here."

"Caldwell isn't due back from Talkeetna until seven o'clock. So, I'd say at least two hours. Maybe three. That doesn't help much, does it?"

"Afraid not," Gus said. "I'm expecting Jong inside an hour. Any advice?"

"Yes," Mournful George said quietly. "The boss anticipated this eventuality, and told me to remind you not to take any chances. For what it's worth, 'Don't be a fool,' were his exact words. Anyway, as soon as we hang up, I'll go tell him. He hates meetings with politicians, so he'll appreciate the interruption."

"Well, George," Gus said, "I'll try to talk him to death if I can. Get somebody out here as soon as possible."

"Don't be a fool," Mournful George repeated, then hung up.

***

The Cobra came around the last bend, swung ashore, and beached his raft on the sandy verge of the landing strip. He checked his watch and was pleased to see he was just slightly ahead of schedule. It must have been the wind pushing him from behind, he thought. It had grown stronger over the past hour, and was now buffeting the tall spruce trees that lined the far bank. He could hear their trunks rubbing and creaking and their boughs swooshing as they whipped about. The day grew darker and he cast his eyes back up the valley. A bank of black clouds now obscured the mountaintops far upstream. They appeared to be tumbling in the sky above the high country.

He stepped over the side of the raft into the knee-deep water, waded up onto the gravel bar and tied the bow line off to a cluster of willows. Although he had arrived a little earlier than he anticipated, the approaching storm imbued in him a sense of urgency. He dragged the empty raft up onto the bar and quickly detached the rowing frame before opening the bladder valves. When the raft was completely deflated, he folded it into a rectangle and left it on the edge of the landing strip.

He opened the backpack, took out his killing knife and strapped it to his right wrist before putting on his lightweight cotton jacket. It had loose sleeves that would conceal his knife, yet allow his left hand to reach in quickly without obstruction. At Clive's insistence, he had packed a wind-and-waterproof pullover but he chose to leave it in the backpack. Its sleeves had tight elastic wrists – wrong for today's work.

He closed the backpack and left it with the raft. He gave himself a quick pat down to make sure he was ready. 'Belt knife – check; wrist knife – check; pocket knife – check; sidearm – check. 'Good to go,' he thought. 'So go!'

He did not know about the trail that went from the landing strip, up through the trees and down to the cabin so he kept to the riverbank. He refined his strategy as he walked downstream. He would hail the cabin when he arrived, and when Gus came out he would pretend to need help.

"I hit a sweeper and punched a hole in my raft," was to be his opening ploy. No Alaskan would refuse help to a stranded floater in the bush. Still, he realized Gus would be wary of an oriental showing up unexpectedly. He would have heard by now that Jackie Sam's killer had been a Korean. 'Not a problem,' he thought. He would say he was Chinese; Americans could never tell the difference.

The temperature was dropping rapidly. He regretted having left the pullover in the backpack and considered going back for it, but felt he needed to keep moving. The gathering storm complicated things. He had wanted to take his time, but now he had to hurry. Gus would certainly have rain gear and warm clothing in the cabin. All he had to do was what he had come here to do – kill Gus. Then he could sit out the storm in the comfort of the cabin until eight o'clock. He kept moving, his mind now fully focused on how to get in close to his enemy.

He would convince Gus to accompany him back upstream to help him with the punctured raft. Somewhere along the way Gus would drop his guard, if he turned his back, that would be all the opportunity he needed. He knew just where to put the blade into a man's back to pierce the heart. But wait – why the rush? He decided not to go for the heart on the first thrust. Even if the storm moved in, he still had two hours to kill. 'Two hours to kill!' he thought. 'Yes! Two hours to kill the fucker.' He would go slow – stick him just enough to put him down and out of action, then have a little fun. Talk to him while he stripped him naked and opened his belly and spilled out his guts like he had done with Malachenko. 'Two hours!' he thought. He got sexually excited just imagining it. 'Thump…Thump…Thump – another one bites the dust!' Damon had said Gus could not be killed. Maybe it just took a little longer to kill him. "I can live with that," he said, and laughed out loud.

***

Gus had decided to wait outside for the Korean. When an enemy was good at up close fighting you did not meet him in a confined space. You needed room to maneuver. After careful consideration, he chose the woodpile near the splitting stump for his blind. He left the axe sticking in the stump because it looked natural, and its handle pointed toward the cabin, subtly guiding the eye in that direction. He repositioned the spruce round Morgan jokingly referred to as his "lawn chair" behind the woodpile where he would sit and wait. He had chosen this position for his blind because it was east of the cabin so anyone coming down the trail from the ridge would not see him until they were out in front of the porch. It also had the advantage of being shadowed by the old porch roof, and the woodpile provided a screen. With all the gaps in it, it probably wouldn't stop a bullet, but he didn't believe Jong was coming to shoot him. The little bastard worked with a knife; it was his trademark.

Gus had a knife too, a big Marine Corps Ka-Bar fighting knife. Nevertheless, he was wearing his .44 Magnum, and had propped the .444 Marlin against the back side of the woodpile within easy reach. Jong had chosen the place for this fight, so it was only right that Gus got to choose the weapon. If his adversary elected to fight with a knife, so be it – but this was to be a gunfight.

As he surveyed his preparations, he noticed that the day had lost its warmth. He looked upstream and saw the storm clouds gathering over the high country. The wind coming down the valley bore the scent of coming rain. He trotted up the steps and entered the cabin.

"You might want to start…" he did not finish the sentence. Morgan was not there, nor was Bosworth. Smoke coming out of the

251

chimney would indicate he was inside. It would serve as a good distraction. He wadded up some newspaper, stuffed it in the stove, added a handful of kindling and a few chunks of firewood, then tossed in a match. He didn't have time to make sure the flame caught; he needed to get settled in his blind and wait for his visitor. He snatched his all-weather camo jacket off a wall peg and headed back outside. There was a small "wumph" behind him as he went out the door. Good omen, he thought. Things were going his way.

Outside the sky was getting darker by the minute. He had a quick look up the path which came down from the overland trail then he grabbed a small blue tarp from under the porch on the way back to his blind. It was common practice in the bush to cover your firewood with a tarp, but Gus wanted it for concealment. As he quickly arranged it over the stacked cordwood, he glanced up at the cabin's roof. An almost invisible column of smoke poured out of the top of the chimney then dissipated downstream in the wind. 'Looks like that Gus fella' is at home,' he said to himself and smiled.

Jong had had more than enough time to float down from the burn, so unless he was belly-crawling through the willows, he should show up pretty soon. A few drops of rain began to fall, so he pulled on his hood and cinched up its drawstrings. He lifted a corner of the tarp and slid his rifle under the edge. No sense inviting rust.

The wind through the trees and the raindrops spattering on the tarp and the hood of his jacket obscured all other sounds so he shifted position a little to give himself a view of everything from the porch steps down to the creek. The rain came down harder as the wind driven squall swept in. Maybe waiting outside hadn't been such a good idea, he thought. Then again, Jong was exposed to the elements too. Perhaps he had not come prepared for bad weather. A vision flashed through his mind and it was as if he were perched high atop a tree, looking down on the Moose Jaw. A small man was crouched in the willows, the neck of his jacket pulled up over his head. The willows offered very little protection from the rain as it beat down upon him. Rivulets of water streamed off the fabric and ran down his forehead, over his closed eyes and dripped from his nose and chin. He was shivering and Gus could see the misery on his face. The man wiped the water from his eyes, then opened them.

They were oriental eyes – the eyes of Jong Min-jun. The eyes of The Cobra.

The squall passed through and the rain moved down the valley, but colder air came in behind it. Tendrils of vapor began to dance above the surface of the river as the water gave up its heat to the icy air. Gus could no longer see the vision, but he knew the terrain around The Varmitage very well. Jong had been crouched in the willows just upstream of his boat launch. He had not known about the overland trail, so he had walked down along the creek bank. Gus could feel him moving again. He did not need to hear the crunch of gravel to tell him Jong was about to appear. It was the same feeling you got just before a big trout came up under your floating fly. You tensed your muscles a microsecond before the fish broke the surface. Gus watched the willows down by the boat launch with the same intensity as he followed his dry fly riding down the current. He remained perfectly still in his blind and could almost hear his heartbeats. Thump…thump…thump, and there he was, right where Gus had known he would be.

Jong stopped near the launch and touched the gun on his hip – Gus did not miss the fact that he wore it on his right hip – then he touched his right wrist and his belt, and finally his left pocket. He was inventorying his weaponry. Gus had heard he always had a knife up his sleeve and another in a belt sheath. He wondered what he might have hidden in his pocket.

When Jong appeared satisfied that everything was accounted for, he came slowly up the bank. As he grew closer Gus could see he was shivering uncontrollably. Was that a cotton jacket he was wearing, Gus wondered? Perhaps he hadn't heard the old outdoorsman's mantra – Cotton Kills. Hypothermia was not subject to the seasons. You could lose your body heat as quickly in summer as you could in the winter. Gus gave the fool perhaps twenty minutes before he would be unable to stand erect. Without dry clothes and hot liquid, Jong was finished.

Gus studied the Korean carefully as he made his way up the slope. He appeared disoriented and was unsteady on his feet. Gus wondered if perhaps this was a ploy, but decided it was not. The cold was taking its toll and Jong's condition was deteriorating rapidly.

As he neared the cabin, Jong did not even glance in the direction of the woodpile. He was momentarily distracted by movement on the roof. A big raven lifted off the peak with a raucous squawk and a flapping of black wings. It seemed to be headed upstream, then banked into the wind and settled on the gabled end of the bunkhouse. Jong followed it with his eyes.

"S-S-Stinking b-bird," Gus heard him stutter. His teeth were chattering so speech was difficult.

Jong remained focused on the bird for a few moments, then continued toward the cabin. He stopped at the foot of the steps and caught the smell of burning wood. He glanced up at the roof and saw a wisp of smoke rising from the chimney into the frigid air. Gus had a fire going in there! All his plans evaporated in that instant. All that mattered now was getting inside near the fire and getting warm.

"Hello in the c-cabin!" he called out as loud as he could. The Sam brothers had advised him to always announce his arrival before getting too close to a bush dwelling. Any sound not accompanied by a human voice might be a bear.

He had just placed his left foot on the bottom step when a voice came out of the shadows to his right. He momentarily lost his balance and staggered backward as if he'd been struck a blow.

"We've been waiting for you," the voice said quietly.

Jong's scalp tingled and a cold hand seemed to grip his heart. 'We?' he wondered. Then he recalled the raven in his dream. It had said, "They are waiting."

He recovered his balance and looked around. He had not been able to tell where the voice had come from.

"W-will you help me?" he said. "The storm c-caught me on the river. I'm w-wet and need to get w-warm."

The voice came out of the shadows again. "You're floating this river alone?"

"No!" He desperately tried to remember the story he had prepared. His thoughts were coming to him slowly. "M-My f-friend stayed with the raft. I c-came for help."

'Enough of this,' Gus thought. He said, "That's not true. Your name is Jong Min-jun. You killed Alexi Malachenko and Jackie Sam. You came here to kill me too. Looks like it just isn't your day."

"Lee!" Jong cried. "My name is L-Lee, I am Chinese n-not Korean!"

Gus could see he was losing it and wondered if he shouldn't shoot him and have done with it. Just as this thought entered his mind, he saw the bear coming up from the creek through the mist. Trilogy stopped halfway up the bank and swung his enormous head from side to side. He made no sound, but Gus knew he was getting ready to charge. He brought his rifle out from under the tarp, pressed the safety to "Fire", and thumbed back the hammer. He knew there was a round in the chamber; he had jacked it in before settling down to wait.

Jong was still standing at the bottom of the steps, apparently unaware the bear was behind him. He started to speak, but Bosworth appeared from under the porch and rubbed himself against Jong's ankle.

"Ah!" Jong shrieked and kicked at the cat. As soon as his foot made contact Bosworth sunk his teeth and the claws of both forepaws into his ankle.

Jong cried out in anger and surprise. A long-bladed knife materialized in his left hand and he struck downward at the cat. At the same moment, Gus saw Trilogy coming in low and fast, another second and he would have Jong.

Gus didn't have time to aim, he just fired. The shot hit Jong's left wrist an instant before the blade sliced into Bosworth. The Cobra screamed as the impact of the heavy caliber bullet nearly tore his hand off. Blood and bone fragments exploded from the bottom of his loose sleeve and the knife went spinning into the fog. He staggered to his left and fell heavily to the ground. Bosworth bolted back under the porch and Trilogy, startled by the gunshot broke off his attack, rose to his full height and looked over toward the woodpile.

Gus levered another round into the chamber. Jong was not dead, but without medical attention, he would bleed out in a matter of minutes. The little Korean looked up from where he had fallen and saw the gigantic bear looming above him. He vomited.

Trilogy swung his eyes from the woodpile and focused them on the human whose scent he recognized. The essence of the man stirred rage deep within him. He dropped down on all fours, lifted his good left forepaw and with his five scimitar claws raked open

255

the stricken man's jacket, chest cavity and abdomen. Remarkably, Jong struggled to sit up. He looked down in horror at his exposed organs. Gus could see Jong's heart beating through his torn flesh, shattered ribcage and shredded lungs. The Cobra had just enough life in him to whimper one last word.

"No!" Frothy blood gurgled out of his mouth making the pathetic plea almost inaudible.

Trilogy opened his huge jaws and let out a thunderous roar. Gus aimed carefully and squeezed the trigger. Jong's barely pulsating heart exploded as the three hundred grain bullet blasted through it and blew a fist-sized hole in his back as it exited.

Trilogy swung his head toward Gus. Gus levered a fresh round into the chamber and waited. The bear focused his black eyes upon him for several heartbeats. Gus' senses became so acute he could smell the beast's wet fur, and hear the mist settling on birch leaves deep in the woods behind him. The fog-laden air vibrated with menace as their feral spirits joined in silent combat on a battlefield not of this world. At length, the bear gave forth a dismissive grunt and returned his attention to the dead human. He clamped his powerful jaws on the left arm. The grizzly's mouth was so wide Jong's whole arm, from shoulder to wrist, disappeared into its maw. With a whip of his broad, flat head, the gigantic bear threw the limp corpse halfway down the bar. Jong's left hand, nearly severed by Gus' bullet, flew off into the fog and his entrails spilled out of his torn abdomen as he whirled through the air.

The big bear turned to face Gus. He seemed to be deliberating upon his next course of action. Gus waited, finger on the trigger. Everything was still as if the valley were holding its breath. Even the Moose Jaw ran silently in the fog. After what seemed an eternity Trilogy shook his ponderous head as though to rid it of a thought, then he turned and proceeded down the slope toward the river. He approached the dead man, sniffed him, then rolled him over with his huge crippled paw. Gus' adrenaline-fueled vision could see every detail of Jong's death mask through the slowly stirring mist that covered the bar. The snake was dead.

The raven swooped down from its perch atop the bunkhouse and settled on the corpse's chest. With a quick bob of the head, it plucked out one still moist eyeball with its ebony beak. Gus could see the eye staring blankly at him from the bird's mouth, then the raven tossed back its head, opened its beak, and let the eyeball drop into its crop. The bear looked on dispassionately as the bird consumed the other eye, then flew over and landed on the handle of Gus' splitting axe.

"Nice touch," Gus told the raven. The bird answered with a single "Glunk".

Trilogy clamped his jaws around the mutilated corpse's midsection, lifted it effortlessly off the ground, turned and went back down toward the river where he disappeared into the vapors. Gus could hear the 'slosh-slosh-slosh' of his massive legs plowing through the water.

When the sound receded into the distance, Gus stood up on shaky legs and left his blind. Morgan sprung out of the cabin, flew down the steps and ran up the bar. He watched her disappear into the mist; swirling tendrils of it roiled in her wake. He didn't call out to her. He knew where she was going.

The raven squawked as it lifted off the axe handle, rose into the fog and, like Morgan, disappeared. Gus remained standing near the splitting stump and listened to the sound of beating wings fading in the distance. He recalled the night he had killed Roy McCaslin. There had been fog then too, and the flapping of wings. And the fog that night, just like this fog, had seemed alive. Perhaps it was. Spirits took many forms on the Moose Jaw.

He did not hear Morgan come up beside him. She just materialized out of the mist. She did not speak, but took one of his hands in hers and gently placed a gold ring in his palm. He looked down at it. The image of the cobra had been embossed in its surface by a master craftsman. It projected a disturbing beauty that only pure malevolence can possess. He had the sense that it squirmed in his hand.

"I thought you said I'd never see another snake in Alaska," he smiled wryly as he said this.

Morgan closed his hand around the ring and kissed him on the cheek. "Not one of any significance," she answered. "He was just a despicable little man who fancied himself a viper."

"I saw him in a vision before he came around the bend," Gus told her. "He was crouched under the willows in the rain. He looked like a miserable little boy, lost and alone and scared. I think he knew then he had come here to die."

257

"Yes," she said. "I saw it too. We've been sharing thoughts all summer. Now we've shared a vision."

Gus nodded his head slowly. "Not just us," Gus said. "It seemed, there at the end, that I was sharing something with the bear too. I'm just not sure what it was. But it was something powerful."

"And the raven?" she asked.

Gus smile. "Yes. The raven also. Now, there is one strange bird."

***

The fog did not lift until just after nine o'clock. Gus had spent a long time scouting the bar and the riverbank to see what there was to see. He gave Jong's severed hand a wide berth because he did not want to leave his footprints near it. He was certain Hard Case would notice the absence of the ring. Footprints near the hand would complicate matters. Mournful George had not told him Hard Case would be coming out with Caldwell, but lately Gus seemed to be sharing a private frequency with his old friend. He didn't know how he knew Hard Case was on his way, but he knew he was, nevertheless.

Once satisfied he had located all the evidence there was to find, he returned to the cabin. When he went inside, Bosworth hopped off the bed and made a few passes at his pant legs.

Gus smiled down at him. "I thought you disapproved of ankle biters," he said.

The big cat looked off into the corner of the room for a moment as if trying to compose an appropriate response. At length, he appeared to decide Gus' sarcasm was not worthy of one. He padded back over to the lady of the house and rubbed his jaw against the wood of her rocker.

Morgan smiled gently, reached down and stroked him from head to tail. Bosworth actually purred. She picked him up and settled him in her lap.

"I told you he'd start earning his keep someday," she said.

"Well, he certainly got the party started this evening," Gus told her.

He crossed the room to the stove and added a few chunks of wood to the fire. Then he went to the counter and poured them each a stiff whiskey. He took Morgan's over to her.

"The fog is lifting," he said. "Caldwell should be able to land by the time they arrive. I'll need to show them all the evidence and walk them through the chain of events. Did the hand look like a gunshot wound?"

Morgan sipped her drink. "No. It looked like a bear bit it off."

Gus nodded, "That's pretty close to the truth. But they'll have to look for the body. If they find it, it will be obvious I shot him. Hard Case won't be able to look the other way this time."

Morgan glanced up at him through a curtain of red hair that partially obscured her green eyes. "They won't find his body, Gus. By the time they get here, there will be little of it left."

Gus shuddered and downed his whiskey in a single swallow. He went back to the counter and was about to pour himself another when he heard the airplane approaching.

"Show time," he said. "I'll walk up and meet them."

"Take your rifle, Gus," she told him.

He looked at her speculatively. She knew – or suspected – something was not right. Perhaps she was thinking Trilogy might still be out there nursing a grudge. He had, after all, stolen a march on the bear when he killed Jong.

"Why…" he began.

"Just take your rifle," she preempted. "This is the Alaska bush. It would be imprudent to walk around out here with nothing but a pistol."

He didn't argue; she was right. He took the box of .444 cartridges off the shelf and pocketed a handful.

"Sounds like they're landing," he said, bending to kiss her. "I'd better get moving."

Outside, he noted that the cloud ceiling was still quite low, but there was enough clear air for an experienced bush pilot to set down on the landing strip. He went back behind the woodpile and fetched his rifle. He picked up the brass of the two spent cartridges he had fired earlier, and thumbed two fresh rounds into the magazine tube before heading up the trail. As he topped the ridge, he sensed there was something out of place. The fog still hung just above the tops of the tall spruce trees giving everything an eerie luminescence. But he had become accustomed to the otherworldliness of the Moose Jaw country – that wasn't it. There was something disturbing the stillness that always pervaded the fog shrouded woods. Then he realized he could still hear an airplane's engine ticking over. That was odd. Caldwell usually rolled out, taxied back down the bar, then killed the engine. He stopped atop the rise and listened. 'Yes,' he thought, 'that's not Caldwell.'

He racked the lever of his Marlin halfway open and confirmed there was a live round in the chamber. Then he started down the trail that would bring him out through the willows to the landing strip.

Chapter 49

"Divert! Divert!" Hard Case shouted as they dropped out of the fog over the river and rounded the bend above Gus' landing strip.

But, Caldwell didn't need to be told. He had already seen the other plane looming in his windscreen, rising steeply from the ground. He banked hard right knowing that the other aircraft would have to bank in the opposite direction if it were to avoid the trees across the river. His instinctive maneuver was all that saved them. The two Super Cubs slid past one another with just a few feet between them.

"Sweet Jesus!" Caldwell cried as the old Super Cub nearly clipped off a wing. "Get the numbers!" he yelled at Hard Case.

It had all happened too fast. Still Hard Case had glimpsed the numbers on the fuselage of the other plane as it went by them. He wasn't able to get them all, but enough to start a search. He fumbled his notepad out of a breast pocket and jotted down what he believed he'd seen. N_28_H.

"You got them?" Caldwell asked, his voice still high and tight.

"Just a partial," Hard Case told him.

"Shit!" the young pilot spat the word. Then, realizing he may have gone too far he said, "Sorry, Boss – I got a little excited there."

"Me too," Hard Case said, breathing a sigh of relief. "That was close. But, forget about that asshole. Gus might be in trouble. Put down as fast as you can. I think that fucker was Jong's transport. Did you see if there was a passenger?"

"No," Caldwell said, obviously still shaken. "I didn't see anything but yellow wings and a propeller."

He climbed to just beneath the cloud cover, brought her around and set down hard on Gus' strip. As they were rolling out, Hard Case saw Gus trotting out of the willows at the top of the bar.

"Thank God," he said. "Thank God."

Caldwell didn't bother bringing his nose around. As soon as he brought the plane to a stop he killed the engine and they both jumped out and ran to meet Gus. Hard Case was the first there and he threw his arms around Gus and crushed him to his powerful chest. Caldwell was only a step behind him. He piled on.

"Gus," he croaked. "We thought…"

Hard Case picked up where Caldwell faltered. "We thought we were too late."

Gus, engulfed in a constricting double bear hug, said, "You thought?" He struggled for breath. "I thought you two were toast! That was the closest thing I ever saw to a mid-air collision in my life."

"You didn't happen to get that guy's tail numbers did you?" Hard Case asked hopefully.

Gus shook his head. "No. He took off going straight away from me. I didn't see the sides. Sorry."

***

On the way back to the cabin Gus told them about his face-off with Jong and hearing an airplane coming in for a landing. He'd thought it was Caldwell – the timing was just about right. He'd gone up the overland trail and was just coming down the last slope when the other plane took off and he watched it rising as they were dropping in out of the low ceiling. He was sure they were going to collide.

"So, Jong's dead?" Hard Case asked.

"Dead and gone," Gus confirmed. "Trilogy made off with his mortal remains," he told them. "All except for his left hand. He lost that in the fight." It was the truth – just not the whole truth.

"But, there's no doubt he was dead?" Hard Case pressed.

"He was dead," Gus said unequivocally. "The bear just fastened his jaws around his waist and carried him off across the river."

Caldwell looked puzzled. "Who's Trilogy?" he asked innocently.

"It's a long story, lad," Hard Case said. "But it's the same bear that mauled Gus last year."

Gus nodded. "He's been around all summer. Old Blue Eye said he was waiting for Jong and the other Sam brother. If it was any other bear, I'd have my doubts, but with Trilogy..." He didn't need to finish.

"Yeah," Hard Case said thoughtfully. "You never know with that one. In any event, I'll have to deal with the inevitable paperwork. When we get back to the cabin, you can take us through it step-by-step and we'll collect whatever evidence your pet bear left behind."

***

As Hard Case had suggested, Gus walked them through it. He didn't mention how he had known Jong had arrived. He simply said he had been ready for his arrival and had prepared a blind outside the cabin. And, of course, he did not mention the fact he had fired the fatal shot an instant before Trilogy delivered his kill stroke. Hard Case wrote it all down in his little spiral bound note pad.

"So," Hard Case summed it up. "He said he got caught out on the river in the storm and put in here for shelter. I didn't see any watercraft up at the landing strip, and none here. If a plane brought him in, you'd have heard it. How do you figure he got here?"

Gus rubbed his chin and tried to remember all that had transpired in those short minutes before the fireworks. "He said something about a raft. I think he said he was coming downstream with a friend and that the friend stayed with the raft while he came for help."

"You think there might be someone else upstream of us waiting by a raft?" Hard Case asked.

"No," Gus told him. "I think he made that up on the fly. If there was a raft – and I guess that was the way he got here – I'd say someone flew him in and set him down on a bar high above us. There are a few good places up there to land a plane. Then he floated down here and left his vessel – probable an inflatable – up at the landing strip. If that plane we saw take off when you were coming in was his transport, the pilot must have returned for Jong on a scheduled run. When Jong didn't show, he loaded the inflatable aboard and cleared out as fast as he could."

"Makes sense," Caldwell said. "He must have figured Jong had run into trouble and decided to pull out while he could."

Hard Case said, "Which reminds me – Gus, is that satellite phone charged?"

Gus nodded and took it off the shelf. "Here," he said, placing the carrying case on the table. "It's got a full charge. Make your call."

While Hard Case called Mournful George to give him the partial tail numbers he had written in his notebook Gus and Caldwell went out on the porch.

"You said something about the Korean leaving a hand behind," Caldwell said. "We'll need it for evidence. We have Jong's fingerprints on file. We can use the hand to positively identify the deceased."

Gus smiled. "Follow me," he told him. He admired the young trooper's professionalism.

***

As he had done with Lindsay's body the previous autumn, Caldwell took a series of photographs of Jong's detached hand from various angles and elevations. Gus assumed it was important to record the gruesome image in situ before collecting it as evidence. Hard Case joined them midway through the "shoot" and gazed thoughtfully at the torn flesh of the wrist.

"It certainly looks like the hand was separated from the wrist by brute force trauma. I'd have thought a bear with jaws like his would have bit clean through."

Gus shifted his feet uncomfortably. "He didn't bite it off per se. It was sort of dangling by its tendons and sinews. I couldn't really tell what was holding it on. Anyway, I'm pretty sure Jong was already dead when the big bastard clamped down on his arm and with one shake of the head flung the whole body down the bar. The hand flew off over here and the rest of him landed over there." Gus pointed to a spot halfway down the bar toward the boat launch. "He'd already ripped him open from balls to briquette and his guts and lungs were spilling out as he spun through the air. You'll find a knife with his fingerprints on it somewhere over near the porch."

Hard Case walked down the bar and stopped at a place where the rocks were dotted with blood and offal.

"Better get a few shots over here too, Caldwell. Looks like maybe some bits of flesh and stomach contents. We'll bag up anything big enough to bother with when you're finished."

He looked at Gus and shook his head. "Kind of makes you realize how lucky you were last year, doesn't it Fergus. If you hadn't got your gun in that monster's mouth when you did, this could have been all that was left of you."

"Yeah," Gus said quietly. "The thought had crossed my mind."

"Be that as it may," Hard Case went on, "I better see if he left anything else behind. Where'd he go from here?"

Gus gestured down toward the river. "He headed off in that direction with the body. You can see smears of blood on some of

264

the rocks and there's a piece of his jacket near the waterline. I checked it out before you arrived. Come on, I'll show you."

He indicated the spots of interest as they proceeded. When they reached the water's edge, Gus pointed to a scrap of torn fabric lying in the mud.

"I'm pretty sure that was part of his jacket," he said.

Hard Case studied it for a moment. "Cotton?" he asked, incredulous.

Gus nodded, "I think so."

"Jesus," Hard Case said. "He didn't have a clue, did he?"

***

By the time Hard Case and Caldwell had photographed the scene and bagged and tagged the evidence it was nearly midnight.

"Well gentlemen," Hard Case said, "I think that's about all we can do on this side of the river. If you'll put us up for the night, Gus, we'll go over to the far bank tomorrow morning and see what else we can find. You mentioned a sidearm and another knife. Maybe we'll get lucky."

Gus said. "There's no bedding on the bunks in the bunkhouse. Did you bring your sleeping bags?"

Hard Case shook his head. "No, we tossed everything out of the rear compartment to make room for a stiff." He went silent after this admission, realizing the implications.

"No matter," Gus told them. "If you help me move the camp bed down to the cabin, you can sleep there. The rain chilled things off quite a bit. The cabin will be more comfortable than the bunkhouse."

They went up to the bunkhouse to fetch the two-tier camp bed before returning to the cabin. Hard Case and Caldwell each carried a section of the frame and Gus toted the mattresses.

As they entered the warm cabin, Hard Case said, "Caldwell, you get the top bunk tonight – I'll take the bottom."

"Sounds good," Caldwell said, winking at Gus. "We don't want to be top heavy."

Hard Case pulled a face and looked sadly at Gus. "You see what a man in my position has to tolerate?" he said. "It's intolerable."

Gus laughed, closed the door and deposited the mattresses on his own bed. Cop humor at the scene of a gruesome death did not surprise him anymore. He understood their need for a little comic

265

relief. He helped Caldwell set up the bunks in the corner while Hard Case tended bar. He poured whiskies for Gus and himself and opened a bottle of beer for Caldwell. The young Trooper rarely drank anything stronger.

They took their drinks out on the porch and sat at the big table. Hard Case pointed at a spot on the ground off the edge of the new deck. "That knife we found could prove to be a valuable piece of evidence. If it's the one he used on Malachenko, the lab boys might be able to extract some trace DNA that will prove it was the murder weapon. I'd like to put that case to rest too."

"I'm sure you would," Gus told him. "I imagine Alexi's clan is still agitating for closure."

"That's putting it mildly. Anyway, even if we don't find the body tomorrow, a DNA match on the knife will pretty much confirm Jong as his murderer. And that hand will be enough to identify your visitor as Jong Min-jun."

Caldwell finished his beer and stood up. "I'm turning in, guys," he said. "See you in the morning."

"Be careful climbing up to your bunk," Hard Case told him. "It might be top heavy without me anchoring the base. Wouldn't want you to tip over and hurt yourself."

Caldwell laughed as he went into the cabin. "Good night, Boss. Good night, Gus."

Hard Case lit up a Camel. "Why don't we have a nightcap and a smoke while Caldwell settles in?"

"My very thought," Gus agreed. "I'll pop inside and fetch my pipe."

When Gus came back out to the porch, he set the bottle on the big table alongside a jug of water. "Just in case we have more to discuss than anticipated," he said. "Wouldn't want to disturb young Trooper Caldwell going in and out."

"That's what I've always admired about you Fergus," Hard Case accepted the fresh whiskey Gus handed him. "Foresight. You always think ahead."

Gus settled down on the top step next to his old friend. They clinked glasses and sipped. Hard Case looked out into the gloaming and took a deep drag on his cigarette.

As the smoke rolled out of his mouth into the cold air, he said quietly, "Shot him, didn't you."

266

Gus lit his pipe before answering. When he had it going to his satisfaction he said, "Don't ask the question unless you're ready to hear the answer."

Hard Case considered this as he had another sip of his whiskey. At length, he sighed and said, "Tell me."

Gus told him. Hard Case never interrupted. When Gus had finished, the old cop lit another Camel and said, "I thought it was probably something like that. Sounds like the bear had already punched his ticket. Why'd you even bother?"

"I did it for Old Blue Eye. He said it was important that I not let the bear kill Jong so I shot him while his heart was still beating. I'm sure the old bugger will be pleased, but I got the sense that Trilogy was not amused. For a while there I thought we were going to tangle again."

Hard Case shook his head and thought about all Gus had been through since he came out here to build his cabin.

"It's a strange place, Fergus my boy."

"That it is, Case," Gus said. "That it is."

Before they retired for the night Gus reached into his pocket and took out an envelope and handed it to Hard Case. The seasoned old trooper read the name written on the front, then tapped it speculatively against the palm of his hand.

"Yuri Malachenko," he said. "Alexi's father?"

Gus nodded. "Yes. Would you give this to Haywood for me and ask him to deliver it personally?"

Hard Case pursed his lips. "I guess I don't need to ask what's inside. If it's what I think it is, I thank you for keeping me out of the loop."

Gus smiled. "Morgan suggested I avoid getting you involved. She's a diplomat's daughter. If Viktor Malachenko wants to stay clear of this little exchange, you should probably follow suit."

"She's more than just a pretty face," Hard Case said, and meant it.

"There's a note of condolence inside for the family – just a simple 'sorry for your trouble' sort of thing. If the father offers any gift in return, tell Haywood not to accept. It was enough to do a favor for the family."

"You're more than just a pretty face too," Hard Case told his friend. "And you don't even have a pretty face."

Hard Case pocketed the envelope and yawned. "Time to call it a night."

Chapter 50

Clive watched the man he called Lee disappear around the bend downstream of the bar upon which he had landed. Giving Lee his revolver had not set well with him. He'd bought it from another guide about eight years back and had never registered it in his own name. He didn't know if the other guide had registered it either, but it didn't matter. He had not thought to wipe it down before he gave it to Lee. Come to think of it, he'd fed all the cartridges into the cylinder that morning; each round would have his thumbprint on the brass butt. If anything went wrong down at the cabin, he could be in deep shit.

He walked back to his old Super Cub and hauled out the plastic tote that served as his camp kitchen. He opened it, took out his little single burner stove and put a small pot of coffee on to perk. He had a few hours to wait before the eight o'clock pick-up run he'd arranged with Lee. But he was good at killing time. He'd eat a sandwich with his coffee, then maybe have a go at the grayling. He kept a fly rod in the plane as part of his survival gear. He also had the little over-and-under in case he decided to bag a few birds. The top barrel was a .223 caliber rifle, but the bottom barrel was a 20 gauge shotgun. It was perfect for spruce hen and ptarmigan. Might as well enjoy yourself while you could.

When the coffee began bubbling up into the little glass dome atop his percolator, he turned down the flame to let it simmer, got his fly rod out of the airplane, assembled it and affixed a dry fly to the tippet. Keeping busy was the best way to while away a few hours – as long as you didn't have to work too hard at it.

***

Clive's wristwatch had an alarm feature. It began vibrating at six o'clock. He woke from his nap, had a cup of cold coffee and loaded all his gear back aboard the plane. He still had two hours before his first recon run over Lee's take-out point, but he always liked to take his time verifying the air-worthiness of his Super Cub. It wouldn't do to wait until the last minute to do a walk-around. A flat tire could set you back a couple hours.

He had just climbed into the cockpit when he noticed the clouds gathering over the high country upstream. The breeze had freshened considerably and was now gently buffeting his grounded aircraft. As he sat watching the sky darken, a few raindrops spattered on his windshield. 'Great,' he thought. 'There's a squall moving down the valley. I'll have to sit it out. If Lee has to wait for me, that's just too damn bad.'

The rain turned into a downpour for a while, then the squall passed through followed by a cold front that was so sudden his teeth began to chatter before he could retrieve his jacket from the rear seat and slip it on. By six-thirty the temperature of the air had dropped into the forties, and the warm water on the surface of the stream was vaporizing into a mist. He watched it rise off the water and coalesce into a thick ground fog. There was no way he could take off in these conditions. 'Lee is going to be plenty pissed if he has to wait long in this,' he thought. 'But, fuck him. I'm not going to risk taking off in this soup, let alone trying to land in it.'

He was forced to remain on the ground for both the eight o'clock and nine o'clock runs. But shortly after nine the fog had lifted enough that he had perhaps a hundred feet of clear air. There was no longer any point in making a high level pass over the landing strip now – either Lee would be there, or he wouldn't. Clive decided to climb up just above the treetops and follow the river down to the pick-up point. If Lee was waiting there, he'd land and pick him up. If not, he'd have to play it by ear.

He cranked up the engine and took off. There were still pockets of mist hanging just above the trees so he ascended until he was above them and cut a bee-line across the bends of the river on his way to the rendezvous. It took him just less than ten minutes to reach Gus' landing strip. As he came over the final rise above The Varmitage, he could see the gravel strip clearly. The raft and the backpack were there, but Jong was nowhere to be seen. "Shit," Clive said aloud. "He botched it."

He had to think fast. If there was still someone at the cabin, they would have heard his approach by now. They'd be coming up to see who was landing on their strip. "Damn it all," he said. There was no choice. He had to recover the raft and the backpack and get out fast. He set her down and taxied up to the raft. At least Lee had had the good sense to deflate and fold it. He cut the throttle to idle, set the brakes and hopped out of the cockpit. The raft was heavy and awkward and Jong had not disassembled the rowing frame.

Clive broke it down as quickly as he could and loaded it, the raft and the backpack into the rear compartment of the plane. The wind had died almost completely since the storm blew through so he could see no advantage to be gained by positioning himself to take off into the wind. He decided to save time and take off downwind. There was plenty of bar and he had lifted off shorter runways before. He revved the engine, let off the brakes, got up to speed and pulled back on the yoke. "Made it!" he said aloud. Then he saw the other plane coming out of the low ceiling straight at him.

"Shit!" he shouted, banking hard right to avoid the other aircraft and the trees along the creek. Had the pilot of the other plane not banked in the opposite direction they would have collided head-on.

As it flashed past him on the left, he caught a momentary glimpse of the blue lettering on the white underside of the left wing – T R O O P E R S. "Son of a bitch," he groaned.

Chapter 51

Gus was at the stove cooking breakfast and Caldwell was sitting at the table drinking coffee when Hard Case stopped snoring and opened his eyes at five-thirty the following morning.

"How's a man supposed to sleep with all that racket going on?" he grumbled.

"Ah," Gus said as he served up a platter of bacon and eggs for Caldwell. "You're in good voice this morning, Case. Welcome back among the living."

"Mornin' Boss," Caldwell said cheerfully. "Sleep well?"

"You're fired," Hard Case growled as he swung his legs out of bed and planted his feet on the floor. He did not attempt to stand up yet. He just sat there and rubbed his face with the palms of his meaty hands.

Gus gave Caldwell a wink. "Pay him no mind," he said. "He fires me on occasion too, and I don't even work for him."

He took Hard Case a steaming mug of coffee. "Here," he said handing it to him. "Get this inside you before you make any more personnel decisions."

Hard Case accepted the coffee and nodded his thanks. Gus went back to the stove and filled his own plate before joining Caldwell at the table. Bosworth emerged from under the bed and walked back and forth across Hard Case's bare feet, giving his ankles a full-length body rub with each pass.

"Morning, Bosworth," Hard Case smiled down at him, obviously in better humor. He finished his coffee, placed the empty mug on the floor and climbed into his pants.

"You ready for some breakfast?" Gus asked him.

"Not yet," Hard Case said, heading for the door. "Have to attend morning devotions first. I'll be back in a minute." With that he went out the door into the crisp morning.

***

After breakfast they crossed the river in Gus' canoe. Trilogy was not hard to track; he cut a wide swath through the tall grass and bushes. Nevertheless, Gus led the way since his .444 Marlin was of larger caliber than the scoped rifles Hard Case and Caldwell carried.

And, it was a short-barreled guide gun, quick in heavy cover, and unencumbered by a scope which was next to useless at close range.

He stopped atop the steep cut bank and followed the bear's clearly visible path with his eyes. It crossed a relatively open muskeg flat, then disappeared into the mixed spruce and birch forest at the base of the hills that bordered the valley on the south side. Hard Case scrambled up to join him, Caldwell close behind. They too studied Trilogy's exit route.

"That little game trail he followed looks like a centerline down the middle of the two lane highway he plowed," Hard Case observed.

Caldwell pointed out a bear track the size of a turkey platter stamped in the mud at the edge of the muskeg. It was so deep in the rain soaked soil the three stiletto-length depressions left by the claws were clearly visible.

He whistled a single note. "Wow," he said. "That's one big bear. I can't believe you lived through a fight with him."

Gus gave a derisive snort. "Some fight," he said. "It was over before it started."

Hard Case was on a mission. He was anxious to get going. "Enough prattle about a little bear track," he growled as he gestured for Gus to get things moving. "Lead on McDuff."

Gus took point with Caldwell right behind him. Hard Case brought up the rear. They followed the trail across the open ground all the way to the tree line. The light was muted in the woods so Gus pulled up for a few moments to let his eyes adjust. He didn't want to miss anything on the ground. When his vision sharpened, he set out again.

He had not proceeded more than fifty yards up the path when he again halted and directed Caldwell's attention to what appeared to be a viscous grey snake stretched across the trail.

"Good God!" Caldwell exclaimed.

Hard Case came up beside them. He looked at the section of large intestine that had obviously become detached from the rest of Jong's entrails.

He sighed. "Better snap a few shots and bag it. I hope we don't find more of the same up ahead."

Caldwell took out his camera and shot the length of viscera from four angles. When he had finished, Hard Case held the mouth of a large evidence bag open while Caldwell lifted the dripping offal with the tip of a stick and dropped it in. Hard Case recorded the date, time, and GPS coordinates on a tag and affixed it to the zip-lock seal at the top of the bag.

"Let's push on," he said. "Might as well see what other goodies dear old Trilogy left behind."

Gus led them uphill for perhaps a half mile before he stopped again.

"Knife," he said, indicating a short bladed belt knife just visible under the low leaf of a devil's club.

Caldwell went through his camera routine again, and Hard Case bagged and tagged the evidence. Fifty paces more up the hill, they came upon the pistol lying in the path.

"Bingo," Gus said.

"Bingo, indeed," Hard Case echoed.

While Caldwell did the honors, Hard Case asked Gus, "Was that the extent of his arsenal?"

"I didn't see anything else, but he may have had a pocket knife," Gus told him.

Hard Case looked up through the woods above them. "Have you been up this trail before?" he asked.

"All the way to the top. It's another couple of miles maybe. I didn't go down the other side. The creek that cut the valley over there dumps into the Moose Jaw from the right a few miles below where Wolf Creek comes in from the left. I don't recall its name."

"Caldwell will know," Hard Case assured him. "He knows every river and stream out here by name."

"Beaver Creek," Caldwell said over his shoulder as he bagged the pistol and slipped it into his backpack. "You think the bear is headed over there?"

Gus considered whether or not he should say what he thought. What he thought was that Trilogy was going to devour Jong's corpse. He decided to keep that to himself.

"Yeah," he said. "I'm pretty sure we've found all there is to find of Jong. That bear can cover a lot of ground fast. If you want to keep going I'm game, but I don't see much profit in it."

Hard Case agreed. "With the evidence we've collected and your eye-witness account, we have enough to confirm this as a bear killing. Let's get back to the cabin and wrap this up. You can give

274

us your statement over a cup of coffee. Then we'll head back to Fairbanks."

They followed their own trail down to the river. Back at the cabin, Hard Case recorded Gus' statement on his portable voice recorder while Caldwell took all the hard evidence they had gathered up to the landing strip and stowed it in the airplane.

"Moose season opens in a couple weeks," Gus said to Hard Case as they walked up the overland trail. "When will you guys be coming in?"

"Probably around the sixth or seventh," Hard Case told him. "When I get back to Fairbanks I'll hook up with Haywood. He can't wait to get back out here. And, I appreciate your inviting Caldwell. I'll call you on the satellite phone when we've settled on a date."

"That's fine," Gus said. "I probably won't hunt until you get here. I'll just scout so I can put you guys on some bulls. I'll find a big one for Caldwell. He's a fine young man."

"He is," Hard Case agreed. "Old school, he likes to call himself."

When they came down the trail and through the willows, Caldwell had everything ready to go. They said their good-byes.

Hard Case looked pointedly at his watch. "Nine-thirty-five," he said. "Time we got out of here, Caldwell. Don't let the bears eat you, Fergus," Hard Case told Gus as he boarded the airplane.

Gus smiled. "See you in a couple weeks."

He sat on a driftwood log at the top of the bar, lit his pipe and watched the blue-and-white Super Cub taxi out onto the landing strip, swing its nose into the wind and take off. He remained there until the sound of their engine faded into the distance, then walked back to the cabin.

Chapter 52

Mournful George was waiting at the boss' desk when Hard Case returned from the Medical Examiner's office.

"We came up with six old Super Cubs with tail numbers that could work with what you gave us. The best bet is registered to one Clive Nelson of Kasilof, Alaska," George reported.

"That fits," Hard Case said. "We thought Jong was holing up somewhere on the Kenai. We got anyone rolling out to Nelson's place?"

"We do," George told him. "One of the units out of Homer was up in Cooper Landing this morning. They dispatched it to check his fishing lodge on Crooked Creek. Haven't heard back yet, but their troopers should have arrived there before noon."

"Anything else?" Hard Case asked.

"We issued a BOLO for Nelson and his airplane a few hours ago. All airfields and refueling points have been notified," George told him.

"Okay," Hard Case said. "Let's say he flew straight over the mountains and topped off his tanks at Chekov. That would put him back in the air no later than eleven o'clock last night. I'm pretty sure he could have made it down to the Kenai without refueling again. If that's what he did, I'm guessing he could have been back at his lodge by four or five o'clock this morning. Let me know as soon as you get word from our Homer guys. It wouldn't surprise me if Nelson's already come and gone."

"Yeah," George said. "You're probably right. If he figured you saw his tail numbers, he'd have wanted to get home as fast as he could and ditch the airplane. According to the DMV there's a 1984 Suburban registered to him. I'll put together a bulletin with its plate number and description. If we strike out at his fishing lodge, I'll release it as an update."

"Good," Hard Case said. "He have a sheet?"

Mournful George tapped a file folder lying on the desk in front of him. "Right here," he said. You can read it at your leisure, but it's nothing to get excited about. He was a licensed hunting and fishing guide until he got busted for poaching and shooting bears over bait back in '96. Never convicted of a felony but he's spent a little time in local lockup for misdemeanor stuff."

"Think he's dangerous?" Hard Case inquired.

"Nothing in his bio that suggests it, but you never know. He's on the run and facing some serious time. If he gets cornered, he probably won't go peacefully."

"Fair enough," Hard Case said. "Keep me posted."

George nodded and headed for the door. "Will do."

When Mournful George had gone, Hard Case walked to the door and closed it. He dialed Haywood's number on his personal mobile phone.

"Caldwell phoned me earlier," Haywood said. "He just wanted me to know Gus was alright and you'd be tied up all day."

"Good," Hard Case said. "If you're going to be home this evening, I'd like to stop by for a drink. Gus made up a laundry list of things he'll need when you go back out to The Varmitage. I told him I'd see you got it."

It took Haywood only a moment to realize Hard Case had something more important than a laundry list to deliver. He never missed a beat. "I'll be home. But, it beats me how you always know when I've laid in a fresh supply of scotch."

"Always the gracious host," Hard Case told him. "I'll see you about eight."

* * *

It was two in the afternoon before they heard back from Homer. Mournful George came through Hard Case's always open door looking more mournful than usual. He had a dispatch on his clipboard.

"Bad news, boss," he said by way of preamble. "Looks like you nailed it. They found the plane in a barn at the back side of Nelson's property. The Suburban was there too. They searched the premises and discovered two bins of camping equipment upended on the floor with stuff scattered all around them. They found a winter-weight sleeping bag and a big wall tent, but nothing a guy might take if he wanted to travel light. No firearms in any of the rooms, but there's a gun safe. Of course, it was locked so no telling what might be inside. One thing they did notice was that a dusty shelf had a rectangular clean spot about the size and shape of a camp stove. That tied in with the fact that the pantry looked like

277

someone had tossed it in a big hurry. They said it appears our boy geared up and made a hasty departure. They're thinking boat."

"Damn," Hard Case said. "What took so long?"

"Everything was locked up," George told him. "They had to wait for the warrant."

Hard Case frowned and shook his head. "He probably realized the Suburban would be as easy to spot as his plane. If he lit out in a boat, we won't find him anytime soon. But, he'll turn up sooner or later. They always do."

"Sorry, boss," George told him. "But, for what it's worth, O'Kelly called in from Chekov. He drove out to the airfield and learned that Nelson landed there last night at ten-thirty-eight, purchased nineteen gallons of Avgas and took off at eleven-oh-two. Your timeline was dead on."

"Sometimes I get lucky," Hard Case told him. "Anyway, thanks for the effort, George."

***

Clive would have preferred to avoid flying over Wolf Creek pass after he refueled at Chekov, but he had no choice. His only hope of making it back to the Kenai Peninsula without another stop was to maintain a direct course south-by-southwest. He did not want to enter the airspace over Fairbanks or any military bases along the way, but he couldn't afford to waste the fuel a serpentine route would require. So flying back over the pass and the valley of the Moose Jaw was a risk he had to take. He just hoped he didn't run into the Troopers again. They'd get his tail numbers for sure this time.

Luck was with him. Sixty miles north of Anchorage he checked his gauges and decided he could vary his course enough to skirt the busy airspace over the city and Cook Inlet. By swinging a little east over the Chugach National Forest, he was able to keep above wild country all the way back to Crooked Creek. Once on the ground, he didn't bother with his post-landing routine, he just grabbed his survival gear and over-and-under, locked the plane in the barn and dashed down to the lodge.

He knew Lee had a hidey hole under one of the floorboards in the closet of the bedroom he had occupied. He went directly there, threw back the small throw rug that covered the floor and took up the loose board he had discovered one day while Lee was practicing with the raft. He switched on his mini-mag flashlight and shone its light into the space between the joists.

"Jackpot," he said aloud as he reached in and pulled out a one gallon zip-lock freezer bag. It was three-quarters full of what he knew to be cocaine. Hidden under it was an old tin cracker box that had gone missing from the pantry shortly after Lee had moved in with him. He bent down and brought it out where he could inspect its contents. It was heavier than he expected.

He settled it on the floor and opened the lid and was astonished at what he found inside. There was a thick stack of one-hundred dollar bills which, when counted, totaled seventeen thousand dollars. Beneath the bills, the bottom of the tin was covered with stacks of solid gold South African Krugerrands, worth about three hundred dollars apiece. There were twenty-five stacks of ten coins each. Clive did the math in his head. He didn't believe the result, so he recalculated. 'Whoa!' he thought – 'seventy-five grand!'

He quickly replaced the board and rug, and ran to the back room where he stored all his camping gear. He tore the lid off a plastic bin and dumped the contents out on the floor. He snatched up a small day-pack, flipped open the flap and dropped in the wad of cash, the tin of coins and bag of cocaine. Then he scattered the contents of another tub on the floor and quickly made a pile of items he'd need for two weeks in the bush. When he had everything gathered, he filled two waterproof river bags with the equipment. He opened the gun safe and took out a .44 magnum handgun and several boxes of ammunition for it, as well as .223 rounds and shot-shells for the over-and-under. It went against his nature to leave his other firearms behind, but there were too many of them and it would have taken too long to get them out of the safe and move them down to the boat. He closed and locked the gun safe and deposited the pistol and all the boxes of ammo in the backpack with the cash, coins and coke.

After staging the river bags and backpack near the front door, he filled a large plastic tote with food from the larder, tossed in a skillet, hanging pot, kitchen knife and a half-bottle of rye whiskey. It wasn't much, but he knew he could live off the land if he had to. He'd done it before. And there was an old hunting camp he knew of up a small tributary where the salmon did not spawn. That meant he could be relatively certain no fishermen or bears would trouble him for a while.

Ten minutes later, with everything stowed in the johnboat, he pushed off his dock and headed downstream toward the confluence with the Kasilof. He knew there would already be a lot of boats on the water down there because the salmon were running. One more wouldn't be noticed. He was home free – and he was rich!

Chapter 53

"So, Mr. Sam, you wanted to see me. I believe we recently met at a potlatch over in Circle – for Mike and Katiana O'Kelly."

"Yes, Mr. Calis. Katiana is my aunt, but very few people know that. After meeting you there I decided it was time to put the past behind me so I can get on with my future. You see, my dream has always been to become ordained as a priest, but in order to do so I need to set something right. Perhaps you can help me."

"Of course, if it's within my power. How can I help?" Hard Case was curious.

"You may have to arrest me. But I accept that," the man said. "You see, my real name is Henry – Isaac Henry. I understand you've been looking for me."

Hard Case smiled and shook his head in admiration. "Henry Sam," he said. "Living and working right there in Chekov, under your mother's maiden name. You never bumped into your cousin Katiana?"

"Many times." Henry Sam said. "She never recognized me. We didn't have much contact when we were young. I was in high school when she was still a little girl. And, of course, she was raised Catholic so we moved in different circles. My family was Orthodox."

Something had been troubling Hard Case since his visitor had arrived in his office. He recalled that two of the poachers had been named Sam.

"Sir," he began. "Would you also be related to Jackie and Damon Sam?"

The man nodded his head sadly. "My sons," he said simply. Hard Case could see the pain in his eyes.

"Forgive me," Hard Case said. "I should have realized. I was involved in the investigation of Jackie's murder. You have my condolences."

"Thank you," the man said. "I was never a very good father to the boys. My wife's brother raised them. Perhaps I was too caught up in my own problems."

Hard Case let a few moments pass to give his visitor time to regroup. Then he asked, "Have you heard from Damon?"

Henry Sam shook his head. "No," he said truthfully. "But, I heard one of my relatives at the potlatch say he was staying with cousins down near Tanana. I'll let you know if he contacts me. Is he a fugitive?"

Hard Case thought about that for a moment. "No," he answered. "Not really. We'd just like to know if he is alive and safe so we can remove him from the missing persons file. I'd appreciate it if you can confirm that he is alright."

Damon's father nodded. "I'll see what I can find out."

"Good," Hard Case said. "That's settled then. Now, let's get back to the reason for your visit. I suspect the thing you wish to put right has something to do with a double homicide that occurred when you were a young boy. Is that the case?"

Isaac Henry – aka Henry Sam nodded. "Yes. It has troubled me since I was in my teens. It's time to put it behind me."

Hard Case smiled. "I appreciate your coming forward. I've been trying to wrap up some loose ends regarding the Rainbow Lodge murders that occurred back in 1959. I'm sure you recall them, since your father was a suspect at the time."

Henry Sam nodded. "I remember."

Hard Case went on. "And I assume the thing you need to put right has to do with your involvement in that old case."

Again, Henry Sam nodded. "Perhaps we can help one another put all that to rest."

Hard Case said, "I believe we can. I understand your reasons for wanting to tell me what happened that night, but before you do I should advise you that there is no statute of limitations on murder. Having said that, I should also tell you that we closed the case last year and, for my own reasons, I have no intention of reopening it. I already know how the McCaslin brothers were killed and that you were present. There is no need for you to confess."

"Thank you," Henry Sam said. "But you see, I must confess my part in it; first to you, then to my spiritual father. There can be no absolution without confession."

Hard Case sat back in his chair and sighed. "Very well, then. Proceed."

Isaac Henry said, "I was there that night. I've lived with the burden of that guilt for more than forty years. It has prevented me from fulfilling my dream of becoming a priest. My teachers at St.

282

Herman's thought I was hesitant to become ordained because I wanted to marry first. That was not the case. I knew then that I could not accept ordination with that sin on my soul. I decided to live the secular life until the time came when I could confess my guilt. The time has come."

"Forty years is a long time to wait," Hard Case said. "Why come forth now, after all this time?" Hard Case asked.

"My uncle Nathan died last month. The clan held a potlatch in his honor after his death. Sergeant O'Kelly was there with Katiana. I overhead them mention my name and yours also. Of course, I knew he had been asking around about me, but none of the family except Uncle Nathan knew who I was. Everyone thought I had become a priest and left Alaska. Anyway, with my uncle dead, there was no one left I needed to protect. Aside from myself, he had been the last one alive who had been at the lodge that night. I've been debating what I should do ever since he died."

"I see," Hard Case told him. "Please go on."

"God works in mysterious ways, Mr. Calis. When we met at the potlatch celebrating my aunt's wedding, I knew he was showing me the way to absolution. Just yesterday, I decided to confess my guilt, accept my punishment, and with God's help, become a priest."

Hard Case was puzzled. "I'm a bit confused," he admitted. "Two weeks ago I interviewed someone else who had been at the lodge that night. He told me that four of the five people that wired up the McCaslins and left the fire bomb were dead. You don't appear to be dead."

Isaac Henry seemed puzzled also. "Who told you this?"

Hard Case's mind went back to the conversation he had had with Old Blue Eye. "I assumed I was talking to a man named Jason."

Isaac smiled and shook his head. "I doubt that, Mr. Calis. Jason died that night. Larry had beaten him badly and was about to rape him when we arrived. We knocked Larry unconscious and tended Jason's injuries as best we could, but he was in a bad way. He'd lost two fingers and half his face was crushed and one eye was hanging out of the socket. I bandaged his head myself. Somehow, he found the strength to help us take vengeance on the McCaslins. He crimped the metal sleeves onto the snare wire we used. Then, later, after a man appeared with a gun and killed Roy, we were going to take Jason upstream to a hunting camp where he could get help. But, he died before we got there."

"Who else was with you?" Hard Case asked.

"My brother Joshua and two of my uncles, Nathan and Johnny. My father wanted to go to the fishing lodge with us, but he was too smart. He knew he would be the first one the Troopers would think of because of the trouble we had with the McCaslins before. His sister, over in Circle was going to have a baby, so he planned everything to happen during the naming ceremony.

He hired an airplane to fly us in to our hunting camp on the upper Moose Jaw to kill the moose for the potlatch. His brother Nathan and one of his cousins met us there. Our mom's brother Johnny lived at the camp year round so he was there too. After we killed the moose my father and his cousin flew back to Circle with the meat. The rest of us waited one day, then went down to the lodge in canoes. It took us one more day to get back to our camp. The plane came back and Josh, Uncle Nathan and I flew back to Circle. We got there for the last day of the potlatch. Uncle Johnny stayed there at the camp."

Hard Case lit a cigarette, inhaled deeply and stared down at the names he had written in his notebook. "Help me out here," he said. "You're telling me Jason died in 1959, and I understand your brother Joshua was killed in 1965. Your father's brother Nathan died last month, and you're clearly alive – what about your Uncle Johnny? What happened to him?"

"Killed by a bear several years ago. He was up at that hunting camp where our family and some others always went to hunt moose and caribou in the autumn. He lived there year round, in the old tradition. A big three-toed grizzly killed him while he was butchering a moose. It was a huge bear, well known to my people. They call him the ghost bear and believe his spirit still prowls that river."

A chill ran down Hard Case's spine. He opened the file drawer of his desk and pulled out the missing person files for Katherine Morgan and Jason Thomas. He flipped a couple of pages and found what he was looking for – Jason's description.

"Ah, sweet Jesus," he said. Then, "I beg your pardon, father." When he realized what he had said, he rubbed a big hand through his salt-and-pepper flattop. "Oh, hell – I'm sorry. It's just that Old Blue Eye…"

Isaac interrupted him. "Old Blue Eye?" he asked.

"The old one-eyed guy I interviewed two weeks ago. I met him out at a friend's cabin on the Moose Jaw."

"And he had one blue eye?" Isaac asked.

"That's right," Hard Case confirmed. "I thought he was the long lost Jason until I just reread this old report. Jason had brown eyes."

Isaac's face lost all color. "Uncle Johnny had blue eyes. At least he did until the bear ripped one of them out when he killed him."

Hard Case stared at him, not wanting to ask, but knowing he had to. "And a crippled right hand?"

Isaac nodded. "Caught it in a salmon wheel when he was a kid. Mangled it pretty bad – he lost two fingers."

Epilogue

Late in the first week of September, they all met out at The Varmitage to hunt moose. The days were colder now, and each morning there was frost on the yellowing willows. Gus spent his nights in the cabin with Morgan, while his three friends enjoyed the comforts of the bunkhouse. The new roof and chinked walls kept the rain off and the winds out, and they'd all gather around the Tin Lizzy in the evenings to sip whiskey and smoke and recount the day's hunt.

Caldwell and Haywood had each killed their moose on the third day, and Hard Case had decided two were enough. He had passed on a very respectable bull on the fourth day, choosing instead to wait for a caribou. He preferred caribou meat anyway, and they were much smaller than moose and therefore easier to pack out of the woods.

On the fifth day, a cold wind came down the streambed and the sun remained hidden behind an overcast sky. The hunters encountered no game in the woods or meadows or along the river banks that day. An eerie quiet settled upon the valley, and no bird calls were to be heard in the willows. When they returned from the hunt late in the afternoon, Gus left his companions at the bunkhouse and went down to the cabin, where he found Morgan weeping silently near the cold stove.

When she told him something terrible had happened down in the Lower Forty-eight, he rushed back up to the bunkhouse with the satellite phone and told Hard Case he'd better call his office. When Hard Case hung up the phone, there were tears in his eyes.

***

Two days later Old Blue Eye reappeared at The Varmitage. Hard Case, Haywood and Caldwell were still there because all air traffic in the United States had been grounded due to the terrorist attacks in New York City. Caldwell's uncle had worked in one of the offices atop the World Trade Center. He was listed among the missing.

Hard Case was sitting alone, down by the river, smoking a Camel and studying the feeding rings on the water. No matter what went on in the world outside, the fish still fed. He turned when he sensed the old shaman's presence behind him.

"I didn't think I'd see you again," he said.

"I went away for a time," the old man told him. "But the world has gone crazy, so I came back here."

Hard Case offered him a cigarette and made room for him on the driftwood log he occupied. The old man accepted it and sat beside him.

Hard Case patted down his pockets and, miraculously, produced a pack of matches. He struck one and held it while his companion lit his smoke. "I guess it doesn't matter at this point," he said. "But, I want to make sure I got it right. You were Charlie Henry's brother-in-law?"

The old shaman nodded. "His wife was my sister."

Hard case took a slow pull on his Camel and exhaled. 'Johnny Sam,' Hard Case thought. 'At least I had that part right.'

The old one smiled. "Yes. But I like it better when you call me 'Sir'. It shows respect."

There was nothing more to say so they sat together in silence for a while, watched the fish feed, and thought their own thoughts.

Morgan came down from the cabin and joined them. "It's good you are here," she told the old man. "We should all be together in this valley now."

"Yes," the old shaman said. "This is home. I saw the bear's track along the river. It will be good to have his strength near us."

She looked off toward the high ridge across the creek where she knew Trilogy liked to keep vigil. "Has he made peace with your nephew?"

The old man too looked up toward the ridge. "I don't know," he said. "But he has not killed him yet. The boy has come back to the Moose Jaw. I see him up in the old hunting camp near the caribou fence. He has returned to the old ways now."

Morgan said, "There is another young man up in the bunkhouse – the pilot. He lost someone yesterday. He does not know this as a certainty, yet he does. He was so alone in his grief I revealed myself to him. I spoke with him face to face. Did I do wrong?"

The old one shook his head slowly. "No, daughter, you did the right thing. If he was not of good heart, he would not have seen your face or heard your words."

Hard Case was new to this himself, but he understood that Morgan had reached out to Caldwell through the nebulous curtain between their worlds, and had helped him find his own passage.

Gus' voice came down to them from the cabin. "Lunch is on the table. May as well come eat."

Morgan turned and started up the incline. "Join us when you're ready," she said over her shoulder.

***

That evening two hunters came downstream in a red inflatable raft. It rode very low in the water and appeared on the verge of swamping, overloaded as it was with moose quarters. Both men bristled with new-growth beards, and their faces and forearms were sunburned. Their rifles and fly rods were nestled in the tines of an impressive rack of moose antlers mounted astern. Another, smaller rack had been positioned as a bowsprit. Neither they, nor their vessel would have seemed out of place navigating the River Styx. As they hove to and pulled ashore Gus and Haywood went down to greet them.

"Hunting was good," Haywood observed.

The tall guy at the oars held the raft steady in the water while the other walked the bow line up to the driftwood log and tied it off.

"Maybe too good," the oarsman said. "Two bulls and a caribou – we've been shipping water for the past couple of days."

Gus said, "Have you heard about New York?"

They looked at one another and shook their heads. "No," the one at the bow line said. "We've been on the river since opening day of moose season. Didn't bring a radio. What happened in New York?"

Gus looked at Haywood. To the hunters he said, "It's not good. You better come up to the cabin and we'll fill you in."

When they had pulled the raft up on the bar as far as they could, the four walked up to the cabin where Hard Case was setting out drinks on the porch table. Caldwell hadn't left the bunkhouse since Mournful George had called last evening with an update of the attack on the Twin Towers and subsequent no-fly restrictions for all non-military aircraft. Hard Case assumed that Morgan and the old man were in the cabin – then again, maybe not. When all were seated at the big plank table he filled five glasses with whiskey while introductions were made all around.

288

The tall hunter was a veterinarian from Eagle River, and the short one a writer from Colorado. This was their first float trip down the Moose Jaw and they'd done very well. It was obvious to The Varmitage contingent that both were seasoned outdoorsmen, very much at home in the bush. Hard Case demonstrated his approval by filling their glasses to the Haywood line.

Formalities observed, Gus raised his glass to the visitors and said, "Gentlemen, if you put in on opening day, you've been on the river two weeks tomorrow. The world you left behind has changed a good deal in your absence." Then he proceeded to tell them all he knew of the terrorist attacks in New York and Washington.

When he was done he could see they were visibly shaken. After he'd given them a moment for their own private reflections, he said, "You'll be wanting to stay the night. You're welcome to sleep in the bunkhouse, or pitch camp down by your raft – whatever you prefer."

"Thanks," the vet said. "We've been roughing it for two weeks. The bunkhouse sounds pretty good."

"Right, then," Gus said. "There are three unoccupied bunks, so take your pick. We bagged two moose ourselves, so my drying racks are full, but we'll throw together a couple more while you get your gear ashore. When you're squared away in the bunkhouse, just line your raft downstream and we'll help you offload and rack your meat."

Later, after all their moose and caribou quarters were spread on two new willow-pole racks, the hunters waded their raft out into knee-deep water, scrubbed it clean and gave it a good rinse. Satisfied no trace of blood or gore remained, they lined it back upstream to the driftwood log, dragged it up on the bar and tied it off.

While they had been tending to the raft, Gus found Morgan inside the cabin, at the stove, over a simmering skillet of moose liver and onions.

"Smells delicious," he said, closing the door behind him. "Will you be joining us for dinner this evening?" Since she had presented herself to Caldwell, he wasn't sure he understood the rules of engagement anymore.

"Maybe. I haven't decided yet. As you heard, the old man doesn't think crossing the line is – well, crossing the line." She stirred the skillet as she spoke.

"Where is he?" Gus asked.

"He is with the bear," she said. Gus still hadn't come to grips with the fact that man and bear – and woman, for that matter – could all belong to the same clan. He understood there was no longer hostility between himself and the bear. And he realized that they had come to share something; he just wasn't sure what that something was. It appeared the old shaman shared it with the bear also. Gus supposed he should ask him about it. Then again, perhaps he wasn't ready to fully comprehend their bond.

"I'll lay the table," he said, heading for the door. "How many plates?"

"Just six," she said. "One for Caldwell, in case he feels up to joining you. Don't set a place for me, Gus. I'm not ready to break bread with strangers yet."

"What about Old Blue Eye?" he asked.

"He never eats," she told him.

Gus took six plates off the shelf over the counter and went out the door.

***

Caldwell had opted to remain in the bunkhouse, so Morgan took him a plate of food. After dinner, Gus and Haywood built a roaring campfire down by the water and the five that had dined together gathered around it on stumps and logs and sipped whiskey and talked deep into the night. Morgan kept to the cabin after clearing the table, but the old shaman materialized out of the darkness just as the party was pulling the cork on a second bottle.

He stood just outside the dome of firelight, but they could see him when a log rolled and sparks flared.

Hard Case left his stump long enough to take him a cigarette and stayed to light it for him. It had become a form of social ritual between them.

When he rejoined the men around the fire, he said, "Old Blue Eye says your bear is on the meat, Gus. But he assured me he would only take one caribou quarter, and we should not challenge him for it."

Gus had been in the process of loading his pipe. "I knew he was around," he said. "We'd do well to heed the old man's advice. It wouldn't be prudent to tangle with a grizzly in the dark over a piece of meat." He turned to his new friends, "If you'll feel the loss, I'll give you a moose ham in the morning."

The vet withdrew a flashlight from his vest pocket and shone the light in the direction of the meat racks. Its beam was strong and concentrated enough that the men could, indeed, make out the shape of the bear.

"Jesus!" exclaimed the writer, "that's the biggest bear I've ever seen."

"Me too," Hard Case told them truthfully. "And I've seen a lot of bears."

The vet took a cigar out of his pocket, slowly removed the wrapper and held a match to the tip until it was suitably lit. He tossed the match into the fire. "I guess a bear that big can take any cut he likes," he said. "I don't fancy fighting him for it. Besides, whatever he eats will serve to lighten our load."

The writer looked at Gus. "Unless I misheard, I thought Case, here, called him *your* bear. What's that all about?"

Gus lit his pipe. "It's a long story."

"We've a new bottle, and it's still early," the vet suggested.

Gus looked at Haywood across the fire. Haywood shrugged his shoulders as if to say, "Up to you".

Hard Case said, "Tell 'em, Gus. I think a lot of people are going to want to escape reality in the days to come. It might help. If you tell it well, perhaps our new friend here will go home and put it down on paper for folks to read."

Gus held out his glass to be refilled. When Haywood had complied, he took a sip, settled back on his stump, and began, "Okay, then. But, as Case often reminds us, strange shit happens in the Alaska bush – and white men too long alone out here go mad."

Without further preamble, Gus told them about his coming into the Moose Jaw last summer, building his cabin and finding Morgan, and his encounter with the bear. Haywood added a detail here and there, and Hard Case also. Even the old shaman, just visible out on the verge of the campfire's glow, could be seen nodding in appreciation now and again. When the whiskey was gone, they'd had the whole story – the McCaslins, the bear, LaGrange and

Lindsay, and of course the recent trouble with the Korean. They were all pretty well in their cups by the time they turned in.

***

The next morning while The Varmitage crew was still fast asleep, the two hunters quietly departed the bunkhouse, loaded their raft and pushed off. They ate a cold breakfast of trail mix and jerky after they had put a few river miles behind them. As they made their way downstream toward their takeout point at Victoria Landing, the vet lit a cigar and settled in among the river bags stacked in the bow while the writer guided their meat-laden raft through the rapids.

"What do you make of all that back there?" he asked.

The writer shrugged. "Strange shit indeed," he said shifting the oars slightly to keep in the fast water. "The guys telling the story were all white men. Maybe they've been out here too long."

"Could be," the vet admitted, exhaling a stream of smoke into the chill morning air. "Still, the redhead had sort of a 'not of this world' quality about her."

The writer nodded. "I felt that too. And the old Athabascan seemed to be somewhere distant, even when you could see him right there in front of you. Did you ever hear either of them speak?"

The vet savored his cigar for a moment as he considered the question. "No, I don't think I did. But, I know I saw them. I didn't imagine them."

"Yeah," the writer agreed. "I saw that bear too. And this morning at the meat rack – that empty meat bag was definitely real. But he left just a single, three-toed track."

"I saw that. Makes you think doesn't it. Still, we don't even know if the terrorist attacks they reported really happened."

"True," the writer agreed. "Guess we'll know tomorrow. In any event, it was one hell of a story."

"Did you believe it?" the vet asked.

"I did last night. Today I'm not so sure," the writer said thoughtfully. "I guess maybe I do."

The vet took a last puff on his cigar and tossed the butt over the side. "I think I do too," he said. "Then again – maybe we've been out here too long."

The End

Made in the USA
San Bernardino, CA
23 September 2017